Lincolnshire
COUNTY COUNCIL

KT-142-864

discover libraries

This book should be returned on or before the due date.

Gainsborough
Library

17 OCT 2019

24 JAN

To renew or order library books please telephone 01522 782010
or visit https://lincolnshire.spydus.co.uk

You will require a Personal Identification Number.
Ask any member of staff for this.

The above does not apply to Reader's Group Collection Stock.

05280253

Also by Jean Fullerton

No Cure for Love
A Glimpse of Happiness
Perhaps Tomorrow
Hold on to Hope
Call Nurse Millie
All Change for Nurse Millie
Fetch Nurse Connie
Wedding Bells for Nurse Connie
Christmas with Nurse Millie
Easter with Nurse Millie
A Pocketful of Dreams
A Ration Book Christmas

A Ration Book Childhood

JEAN FULLERTON

CORVUS

First published in paperback in Great Britain in 2019
by Corvus, an imprint of Atlantic Books Ltd.

10 9 8 7 6 5 4 3 2 1

A CIP catalogue record for this book is available
from the British Library.

Paperback ISBN: 978 178 649 6072
E-book ISBN: 978 178 649 6089

Printed and bound by CPI Group (UK) Ltd, Croydon, CR0 4YY

Corvus
An imprint of Atlantic Books Ltd
Ormond House
26–27 Boswell Street
London
WC1N 3JZ

www.corvus-books.co.uk

*To my seven grandchildren, Hannah,
Nathan, Sarah, Imogen, Amelia, Annabelle and
Tabitha, who I love to the moon and back.*

A Ration Book
Childhood

Chapter One

AS EVER, AT seven thirty on a working day, the signature tune of the BBC Home Service's *Up in the Morning Early* programme drifted out from the Bush radio on the dresser. Ida Brogan, already dressed in her workday skirt and jumper and with her bouncy chestnut-brown hair encased in a turban scarf, flipped a slice of yesterday's bread in the frying pan.

It was the second Monday in October and Ida was standing in the kitchen of number 25 Mafeking Terrace, the three-up three-down Victorian workman's cottage that had been her family's home for the past dozen years.

Mafeking Terrace was situated between Cable Street to the south and the Highway to the north, just a short walk from London Docks. The narrow street was lined on both sides by houses identical to Ida's. Every front door opened straight on to the pavement, without the benefit of a small garden or railing for privacy, while at the rear, each house had just a square paved yard with an outside toilet. A shared alleyway ran between each house and the one either to the left or to the right of it.

Before Chamberlain announced the country was at war with Germany a little over two years ago, families used the open space behind their homes to store their prams, tools and bicycles, but now the small yards were cluttered with stirrup pumps and sand-filled buckets ready to extinguish incendiary bombs, while barrels filled with soil were used for

1

growing potatoes and iron drinking troughs for sprouting winter cabbage.

Life in the street had changed, too, since that fateful broadcast to the nation. Men had received their call-up papers and had gone off to the army, Ida's eldest son Charlie among them, while children and expectant mothers and those with babes in arms were evacuated to the country.

Last year, when the Luftwaffe blitzed East London nightly, the Brogans' terraced house had been packed to the gunnels as all the family took shelter there, but now that her two eldest daughters, Mattie and Cathy, were married with babes of their own, there was more room to spread out. Jo, her youngest daughter, had a bedroom to herself at the front of the house while Billy, the baby of the family, no longer had to share with his big brother.

Of course, as Queenie, Ida's argumentative and contrary mother-in-law, occupied the front parlour, it was still a bit of a squeeze, but they were better off than many of their neighbours, who might emerge from their shelters after a visit from the Luftwaffe to find their houses reduced to a pile of rubble and all their worldly goods gone.

The blackout would still be in force for another hour, so the curtains across the window overlooking their backyard were closed as was the one across the back door. Therefore, the room where the Brogan family ate their meals, drank tea and exchanged gossip was illuminated by a 40-watt bulb which hung from the ceiling above. What with the blackout coming into force at half five in the evening and lasting until most people were arriving at work in the morning, you barely had time to draw back the curtains before you had to shut them again. What with that and the low-wattage output from the power station to conserve coal for the factories, the inhabitants of East London – well, in fact the whole country – were living in a dull twilight land.

'Looks like the fog's lifting,' said Jerimiah, dabbing his freshly shaven face as he stood by the sink in his trousers and vest.

Ida raised her eyes from his breakfast sizzling in the lard and studied her husband of twenty-five years.

At forty-four Jerimiah Boniface Brogan was two years older than her and although he sported a few grey hairs at his temple and amongst the curls on his chest, he was as easy on the eye as he had been when they'd met all those years ago. A lifetime of heaving discarded household items on and off the back of his wagon meant his big-boned frame was still tightly packed with muscle and he towered above most of the men in the area by a good three inches.

'Pity,' said Ida. 'The German bombers are bound to be back tonight, then.'

'Pity too,' he winked, 'because I was hoping perhaps to have another night with you in the same bed.'

Suppressing a smile, Ida turned her attention back to the frying pan. 'Honestly, Jerry, fancy thinking of such things and at your time of life!'

'What can you be meaning, woman?' he replied, an expression of incredulity spreading across his square-boned face. 'I'm as frisky as a man half me age.'

'Are you now?' said Ida, making a play of moving the pan on the gas.

He flipped the towel over his shoulder and, striding across the space between them, grabbed her around the waist.

'Sure, don't you know the truth of it, me lovely girl?' he said, pressing himself against her. 'And a woman of your age shouldn't be complaining either.'

'Get away with you,' she laughed, shoving him. 'I'm the mother of four grown-up children not some slip of a girl to be dazzled by your Irish charm.'

'That you may be,' he replied, nuzzling her neck, 'but you're still a pleasing armful.' He gave her an exaggerated kiss. 'And as to my Irish charm: isn't it the very same reason we have a quiverful in the first place.'

Laughing, she pushed him away again and he released her.

With his dark eyes still twinkling, Jerimiah grabbed his canvas shirt that was draped over the back of the chair and shrugged it on.

The back-door handle rattled and the curtain covering it billowed out as Queenie and a chill of icy air came into the room.

''Tis cold enough out there to freeze the hooves off the devil,' she said, stomping into the room from her daily trek to the Jewish baker in Watney Street. She dumped her basket on one of the kitchen chairs and took out a tissue-wrapped tin loaf which she placed on the table. 'Is there a cuppa in the pot going spare?'

Small and wiry and with her head barely reaching her enormous son's shoulders, Jerimiah's mother was in her sixty-fourth year. She had moved in with the family a decade ago after her husband Fergus was found face down in the mud at low tide having drunk his own body weight in Guinness after a three-day drinking spree.

At first glance, with her wispy white hair, twig-thin legs and a face like an apple left out in the sun, you'd be forgiven for thinking Queenie Brogan was one of those soft and gentle sorts of grannies who tickled babies under the chin and fed stray cats, but that's where you'd be wrong.

4

From the time the first air raid had sounded, Queenie had refused to go to the air raid shelters. Her only concession to having the Luftwaffe rain death down on her each night was to pop in her false teeth when the siren went off so that if she arrived at the Pearly Gates before dawn she wouldn't be embarrassed to greet St Peter.

Like Ida, Queenie was kitted out in her workday attire: a seaman's greatcoat, so large it skimmed the floor as she walked; a brown serge dress and lace-up men's boots, which looked way too heavy for her spindly legs to lift off the floor. To keep the cold at bay, she also wore the balaclava Mattie had knitted for Charlie, one of Jo's old school scarves around her neck and fingerless leather gloves like the market traders wore.

'The tea's just brewing,' Ida replied, as Queenie hung her outer garments on the nail behind the door. 'I'll pour you one after I've dished up Jerry's breakfast.'

'Well, before you do, you might want to throw one of these in for good measure.' Reaching into the basket again she pulled out a screwed-up sheet of paper with three eggs nestling in the middle.

'Where did you get those?' asked Ida, scooping the fried bread out of the pan and on to a plate.

Queenie's wrinkled face lifted in a toothless grin. 'I found them.'

'Where?'

'Probably better not to ask,' said Jerimiah, fastening the top button of his collarless shirt and winding his red neckerchief around his throat.

Ida regarded the precious eggs for a moment then picked up the large brown one. When all was said and done, Jerimiah was a working man with a hard day's graft in front of him, plus a patrol with the Wapping Home Guard in the cold later, so he needed to be fed.

Ignoring her conscience about where the egg might have been found, Ida broke it into the pan and while it was crackling in the fat she poured Jerimiah and her mother-in-law a mug of tea each.

'You'll have to have it without sugar as I'm saving the rations for Christmas,' she said, placing the steaming mugs in front of them. 'And no, don't see if you can "find" me some, Queenie, as I don't want the police knocking at the door asking about the black market.'

'Sure, don't you be worrying about the police now, Ida,' said Queenie, in the soft Irish brogue that forty-plus years in London hadn't yet softened. 'For aren't I on the best of terms with all those lovely lads at the station?'

'Only because they're forever arresting you for running bets for Fat Tony,' replied Ida. 'And I doubt that poor wet-behind-the-ears lad they sent down last time has recovered from the experience yet.'

A soft look stole across the old woman's face. 'Ah, he was a sweet lad, right enough, and very polite, too.'

'Well, if that's the case why did you scare him half to death by pretending to have a funny turn when he locked you in the cell?' said Ida, splashing fat over the top of the egg.

Queenie waved her words away. 'Because, Ida, a run-in with the law would be no fun at all if you didn't get one over on a rozzer from time to time.'

Ida rolled her eyes and turned back to her task. Satisfied the egg was cooked she scooped it out of the pan and deposited it on the fried bread just as the eight o'clock pips sounded out from the wireless.

'I ought to be off,' she said, placing her husband's breakfast in front of him. 'I've put your sandwiches in the tin and topped up your flask.'

'You're a grand woman, so you are,' said Jerimiah, spearing a piece of eggy bread with his fork.

As he ate his breakfast Ida pulled down a plate and bowl in readiness for their son Billy's breakfast. Then she put the cover over the butter dish and wiped the crumbs from the breadboard.

'Are you back for tea or going straight to the Methodist Hall?' asked Ida, taking her coat from the back of the door.

Putting the last morsel of his breakfast in his mouth, Jerimiah stood up.

'Our squad's not on patrol until seven so I'll have a jar in the club then I should be back before the blackout starts. In fact,' he knocked back the last mouthful of tea, 'what with the government fixing the price of metal it's hardly worth putting Samson in harness these days.'

Ida bit her lip.

'Now, now, don't you start fretting,' Jerimiah said, taking his thick sheepskin jerkin from the back of the chair. He sidestepped out from behind the table, squeezed behind his mother and came over to Ida.

'You and me have got through lean times before, have we not?' he said, shrugging on his top coat.

Ida forced a smile. 'We have, but what with the price of everything in the shops going through the roof and Christmas just two months away and—'

'And in all these years,' he cut in, giving her that sideward cheeky grin of his, 'when have I ever let you or the kids go short?'

Gazing up into his sea-grey eyes, Ida's shoulders relaxed and she smiled in reply.

'That's better.' He gave her a quick peck on the cheek. 'Mind how you go and I'll see you at tea time.'

Taking his leather cap from his pocket Jerimiah flipped it on the back of his still abundant curls and left the kitchen, leaving a blast of cold air and an empty space behind him.

Queenie heaved herself to her feet.

'Well, I ought to make a start on the day, too, as that lot' – she indicated the enamel bucket piled high with the family's weekly smalls under the sink – 'won't wash themselves.'

Buttoning up her coat, Ida moved the blackout curtains aside a little and gazed through the kitchen window at the receding figure of her husband as he headed off to work.

She'd known from the first moment she set eyes on him walking into St Bridget's and St Brendan's that she was going to marry Jerimiah Brogan.

Although her family, like many in East London, had come from Ireland a hundred years earlier, they still counted themselves a cut above those newly arrived from the Old Country. And so they hadn't wanted Ida to marry Jerimiah, calling him a thieving gypo tinker with a crazy mother.

Her mother, God rest her soul, had told her he'd never amount to much, while her sister Pearl had predicted he would beat her when he was drunk and pinch her housekeeping when he was sober. Her brother Alfie had threatened to punch his lights out for setting his pikey sights on Ida, until he saw Jerimiah and thought better of it.

Her father had refused to give his consent so in the end she'd had to fall back on the age-old remedy for young couples with uncooperative parents: she'd got herself in the family way. They were married the day before Whit Sunday, six months later.

Well, other than the comment about his crazy mother, everything her family had said about Jerimiah had proved to be completely wrong.

Unlike many men who left their wives hiding from the rent man and their children hungry to ensure they had their beer and tobacco money, Jerimiah had always provided for his family. More then provided, in fact. He, as much as she, had worried over their children when they were raging with fever and had sat by their bedsides through the night. In twenty-five years of marriage her husband had never raised his hand to her, and there weren't many women who could make that boast.

Tucking up her collar, Ida hoped she could sweet talk the butcher into giving her a pork chop with a bit of kidney. After six hours trudging around the streets on top of his wagon in the freezing cold, Jerimiah would surely deserve a bit of a treat.

The queue shuffled forward and Ida did too, thankful that after twenty minutes of waiting outside the shop she was now through the butcher's door.

'Will you look at the price of that liver,' said Winnie Munday, who was behind her in the queue.

It was now almost midday and some forty-five minutes since Ida had left Naylor, Corbet and Kleinman's, the three-storey, double-fronted law firm on Commercial Road where she cleaned each morning. Although there were still three women in front of her, the tray of pork chops in the window was still half full, meaning she had a good chance of getting Jerimiah one for his supper.

The line of women outside Harris & Son, where the family's meat ration was registered, had already been halfway down Watney Street Market when Ida arrived, so she had popped into Sainsbury's first to see what was on offer there. She was glad she had because they'd just had a delivery of split peas and national flour, so she'd loaded them, along with a block of marge and a tin of salmon and another of golden syrup into her bag. Luckily, she'd remembered her greaseproof paper to wrap her purchases in as the store had already used its monthly allocation. The butcher's queue had shrunk by the time she'd emerged, so she'd decided to get her meat before visiting the greengrocer's stall.

'Shocking,' said Ida, glancing at the quivering mass of reddish-mauve offal sitting alongside a tray of pigs' trotter in the window.

'Criminal is what I'd call it,' Winnie replied, her close-set eyes looking at Ida through the thick lenses of her round-rimmed glasses. 'God only knows what a turkey for Christmas dinner will cost us.'

Winnie and her family of three boys and one girl lived in Alma Street, three streets down from Mafeking Terrace. Her husband worked for the gas company, a reserved occupation.

'That's assuming there are any,' said Ida. 'I had to make do with an ox heart last year.'

'Have you got much so far?' asked Winnie as they shuffled forward again.

'A few bits,' said Ida, 'plus enough dried fruit to make me Christmas cake, but I'll have to add some apple to bulk it up.'

'Better that than spuds,' said Winnie. 'I had another blooming Ministry of Food leaflet bunged through me letterbox yesterday with holly on it telling me 'ow to make shortbreads and marzipan with potatoes.'

'Hopefully, when the government's new extra-points rations come in next month, I'll be able to splash out on a few luxuries to cheer us all up,' said Ida, as the woman in front of her stepped forward to be served.

Winnie rolled her eyes. 'I'm sure I don't understand what all that's about.'

'It's the food and stuff the Americans are sending us; you know, dried milk and powdered egg,' Ida explained. 'We're getting an extra ration book with points and depending on what arrives and what ends up at the bottom of the Atlantic each week, they will let us know how many of these extra points we'll need to buy it.'

'For Gawd's sake,' said Winnie. 'My brain's scrambled enough trying to add up coupon points for this without totting up another lot of numbers. I suppose you've got everyone at your place for Christmas again.'

'All except my Charlie,' Ida said, as an image of her strapping son flickered through her mind. 'He's out in North Africa, so God himself knows when he'll be back. I won't see his Stella or the baby either as she'll no doubt spend the day with her family. Although I said I'd take Patrick to Midnight Mass with the rest of the family.'

Winnie pulled a face. 'I'm surprised she didn't argue.'

'She tried,' said Ida, thinking of the look on her daughter-in-law's flat face when she announced it. 'Said it'd be better for him to sleep in his own pram and all that but as I pointed out to her, he's with me most nights down the shelter while she's working so I don't see how him being with me at St Bridget's and St Brendan's is any different. He's only six months so he won't know anything about it anyhow.'

Winnie gave her a sideways look. 'I saw her the other morning getting off the last night bus at the Troxy.'

'I expect she was coming home from a night shift at the factory,' said Ida.

'What in high heels with her lipstick all rubbed off her mouth?' said Winnie.

Ida didn't reply and thankfully the woman in front of her collected her change and moved aside.

''Ello, Mrs B,' said Ray Harris, wiping his chubby hands on his blood-stained apron. 'How are you this fine morning?'

Ray was the son referred to in the Harris & Son sign painted above the shop. In fact, he resembled his red-headed father so closely sometimes you had to look twice before you were certain which one of them you were talking to . . .

Ray had always fancied himself as a bit of a ladies' man but until recently, with heavy features and crinkly ginger hair, he'd been unlucky in love. Now, however, with the meat ration recently cut again, he had dozens of women keen to walk out with him.

'Well enough,' said Ida. 'And all the better for seeing you've got some decent pork chops for once. I'll have five, and a bit of kidney on one of them would be welcome.'

'Right you are, Mrs B,' he said, licking his fingers and scooping up a sheet of paper from the pile next to the scales. 'Five pork chops coming up.'

Leaning into the window, he scooped up the cuts of meat and plonked them on to the paper.

'Just over the half and a bit of squiddly-diddly, too.' He looked at Ida.

She nodded. 'And I'll have three-quarters of braising steak, but make it lean.'

Wrapping the chops up with a deft twist of his hand, Ray put the parcel to one side of the till. He slid another sheet of paper from the pile then leaned back into the window.

'Your Cathy was in earlier,' he said, dropping the paper and cubes of beef on the scales. 'I managed to find her a nice bit of shin and a spare sausage for that little lad of hers.'

'That was good of you,' said Ida.

'Well, it can't be easy for her all by herself, like, with her husband away,' the butcher continued.

'Plenty of women around here are in the same boat,' said Ida.

'You have the right of it there, Mrs B,' said Ray.

Of course, Cathy wasn't in the same boat because although there were thousands of young mothers like her up and down the country, most of them were raising toddlers alone because their husbands were in the army not, like Stan Wheeler, in prison.

Ray slid the weights on and off to bring the central needle on the scales upright then he wrapped the rest of Ida's order and placed it alongside the chops.

He looked at her expectantly. 'Anything else, Mrs B?'

'A quarter of suet,' she said. 'And that should do me until Wednesday.'

Ray grabbed a waxed tub from the small stack behind him and placed it with the rest of her order then took the stubby pencil from behind his ear.

'Two and a tanner,' he said, after scribbling the sum on a tatty pad next to the till.

Opening her bag Ida took out her purse and handed him her ration book. He marked off her meat allocation then, shoving the pencil back where it came from, returned her ration book. She handed over half a crown and got her purchases in exchange. Popping them in her bag, she squeezed her way along the queue and out through the door.

Wondering if there would be more than just cabbages and carrots on the greengrocer's stall, Ida skirted around the men from Truman's who were unloading barrels outside the Lord Nelson and headed towards the cluster of barrows under the railway arches at the bottom of the market.

She'd just reached Feldman's stationers on the corner of Chapman Street when a woman walked out of the Post Office on the other side of the road.

Ida could hardly believe her eyes.

'Ellen,' she shouted. 'Ellen!'

The woman looked up. Ida waved and hurried across the street. 'Ellen,' she said breathlessly, stopping in front of the other woman. 'I can't believe it's you.'

'Ida,' she said, looking incredulously at her.

'Yes, it's me,' laughed Ida. 'And I'm glad you recognised me after all this time.'

Ellen's eyes flickered behind Ida and then back to her face.

'Of course I did,' she said, giving her a guarded smile. 'You haven't changed a bit.'

'You neither,' said Ida, looking her up and down.

Actually, that wasn't strictly true. Although she couldn't see any grey in Ellen's light brown hair, its bounce had disappeared. Her eyes, too, were dull, with dark shadows surrounding them. In addition, her cheekbones stood out in sharp relief. Unsurprising, really. After two years of food rationing and disturbed nights, everyone was sleep deprived and had shed a few pounds.

'How are you?' asked Ellen.

'Well,' said Ida. 'Very well.'

Ellen's eyes flickered down the road again. 'And the children?' she said, giving Ida a tight smile.

'All grown,' said Ida. 'Charlie, Mattie and Cathy are married with babes of their own and Jo's engaged. Billy's eleven now and a bit of a handful, but there's no harm in him. Of course, we have Jerimiah's mother Queenie living with us, cantankerous old so-and-so, but—'

'How is Jerimiah?' asked Ellen.

'Fit as a fiddle,' Ida replied. 'But never mind about us. How are you? I thought you were in Sevenoaks?'

'For a couple of years then we moved to Hastings.' Ellen glanced down the road again. 'Paul was promoted to deputy station master there but unfortunately even with the sea air to help, his condition got worse soon after he took the job and he died.'

'Oh, I'm so sorry,' said Ida.

'It was a few years ago now…' Ellen gave her a brittle smile.

'So where are you living?' asked Ida.

'I've got a couple of rooms in Juniper Street,' Ellen replied.

'You should have written and told me about Paul,' said Ida, her heart aching for her old friend's loss.

'I didn't want to trouble you, not when you had your own family to worry about,' said Ellen.

'Perhaps not, but we were so close once, me and you,' said Ida.

'Yes, we were,' said Ellen softly, a sad smile lifting her thin lips.

Ida's gaze ran over her old friend's face as long-buried images and unbearable emotions surged up. Her hazel eyes captured Ellen's grey ones and the years since they'd last met disappeared for a heartbeat or two. Then her friend glanced up the street once more.

'Look, Ida,' she said nervously, 'I need to tell you something. Something important. The reason—'

15

'Mum!'

Ida turned to see a young lad of about Billy's age, dressed in a green school uniform, scooting down the road towards them.

Darting between the shoppers and stall holders, he skidded to a halt beside Ellen.

'I got the last one, Mum,' the lad said, waving a copy of *Boy's Own* with a Spitfire shooting down a German bomber on the front cover. 'Look!'

Fear flashed across Ellen's face but then she turned to the boy.

'Well done,' she said, smiling at the lad. She took his hand. 'Michael, this is my oldest friend Ida.'

Michael turned his snub-nosed, freckled face to Ida.

'Hello, Auntie Ida,' he said, smiling innocently up at her.

Ida opened her mouth to reply but the words stuck in her throat. Staring down at the lad's square jaw, broad forehead, black curly hair and soft grey eyes, the blood drained into her boots.

'Be a luv, Michael,' said Ellen, cutting across Ida's chaotic thoughts. 'Pop over and buy me a couple of apples from the stall across the way.'

'Right you are, Mum,' he replied, giving her a smile that ripped through Ida's heart.

Taking the couple of coppers from his mother, the lad dashed across to the greengrocer's barrow. Ellen watched him for a second or two then she looked back at Ida.

'I'm sorry you had to find out like this, Ida,' she said, in a tone that belied her words.

Ida stared incredulously at her. 'Is he—'

'Yes, Ida,' Ellen interrupted. 'Michael is Jerimiah's son.'

Chapter Two

JERIMIAH BROGAN PATTED Samson's piebald rear as the sixteen-hand gelding buried his muzzle in his supper.

'There you go, me fine lad,' he said to the horse as he filled the overhead manger with sufficient hay for the night. 'We'll be having a better day tomorrow, so we will.'

The draught horse flicked his ears in response but continued to munch away. Jerimiah patted the horse's rump again, checked the water in the drinking trough and left the stall.

Securing the bolt across the door, Jerimiah hung the bridle and tack on the wall hook next to the horse's cart collar and harness. The railway arch where he stabled Samson and stored his wagon was situated within sight of Shadwell Station in Chapman Street, under the Blackwell-to-Minories railway. Samson's stall was at the far end of the arch, constructed to keep him dry and out of the wind that cut like a knife up the Thames some nights.

Next to Samson's stall was an office that Jerimiah had built out of a couple of old door panels and windows. Furnished with a school desk that could have come from the ark, a clerk's chair with no arms and a kitchen dresser without any doors in which he stored his accounts book, it was nonetheless comfortable, especially after a long day scouring the streets for scrap metal or any other odds and ends that Jerimiah could sell on.

To be truthful, it had been a better day than many he'd known in recent times.

As the fog meant the Luftwaffe hadn't come calling last night, for once he hadn't had to coax Samson through the emergency crews as they cleaned up after a night's bombing. What's more, he'd been able to search unhindered for fragments of shell cases and twisted metal amongst the debris. He'd discovered a tail fin and a long section of brass casing amongst the rubble along with melted house railings and warped coal-hole covers. Under the Ministry of Defence directives, he would get nothing for the railings as all unclaimed metal was deemed to be government property and vital to the war effort, but he would be paid for collecting the remains of the German armoury although, sadly, he wouldn't receive what the brass and copper were actually worth.

He'd made light of it to Ida that morning, but in truth, with furniture and household goods being either unobtainable or extortionately expensive, no one was throwing out household items any more so some days he barely scraped together enough to feed Samson let alone give Ida her weekly housekeeping. The small allowance he received for being a member of the Home Guard helped a bit, but the fact of the matter was he'd have to put his thinking cap on to figure out a way of increasing his income. Easier said than done for an Irish rag-and-bone man who left school at twelve.

Casting his worries aside, he kicked the wedges under the wagon's back wheels. He opened the door cut into the left-hand double gate, ducked his head and stepped out into the street outside.

Although it was only just after four, the blackout was already in force so taking his muted torch from his sheepskin pocket he pointed it at the floor and headed along the street towards his end-of-day watering hole.

In truth, his boots could probably find the way by themselves as the Catholic Club that backed on to St Bridget's and St Brendan's was the Brogan family's second home. Not so much for the bar on the first floor but for things like Irish Dancing classes, young mothers' groups, wedding receptions, birthday parties and funeral wakes, which all took place in the main hall below.

With the beam of light just in front of his toecaps, Jerimiah joined port workers in donkey jackets and heavy boots as they trudged home after a twelve-hour shift unloading vital food supplies in the docks. Mingling amongst them were dozens of women pushing prams loaded with toddlers, sandwiches and flasks of hot drinks: although the air raid warning had yet to sound, they were on their way to a bomb shelter or an underground station to bed down for the night.

Turning the corner into Dean Street, Jerimiah strolled on towards his well-earned end-of-the-day Guinness and within a few moments he reached his destination. Situated around the corner from the church, the Catholic Club had been built fifty years ago and was a square, functional building typical of the Edwardian period. Of course, the windows now had the extra protection of gummed tape criss-crossing them to stop shards of broken glass littering the room in the event of an explosion.

The main hall on the ground floor, where the Brownies and Scouts met and the club's Shamrock League held their ceilidh dances, was now one of the local rest centres. It was manned by the WVS and gave shelter to those who had been bombed out.

As there hadn't been any bombing the night before the rows of camp beds at the far end of the hall were currently empty, with a brown, government-issue blanket neatly folded on each one. There were a handful of people sitting at tables drinking tea while mothers with babies balanced on their hips or hanging on their skirts were sifting through the rails of second-hand clothes looking for bargains.

Jerimiah pushed open the brass-plated door that led into the entrance hall. Passing the noticeboard with a poster showing a German soldier surrendering with the caption 'We Beat 'em Before; We'll Do It Again', he headed along the concrete-floored passageway to the stairs at the far end.

Taking them two at a time he soon found himself in the club bar on the first floor, which already had a good number of his fellow members supping pints within. With its scrubbed wooden floor and private booths, this bar was like many others in the area. There was a dartboard in a wooden frame with a chalk scoreboard on one side and an advert for Jameson whiskey painted on the other. There was a worn rubber oche on the floor showing the required throwing distances, and a couple of sets of darts jammed into the bottom on the surround.

Greeting old friends as he passed by, Jerimiah strolled between the tables to the bar and slid on to a vacant stool.

'The usual, Jerry?' called Pete Riley, the club manager, who was drying glasses at the other end of the bar.

'When you're ready,' Jerimiah replied.

He and Pete's families had lived a few doors apart in Pennington Street. They had been snotty-nosed, barefooted kids running the streets during the last few years of the Old Queen's reign. Mostly, trying to keep out of sight of PC McDuff, the keen-eyed heavy-handed beat bobby.

Like Jerimiah, Pete was the father and grandfather of an ever-expanding family but whereas a lifetime of heaving household items on and off a cart had helped Jerimiah avoid middle-age spread, Pete's buckle was strained to its last notch.

Miraculously, both had survived the trenches, leaving Pete with a lump of shrapnel embedded in his right thigh and Jerimiah with the unswerving conviction that the officer class, their self-styled betters, were nothing more than a collection of inbred, fecking idiots.

Hooking the last couple of glasses on the brackets above the bar, Pete flipped the tea towel over his shoulder and took down a pint glass.

'Good day?' he asked, putting the glass under the brass spout and grasping the pump on the top of the counter.

'So so.' Jerimiah pulled a couple of coins from his trouser pocket and put them on the counter. Taking his drink, he raised it to his lips and took a long swallow, enjoying the rich bitterness as it slid down his throat.

Smacking his lips, he placed the glass on the polished mahogany counter and looked at his old friend.

'How's the family?'

They exchanged anecdotes about their respective offspring for a couple of minutes until the door of the bar opened and a chap Jerimiah vaguely recognised entered. He spotted Jerimiah and strolled across.

'Jerry Brogan,' he said, stopping next to him.

'The very same.'

'Brian O'Connor,' he said, offering his hand. 'We met when the St Patrick team played St Bridget's and St Brendan's a few months back.'

'Yes, we did,' said Jerimiah, shaking his hand. 'I remember it well. Four–three to us, if my memory serves.'

Brian smiled. 'Indeed, although a blind man could see your last goal was offside.'

They laughed.

'Can I buy you a pint?' asked Jerimiah.

'No, I'm grand, thanks,' said Brian. 'But am I right in thinking you helped move the Ibbertsons from Diggon Street to Fairfield Road?'

'You are, just last week,' said Jerimiah, slurping the froth off his drink.

'Well, I wonder if you could do the same for my sister,' said Brian. 'She was bombed out and is staying with us but you know what it's like having two women in a kitchen . . .'

'I most certainly do.' Jerimiah laughed, thinking of the daily ding-dongs between Ida and his mother.

'Well, thankfully,' continued Brian, 'Mary's found another house for her and the kids in Chigwell.'

Jerimiah pursed his lips. 'That's a bit of a trek from here, isn't it? I mean, it would take me a day there and back.'

'How much?'

'Well, now.' Jerimiah took another mouthful of his drink. 'What do you say to three quid if there's someone to load with me or four if not. And I could take her on Wednesday?'

Brian chewed his lips for a moment. 'Done, it'll be worth it just to have me tea in peace and I'll send my lad to help out. We're in Thurza Street, number twelve.'

Jerimiah offered his hand. 'I'll be there at eight on Wednesday.'

Brian took it and then strolled back to the door.

'Not bad for a day's work,' said Pete after he'd gone.

Jerimiah took another mouthful of beer. 'I'm not complaining.'

'That's four you've moved in as many weeks, isn't it?' said Pete.

'It is,' said Jerimiah. 'But sure, I'm only doing it so old Samson can have a day out in the country.'

'And three nicker,' laughed Pete. 'You carry on like this and you'll be able to retire to the country yourself.'

Jerimiah smiled, and Pete went off to serve another customer.

Lifting his pint to his lips Jerimiah took another large mouthful. He didn't know so much about retiring to the country but perhaps having the horse and cart might provide a way of keeping the wolf from his door for the duration.

As he'd promised Ida that morning, Jerimiah pushed open the back door and entered the kitchen just as the last five o'clock pips fell silent.

The aroma of simmering cabbage and roasting meat were all but swamped by the starchy smell of the washing that hung from the dryer hoisted above the kitchen range and the family's smalls draped over the clothes horse in front.

This was only to be expected, given it was a Monday, but what was a surprise was that Ida wasn't in the kitchen to greet him with a cup of tea. In fact, he couldn't remember the last time he'd walked into the house after a long day's work and not found her getting supper ready.

Frowning, he took off his coat and hung it over several others on the back door.

'I'm home,' he shouted.

'I thought I heard you,' said Queenie, as she came through from the parlour. 'Good day?'

'Not bad,' he replied. 'Where's Ida?'

'She came home a couple of hours ago with a face like thunder saying she had a headache and she was going upstairs to lie down,' Queenie replied. 'Supper won't be ready for an hour yet so why don't you put your feet up in the other room and I'll bring you a cuppa. Jo's in there.'

'Thanks, Ma,' said Jerimiah.

They exchanged a fond look. Jerimiah loosened his neckerchief and went into the back parlour.

One of the advantages of the work he did was that he was able to furnish the family home with quality items which he acquired on his travels. The massive dresser in the kitchen was one such item, as was the button-back leather porter's chair that he relaxed in each evening. It had a wobbly arm, true enough, but you can't have everything.

He'd found a carved wooden chair with a padded seat for Queenie but he'd had to saw two inches off each leg so her feet could touch the floor, but his best find was the tapestry armchair with padded arms that he'd got for Ida. It had cost him double what he'd usually have paid but it was worth it so that after a long day scrubbing other people's floors and caring for the family she could sit in comfort by the fireside each night.

With Ida in mind and knowing she had a soft spot for them, he'd also gathered a collection of figurines for her to display on the mantelshelf. To his way of thinking they would have been more suitable as substitutes for coconuts in a coconut shy for the church's summer fair, but Ida thought they looked nice and that's what mattered.

And he could understand his wife's attachment to her mantelshelf trinkets because he felt the same about his greatest find: a 1913 edition of the *Encyclopaedia Britannica*.

This sat proudly in the tall mahogany bookcase, dominating the whole room.

Sadly, volume twenty-five was missing but even so he'd spent many a happy hour when the children were young reading to them from the various volumes.

As he walked in to the comfortable family room, Jo, his youngest daughter, looked up.

'Hello, Dad,' she said, giving him a weary smile. She was sitting in her mother's chair with her feet up on the battered leather pouffe. A few months short of her nineteenth birthday she was a member of the Auxiliary Ambulance Service and had worked her way up from driver's assistant to a fully fledged ambulance driver. She had been on the day shift, which didn't start until nine, so she'd still been in bed when he'd left this morning. Although she had loosened her tie she was still in her navy uniform and could have only been in a little while as she was holding a steaming cup of tea.

Like her oldest sister Mattie, Jo took after his side of the family, and in more ways than just her dark colouring and turned-up nose. Jo had the look of an angel from above, but she could send you spinning with a flash of her sharp green eyes. Truth be told, like her two sisters, Jo could twist him around her little finger but that was one of the joys of being a father of girls.

'Hello, me darling,' said Jerimiah, sinking into the chair opposite her. 'Have you had a good day?'

'Busy,' Jo replied. 'But thankfully routine stuff like fetching people back and forth to hospital for appointments. I did get called to a woman in labour but the midwife was already there when I arrived, so I left her to it.'

'You going out later?' asked Jerimiah.

'Only to phone Tommy.' She twisted her engagement ring with her thumb. 'Mum told you I'm going to visit him the weekend after next, didn't she?'

'She mentioned something about it,' Jerimiah gave her a severe look, 'and promised me you'd be in separate rooms.'

'Of course, Dad,' Jo replied, giving her father a wide-eyed, innocent smile.

'That's all right, then,' he said, hoping he sounded as if he believed her.

Jo took a mouthful of tea.

'I was wondering, Jo . . .' said Jerimiah. 'If I knocked up a couple of sign boards in the next day or so, could you paint notices on them in your best handwriting?'

She laughed. 'I don't know about best handwriting. My English teacher Miss Wood used to say my script was like a drunk spider who'd fallen in an inkwell, but I'll have a go. What's it for?'

'Oh, just an idea that's come to me,' he replied.

Queenie came in from the kitchen and handed him a cup.

Jerimiah glanced at the door leading out to the hall. 'Has Ida been up there all afternoon?'

'She has,' said his mother. 'Although I thought she might have roused herself when she heard you come in.'

Jerimiah put his drink on the floor and stood up. 'I think I'll just go and see if she's perhaps sickening for—'

The door burst open and Ida walked in. She'd changed from her work clothes and was now wearing a pair of trousers and a thick jumper and carrying the briefcase that contained all the family documents, ready for another night in the shelter.

'Hello, me darling,' Jerimiah said, giving her a warm smile. 'Ma said you had a headache.'

Ida gave him a look that could have cut tempered steel then barged past him and into the kitchen.

He looked at Jo, who shrugged. Searching his brain and finding nothing that he knew of that might have upset his wife, Jerimiah followed her through. By the time he got into the kitchen Ida had put the old picnic basket she took to the shelter with her on the table and was packing the sandwiches for her and Billy's night underground.

'Isn't it a bit early to go to the shelter?' he asked, as she slammed the Thermos flask in beside the tins of sandwiches.

'Might as well beat the rush,' she replied, without glancing at him.

'Good idea,' he replied, watching his wife's sharp movements and tightly drawn face.

She looked up and he noticed her eyes were red-rimmed.

'I saw Ellen today in the market,' she continued, as her stare bore into him like two hot needles.

'Ellen?'

'Yes, Ellen Gilbert,' she said. 'Surely you remember her?'

'Yes, of course I do,' said Jerimiah, unease creeping up his spine. 'She was a good friend to you, to both of us.'

'Yes, she was, wasn't she?' Ida gave him a brittle smile. 'She had Michael with her.'

Jerimiah frowned. 'Michael? Michael who?'

His wife's hazel eyes, flint-like with pain, fixed on his face. 'Michael. Your son.'

The breath caught in Jerimiah's lungs and the blood stilled in his veins.

'My . . .'

'Son,' Ida repeated. 'Michael. That's what she called him. He's about ten and so like our Charlie at that age he could have been his twin.'

27

Jerimiah's jaw dropped. 'Ida, I—'

'Aren't you going to say there's some mistake,' Ida cut in.

Jerimiah opened his mouth, but no words came as jumbled images, long buried and forgotten, resurfaced in his mind.

'Or perhaps, "He couldn't possibly be mine, Ida, because I've never been with Ellen,"' she continued, tears springing into her eyes again. With pain and anger reddening her face she glared at him, daring him to say something. Several heartbeats passed before Jerimiah found his voice.

'Let me explain, Ida,' he said. Crossing the space between them, he tried to capture her in his arms.

She stepped back. 'Don't you touch me.'

Jerimiah let his arms fall to his sides and he stood there, helpless, as she dragged her coat from the nail at the back of the door and put it on. She snapped the hamper shut and heaved it off the table.

She opened the door to the parlour. 'Tell Billy to meet me at the shelter, Jo,' she shouted through to her daughter.

'Righto, Mum,' Jo called back from the living room.

Ida closed the door then giving him another murderous look she crossed the kitchen and went out into the backyard. She marched across to the gate, but Jerimiah got there first.

'Ida, please,' he said, trying to take her arm but she knocked his hand away.

She spun around to face him, tears glistering on her cheeks. 'By my reckoning you and she must have had your bit of fun about eleven years ago. Eleven years ago, when James died. I hate you, do you hear? I hate you, so don't you dare touch me, Jerimiah Brogan. Not now, not ever again!'

Tearing the gate open she stormed out.

With a yawning chasm opening in his chest, Jerimiah stared helplessly into the dark side alleyway as the woman he'd loved from the first moment he'd laid eyes on her marched away, taking her love with her.

Chapter Three

'THAT'S THE LAST of them,' said Jerimiah, heaving the cardboard box of Player's cigarettes he was carrying on to the corner shop's counter.

'Thanks, Mr Brogan,' said Lena Robinstein, the shopkeeper. 'You're a lifesaver. There'd have been a riot if they hadn't arrived today.'

It was late morning on the next day and he was standing in Robins & Sons general store between an artistically arranged pile of OMO washing powder and a stack of galvanised buckets.

Lena and her husband Morris had owned the shop at the corner of Tailor Place and Ben Johnson Road for as long as Jerimiah could remember; they had also been leading lights in the Brady Boys' Club in Durward Street before it closed at the outbreak of war. They now put their considerable philanthropic efforts into finding homes for Jewish children who had been smuggled out from the horrors across the Channel.

Like many shops of its kind, Robins, which served several local streets, was crammed full of household essentials, from arsenic-coated fly paper to dried baby milk and everything else in between.

Jerimiah had just arrived at the Methodist Hall to parade with the Home Guard the night before when the potman of the Old House at Home public house around the corner came into the yard. He'd had a frantic telephone call from Morris saying he was clean out of fags and urgently needed his monthly supply of cigarettes collected from the warehouse in Canning Town; his van's radiator had sprung a leak and he wondered if Jerimiah could help.

Jerimiah had been happy to oblige: it would give Samson an easy day plus it was thirty bob for half a day's work.

'Any time,' Jerimiah said now, as Lena handed him his money. 'I've given you my girl Mattie's telephone number so just ring if you need anything else and she'll pass on the message and,' he pulled a postcard from the breast pocket of his waistcoat and offered it to her, 'if you wouldn't mind putting this in your window, I'd be much obliged. It's tuppence a week, isn't it?'

She nodded.

Jerimiah fished a shilling from his trouser pocket and handed it to her. 'I'll be back in six weeks with another.'

Lena scanned the details of Jerimiah's new business.

'You're branching out,' she said, giving him an impressed look over her half-rimmed glasses.

'I am.' He touched his cap. 'Good day to you, Mrs Robinstein, and give my regards to your husband.'

After holding the door open so a mother with a toddler in tow could enter the shop, Jerimiah left. He had nothing much to do until the auction of unclaimed goods at Bethnal Green Council's depot at three so he decided to head back to the yard. Usually, it would have been to have a swift half and a pie in the Lord Nelson, but today he just wanted to be alone and think. Think about the trouble he was in.

Not so much how he'd got himself in such a mess, he knew that fine well, but how, if he was ever going to have a day of joy in his life again, he could persuade Ida to forgive him.

Giving Samson an affectionate pat on the neck as he passed, Jerimiah freed the horse's tether from the lamp-post, put his foot on the wheel hub, and leapt on to the front of the cart. Sensing the shifting weight, the gelding pricked up his ears as Jerimiah took up the reins. Kicking off the brake, he shook the leather straps and the horse set off along the familiar road towards home.

Tucking his sheepskin jerkin around him and holding the reins lightly in his hand, Jerimiah put his feet up on the wooden guard, and rested back. He let his mind wander through the increasing list of people wanting to be moved over the next few weeks as Samson plodded homeward at his own steady pace with only the occasional tug on the reins to turn him as necessary.

He was just wondering if he could squeeze in a quick delivery to East Ham the following Tuesday when he saw Ellen. She was sitting on the low wall by the bus stop at the corner of the street and when she spotted him she stood up.

Queenie and Ellen's mother had become friendly through the mothers' group at the church, so he had known Ellen more or less all his life. She'd been a pretty enough child who turned into a pretty enough young woman with gentle blue-grey eyes and a sweet temperament. They'd had a jig or two at Shamrock League dances with the odd kiss added in, but that was before he'd met Ida.

Ida had joined Ellen's class in the third year of elementary school when her family moved into the area. She and Ellen had become fast friends from the first, always together, arm in arm. And to him Ellen had always been Ida's friend who popped in occasionally for a cuppa and a gossip. Even with the few moments of madness they had shared ten years before, that's how Jerimiah thought about Ellen, nothing more.

Pulling Samson to a halt, Jerimiah jumped down from the front seat as Ellen crossed the road.

'Hello, Jerimiah,' she said a little breathlessly, as she stopped in front of him.

'Hello, Ellen,' he replied, noting the half a dozen people waiting at the bus stop who looked their way. 'I hope you've not been waiting long?'

She shook her head. 'I need to talk to you.'

'You most certainly do.' Jerimiah took hold of Samson's halter. 'You'd better come inside.'

Taking the key from his trouser pocket, he unlocked the padlock and threw open the double gates. Eyeing his manger at the far end of the yard, Samson shook his head and ambled through the gates without urging. Jerimiah stood back as Ellen followed the wagon in and then did the same, leaving the gates open so those on the other side of the road didn't get the wrong idea.

Catching hold of a dining chair from the pile of furniture he had for sale, Jerimiah carried it across and set it beside Ellen. She gave him a grateful look and sat down.

Leaving her to catch her breath, Jerimiah replenished Samson's manger with fresh hay and started loosening the horse's harness so he could rest before his three-mile trot to Bethnal Green after lunch. Free of the wooden shafts of the wagon, the horse started munching on his lunch.

Jerimiah lowered the shafts to the floor then, walking around to the other side of the horse, he glanced across Samson's tufty withers at Ellen as he unbuckled the girth.

'I'm sorry to come to the yard and give people something new to talk about,' she said, twisting her fingers together.

'Sure, don't you worry about that,' he replied lightly. 'It's been my aim for some time to give the gossips something fresh each day.' Lowering his eyes and taking up a brush,

Jerimiah started brushing the horse's flanks. 'Ida told me she'd seen you and about the boy—'

'Michael,' Ellen cut in.

'Michael.' He regarded her steadily. 'Is he mine?'

She smiled, and Jerimiah caught a fleeting glimpse of the woman he'd once known so well.

'Yes,' she replied. 'You only have to look at him to see that and you know yourself Paul was not a well man, so I'd not been a wife to him for a year before we—'

She lowered her eyes, then, after studying his steel-toe-capped boots for a moment, she raised her head.

'I'm sorry,' she said, her deep-set eyes holding his. 'I didn't mean you to find out like this.'

'You mean by me having my wife tell me I've a son by the woman who was her best friend,' he said.

Ellen flinched.

Shame washed over Jerimiah. 'No, 'tis I who should be sorry, Ellen,' he said with a heavy sigh. 'This is a storm of my own making.'

'You didn't force me, Jerimiah,' she said quietly. 'I'm as much to blame as you, and it can't be easy for you to find out you have another son.'

'It's not,' Jerimiah replied. 'But it's a whole lot harder for Ida.'

'I'm sure,' said Ellen. 'I suppose she was furious.'

Jerimiah didn't reply. He didn't have to as they both knew Ida well. They stared at each other for a moment then Jerimiah moved to Samson's shaggy head and unfastening the horse's blinkers. For a long moment only the sound of the horse's teeth munching on the hay punctuated the silence and then Jerimiah spoke again.

'Well, then,' he said, stepping out from behind the horse,

'after keeping Michael a secret from me for all this time I'm wondering why you feel the need to tell me about him now?'

Yawning, and with her arms aching from the two heavy shopping bags hanging from them, Ida turned into Mafeking Terrace just after twelve thirty.

The sky was iron grey and she'd hoped to be home from work before the weather broke. She had only popped to the market on her way home to pick up something for tea but when she got there the Home and Colonial had just had a consignment of tinned peaches and corned beef, so Ida had bought three of each to stash alongside the rest of the tins and packets she was putting by for Christmas. What's more, Feltons had just found some Christmas wrapping paper from somewhere. It was dull stuff, really – you could hardly distinguish the robins from the holly leaves and it had probably been tucked away in their storeroom for years. Although she had barely anything to wrap in it as yet, she spent her last few coppers on half a dozen sheets.

The Luftwaffe had decided to make up for lost time the night before, sending wave after wave of bombers throughout the night until they ran out of either bombs or fuel and disappeared back to France. The all-clear had sounded just before dawn. She'd arrived home with Billy and baby Patrick twenty minutes later to find Queenie had already been out and about getting the family bread from the Jewish baker around the corner.

Stella finished work sometime after midnight so wouldn't be around to collect Patrick until at least ten, so while Ida went to work Queenie tended him. It wasn't ideal, given that Queenie was completely potty, but there was a war on. Leaving Billy having breakfast and Patrick asleep in his pram, Ida had downed a quick cup of tea and hurried off to work.

She yawned again, weariness washing over her. Of course, everyone was tired after a full night of bombing. In fact, they'd been exhausted from lack of sleep since the Germans started their nightly bombing raids last September, but Ida was bone weary for a very different reason. Michael, with the dark grey eyes of his father, had ripped her life and heart apart.

How could he? How could Jerimiah have done this to her? And with Ellen, of all ruddy people, and their James not yet cold in his grave.

Feeling tears pressing the back of her eyes again she hurried on and turned into the alleyway between the houses just as the first spot of rain hit the pavement.

Dragging her feet, Ida went through the back gate, across the yard and in through the back door, heaving the two canvas shopping bags on to the kitchen table with a heavy sigh. Unwinding her scarf, she shoved it in the pocket of her coat which she hung on a free peg.

By rights, the family's main living room should have been the one at the front of the house, but Queenie and her moth-eaten parrot, Prince Albert, had taken up residence there. Since her mother-in-law's arrival, the rest of the family had had to squash into the back parlour for everything, including entertaining Father Mahon when he called for his twice-a-month visit. However, the back parlour had the door to the kitchen opening into it so was a great deal warmer than the front room, even before she lit the fire in the morning.

Wondering if Billy's school trousers would last him until Christmas or if she'd have to apply to the council for extra coupons and get him a new pair, Ida walked into the back room to find Jerimiah sprawled out in his chair asleep.

He was dressed in his version of the Home Guard uniform, which consisted of full battle dress but with his blue paisley waistcoat beneath and the sheepskin jerkin he wore on the wagon over the top. His combat trousers, secured with a wide brown leather belt with a stylised buckle, were tucked into his hobnail boots, while around his neck was a red neckerchief, tied in a dapper knot at his throat.

He was lying with his head back and his hands resting lightly on the arms of the chair, his long legs stretched out in front of him.

There was a hint of silver amongst the bluey grey of his afternoon bristles and the lines around his mouth were deeper than usual; his hair, still abundantly curly and a little longer than most men wore it, was dishevelled.

It had clearly been a hard night for those working to keep the capital and the people dwelling there safe, and he'd gone straight from that on to the yard to start his morning's work.

The familiar feelings of compassion for the man who'd shared her life and bed for a quarter of a century started to rise within her, but she cut them short.

With imagined pictures of her husband entwined with Ellen playing in her head, Ida's eyes returned to Jerimiah's hands. She studied those strong, square fingers that had caressed and pleased Ellen Gilbert.

He opened his eyes. 'Hello, luv.'

'I thought you were going over to Bethnal Green this afternoon,' she said, the corners of her mouth downturned.

'I am,' he said, stretching his face to wake himself up. 'But the council sale isn't until three.'

'Well, I haven't got you any dinner,' Ida replied.

'It's all right,' he said, 'I'll get something on the way. I wanted to see you, though, before I headed off.'

He stood up and crossed the space between them in two strides.

Despite her pounding heart, Ida gave him a chilly look. 'I suppose you want a cup of tea.'

'Only if you're making one.'

He gave her a tentative smile, which Ida answered with a glacial stare.

'If you don't mind,' she said flatly, indicating that she wanted him to move out of her way.

He stared down at her for a second then stepped aside. Ida brushed past him into the kitchen and he followed her.

Painfully aware of him standing behind her, Ida took the kettle to the tap to fill it then returned it to the stove and lit the gas beneath it.

As the gas popped and spluttered, and feeling his eyes boring into her back, she started to unpack her shopping.

'Ellen was waiting when I got back to the yard,' he said, as she pulled a tin of corned beef out of the bag.

She slammed it on the table, feeling something akin to a double-edged saw cut through her heart. Then she hung her head and stared at a whirled knot on the table's surface, images of Jerimiah holding Ellen, kissing Ellen, flaring up once more in her mind.

'Ida,' he said softly.

Straightening up, she turned and faced him. 'What did she want?' she said finally.

'To talk,' he replied.

Ida raised an eyebrow. 'Just talk? Not for a quick one in the office for old times' sakes, then?' she said, twisting the knife buried in her heart.

'Ida.'

'I hope she ain't after money,' she snapped, thumping another tin next to the first.

'She's not,' said Jerimiah.

'Cos we've got precious little of that,' Ida continued.

Jerimiah sighed. 'She's not after money.'

'Well, what's she after then, you?' said Ida. 'Maybe widowhood don't suit her, and she's after a bit of the other. It wouldn't surprise me. She always did have a hankering after you.' With tears shimmering on her lower lids, Ida gave him a brittle smile. 'And now it would seem you had a bit of a hankering for her, too.'

He frowned. 'That's not true. From the moment I saw you with that red ribbon in your hair at the St Patrick's Day dance there's been no one else.'

'Except Ellen,' Ida snapped back. 'Anyway.' She turned back to her shopping and pulled out the rolls of wrapping paper. 'If it's not you or money then—'

'She's dying,' said Jerimiah softly.

Feeling as if she'd just had ice water tipped over her, Ida turned and stared at him.

'Some tumour in her lung,' he continued. 'She's got a few months, if she's lucky. That's why she came back. To find me, to tell me about Michael and . . .' His dark grey eyes that sent her heart fluttering held hers. 'To ask me to look after him when she dies.'

'What did you say?'

His gaze didn't falter. 'I said I'd have to speak to you.'

Fury gripped Ida. 'Well, that's good of you.'

He held his calloused hands out in supplication. 'What could I say, Ida? It's us or some orphanage somewhere and I wouldn't want to condemn any child to that.'

Neither would Ida, usually, but at the moment she'd happily tie a lead weight to the boy, Ellen and Jerimiah too and pitch them off Southend pier.

She stared wordlessly at him for a moment then the kettle whistle started. Turning her back on him, Ida went to the cooker and turned off the gas.

Painfully aware of her husband standing just behind her, she spoke again. 'You'd better be off to your sale, then.'

After what seemed like a lifetime, a gust of cold air shot across the room before the back door slammed shut as Jerimiah crashed out of the kitchen.

Forcing her gaze to remain on the kettle, out of the corner of her eye, Ida watched her husband stride across the yard but as he banged the gate behind him Ida staggered back. Falling on to the chair, she rested her elbows on the table, covered her face with her hands, and sobbed.

'Can I, Mum, pleeeeeease?' Billy whined, his voice cutting through the fog in Ida's head.

'Can you what?' she asked, forcing herself to concentrate on her son, who was bouncing along beside her.

'Go and knock for Keith?' asked Billy.

'All right, as long as you're in the shelter by the time I get there,' Ida replied, adjusting her grip on the picnic basket.

'Thanks, Mum,' Billy shouted as he dashed off.

It was just gone six o'clock and more than three hours since Jerimiah had told her why Ellen had returned. It was also ten minutes since she'd closed her back door, but it might as well have been ten hours or ten days. In fact, in the short walk from her house to her son's house two streets over, Ida had seriously considered just lying down in the road and to hell with the Luftwaffe and their bombs.

Forcing the images of Ellen and Jerimiah in each other's arms out of her head, Ida turned the corner of Ladysmith Terrace where her daughter-in-law lived.

Charlie himself had joined up as soon as war was declared and was currently with the 8th Army in North Africa, but his wife of nine months, Stella, and his six-month-old son, Patrick, lived halfway down on the east side of the two-up two-down terraced cottages.

As the light was now all but gone, Ida took the torch from her pocket and switched it on. Pointing it downwards as the blackout regulations demanded, she continued until she found herself outside the red-painted door of number 43.

Grasping the knocker, she banged on it twice and stood back, noting that, as always, every housewife in the street had scrubbed a half circle on the pavement outside their front door that day. Every housewife, that is, except her daughter-in-law.

The lock rattled, and Stella stood illuminated by the low-wattage hall light in the door frame.

The only average thing about Stella was her height, everything else was greatly exaggerated. The bright auburn victory rolls at her temples were larger, her pencilled eyebrows were higher and her lipstick redder. Even the cigarettes she smoked were cork tipped whereas most people made do with rough cut. Despite having had a baby only six months before, her corseted waist was drawn in an inch

41

or two tighter, thereby emphasising the most prominent feature she possessed: her breasts.

Tonight, like a pair of pink torpedoes, these were pushed up beneath the tight, sweetheart neckline of her figure-hugging dress as if ready to fire at someone. Someone, that is, wearing trousers.

'Oh, it's you,' Stella said, regarding her mother-in-law from beneath heavily mascaraed eyelashes. 'I've not got Patrick ready yet.'

'That's all right, I'll wait,' said Ida. 'You'd better let me in before you have the warden after you for showing a light.'

'Not unless he wants another mouthful from me, he won't.' She stepped back from the door. 'I suppose you'd better come in while I fetch Patrick. I was just getting him up when you knocked.'

'I'll come around the back next time if you like,' said Ida.

Stella threw her a sour look. 'You know I prefer visitors to knock.'

Of course she did: Stella thought friends and family letting themselves in around the back of the house was common.

'Wait here and I'll get him,' she added.

She left the room and her high-heeled footsteps could be heard going up the stairs. Ida looked around the small front room, which was about the same size as Ida's back parlour. It was immaculately kept, thanks to the woman two doors down, who Stella paid to clean for her.

Unlike the living room in Mafeking Terrace, which was crammed with an assortment of chairs, table and, of course, the oversized bookcase, Stella's main room was furnished like one of those houses you saw in the dog-eared glossy magazines at the doctor's surgery.

A matching pair of sage-coloured roll-armed easy chairs

sat either side of the fireplace with a matching sofa against the wall opposite. There was also a sideboard with a walnut veneer gramophone on it and a dozen or so records slotted upright in a rack beside it plus an oval mirror with bevelled edges above.

The hearth was surrounded by tawny marbled tiles. Instead of the usual family portraits on the mantelshelf, Stella had a heavy onyx clock on a stout plinth with a scantily clad nymph pirouetting on top and two greyhounds either side watching her.

There was a photo of her and Charlie on their wedding day on the wall in the alcove to the right of the chimney breast, with another of a very new-born Patrick alongside. On the wall of the opposite alcove, instead of an image of Charlie in his uniform, there was a photo of Stella perched on a bar stool; she was dressed in a skin-tight evening gown, leaning forward and showing cleavage down to her navel. She had jewels at the throat and ears and a wanton invitation spread across her face.

Her daughter-in-law's shoes clip-clopped down the stairs again and Stella walked back into the room holding Patrick.

He was wrapped in the pale blue pram set, with the matching bonnet and bootees secured by pom-pom ties that Mattie had knitted for him.

He rubbed his eyes and blinked a couple of times then, seeing Ida, he smiled and stretched out his arms.

Ida did the same and his mother promptly handed him over.

'How is he?' asked Ida, settling him on to her hip.

Delving into her handbag on the sideboard Stella took out a silver cigarette case and shrugged. 'Same as ever: grizzly. Why?'

'I just thought he had a bit of a snuffle last night, that's all,' said Ida, pressing her lips on to her grandson's cheek and enjoying its softness.

'Can't say as I'd noticed,' her daughter-in-law replied.

'Have you heard from Charlie?' Ida asked.

Flicking a flame from her lighter Stella lit her cigarette and nodded. 'I got one in the afternoon post yesterday.'

'What did he say?' asked Ida.

'Not much. Just army stuff,' Stella replied, spreading her mouth wide as she checked her lipstick in the mirror. 'I only skimmed it.'

Ida studied her for a second or two and spoke again. 'You're a bit dressed up for a night shift in a factory canteen, aren't you?'

Pressing her lips together in the reflection, Stella turned. 'Oh, didn't I tell you?' she said, all wide-eyed innocence. 'I've got a new job.'

'Oh, yes,' said Ida. 'Where's that?'

'Just a dining club up West,' Stella replied. 'It's for officers and government top brass only. Very exclusive. I change when I get there but I can't turn up looking like I'm there to scrub the floors.' She turned back to the mirror and gave Ida a sweet smile. 'Can I?'

'If you say so,' Ida replied.

Annoyance flashed across Stella's powdered face for a second then she gave Ida a sweet smile. 'Fancy me yakking on about my new job hob-knobbing with the squadron leaders and generals and keeping you from your nice dry spot in the shelter.'

'Give Mummy a kiss, Patrick,' said Ida, giving her daughter-in-law a tight smile. 'And we can go and have a nice time with our friends.'

She held him towards his mother who, blowing a steam of cigarette smoke out of the side of her mouth, kissed the air next to her baby's cheek. Patrick reached for his mother's cigarette, but Ida caught his hand. Taking Patrick's white crochet blanket that was draped across the back of the sofa she wrapped it around the baby and laid him in the pram tucked in the corner of the room.

'And he might need changing,' said Stella, turning back to the mirror.

Ida kicked off the brake and manoeuvred the pram's front wheels between the furniture.

Pushing the pram into the dimly lit hallway, Ida stopped.

'There you are, my little sweetheart,' she said in a low voice as she tucked one of her own blankets around him to keep out the chill. Realising he was about to set out on his nightly jaunt with his gran, Patrick kicked his legs and smiled at her.

Pain cut through Ida's chest as the image of Ellen's son Michael flashed through her mind. Raising her eyes to stop the threatening tears from forming, she opened the front door and pushed the pram out into the cold night air.

As the low boom of the ack-ack guns on Tower Hill shook the ground in the Tilbury Shelter, dislodging specks of dust from the high roof over her, Ida pulled the hood of the Silver Cross pram a little further over the baby sleeping peacefully beneath.

The Braithwaites, Rose on the tambourine and her husband Eric on the accordion, had just finished leading the evening's communal singing, and all around mothers were calling the younger children back from their games to bed them down for the night. The older children, Billy included, were amusing themselves under one of the arches at the back, playing board games or shove ha'penny until the main light went out.

Tilbury Shelter, under the warehouse of the same name, on Cable Street had been taken over by the council to shelter the population of Stepney. Unfortunately, whoever's job it was to get the shelter in order had forgotten to clear out the stock of rancid margarine left in the basement. What with that and the stink from the shelter's three over-flowing toilets – planks of wood over buckets that the council deemed sufficient for six thousand men, women and children – the smell in the shelter had left them all gagging. How anyone had managed to eat the 'Shelter Picnic' that the Ministry of Information had advised people to take with them when they heard the siren was beyond Ida.

However, after a year and a half of nightly bombing raids, life in the shelters had taken on a much more civilised existence for a number of reasons. For a start, there were fewer people using them each night. Even as houses were destroyed around them, many people just stayed at home. What's more, while it was considered the duty of women to ensure children and babies were safe in shelters each night, people tended to regard any working men who cowered underground as cowards who should be up top helping to defend the city.

These days, the women who spent each night in the shelter had got themselves organised, too. Along with the official ARP wardens there were section marshals like Ida, who made sure people kept to their designated area. This allowed people to leave items like deckchairs or camping chairs in the shelter instead of carrying them to and fro. So now, although spaces were still supposed to be allocated on a first come, first served basis, many families, like Ida's, had their regular spots. And although the walls were still rough brick, people had pinned up family photos, giving the place a homely feel.

The upshot of all this was that the Tilbury, which had been so notorious that toffs and nobs from up West had taken sightseeing trips to see its squalid conditions, now had a permanent WVS canteen and a designated washing area so people could do their morning ablutions before going to work. The chief librarian at St George's library had even set up a lending library there so, along with the nightly sing-songs and parlour games, there were plenty of ways to help people while away the idle hours.

To be honest, though, despite the relative comfort and the good-natured camaraderie of the shelter, Ida would have rather taken her chances, like thousands of others, in her own bed. However, Billy and Patrick were another matter so, unless London was blanketed in thick fog, every evening just after six, she made her way to the shelter to bed herself, Billy and Patrick down for the night.

'Is that your Charlie's boy?'

Ida raised her head and found herself looking into the very familiar face of Mary Unwin. Her erstwhile neighbour was about a year or two older than Ida and the mother of three strapping lads, all of whom had joined up the same time as Charlie.

'Yes, he is,' said Ida, gazing down adoringly at her grandson. 'This is little Patrick.'

Patrick's almost transparent eyelids fluttered for a second, squeezing at Ida's heart. His lips sucked on air for a moment or two then he gave a little sigh and settled back to sleep.

'He looks just like your Charlie,' Mary said, the strip light above shining on the lenses of her spectacles.

'He does, doesn't he?' said Ida.

'How old?' asked Mary.

'Six months.'

'Aw, God bless him and keep him. And such a beautiful pram,' said Mary, casting an admiring gaze over the coach-built body of the stroller. 'It's a Silver Cross, isn't it?'

Mary was right. It was a real beauty, with a grey body and blue interior, chrome swirls on each side, C-sprung wheels and mock-ivory handle. Ida wondered, not for the first time, how in the midst of rationing and shortages, her daughter-in-law had managed to get her hands on it.

'Yes,' said Ida tightly. 'So when did you get back?'

'Last week,' said Mary. 'My Reg said now the bombing's eased up a bit we should be safe enough but to be honest I think it's cos he got sick of living at the back of beyond with my sister and her screaming kids.'

'Where were you?' asked Ida, as distant booms indicated a German bomb had landed close to the Shadwell Basin half a mile away.

'Somewhere near Billericay but you had to walk half a mile to fetch a loaf of bread,' continued Mary. 'And the locals all looked down their blooming noses at us and called us common, ruddy cheek. I tell you, I couldn't wait to get back. As soon as Reg said we were off I had my bags packed and by the door. We tried to get our old house back but the bloke at the Chapman estate office said some young family has moved in.'

'Yes, the Pierces,' said Ida. 'Nice couple with three little 'uns. He works on the railways and she always says hello.'

'Well, we've got a couple of rooms in Perth Street, but we're top of the list if one comes up in Mafeking.' Mary glanced around the vaulted ceiling. 'This old place has changed a bit since I was last here.'

'We've got proper toilets, for a start,' said Ida, indicating the tall cubicles tucked away in an alcove at the back of the shelter.

The guns on Tower Hill let off another round as a bomb found its target close by and the floor trembled.

'So did your Charlie marry that nice Italian girl whose family had the fish bar on Commercial Road?' asked Mary when the ground stopped shaking.

'You mean Mattie's friend Francesca?' asked Ida, somewhat surprised at the question.

Mary nodded.

'I wish he had.' Ida's mouth pulled into a hard line. 'He married Stella Miggles.'

'Stella Miggles from Castle Street?' asked Mary, her eyes wide with horror.

'The same.'

'Oh, well,' said Mary brightly, forcing a smile, 'people change.' She gave a light laugh but Ida didn't join in. Mary blinked a couple of times then glanced at the pile of blankets. 'Is she with you?'

'No,' Ida replied. 'She got a job up West, so I bring Patrick with me and Billy.'

'Jerimiah's not with you, then?' said Mary.

Pain ripped through Ida. 'No,' she said, over the lump in her throat. 'He's out with the Home Guard.' She looked away and started fiddling with the blankets. 'I ought to get things—'

'Course,' said Mary. 'I better get back, too.'

'Yes,' said Ida. Her eyes felt suddenly tight. 'Mind how you go.'

Mary gave her a quick smile and then made her way back to her own space.

Stretching her eyes and telling herself not to be so soft, Ida shook out the blankets and folded them ready for later. Patrick gave a little cry and Ida glanced at her watch. It was almost time for his night bottle, so Ida rested her hand on the side of the pram and stared down at the sleeping baby. Bringing his little fist up, Patrick arched his back and yawned. Tears sprang again into Ida's eyes but this time she couldn't hold them back. Staring down at her sleeping grandson she wiped them away with the heel of her hand.

As another blast rocked the earth, a bitter-sweet smile spread across Ida's lips. Mary was right. Patrick did look exactly like his father but heartbreakingly also very like little James, the baby she'd lost eleven years ago.

Jerimiah had always maintained that being an only child, like him, was a lonely existence so he'd been keen to have a large family. Ida, who had always thought half a dozen was a nice round number, had been more than happy to oblige. She'd expected to become pregnant again after weaning Jo but after six years she and Jerimiah had given up hope of more children when to both their delights they discovered Ida was carrying again. They thought their joy complete when after a long labour James came, feet first, into the world. But sadly, despite theirs and the family's fervent prayers, James stayed with them for just six short days.

Oddly, at the same time as they were weeping over James's small white coffin, her sister Pearl had dumped a baby boy that no one knew she'd been carrying at the old workhouse. Ida, deep in grief, went and fetched him out. Nursing Billy with James's milk helped Ida come back from the hell of her loss and come to terms with the fact she and Jerimiah would have only four children. Except, of course, now it seemed that while she was the mother of four of Jerimiah's children, Ellen Gilbert was the mother of his fifth.

Chapter Four

HOLDING THE BOARD against one of the yard's gates with one hand, Jerimiah took one of the four nails he held between his lips with the other.

Using his elbow to anchor the board firmly against the wood, he positioned the nail into the right-hand corner then, taking the hammer from his back pocket, he whacked it into place. Repeating this action with the other three nails he fixed the sign Jo had painted into place.

'Oi, oi, that looks a bit fancy for an old Paddy like you, Jerry,' someone called behind him.

It was Wednesday and just after four thirty in the afternoon and the October light was already fading. Last night, when the air raid siren went off at seven followed by at least a dozen waves of enemy bombers, they'd thought they were in for a full night's action. However, for some unfathomable reason by three in the morning they'd stopped, allowing Jerimiah and the rest of the Home Guard platoon to grab an hour or so of kip on the Methodist Hall floor between patrols.

It was a double blessing as today was when he'd agreed to move Brian O'Connor's sister into new accommodation in Chigwell; he'd got back from the job half an hour ago. Having settled Samson in for the evening he'd just had time – and enough light – to put up the advertisement board.

Jerimiah turned and smiled. 'No so much of the "old" now, Murphy, for I've still a year or two before I catch up with you.'

Keith Murphy, the foreman at the packing factory and Jerimiah's longstanding friend, laughed.

'You're right there,' he said. 'You walking my way home?'

'In a while,' Jerimiah called back. 'I've some things to take care of first.'

Keith waved and continued on his way.

Jerimiah stood back and read the freshly painted board he'd just fixed in place:

J. B. Brogan & Sons Removals
Friendly Service at a Reasonable Price
Enquire at: 25 Mafeking Terrace or leave a note under
the gate or with the barman at the Catholic Club
No job too small

Keith was right, it was a bit posh for a Paddy's rag-and-bone yard, but Jo had done a grand job and hopefully it would attract trade as well as attention, which was, after all, the whole reason for him fixing it there.

Swinging his hammer in his hand, Jerimiah went back into the yard. In his stall Samson was already munching away at his oats so, grabbing the tarpaulin as he passed, Jerimiah headed for the stack of furniture he'd bought at the bomb sale at Bermondsey the day before.

He'd just had wind of another sale over Haggerston way on the following Tuesday. It was a bit early but if he headed across the marches as soon as he finished Home Guard duty he should get first pickings.

Putting the hammer back in his tool box and snapping closed the lid, Jerimiah cast his eye around again. Leaving the dim lamps casting a pale light over the horse resting in the stall he took the padlock from the nail in the wall and left the yard, locking the double gates securely behind him.

As he turned to walk away he caught sight of the sign again and his eyes fixed on the word 'sons'. Just two short days ago, that would have meant Charlie and Billy but now . . .

Flipping his collar up against the biting wind whipping up off the river, Jerimiah turned in the direction of Shadwell Basin. Within half an hour or so, he was in sight of the Edward's Memorial Gardens, which was all that remained of Shadwell's fish market. A mountain of rubble that had once been a row of terraced houses was swarming with soldiers from the Pioneer Corps trying to clear the road, while a team from the water company were trying to stem the water gushing from the bomb crater.

Skirting around the desk on the pavement where two ARP wardens were directing those whose homes had been obliterated to rest centres, Jerimiah continued on for a few yards before turning into Juniper Street.

The cobbled street was lined on both sides by early-Victorian three-up three-down cottages, much like his own, with bay windows at the front and small yards at the back. Although the far end of the street looked as if it had escaped the blast, every window this end had blown out and glass lay shattered on the ground. Residents were out in the street with brooms and shovels, tackling the mess.

'I hope you'll forgive me for taking you from your task,' Jerimiah said, as he reached a woman wearing a greatcoat and her hair in curlers, 'but I'm looking for Mrs Gilbert who's recently moved in to the street.'

'Does she have a little lad?' the woman asked.

'Yes, she does,' said Jerimiah, an odd feeling passing through him at the thought.

'Number seven. Fourth house before you reach Woodman's on the corner,' she said, nodding towards the shop at the far end of the street.

'My thanks to you,' Jerimiah replied, touching his cap as he strolled on.

Crunching over shards and with neighbours giving him the once-over as he passed, Jerimiah was in front of the house he was seeking within a dozen strides.

He hesitated for a second then grasped the knocker firmly and rapped on the door twice. There was a long pause but just as he was about to knock again the door was opened by a thin woman wearing a colourless apron and down-at-heel slippers. She had curlers in her hair and a roll-up dangled from the corner of her mouth.

The hallway she was standing in matched her rundown appearance, with peeling wallpaper, filthy paintwork and the odd mouse dropping scattered across the bare boards.

Her thin lips pulled into an unfriendly line. 'Yes!'

'I'm looking for Mrs Gilbert.'

The woman looked him over then stood back.

'Upstairs,' she said.

'Thank you.'

Jerimiah stepped inside, catching a whiff of tom cat as he brushed past her. Thinking it safer not to grasp the wood-wormy banister, he made his way up to the first-floor landing.

If the décor downstairs was neglected, the condition of the walls and floor upstairs was disgusting. There was a turn in the staircase halfway up and the window there, which was supposed to illuminate the stairs, was so grimy you could barely see the backyard through it.

At the top of the stairs was a decrepit marble-top table with a two-ring primus stove on it. Jerimiah headed for the room at the end of the landing which overlooked the street.

His heart beating wildly in his chest, he pushed open the door. The room he stepped into would have been the front bedroom but was now being used as a living space. It was sparsely furnished with a beaten-out old sofa he wouldn't have given tuppence for, one easy chair with a few cushions on it and a rickety pair of straight-back chairs. The wallpaper was so faded it was devoid of colour; black mould dotted the top and corners. The curtains at the windows were chenille but so old the velvety pile had been rubbed away. On the mantel above the fireplace was a photograph of a baby and another of a wedding, while at either end of the shelf a pair of cheap porcelain dogs with Southend stamped across their hind quarters faced each other.

Jerimiah noticed all these things in passing even though, from the moment he stepped over the threshold, his focus was on Ellen who was sitting in the tatty chair beside the unlit hearth.

'Hello, Jerimiah,' she said softly. 'It's nice to see you again.'

'Hello, Ellen,' he replied. 'I've come to meet your lad.'

A ghost of a smile lifted her colourless lips.

'He's your lad too, Jerimiah,' she replied, her gaze softening as it ran over him.

Jerimiah forced a smile. 'Is he—'

The door behind Jerimiah opened and he turned as a boy with black curly hair and wearing a green school uniform walked into the room.

'Sorry I took so long, Mum,' he said, walking past Jerimiah and over to his mother's chair. 'There were a lot of people in the chemist and I had to wait for Mr Lachman to make it up.' He handed her a paper bag. 'He said one teaspoon every four hours should do the trick.'

'Thank you, Michael.' She took the boy's hand. 'Sweetheart, this is Mr Brogan. He's an old friend of mine and he's popped by to see us.'

Michael looked up at him and Jerimiah looked into the face of his childhood self.

'Hello,' Michael said, giving Jerimiah a friendly smile.

'Hello, lad,' said Jerimiah, as fatherly emotion stirred in his chest. 'I see you're at Greencoat.' He indicated the embroidered badge on the boy's blazer pocket. 'How do you like it?'

'It's all right now, after I thumped Ron Murphy,' Michael replied.

'Is it now?'

'Yeah,' the lad replied. 'Sister Evangeline gave me six of the best for fighting but Ron don't pick on me any more.'

Jerimiah suppressed a smile.

Michael turned to his mother. 'Can I play out until supper?'

Ellen nodded. 'As long as you stay in the street. But put your duffel coat on and if the siren goes off you're to come straight back.'

Michael grinned. 'Thanks, Mum.'

He snatched his coat from the back of the chair.

'Nice to meet you, Mr Brogan,' he said, as he dashed past.

'You too, lad,' Jerimiah replied.

Michael glanced fondly at his mother and then left the room, his footsteps echoing down the stairwell as he went to join his friends.

Jerimiah stared after him for a long moment then turned to face Ellen. 'He's a fine lad.'

'He is,' said Ellen, motherly pride shining in her eyes. 'And there's no doubting who his father is, is there?'

Jerimiah held her gaze for a moment then sighed. 'No, there's not.'

Feeling the world pressing down on his shoulders, Jerimiah strolled over to the mantelshelf and picked up one of the photo frames.

The image was of a chubby baby lying on his tummy, naked, with a fur rug beneath him. There was one almost identical on the mantelshelf at Mafeking Terrace, of Charlie in the same pose.

He gazed down at it for a long moment then, returning the photo to its place of pride, turned back to face Ellen.

'I've told Ida about your condition,' he said. 'And what you've asked.'

Anxiety showed in Ellen's face. 'Did she agree?'

'Not yet,' Jerimiah replied.

Tears sprang into Ellen's eyes and she covered her mouth with her hands. 'But if he—'

'She needs time,' he said.

'But I haven't got time,' said Ellen, a tear rolling down her cheek. 'Can't you just tell her? He's your son, after all.'

'I know,' he replied. 'And I understand your worry, Ellen, but you can't just expect Ida to welcome Michael with open arms, especially given how he got here.'

'But he's your son,' she repeated.

'And Ida's my wife,' Jerimiah said firmly. 'I let her down, let her down badly, and I'm asking a hell of a lot of her now so she has the final say in all this.'

They stared at each other for a moment then Ellen nodded.

'Good,' said Jerimiah, his grim expression lightening a little. 'I think you know me well enough to know I'm not a man to shirk my responsibilities.'

'No,' Ellen replied with a heavy sigh. 'No, you're not.' She gazed across the space at him for a long moment then adoration filled her eyes. 'Oh, Jerimiah, if only you and I had—'

'I'll let you know what Ida decides,' Jerimiah cut in.

Pain flickered across her face but she gave him a sad smile. 'Give her my regards.'

'I will,' he replied.

He walked to the door but as he turned to wish her good day grief and pity swirled in his chest: grief because forty-two was just too young to die and pity because he never had and never could return Ellen's love.

The searchlights on the Isle of Dogs were already cutting across the clear sky hunting for enemy aircraft when Jerimiah turned into the alleyway that ran between his house and number 23.

Feeling as if he could sleep for a thousand years he opened the rear gate and trudged the last few yards to his back door. Turning the handle, he walked in to the mellow sound of Ethel Waters singing 'Stormy Weather' on the wireless, which seemed very apt.

With two pots simmering on the stove and the table set out for tea, the kitchen was as he'd expect to find it on his return from work, except it was his mother not his wife at the sink.

'Where's Ida?' he asked, taking off his coat and hooking it up.

'She's already gone to the shelter,' his mother replied.

'But it's not six yet,' he said.

His mother shrugged. 'Said she wanted to make sure no one pinched her spot.'

Jerimiah sighed and sank into the chair at the top end of the table. Letting his head rest back against the wall, he closed his eyes and listened to the familiar sound of his mother dishing up the evening meal.

The music drew to a close and the plummy tones of the BBC presenter announced the six o'clock news. He gave them a rundown of Germany's push into Russia and also news of a successful bombing raid carried out by the RAF over unspecified targets in Germany's heartland. In addition, there was welcome news from the Ministry of Food: following America's agreement to send vital supplies to Britain, the first consignments of food would be released to the shops at the end of the month, in time for Christmas. It concluded with a reminder that conserving coal would help build fighter planes.

'There you are, boy,' his mother said, as the *Variety Bandbox* signature tune started.

Jerimiah opened his eyes.

'It's hotpot,' she said, placing the bowl before him.

'That looks grand, Ma.' He gave her a weary smile. 'Has Jo gone too?'

'Just after Ida,' said his mother, returning to the stove. 'Said something about phoning Tommy on the way to work. I reckon, with a full moon and not a cloud in the sky, she and everyone else around here will be having a busy night.' His mother crossed herself. 'Mary bless and keep them.'

'Amen,' said Jerimiah, automatically doing the same as the faces of his children flickered through his mind.

He speared a chunk of turnip with his fork and popped it in his mouth.

Queenie spooned tea leaves into the pot then filled it from the kettle. Stirring it a few times she poured it into two mugs and brought them over.

'Did you get on all right with moving that family?' asked Queenie as she slid his tea across the table.

'More or less,' Jerimiah replied. 'A high explosive bomb had hit the shops at Maryland Point so that held us up for half an hour but once we got past the Green Man at Leytonstone it was pretty straightforward and we were in Chigwell by midday and off-loaded by two.'

'Did they have much?' asked Queenie.

Jerimiah shook his head. 'They had a few bits from downstairs and the relief centre had given them some linen and some basic kitchenware but the blast that demolished their house blew off the roof, so all the wardrobes and beds were destroyed. Luckily, I'd bought a double bed and mattress plus a couple of kiddies' beds in a bomb sale only the day before so I sold them those. Poor old Samson was puffing when I got back but a bellyful of oats should sort him out. It's worth it, though – twice as much as I'd get a week from the government for scrap metal. I'm going to try and get more work like that.'

'That explains the sign you had Jo paint,' said Queenie.

Jerimiah nodded and smiled at his mother. 'I don't suppose there's a letter from Charlie, at all?'

Charlie had volunteered a few weeks after war was declared and was part of a gun crew in the artillery. He'd been one of the last off the beaches at Dunkirk as his regiment had been trying to hold the Nazis back to allow as many men as possible to escape. He was now in the heat and dust of a different continent, getting ready to push the Germans and Italians back into the Mediterranean at Benghazi.

'There was a letter this morning,' his mother said.

'At last,' he said, spearing a slither of meat. 'I was starting to think the boy had lost the use of his hands.'

'Sure, weren't you the same at his age?' His mother smiled. 'I tell you, I counted myself lucky if I got a letter a month while you were away in France. Ida left it on the sideboard for you.'

She took a sip of her tea and they sat in silence until he polished off the last few scraps.

'Well, now,' she said, regarding him over the rim of her mug, 'are you going to tell me what's had Ida glaring at you all the day long and why you're walking around with your tail between your legs?'

Jerimiah knew there was no point trying to convince his mother she had it all wrong, so he told her about Ida's encounter with Ellen. A look of astonishment spread across Queenie's wrinkled face.

'So, let me get this right,' she said, when he'd finished. 'You're this boy's father?'

'Yes, I am,' he said, holding his mother's penetrating gaze.

'For mercy's sake!' she said, staring across the table at him in disbelief. 'No wonder Ida's had a face like a scalded goblin all week.'

'Can you blame her?' Shame surged up in Jerimiah and he raked his fingers through his hair. 'But I only . . . me and . . . it was only the once!'

His mother gave a mirthless laugh. 'For sure, don't I know it only has to be the once? Are you positive you're the father?'

Jerimiah nodded. 'You only have to look at the boy to see he's mine.'

'But if he is your lad, why in the name of all that is holy hasn't she come back to tell you before?' asked his mother.

'Because . . .' He told her about Ellen's condition.

'God and all the saints have mercy,' said Queenie when he'd finished. "'Tis bad enough for one so young to be facing Eternity, let alone to leave a child alone in the world, too.'

'Which is why she's asked me to care for him,' said Jerimiah.

Queenie chewed her lips. 'And what does Ida say to that?'

'She hasn't; not yet,' Jerimiah replied.

Shoving his bowl away, Jerimiah covered his face with his hands as the weight that had been pressing down on him since Monday became even heavier.

He felt his mother's hand on his arm and he looked up.

'What's the lad's name?' she said, her grey eyes filled with love.

'Michael.' Jerimiah held his mother's gaze for a second or two then spoke again. 'I can't undo what's done but I will have to face up to my responsibility—'

The wail of the air raid siren on the top of St George's Town Hall cut off Jerimiah's words.

Throwing back the last of his tea, he stood up. 'But just for now I'm going to get into my Home Guard uniform, grab my rifle and report for duty.'

Chapter Five

GRIPPING ON TO Tommy's upper arms, Jo gasped as the wave of pleasure washed over her. His arms tightened around her for a second then he relaxed and rested his head on her shoulder.

Jo smiled and opened her eyes. She studied the fringed lampshade above the bed for a little while before shifting her gaze to her weekend case on the floor. Her winter coat was thrown over the chair and her clothes and Tommy's khaki uniform formed a haphazard trail to the bed.

It was the last Friday in October and she was lying on the double bed in room sixteen in the Old George Hotel on Stoney Stratford High Street just ten miles from Bletchley Park where Tommy was stationed.

He'd borrowed a friend's Rover 10 and had met her off the London train when it arrived at six fifteen. After half an hour's drive through icy country lanes Tommy had signed them into the hotel's register as Mr and Mrs Sweete. It had taken them five minutes to get to their room and only three minutes to remove each other's clothes before hurling themselves, naked, on to the bed.

Turning her head slightly Jo studied her fiancé's angular face then kissed the bit of him nearest to her lips, which happened to be his shoulder.

He opened his eyes and he smiled.

'I love you,' he whispered.

'I could tell,' Jo replied, pressing her pubic bone on to his thigh.

'Well, what do you expect,' he laughed, 'handing me your still-warm knickers when you greeted me at the station?'

Jo laughed. 'I just thought I'd give you some encouragement.'

'Believe me, my love,' he said, tucking her into him, 'after nearly thirteen weeks I don't need any encouragement.'

Reaching up, Jo ran her hand along his square jaw, enjoying the feel of his evening bristles under her fingertips. 'Twelve weeks and three days, actually.'

His dark eyes captured hers. They gazed silently and lost in love for a couple of heartbeats then Tommy lowered his mouth on to hers, setting her recently sated needs trembling again.

After a moment he released her lips and sat up on the side of the bed. Having dealt with the French letter he swung his legs back on to the bed then, gathering her to him, he rolled on his back. Snuggling closer, Jo rested her head in the dip between his shoulder and neck, sliding her smooth leg over his hair-roughened one.

The winter wind rattled the casement window and Tommy pulled the sheet and blankets over them to keep out the chill.

'Well, as my leave starts the Saturday before Christmas,' he said, 'at least it won't be as long before I see you next time.'

'There might be a bit of a problem with you kipping on the sofa at mine, though,' Jo said, idly twirling her fingers through his chest hair.

'Why, has your mum gone off me or something?' he asked.

'No. She's gone off Dad.' Jo told him about her parents' argument.

'Blimey,' he said when she'd finished. 'And you don't know what it's about?'

Jo shook her head. 'But I hope they sort it out soon. Mum's snapping everyone's heads off while Dad's just moping with his chin scraping the floor. Gran knows what's up but she's not letting on. Whatever Dad's done it must be pretty bad – I've never seen them at odds for this long before. It'll be bad enough having Mattie and Cathy not speaking at the dinner table without Mum and Dad looking daggers across the Christmas pudding at each other.'

Tommy pulled a face. 'It's a pity your mum and dad have fallen out,' he said, 'because I was hoping I could persuade your mum to help me with something.'

'Sounds intriguing.'

He grinned. 'I'm being transferred back to London.'

Jo's eyes flashed open. 'Oh, Tommy, that's wonderful.' She raised herself on to her elbow to look at him. 'When?'

'At the beginning of February.' He grinned. 'Pleased?'

'Of course I'm please.' She kissed his blunt chin. 'If you've got your own place I won't have to creep downstairs when the family are asleep.'

'Well, Jo, I was thinking perhaps we should stop sneaking around altogether and get married. I know your dad said he wouldn't allow us to marry until you were twenty-one but as I'm being transferred to head up a new team and I've all but been told I'll be up for promotion in a month or two, I'm more than able to support you. Plus,' he gave her a wry smile, 'I just don't want to wait any longer.'

Slipping her arms around his neck Jo hugged him. 'Me neither. When?'

'I thought perhaps after your birthday in March,' said Tommy. 'I had hoped to persuade your mum to speak to

66

your dad about it, but if he's in the dog house then—'

'But it might be better for us that he is,' cut in Jo. 'Don't you see? If we can persuade Mum to agree to us getting wed, then perhaps he will too, just to get back in her good books. I'm sure Mattie and Cathy would be on our side too. Dad would have all of us on at him so he'd have to give in. Don't you think?'

'Well, I know I would,' said Tommy, 'if I had all you Brogan women set against me.'

Jo laughed and kissed him. 'You'll have to speak to him, though,' she said.

'I intend to,' said Tommy. 'I'll put in for a forty-eight-hour pass when I get in to work on Monday.'

Jo giggled. 'Shouldn't that be report for duty? You make it sound as if you're working in an office all day.'

He smiled. 'Do I?'

Sliding her leg further over, she sat up, straddling him. His eyes flickered down on to her breasts and his face went from relaxed to alert in an instant.

'Yes, you do,' she said, leaning forward and running her hands over his chest. 'And I worry sometimes that whatever it is you and your chums are doing in that old country house it's something dangerous.'

'Do you?' he replied, resting his hands lightly on her thighs.

'Yes, I do,' said Jo.

'Well, do you know what worries me?' he asked, as an expression that sent her pulse racing crept into his eyes.

'No, what?'

Gripping her waist, he flipped her over on to her back and, parting her legs with his, covered her with his body.

'What worries me, Josephine Margaret Brogan, is where

67

exactly you took your knickers off on a train packed with soldiers,' he said.

Jo laughed and as his hand cupped her left breast, she stretched across to retrieve the open packet of French letters on the bedside table.

Finally, Jo thought, as she spotted her mother come out of the Home and Colonial Store, situated halfway up the market.

It was the first Thursday in November and just after eleven thirty in the morning and she'd been pretending to study the display of ration-style underwear in Shelston's haberdashery window for almost twenty minutes. She was beginning to worry she might have missed her mother.

It was four days since she'd kissed Tommy goodbye and got on the last London-bound train from Bletchley and although she didn't know if or when he would get a weekend pass, she wanted to get her mum on her side ready for when he did.

Unfortunately, between her WVS duties and working double shifts at the station, her mother's work and the nightly bombing raids, this was the first opportunity she'd had to catch her alone.

Leaving her contemplation of lisle stockings, vests and underslips, Jo turned and, dodging between the stalls and women pushing prams, hurried towards her mother.

'Mum!' she shouted, as her mother reached Carswell the chemist's.

Ida turned and waved when she spotted Jo. 'Hello, luv,' she said as Jo arrived by her side. 'I thought you were on duty at twelve thirty.'

'I'm just on my way,' Jo replied.

'Well, you'd better get your skates on,' her mother said. 'Whitehorse Lane is a good thirty minutes' walk from here.'

'I know,' said Jo. 'But what with me doing double shifts since Monday I've hardly seen you this week, so I thought I'd just try and catch you in the market.'

'Well, that's nice,' Ida said, as they joined the queue outside Pollock's fish and chip shop. She acknowledged a couple of acquaintances in the line as it shuffled forward then turned back to Jo and smiled.

'So did you have a nice weekend with Tommy?'

Jo told her mother selected highlights of what she and Tommy had got up to during her visit the weekend before.

'And although they were a local band they were very good,' Jo concluded. 'They knew all the latest American dance tunes.'

'Sounds like you and Tommy enjoyed yourselves,' Ida said.

'We did,' said Jo, hoping her mother didn't notice her warming cheeks. 'And although he seems to be working all the hours God sends, he loves it, and the chaps he's stationed with are a great bunch.'

'Well, I'm glad he's getting on well in the army,' Ida added. 'Pity he's stationed so far away.'

Jo slipped her arm through her mother's. 'Funny you should say that, Mum, but . . .' She told her mum about Tommy's transfer back to London.

'So because of that rather than wait another two years until I'm twenty-one we wondered if Dad would give his consent for us to get married at Whitsun. Tommy's going to talk to Dad when he comes back next month on leave but . . .' She gave her mother an imploring smile. 'Well, we wondered if you could soften him up beforehand.'

A bleak look flashed across her mother's face.

'Your dad's got a lot on his mind at the moment,' she said flatly. 'Perhaps it would be better for you and Tommy to wait for a bit.'

Jo's shoulders slumped. 'It's not fair,' she said, not caring if she sounded like a five-year-old. 'Dad let Cathy get married at nineteen, so why can't I?' She kicked a pebble and sent it skittling across the pavement.

'Please, luv,' her mother whispered. 'Just wait a week or so.'

Jo's gaze flickered over her mother's face. 'You all right, Mum?'

'Of course, I'm fine,' her mother said, blinking away what looked suspiciously like a tear. 'I've just got a bit of a headache and—'

'You're not sick or something, are you?' Jo cut in as fear flared in her chest. 'Because Mary Fletcher's mother kept saying she was all right and now she's in the London with her family sitting at her bedside.'

Her mother placed a work-worn hand on Jo's arm. 'Jo, it's just a monthly headache and, like everyone else, I haven't had a full night's sleep since I can't remember when, that's all.'

'All right, Mum,' said Jo, feeling a little foolish for letting her imagination run away with her. 'Tommy's not back for a few weeks so there's nothing to be done right now but—'

The blast of the midday hooters at the surrounding factories and warehouses cut off her words.

'You'd better go or you'll be late,' said her mother when the racket ceased.

'You're right.' Jo adjusted her canvas first-aid bag across her. 'But, please, Mum, if you get a chance, will you talk to Dad?'

'I'll try,' said her mother, shuffling forward with the queue.

'Because if you tell him to let us get married, he'll agree,' Jo persisted. 'You know what he's like.'

'I thought I did.' An odd look flitted across her mother's face for a second then she let go of Jo's arm. 'Now off you go.'

Leaning over, Jo gave her mother a peck on the cheek.

'Thanks, Mum,' she called over her shoulder as she hurried off. 'I'll see you when you get home from the shelter in the morning.'

As she hurried towards Commercial Road at the top end of the market, Jo grinned. The war might be turning the whole country upside down but there was always one thing that would never change: although her dad could beat a man half his age in an arm-wrestle, as far as the Brogan household was concerned, her mother was the one in charge.

With the pain slicing across the back of her eyes, Ida snapped the lid on the tin then glanced up at the clock. Four thirty. Where was that blasted boy? She placed Billy's lunch box in the basket on the kitchen table.

Jo was right. Jerimiah had agreed to Cathy getting married at nineteen but given Tommy's brother Reggie's criminal reputation she could understand why her husband had been reluctant to let Jo and Tommy marry straight away. They'd been engaged for nearly a year now and with Jo turning nineteen at the end of March, Ida felt he ought to give way and let them marry.

Ordinarily, she would have been arguing Jo's corner but as for the past three weeks she'd had to force herself even to look at Jerimiah, let alone speak to him, Jo and Tommy weren't her priority just at the moment.

71

Wiping her hands on her apron, she walked through the door leading from the kitchen to the back parlour.

Queenie was sitting in her chair by the fire studying the back page of yesterday's *Sporting Life*. She looked up as Ida walked through.

'Isn't it a bit early for you to be going to the shelter?' she asked, peering over her half-rimmed spectacles.

'I'm picking Patrick up from Stella's on the way,' Ida replied as she passed her mother-in-law.

'She doesn't have to catch the bus until eight,' said Queenie.

'Madge Smith tried to nick my spot twice last week,' Ida replied, not meeting her mother-in-law's eye. 'So, I want to get there early to make sure she doesn't try it on again.'

'But—'

'And if I don't get Patrick down before the siren goes off, he's unsettled all night,' Ida added, as she went out into the hallway.

Closing the parlour door behind her, Ida took the torch from the hall stand. Switching off the hall light she pulled open the front door. Although the blackout had come into force thirty minutes before, there was still enough late-afternoon light to see, so stepping out Ida peered down the street towards the river.

To conserve energy and to ensure pupils were home before the blackout started, Stepney Council had decreed that when British summer time ended in October, school should finish an hour earlier at three. That was nearly two hours ago so where was that blasted boy?

Jerimiah was late too, not that she cared. He was usually home by now. A cold feeling started behind her breastbone. What if he'd gone around to see . . .?

72

'All right, Ida?'

She looked around. 'Oh, hello, Doll,' she said, shoving aside her unsettling thoughts. 'I was miles away.'

Dolly Tucker was wrapped up against the cold in a brown and mustard checked coat with a scarf over her head. The old battered pushchair she had with her was loaded with bags so she was clearly on her way home from the market. Ida had been in the same class at school as Dolly, who now lived in Kimberly Terrace, the next road over. Her husband was a docker and, like Ida, she had a son in the army and two working-age girls still at home.

'I could see that,' her neighbour replied. 'You going down the shelter, then?'

'I am when that blasted son of mine gets back,' Ida replied. 'You going tonight?'

Dolly looked up at the wispy clouds gathering overhead. 'I might if it don't cloud over soon.'

'Do you want me to save you a space near me?' asked Ida.

'Thanks, but my sister keeps me a dry spot,' Dolly replied. 'Hey, you'll never guess who I saw yesterday?'

Ida's heart thumped painfully in her chest. 'No, who?'

'Ellen Dooley,' said Dolly. 'You know, her who married Paul Gilbert who was in the year above us in Miss Roger's class.'

'Did you?' said Ida flatly.

'Yes,' laughed Dolly. 'You could have knocked me down with a feather when I came out of the grocers and walked straight into her.'

'Did she say anything?' asked Ida.

'Not much but I was surprised to see she's had a little lad.' Dolly laughed. 'After all, her and Paul had been married for years without Ellen falling for a nipper once. Plus, with his

73

wheezy chest and all I didn't think Paul had it in him. It must have been his parting shot before he dropped off his perch. After all the candles she'd lit for the Virgin over the years, she got her wish in the end. He put me in mind of your Charlie when he were a nipper.'

'Fancy that,' said Ida.

A worried look creased Dolly's fair brow. 'Mind you, she don't look well.'

Ida gave her a tight smile. 'Well, I best get on. Don't want to find myself up top when the Luftwaffe arrives.'

'Me neither, I'll see you later.' Dolly kicked off the brake and continued along the street.

Ida went back inside and closed the door. Leaning back against it she closed her eyes as the images of Jerimiah and Ellen that plagued her awake and asleep flooded back into her mind. Did he smile that crocked smile of his at Ellen? And did her heart skip like Ida's did when his dark eyes locked with hers at the climax of their lovemaking?

Tightness pinched her nose and the corners of her eyes as tears pressed to be released. I'll never forgive him, she told herself. *Never!*

Squeezing her eyes tight, Ida rubbed them with the heel of her hand and then willing her legs to work she walked back into the parlour.

'Any sign of Billy?' asked Queenie.

Before Ida could answer, the kitchen door burst open and Billy stormed in. He was wearing his grey school uniform, but in his own inimitable style: the shirt collar turned up, his tie skew-whiff, a grubby handkerchief dangling from his knee-length trouser pocket and his socks at half-mast.

'Cor, I'm starving, Mum,' he announced, throwing his satchel on the chair opposite. 'Any chance of a—'

'Where the hell have you been?' shouted Ida.

'Playing with Smudge and Ernie,' Billy replied, looking surprised at her outburst. 'The sweetshop on the corner of Albert Square had its window blown out last night so we had a quick shuftie.'

'Did you find anything?' asked Queenie.

'A couple of bars of chocolate and a dead cat,' said Billy.

'Never mind all that,' said Ida. 'I told you to come straight home from school this morning.'

A cherub-like expression spread across Billy's freckled face. 'Did you?'

'You know full well I did, Billy Brogan,' Ida snapped, feeling her temples throb. 'And look at the state of your shoes.'

Billy glanced down at his scuffed toes then back at her. 'Sorry, Mum.'

'Don't worry, lad,' said Queenie. 'A bit of polish will have them looking like new—'

'I'll give you sorry,' said Ida, storming across the room. She grabbed him by the arm. 'Seven and six those shoes cost me. Seven and six!'

'Mum, you're hurting,' he cried.

'I've a good mind to take it out of the money the Cohens and Greenbergs give you for lighting their Saturday-morning fires,' she continued, as her son struggled to free himself.

Setting aside her newspaper, Queenie rose from her chair. 'Let the boy be, Ida.'

'It's all right for you,' said Ida, the pain behind her eyes biting deeper as she glared down at her mother-in-law. 'It's not you on your knees scrubbing floors each—'

'Let him be,' Queenie repeated.

Ida released him.

Billy snatched his arm back, rubbing it and giving her a wounded look.

'It really hurts,' he whined.

'It's no more than you deserve for not coming straight home as your mother told you,' said Queenie. 'Now go up and get what you need for the night.'

With his lower lip jutting out and still rubbing his arm, Billy skulked out of the room and thumped upstairs.

As her son's bedroom door slammed, Ida looked at her mother-in-law. 'You've changed your tune, haven't you? Aren't you forever telling me I'm too soft on Billy?'

'You surely are,' Queenie replied. 'But I don't like to see any child made a whipping post for their parent's bad mood.'

Ida closed her eyes and rubbed her temples with her fingers in the hope of easing the pain. Tears pressed at the back of her eyes again, but she forced them away and looked up.

'I suppose you know,' she said.

'About Ellen?'

'Of course about Ellen,' barked Ida, as images of her husband embracing her best friend slid back into her mind. 'Unless your son's fathered some other woman's child.'

Queenie matched her angry stare. 'Well, if you must know, Ida, I had no knowledge of Ellen or her boy until recently, just like you.'

A tear tried to escape from Ida's right eye, but she dashed it away and gave a mirthless laugh.

'I'm surprised you didn't get one of your "visions".' She wiggled her fingers, indicating her mother-in-law's so-called second sight. 'Or see it in your blasted tea leaves.'

'Well, as it happens,' Queenie replied, crossing her arms firmly across her sparrow-like chest, 'I did a few weeks back but the leaves were after showing me a girl-child.'

Ida rolled her eyes.

'Mock if you like, Ida,' said Queenie, 'but me knowing or not knowing won't change the bare fact that Ellen Gilbert has a boy called Michael and Jerimiah is the fath—'

The old woman's eyes shifted on to something behind Ida and she looked around. Jerimiah was standing in the kitchen door frame wearing his work clothes under his old sheepskin jerkin.

Ida stared up at him for a second then she turned away, vivid images of him holding and touching Ellen in the same tender and loving way he'd held and touched her over the years danced back into her mind.

'I've got to get to the shelter,' she said, pushing past him as she hurried towards the kitchen with tears blurring her vision.

'Ida, please,' Jerimiah said, catching her arm. 'I'm sorry, so—'

'I don't want to hear how sorry you are,' she yelled, snatching her arm back.

Giving him a contemptuous look, she grabbed her coat from the nail in the back door.

'Billy!' she screamed, as she shrugged it on.

Billy dashed into the kitchen as she fastened the top button.

'Ready?'

Billy held up his duffel bag by way of reply.

'Right, then let's go,' she said, buttoning her coat.

Billy opened the door and as Ida turned, she caught sight of Jerimiah standing with his chin on his chest and his shoulders slumped. As she had done for the past twenty-five years, Ida found herself aching to take him in her arms to ease his pain, but she damped it down. After all, while her breasts were hard with milk for their dead son James, he had slept with her best friend.

Ethel Flannigan shoved her empty teacup across the table towards Queenie.

'Go on,' she said. 'Just have a quick look.'

Glancing over her to where Father Mahon was standing chatting to a couple of the old men of the parish, Queenie took the cup.

It was Friday lunchtime and Queenie was at St Bridget's and St Brendan's weekly lunch club. Before the war the Friday menu would have been fish and chips but now the ladies who cooked each week had to make do with whatever they could get hold of, like everyone else, so this week it had been tripe and onions followed by sponge pudding and custard.

Like most of the churches in the area, the Brogans' parish church ran a lunch club for the elderly members of the congregation. It gave Queenie and her friends a chance to share a hot meal, boast about their grandchildren and complain about their neighbours. They could also find out without waiting for the *East London Advertiser* who would be in the obituary column that week and share fond memories of the newly departed. However, whereas in times past this had usually been one of their contemporaries, sadly now it was more often than not a young life cut short.

As the main church hall had been commandeered as a rest centre for those bombed out of their houses, the parish pensioners' weekly lunch club had been moved into the smaller committee room on the opposite side of the corridor.

Queenie was at her usual table at the back of the room with Ethel, a widow with six children; Vi Riley, a mother of three girls and a boy, and Olive Cotton, who had been blessed with one of each.

Swilling the grouts at the bottom of her friend's cup, Queenie tipped them into the saucer then tilted the cup to the light.

She tutted and drew her brows together.

'What is it?' asked Ethel, her watery grey eyes full of concern. 'It's not one of my boys, is it?'

'No, not as such, although one of them is going on a long journey,' said Queenie. 'It's a relative, though, a woman, but she's not happy.'

'That must be your sister,' said Vi, her wispy white hair floating back and forth as she spoke. 'You said she was having trouble with her old man last week, didn't you?'

'Yeah,' agreed Ethel. 'Bloody workshy bugger.'

'No, it's a younger woman,' Queenie said, peering at the damp tea leaves stuck to the glaze. 'And I think she's unsettled rather than unhappy. She feels she's in a rut and wants a change.'

'Must be my granddaughter,' said Ethel. 'She and my Sheila had a right barney about her signing up for the ATS.'

Queenie continued to peer into the cup.

'What do you say, Queenie?' asked Ethel. 'Should she join?'

'Yes,' said Queenie. 'It'll be the making of her and no mistake.'

'Anything else?' asked Ethel.

79

There was but there was little point heralding troubles that couldn't be avoided. Queenie put down the cup.

'Well, sad as I am to give you the news, Ethel, but Clark Gable's not coming to sweep you off your feet.'

'Well, thank the Lord for that,' chuckled Ethel, flashing her few remaining teeth at them in the process. 'I've all but forgotten what to do with a man.'

'Well, if you don't want him send him my way,' said Vi. 'But tell him to bring his ration book.'

The old ladies at the table laughed and Queenie smiled.

'Do mine,' said Vi, thrusting her cup towards Queenie.

'And how are we this fine afternoon, ladies?' said a deep voice from behind her.

Queenie turned to find Father Mahon, in his black cassock and dog collar, standing behind her. He was but a few years older than her and had been the parish priest at St Bridget's and St Brendan's for over forty years.

When Queenie had walked into the church for the first time carrying six-month-old Jerimiah, Father Mahon had had a full head of wavy black hair, but time and worry had stripped that away, leaving an almost baby-fine layer of wispy white hair.

Although never robust, the skin on his face was so tightly drawn across his nose and cheeks it was a wonder the bones beneath didn't slice through. However, although the years of caring for his parishioners through good times and bad had taken their toll on the rest of him, his coal-black eyes still danced with merriment when they looked at a baby and filled with compassion for those gripped by grief.

His gaze flickered on to the grouts from Ethel's cup sitting in the saucer and back to Queenie.

'Mrs Brogan, I wonder if I could drag you away for a moment or two,' he said.

'Of course, Father,' said Queenie. Picking up her expansive carpet bag at her feet she stood up and followed the parish priest out of the hall.

'I thought as the Civil Defence are in possession of the main hall and the WVS committee are in the parish room we might avail ourselves of the peace and quiet of the church,' he said as the door swung shut behind them.

As he led the way down the side of the church, Queenie brought the priest up to date on Mattie's daughter's latest tooth, Jo's long hours and Cathy's recent clash with her dragon of a mother-in-law and by the time they walked through into the cool quietness of the stone-built mock-medieval Victorian church, she was filling him in on her parrot's recent antics.

'But how are you yourself, Patrick?' she asked as they slipped into the back pew.

'Aching a bit with the cold, as always this time of year,' said Father Mahon.

'Well, make sure you have your scarf before venturing out,' said Queenie. 'For if there's but a trace of damp in the air it'll go straight to your chest.'

'So, you're forever telling me, Queenie,' he said, the sunlight shining through the stained-glass window, throwing muted colours across his face. 'And Mrs Dunn looks after me well enough for you not to worry.'

At the mention of the rectory's housekeeper Queenie's mouth pulled in to a hard line but then she noticed the weariness on Father Mahon's face and her expression softened.

'Well, I'm sure she tries,' Queenie said, 'but she doesn't

know like I do that your mother and sister Colleen were martyrs to the damp.'

Father Mahon smiled fondly. 'Well, I'm glad to hear the family news but I can't help but notice you haven't told me how things are with Jerimiah or Ida.'

Queenie forced herself to hold the priest's penetrating gaze for a moment longer then let out a long sigh.

'Why wouldn't you have heard?' she said, throwing up her hands. 'Mustn't we be the talk on every street corner? Sure, haven't I heard as much meself these past three weeks?'

'So, it's true,' he said. 'Ellen Gilbert's child is his.'

Queenie nodded and told him about Ellen's condition and her desire that Jerimiah care for Michael after she died.

'And what does Ida say to all this?' Father Mahon asked when she'd finished.

'Well, she's fair spitting mad,' said Queenie. 'But as yet she's not said yes to taking care of the lad.'

The elderly priest's bushy eyebrows rose. 'It's not a thing every woman could do, that's for sure.'

'As you know full well, Patrick, me and Ida don't always see eye to eye,' said Queenie. 'But it would be a surprise to me if Ida could stand by and see a child suffer if she could prevent it.'

A grave expression settled on the old priest's face. 'I hope you're right, Queenie, and if she does I hope Jerimiah is suitably humbled by his wife's understanding and compassion.'

'I'm sure he will be but don't judge him too harshly,' said Queenie. 'For couldn't he have given Job a run for his money in regard to the trials and sorrows he suffered after James died?'

'Ha, well now,' said Father Mahon, sadness softening the deep lines of his face, ''twas a terrible time and no mistake.'

'There were many who said he should have had Ida put away like Ken O'Farrell did when his wife went barmy after she lost a babby,' said Queenie. 'But my boy wouldn't hear of it. "For better or worse, Ma," he said to me. "And I'm a man of me word."'

'Well, he's to be praised for that, I'm sure,' said the priest. 'But even so—'

'You're right, of course,' cut in Queenie, matching his sharp gaze with her own. 'But don't you know yourself how easy it is to give in to the flesh, Patrick?'

Father Mahon held her meaningful stare for a moment then swallowed. 'Indeed,' he said, looking down and making a play of adjusting the folds of his cassock over his knee.

'Well,' said Queenie, picking up her handbag and rising to her feet, 'I'm sure you've a cart load of things you should be doing and I shouldn't be keeping you from them.'

'I have too; God's work is never done.' Grasping the back of the pew in front to lever himself up, Father Mahon stood up. 'Will I see you tomorrow at confession?'

'For sure,' said Queenie. 'But mind my words, Patrick, and be sure you guard your chest against the damp.'

'That I will, but you know you're not really supposed to be calling me by my baptised name,' he said.

'I know, and sure haven't you reminded me of the same a hundred times or more.' She placed her hand on his arm and smiled fondly up at him. 'But it's the name I called you when we ran barefoot amongst the low meadows of Kinsale so it's a habit I find hard to break.'

Father Mahon covered her bony hand with his gnarled one and smiled briefly then turned and strolled away.

As Queenie watched his stooped frame shuffle down the aisle, his cassock collecting dust from the tiles as he progressed towards the sanctuary, she smiled fondly. Truthfully, time had taken its toll on both of them, but she didn't need to plumb the depths of her memories to recall the tall youth with a full head of springy black hair that Patrick had once been. All she had to do was look across the room at her son Jerimiah.

Chapter Six

LIFTING THE LATCH of the back door, Jo Brogan stepped inside her sister Mattie's home. The sounds and smells of a late Saturday afternoon, of supper in the oven and fresh washing drying above the stove, enveloped her in a comfortable domestic fug, while *Variety Bandbox* played softly out of the Bush wireless propped up on the window sill. Of course, there was just the faint smell of nappies soaking in the enamel bucket under the sink ready for the Monday wash day but that was to be expected with a baby in the house.

'Only me,' she called, shutting the door behind her before moving the blackout curtain aside.

'I'm just changing Alicia,' her sister called back from her front room. 'Put the kettle on and I'll be with you in a moment.'

Collecting the kettle from the cooker Jo filled it under the tap then returned it to the hob. She struck a match and, turning the knob, held it to the gas, which popped a couple of times then settled down as the blue flame ignited.

Mattie's house was on Jo's route home from the ambulance post in Trafalgar Gardens so she dropped in a couple of times a week for tea and a chat. It was situated in Belgrave Street just a stone's throw from St Dunstan's Church in Stepney, a mile or so from Mafeking Terrace.

Unlike the old workman's cottage which was the family home, her sister's house, although the same age as the one in Mafeking Terrace, was a bit more up-market. With three good-size bedrooms and a separate lounge and dining room, it also had a modern kitchen with a closed-in sink, an air-cooled larder and a gas ascot, which provided hot water on tap, something her mother would give her front teeth for. More usefully in these troubled times, it also had a basement in which Mattie's husband had installed one of the cage-like Morrison shelters so that the family could spend their nights in there rather than in an overcrowded shelter or underground station. But the thing Jo coveted most about her sister's house was the bathroom, with its immersion heater for the bath water and an inside toilet. Unlike when the three sisters had shared a bed as children, Mattie didn't have to use a gazunder at night, instead she just had to walk a couple of steps along the landing.

As the first few wisps of steam started curling from the spout, Mattie walked through from the hall passage, carrying her ten-month-old daughter on her hip.

Like Jo, she had abundant brunette hair, green-brown eyes and a curvy figure. People often remarked how much she looked like her oldest sister, which Jo didn't mind a bit as Mattie was absolutely gorgeous.

Jo crossed the room and after giving Mattie a peck on the cheek, turned her attention to her niece.

'How's my best girl today?' Jo asked, pulling a happy face at the baby.

'Teething,' her mother replied. 'Can you take her while I put this in to soak?'

She held up a damp nappy in her other hand.

'Try and stop me,' said Jo, taking Alicia from her sister.

Sitting down on one of the chairs at the kitchen table, Jo bounced the baby on her knee to make her laugh.

Alicia obliged and started giggling.

'The gas seems low,' said Jo as her sister went to check the kettle's progress.

'It's been like that all day,' said Mattie. 'I expect the gas station is conserving coal stocks. Have you only just finished?'

'Yes,' said Jo with a sigh. 'The ARP wardens and the heavy rescue were still mopping up after last night's raid when I got to the station this morning.'

'Yes, it was a bad one last night,' said Mattie. 'The ground didn't stop shaking all night. At one point I thought we'd been hit but I found out this morning they had a high explosive bomb land in Grosvenor Street.'

'There were two like that landed in Mile End New Town and we spent all morning ferrying the last few with broken bones and glass injuries to hospital then we got a message that one of the West Ferry Road ambulances had shredded their tyres on some debris, so we went over to give a hand fetching people home from St Andrew's. What about you?'

'The usual exhilarating day of a housewife,' said Mattie, taking the kettle off the hob as it started whistling. 'Queuing at the butcher's, queueing at the baker's, queueing at—'

'The candlestick maker's?' suggested Jo.

'Lipton, actually,' said Mattie, with a raised eyebrow. 'And then they were only giving out half tea rations because they were low on stock. And when I got back I found Alicia's dirty nappy has soaked right through to her clothes, which means another lot of washing.' She set a cup of tea in front of Jo. 'I tell you, Jo, some days I wish I was still the coordinator at CD Post 7. At least then I'd only have stroppy ARP personnel to sort out rather than running a house and feeding a family on rations.'

'I can imagine,' said Jo. 'I take my hat off to you, though, Mattie, because despite all that you've managed to get another one of your Needles and Pins tips printed in the local. I showed it to the chaps at the ambulance station.'

'Well, it's only a few patterns for children to sew tree decorations out of scrap,' said Mattie. 'I might as well put all those years making garments for Gold and Sons to good use.'

'It's clever of you to think of it, even so,' Jo replied.

'Perhaps.' Her sister smiled. 'But with Daniel working all hours I'm still going stark-staring mad stuck in the house all day.'

'I'm not surprised,' said Jo. 'I know I'd be bonkers by now.'

'I am,' said Mattie. 'Which is why after Christmas I'm going to have a word with Mr Granger, the area coordinator, about helping out in the ARP control at the Town Hall.'

'What about Alicia?' asked Jo.

'She'll be a year old, so she'll be able to go into the WVS nursery in the Temperance Hall opposite,' said Mattie. 'It would only be for a few hours each day.'

'Won't Daniel object?' asked Jo.

Mattie raised an eyebrow. 'He wouldn't dare.'

Jo grinned.

Her sister turned her attention to making the tea, leaving Jo to bounce her niece on her knee and play pattercake.

Putting the kettle on the back hob, Mattie moved the saucepan of potatoes over the gas. She opened the oven and peered in.

'That smells nice,' said Jo, as the meaty aroma of her sister's supper wafted across.

'It's baked hearts,' said Mattie, putting a cup of tea in front of her. 'The butcher put a fresh plate out as I arrived.'

'Sounds delicious,' said Jo, pulling a blissful expression.

'Would you like to stay for supper?' asked Mattie.

'Could I?' said Jo, putting her cup on the table and making

sure it was out of her niece's grasp. 'I mean, as long as Daniel won't mind.'

'I'm not sure what time he'll be in,' said Mattie. 'But he won't mind.'

'And I'm not getting in the way of your canoodling,' said Jo, shifting Alicia into a more comfortable position on her lap.

'We're sleeping in a cage in the basement with a baby,' said Mattie, raising an arched eyebrow. 'There's not much canoodling going on, I can tell you.'

Jo held her sister's gaze for a second or two then Mattie laughed. 'Well, not as much as I'd like.'

'How is Captain McCarthy?'

Mattie's husband, Daniel, worked for MI5. It was something the whole family knew but never spoke about even amongst themselves.

'Busy as always,' said Mattie. 'In fact, he hasn't been in before midnight all week. What about Lance Corporal Sweete?'

'Tommy's unit are practically working around the clock at whatever it is they're doing in Bletchley,' Jo replied. 'And, in his own words, he's "counting the seconds" until he sees me again.'

'I bet,' said Mattie. 'I'm guessing you had a nice time last weekend.'

'Blissful,' said Jo, with a sigh.

'Was it a nice hotel?' asked Mattie.

'It was,' said Jo. 'At least what I saw of it was.'

Mattie raised her eyebrows again.

'Well,' said Jo, as images of her and Tommy flashed through her mind, 'we only had two days.'

'Is Tommy coming back before Christmas?' asked Mattie.

'He's going to try because . . .' She told Mattie about her fiancé's transfer to London and cornering her mother in the market a couple of days ago.

'I don't see why Dad won't relent,' said her sister when she'd finished, 'especially if Mum's on your side.'

'He might if they were actually talking,' said Jo.

Mattie looked aghast. 'Don't tell me they're still fighting!'

'No, I wish they were,' said Jo. 'At least if they had one big row like they usually do then it would be over, but all this silence is worse and me and Gran are stuck in the middle.'

'Have you managed to find out what it's about yet?' asked Mattie.

Jo shook her head. 'But I overheard Mum say something about an Ellen somebody or other who's moved back into the area.'

Mattie looked puzzled. 'She must mean Ellen Gilbert.'

'That's her,' said Jo. 'Do you remember her?'

'I do, Auntie Ellen we used to call her,' said her sister.

'I remember her, although not much more than the name,' said Jo. 'And that she was forever making a fuss of us because she didn't have any kids of her own.'

'Probably,' said Mattie. 'But she was good after baby James died and Mum wasn't well.'

'I can't say I remember James,' said Jo. 'Or Mum being poorly.'

'I shouldn't think so, you were only seven when it all happened,' said Mattie. 'But I do. I remember Mum sitting in the chair crying and poor Dad trying to look after us kids after being out on the wagon all day and Auntie Ellen cooking our tea. Looking back, I reckon if it hadn't been for Ellen we would have all ended up in the workhouse, Mum included, so I can't understand how her coming back can have caused Mum and Dad to fall out.'

*

'Three, three, any advance on three?' ask the auctioneer, his eyes skimming over the small crowd as he balanced on the wooden beer crate.

Jerimiah raised his hand. 'And a tanner, if you will.'

It was three thirty in the afternoon on the second Tuesday in November and he was in the playground of Fairclough Street School at the west end of Cable Street.

The old Victorian building, which had been the local schoolhouse for almost a hundred years, had been taken over by the council when the school children were evacuated out of London en masse. It now served as a supply depot for the council's road and buildings department, as the huge support joists and metal girders stacked at the far end of the playground testified.

However, this afternoon, the open space that once had boys kicking balls across it and girls turning skipping ropes was hosting a more sombre event: a bomb salvage sale.

A year ago, at this time of day, he'd have been setting out for a last trundle around the streets on his final collection before his well-earned end-of-the-day pint in the Catholic Club when it opened at four.

Today he was standing in a freezing-cold school yard beside a pile of household items and a handful of other local traders and he still had another two hours' work ahead of him before he could sink his first Guinness of the day.

Over the past year, with the government gathering every bit of scrap metal for the war effort, Jerimiah's livelihood had practically disappeared.

However, as Father Mahon often remarked, when God closes one door he opens a window. It was true, albeit in often sad circumstances, for the nightly destruction had opened new possibilities for Jerimiah.

Items such as beds, furniture, crockery and the like that had been salvaged by the council from bombed properties where the owner was deceased were put up for sale. These, of course, were the very same items that people who had lost everything but their lives after a raid desperately needed.

'Three and six, three and six . . .' the auctioneer surveyed the handful of men surrounding him. 'Any advance?' No one answered, he clapped his hands. 'Sold to Jerry Brogan.'

The auctioneer's assistant, a spotty youth with a West Ham scarf wrapped around his neck and wearing an oversized overcoat, handed Jerimiah a chit.

'Lot twenty-three,' shouted the auctioneer.

Shoving the ticket in his trouser pocket with the other half-dozen, Jerimiah strolled over to the wooden hut by the school gate. The door creaked as he walked in, causing the young girl sitting hunched over the desk at the far end to look up.

She was about Jo's age and was one of the Kemp brood who lived in Three Colts Lane in Limehouse. She was wrapped in a camel-coloured overcoat with her reddish hair poking out from under her knitted beret. Despite the fierce blue and orange light flickering behind the paraffin stove's small window she was wearing fingerless gloves.

'Afternoon, Maureen, me darling, and how are you this fine day?'

'Fine day?' She gave a hard laugh. 'After sitting in this hut all day, if I was a brass monkey I'd be ball-less by now. You settling up?'

'I am indeed,' said Jerimiah, pulling the dozen or so auction receipts from his pocket. 'Did I hear a little whisper going around that there's another one next Tuesday in Fairfield Road?'

Blowing on her hands, she nodded. 'There's a notice in the *Advertiser* today.' She held out her hand.

'Do you happen to know what they're putting under the hammer?' asked Jerimiah as he handed her the tickets.

'Now you know I'm not supposed to let dealers know what's on the books before the Monday viewing.'

'Sure I do and I wouldn't want to be getting you in trouble at all,' he replied. 'But could you not do a kindness to a poor old tinker like meself?'

A wry smile lifted the corners of Maureen's orange-lipsticked mouth. 'As long as you don't let on who told you.'

'Wild horses couldn't drag it out of me,' he replied.

She studied him for a moment then spoke again. 'All right, the St Bart's rest home at the back of the church in Roman Road had its side blown off so along with the usual stuff there's a dozen beds and chairs, bundles of linen and towels plus a couple of boxes of china. Now stop badgering me and let me tot up what you owe.'

Jerimiah grinned.

Dipping her nib in the inkwell, Maureen turned her attention to the enormous ledger spread on the table before her.

Leaving her to her sums, Jerimiah gazed through the dirty window to where the auctioneer was selling the last few lots.

'Three pound, twelve and thruppence,' Maureen announced, cutting through his heavy thoughts.

Delving into his other pocket, Jerimiah pulled out his wallet and took out four green pound notes. He handed them to Maureen who unlocked the cash box at her elbow and tucked the money beneath the coin tray.

'Seven shillings and nine pence,' she said, dropping the collection of silver and copper coins in the palm of his hand. 'If you could just check and sign.'

Swivelling the accounts book around to face him she pointed to the line beneath a row of figures.

Casting his eyes over the coins and finding them correct he put them in his pocket and looked down at the page.

Although he knew to the last penny what he'd spent, Jerimiah cast his eyes down the numbers just to check. Satisfied she'd entered them correctly, he took the spare pen from the inkwell and scrawled his signature across the bottom.

'Ta very much,' she said, turning the ledger back the right way.

Jerimiah returned the pen to its pot. 'And to you, me darling.' He winked. 'There'll be a drink waiting for you in the club.'

He touched the peak of his leather cap again and left the hut.

With the ice-skimmed puddles crunching beneath his hobnail boots, Jerimiah crossed the playground to where Samson stood patiently waiting for him. He took his bridle.

'Just let me load all this stuff up on me wagon, old boy,' he said, leading the horse towards the pile of furniture he'd just paid for. 'And I'll soon have you tucked up in your stable.'

'Evening to you, Father,' Jim Bridge called down from his driving seat as the horse plodded by pulling the Meredith and Drews wagon behind it.

'And to you,' Father Mahon called back, raising his gnarled hand in greeting. 'And how's that fine boy of yours?'

It was five fifteen in the afternoon and the sun had just disappeared. Usually, at this time in the evening, Father

Patrick Mahon would be in the cool of the church getting ready to recite his evening prayers, but today he had something to do before ending his day.

'Well, he's got a good pair of lungs on him, I can tell you,' Jim called back.

'Much like yourself as a babe,' Father Mahon replied, 'if I recall correctly.'

Jim, who was a driver for Meredith and Drews biscuit factory on the Highway, laughed. 'So me ma tells me. My Mary will be wanting him baptised soon.'

'Just pop around to the rectory and I'd be mighty happy to oblige,' said Father Mahon.

Jim waved again and then pulled on the reins as the chestnut gelding turned the corner.

Father Mahon continued on past the Britons' garage and towards his destination at the end of the row of railway arches. Reaching number 125 he read the notice nailed up outside before pushing the doorway cut into the gate. Lifting his cassock, he stepped over the threshold and walked into the space beyond.

As always, the space under the arch was crammed with all manner of things but whereas before the war it would have been battered prams, dismantled iron bed frames and handleless saucepans, now the small yard was filled with double wardrobes, chests of drawers, rolled-up rugs and mismatched chairs. In addition, there were smaller day-to-day items that housewives needed to run a household like scrubbing boards and zinc tubs. Everything was stacked on and around the wagon, which was parked, shafts tipped back, against the far wall.

Beyond that stood a piebald horse munching his way through a net of hay suspended at head height on the wall in front of him, while the man Father Mahon had come to see brushed him down.

Hearing someone behind him, Jerimiah Brogan straightened up and turned.

'Father Mahon,' he said, his face creasing into an easy smile. 'What brings you down to this neck of the woods?'

'Oh, I was just passing and as I haven't seen you in church for a few weeks, I thought I'd drop by and see how you're faring,' Father Mahon replied.

'Me?' An ingenuous expression settled on Jerimiah's rugged face. 'I'm grand, so I am.'

'What about Samson?' asked Father Mahon.

'Oh, he's grand too.' Jerimiah slapped the horse's hairy flank affectionately.

Heedless of his cassock skimming across the beaten earth floor, Father Mahon strolled across to the horse's head.

'You know, my father had one just like Samson when I was a boy,' he said, stroking the gelding's whiskery muzzle.

Jerimiah grinned. 'So me ma told me.'

An image of a slender young girl, her dark hair bouncing down her back as she sat astride his father's old workhorse, flashed through Father Mahon's mind. Pulling himself back to the present, he raised his almost invisible eyebrows. 'I'm surprised your mother remembers, it's so long ago.'

'It was the first thing she told me when I brought him home from the auction,' Jerimiah replied.

'How old is he now?' he asked.

'Twelve,' said Jerimiah.

'So he's a few years in him yet?' said Father Mahon.

'I hope so,' said Jerimiah, coming to stand on the other side of the horse's head. 'He's got a steady temperament and a strong back, which is as well now because . . .'

Father Mahon listened while Jerimiah told him of his venture into the removal and second-hand furniture business.

'Yes, I noticed your new sign,' said Father Mahon.

'Our Jo did it,' said Jerimiah, his face creasing again in a friendly smile.

Father Mahon looked suitably impressed.

'She's a bright girl,' Jerimiah continued, his chest swelling a little.

'Just like the rest of your and Ida's young 'uns,' said Father Mahon.

'Even Billy,' said Jerimiah, with a wry smile, 'if he did but apply himself to his school work instead of bedevilling his teachers.'

Father Mahon's gaze fixed on the younger man's face.

'And what about Michael?' he asked softly. 'Do you think he'll take after you for the love of learning?'

Jerimiah looked surprised for a second but then he gave a heavy sigh. 'Sure, you must have had a hundred people give you the news.'

'A hundred and one,' said Father Mahon, with a compassionate smile. 'But your mother told me not to be too harsh.'

'Well, feel free to ignore her, Father, because you could be no harder on me than I've been on meself.' Pain flitted across Jerimiah's rugged features. 'I deserve no less after what the whole business is doing to Ida.'

Stepping forward, Father Mahon placed his hands on his shoulder. 'Why don't we sit a while?'

Jerimiah nodded and led the way to the old leather sofa in front of the small back office.

Tucking his cassock under him, Father Mahon sat down at one end and Jerimiah the other. He waited and after a long moment Jerimiah spoke.

'I want to tell you, Father, I'd never been unfaithful to Ida before I went with Ellen; nor since, in fact.' A wistful smile lightened his expression a little. 'Since the moment I saw Ida with that bright red ribbon tied in her hair, there was no one else. As God and all his saints are my witness, Father. I didn't plan it or want it and as soon as I came to my senses I was so ashamed I . . .' Placing his hand over his eyes, Jerimiah paused for a moment and then looked up with tears sparkling in them.

'And your ma tells me this all happened around the time James died,' said Father Mahon.

'It did but 'tis no excuse,' said Jerimiah.

'No,' agreed Father Mahon. 'But you're only human, my son, and as I remember it was when men stood idle on corners for want of work and the church kitchen fed hundreds each day and your poor wife was fair out of her mind with grief.'

Jerimiah nodded. 'True, they were hard times, Father, the worst I can remember before or since. Some days me and Ida went hungry and had nothing but potatoes to feed the children . . .' Sadness flicked across his face again. 'The fourth of October. I remember it as if it were yesterday; the day James was born. Ida woke me at four, telling me her pains were on her and sent me to fetch Mrs Callahan, the mothers' helper, from Cartwright Street. It had rained that morning and I still recall running through the puddles to fetch her and the struggle she had to get him out. I remember holding him in our front room as I'd held all the others and he greeted me with a damp arm where he'd wet through his nappy. He was dead a week later; those tiny fingers that had gripped mine cold and still for ever . . .' He pressed his lips together for a moment then took a breath. 'To be truthful, with Ida so lost in grief and with Ma not able to do anything because of the way me dad was with the drink, if it hadn't been for Ellen helping me with the children I think the council welfare officer would have come and taken them away . . . Well, somehow – and even now I can't clearly recall how, me and Ellen ended up—'

'Indeed,' cut in Father Mahon. The image of the young dark-haired woman on the horse galloped through his mind again. 'As the Good Book tells us, frail flesh is weak.'

'But that's not the whole tale, Father,' Jerimiah continued. 'Because . . .'

Father Mahon's listened in silence as Jerimiah told him more or less what Queenie had told him about the reason for Ellen's return.

'May the Lord have mercy on Ellen's soul,' said Father Mahon, crossing himself when Jerimiah had finished.

'Amen,' said Jerimiah, doing the same. 'And when all's said and done, Michael is my son and responsibility, which is why I just pray to God and all his saints that Ida will not only forgive me but agree to care for him. However he arrived in this world, Michael shouldn't suffer for it.'

'No, the poor lad is the innocent party in all this,' said Father Mahon. 'But you are asking a great deal of Ida.'

Jerimiah nodded. 'I expect with all this blackening of my soul, I should find my way to the confessional.'

'You should,' said Father Mahon. 'But it is a great deal more comfortable here.'

Jerimiah gave Father Mahon a sheepish look and bowed his head, causing an ebony curl to fall across his forehead.

'Forgive me, Father, for I have sinned; it's been . . .'

As Jerimiah recounted his fall from grace over ten years ago, Father Mahon contemplated the man with his head bowed before him. Father Mahon had first set eyes on him as a six-month-old when Queenie Brogan walked into St Bridget's and St Brendan's for the first time. Looking at him now, with shoulders like an ox and hands the size of a navvy's shovel, Father Mahon mused, not for the first time, how the slightly built, red-haired Fergus Brogan, a man more drunk than he was sober and who would have pushed Judas Iscariot aside had there been thirty pieces of silver for the taking, could have produced a son such as Jerimiah.

Wearily dragging herself through the back door, Ida plonked her shopping bag on the table. Christmas would be here before she knew it and although she was feeling anything but festive, she'd managed to pick up a few extra bits to add to her stash of food.

'Anyone in?' she called through the door to the back parlour as she unbuttoned her coat.

Thankfully, no one replied.

She hadn't really expected to find anyone at home at this time on a Thursday morning. Thanks to a high explosive bomb landing on the parade of shops opposite Naylor, Corbet & Kleinman the night before and blowing every window in the solicitors out, Ida had finished work an hour and a half later than usual.

Jo was on a day shift at the ambulance station and Stella would have picked Patrick up an hour ago. Having been released from her great-grandmotherly duties, Queenie would be on her round collecting bets for Fat Tony at the various pubs along the Highway and sinking the odd Guinness or two 'to keep body and soul together' while she did.

Jerimiah, who came home as regular as clockwork at midday for his dinner, would have been and gone too. However, since he'd turned her world and mind upside down and inside out by telling her the reason for Ellen's return, she wasn't totally upset at missing him. It saved her seeing the look in his eyes that almost willed her to tell him she would accept Michael and care for him once Ellen was gone.

Going to the stove, Ida held her hand over the kettle for a second. Finding it still warm, she relit the gas. Leaving it to boil, Ida took off her coat and hung it on the nail behind the door. Yawning, she added a spoonful of National tea to the pot then, snatching the kettle from the heat as the whistle started to rattle, made herself a well-earned cuppa.

Holding the cup in one hand and taking the copy of *Home Notes* she'd picked up from the newsagent's on the way home in the other, Ida strolled through to the parlour and headed for her easy chair by the fire. Shifting her knitting bag to the side, she sat down.

Putting her drink on the occasional table at her elbow, Ida kicked off her shoes and rested her feet on the fender. Queenie had left the fire banked up so within a moment or two Ida felt the heat on her frozen toes.

She glanced at the clock on the mantelshelf: a quarter past one. A full hour before she had to change into her WVS uniform and take over from Mrs Finkelstein at the rest centre tea bar for the teatime stint.

Ida yawned again. She switched on the wireless and as the warmed valves released the soothing strings of the BBC concert orchestra, her eyelids flickered down.

She must have drifted off because a sharp rap on the door brought her back to the here and now with a start. Blinking the sleep from her eyes Ida stood up and, knowing she was paid up with both the rent and the milkman, wondered who it could be banging on her front door. She padded barefoot across the carpet and opened the door. The chilly hallway drove the last remnants of weariness from her mind but even so, when she opened her front door, Ida wondered if she wasn't dreaming, as standing on the scrubbed doorstep was her younger sister, Pearl.

Ida's heart sank.

Three years Ida's junior, Pearl, with blonde hair and blue eyes, had always been the pretty sister and their mother's favourite. Ever since she could remember, Ida had been instructed to 'look after your sister and don't let her get into trouble'. Something Ida always tried but failed to do.

Hardly surprising, really, given that as soon as she was able to totter about on her chubby legs Pearl had left havoc and conflict in her wake. If Pearl wanted it then she would raise hell and high water until she got it, regardless of who suffered along the way.

These days, she was what the locals called 'well preserved'; at a distance she looked a decade younger than her thirty-nine years but close up was a different matter.

Thanks to her monthly trips to the hairdresser Pearl was still blonde but she was now platinum with a hint of blush, and although the waves on her shoulder looked like a cascade of curls they were in fact held rigidly in place by setting lotion. Her smooth complexion and youthful blush owed more to Max Factor than fresh air and the red lipstick flashed like a warning sign across the centre of her face.

Unlike Ida who had carried and delivered five children, Pearl's solitary brush with motherhood hadn't altered her shape at all. Unsurprising really, considering she'd kept her girdle on the tightest notch for most of the nine months and had never put the child to her breast.

She was wearing a full-length mink coat over a navy suit, her wide-brimmed hat trimmed with a spray of feathers.

Behind her sister Ida could see her neighbours pausing in their workday chores to stare across at her unexpected visitor. She didn't blame them. After all, Pearl was dressed for a visit to an ancestral pile in the country rather than a stroll through the bombed wreckage of East London.

Pearl studied Ida for a moment then flung her arms wide.

'You poor, poor thing,' she yelled, engulfing Ida in a perfume-soaked embrace. 'I came as soon as I heard.'

Ida untangled herself from her sister's clutches. 'Heard what?'

'About Jerimiah and—'

'You'd better come in,' said Ida, noting the people in the street, sensing some drama in the offing, gathering closer.

Grabbing her sister's arm, Ida pulled her through the door and slammed it shut behind them. 'I'd rather not have the street know our business.'

Pearl raised a pencilled eyebrow. 'Seeing how I heard in deepest, darkest Leytonstone about what your husband's been up to, I'd say it's a bit late for that.' She jabbed a nail-polished finger at Queenie's door. 'Is the old bat in?'

'If you mean Queenie,' said Ida, 'no she's not so why don't we go through.'

Shrugging off her fur coat, Pearl handed it to Ida then swept into the parlour. Hooking her sister's coat, which probably cost more than the entire family's wardrobe, on the hall stand, Ida followed her into the snug back room, closing the door behind her to keep in the heat.

Ida forced a smile. 'The kettle's just boiled so would you like a drink?'

'Only if it's Nescafé and not that vile Camp stuff,' said Pearl.

'I'm afraid there hasn't been any coffee in the shops around here for weeks, so I can only offer you tea,' said Ida.

'I won't bother, then,' said Pearl. 'I don't want Gypsy-Lil-from-over-the-Hill nosing through the grouts when she gets back.' A mawkish expression settled on her sister's powdered face. 'Is my precious boy around?'

'He's at school,' said Ida flatly.

'What time is he home?'

'About three,' Ida replied.

'Pity,' said Pearl. 'Lenny's got to be in Hackney by then so he'll be picking me up at two. He's got a new car, you know, a Ford Pilot. Top of the range.'

'That's nice,' said Ida.

'I bet Billy's shot up since I last saw him.'

'Yes, he has,' said Ida.

Her sister sighed. 'I can't believe he's almost ten.'

Billy was, in fact, eleven, but you couldn't expect Pearl to remember that. After all, since she'd squeezed him from her body in a toilet in Liverpool Street Station, her only contribution to his upbringing was a ridiculously lavish present at Christmas and on his birthday if she remembered it.

'Why don't you take the weight off your feet?' said Ida, wishing not for the first time she'd been an only child.

Taking a lacy hanky from her suit pocket Pearl flicked it over one of the upright chairs and perched on the edge.

'Oh, that's better. These might come from Bond Street,' she said, indicating her red patent stilettos, 'but they do

104

pinch. Now,' she continued, crossing one leg over the other and resting her elbow on her knee, 'tell me all about Jerimiah and his bit on the side.'

'Jerimiah hasn't got a bit on the side,' said Ida.

Pearl frowned. 'Are you sure? I mean, they say the wife is always the last to know.'

'Well, you'd know more about that than me,' said Ida.

Pearl shot her a sharp look but continued: 'Well, the way I heard it was that your Jerimiah's been over the side with some woman who's had a kid who looks a dead ringer for him.'

Pain shot through Ida so ferociously it must have shown in her face because Pearl's mascaraed eyes stretched wide.

'So, it's true,' she laughed. Unclipping her handbag, she took out a silver cigarette case. 'Your old man's got his fancy woman up the duff and now she's making him own up to it.'

'It's not like that,' said Ida, cutting across her sister. 'And it was only once.'

'That's what he told you,' scoffed her sister.

'And I believe him,' snapped Ida, realising that she actually did. 'Jerimiah didn't even know Michael existed until a few weeks ago.'

Pearl's powdered face pulled itself into an excessively sympathetic expression. 'You poor thing. Of course' – she drew deeply on her cigarette then blew a lungful of smoke upwards. Her mouth pulled into a bud as she gave Ida the once-over – 'if you'd looked after yourself a bit more he might not have developed a wandering eye.'

'Is that a fact?' Ida snapped.

'It stands to reason,' Pearl replied. 'No man wants a woman on their arm who doesn't look after herself, do they? I know you haven't got much grey but if I were you I'd treat myself to a trip to the hairdresser and have a more modern style. One with a bit of bounce in it; men like that. And let's be honest. Having kids has taken its toll, hasn't it?'

'It's what happens, Pearl,' said Ida.

Her sister placed her manicured hands on her stomach. 'Which is why you need to get yourself a girdle: to pull it all in.'

Holding on to her rising temper, Ida gave her sister a brittle smile. 'Well, thanks for the advice.'

'Glad to be of help.' Standing up, Pearl tapped her ash into the ashtray on the mantelshelf. 'Who is this woman, anyway?'

'Ellen Gilbert,' said Ida. 'Dooley as was.'

Pearl pulled a face. 'That skinny girl from Planet Street you used to knock around with?'

Ida nodded.

Pearl's top lip curled. 'Well, she always had a bit of a soft spot for your wild gypsy rover. I suppose she's come back cos she's after some money.'

'No, she's not well . . .' Ida told her about Ellen's condition.

'So now she's about to snuff it, she wants you to bring up her snotty tin-lid,' said Pearl. 'Bloody liberty.'

'It's what any mother would want in the same situation,' said Ida. 'To know their children will be properly looked after.'

'Well, I hope you told her to sod off,' said Pearl.

Ida shifted in the chair. 'Not exactly.'

Her sister's unnaturally red mouth dropped open again. 'Ida!'

'It's bad enough that the poor little lad is going to lose his mum let alone being sent to live in some godforsaken orphanage,' Ida replied.

'But you can't just take in any old waif and stray off the streets,' said Pearl.

'It's lucky for you that I did,' said Ida. 'Or your "precious boy" would be in an orphanage.'

Pearl gave her a look that had they still been children would have been swiftly followed by a tear-inducing bout of hair-pulling.

'This is different,' she said.

'Yes, this time we know who the father is,' Ida replied.

'Yes.' Pearl jabbed her nicotine-stained finger at Ida. 'It's that bastard husband of yours!'

Although she'd called him that and worse over the last few days, anger flared in Ida's chest.

'Me and Mum never liked him,' her sister went on. 'We tried to warn you about getting tangled up with the likes of Jerimiah Brogan, with his drunken father and barmy mother.' She blew a stream of smoke from her freshly lit cigarette towards the ceiling rose. 'Dazzled you were, dazzled by his "grand curly hair" and "strong arms", as I recall you telling us. Dad was a waterman and we were thought highly of along the river, so you could have done so much better for yourself than a grubby tinker, Ida, had you listened to me and Mum. But no. And now here you are: the talk of every street corner because your Irish scum of a husband has—'

'Well, by the devil himself, look what the cat dragged in,' said Queenie, standing in the kitchen doorway, arms akimbo and eyes blazing.

She was wearing an ankle-length skirt, one of Jerimiah's old jumpers and her cloche hat with a felt rose over each ear. It had been raining earlier so she had put on her hobnail boots which were now mud-caked while her lisle stockings gathered in wrinkles around her spindly ankles. Like Pearl, the old woman was wearing a fur coat but instead of a chic mink, Queenie's was a moth-eaten beaver with a shredded lining, three sizes too big and almost as old as she was.

A nerve in Pearl's right eye started to twitch. 'Mrs Brogan, I didn't hear you—'

'I'm sure you didn't but I heard you,' said the old woman in a pleasant sing-songy voice.

A crimson flush crept up Pearl's throat.

'"Grubby tinker", wasn't it?' Queenie continued in the same friendly tone. 'And Irish scum?'

'Didn't anyone ever tell you that it's wrong to eavesdrop?'

'And didn't anyone tell you it's wrong to be tupping another woman's husband?'

Pearl's neck went from red to purple.

Crushing her half-smoked cigarette in the ashtray she looked at Ida. 'I've got to go. Lenny will be waiting for me.'

'How is Lenny's wife keeping?' asked Queenie, a sharp glint in her black eyes.

'It was good of you to come,' said Ida, for want of anything else to say.

Picking up her handbag from the table, Pearl opened it. 'Me and Lenny are going to stay with friends in the country for a few weeks—'

'Anywhere near his wife and kids at Southend?' chipped in Queenie.

Ignoring her, Pearl took out a ten-shilling note from her purse. 'Could you get Billy something nice for Christmas from me,' she said, handing the note to Ida. 'But remember, only the best for my darling boy.'

'Is this the same "darling boy" you tried to poke out of you with a knitting needle and then abandoned when he was two days old in Bancroft workhouse?' asked Queenie.

Ida glanced at the money then screwed it up in her fist. 'I think he'd like a cowboy outfit.'

'I'm sure you know best,' said Pearl, giving her a condescending smile. 'But make sure you wrap it in new paper not that creased stuff you've saved from last year.'

Snapping her bag shut, Pearl glanced around the room and gave an exaggerated shudder. 'Honestly, Ida, I don't know how you can live in this junk yard.'

Fury like a firecracker shot across Queenie's wrinkled face for a second before being replaced with her sweetest little-old-lady expression. 'Sad as I am that you're going so soon,' she said, 'sure, let me fetch your coat for you.'

She went into the hallway and returned a second or two later carrying Pearl's luxurious mink.

''Tis a fine coat,' said Queenie, smoothing her gnarled hands over the rich pelt. She rubbed it against her cheek. 'And so soft. Bet it cost Lenny a king's ransom.'

Pearl looked smug. 'Well, it wasn't cheap.'

Queenie maintained her gummy smile for a couple of moments then her face turned into that of an enraged gargoyle.

'Which is more than could be said of you, Pearl Munday,' she screamed. 'You fecking gobshite.'

Queenie threw the mink on the floor then, like a child leaping into a puddle, the old woman jumped on to the middle of the garment with both feet. With her eyes fixed on Pearl's horrified face she wiped her muddy boots across the glossy pelt a few times then stepped off.

Dragging the coat across the floor behind her, Queenie stormed out of the room, down the hallway and opened the front door.

'You want your coat, do you?' she shouted, marching into the street and pricking up the ears of the neighbours. 'Well, fetch it, you fecking cow.'

Swinging the now filthy coat around her head like a lasso, Queenie hurled it into the middle of the road.

Pearl screamed and dashed after it but couldn't reach it before it landed in a pool of rainwater with an oily slick swirling on its surface.

'You want to be calling names, do you?' yelled Queenie as Pearl snatched her coat from the cobbles. 'Well, I'll give you a few to be taking with you: tart, trollop, slut. That's what you are, Pearl, and everyone knows it.'

'How dare you?' screamed Pearl, clinging to her ruined fur.

Out of the corner of her eye, Ida noticed a couple of neighbours whispering behind their hands while casting amused glances across at her.

'You come swanning around here all la-di-da when the world and his wife know you've been dropping your knickers for every Tom, Dick and Harry since you had fuzz between your legs,' Queenie yelled. 'There can't be a man this side of the Aldgate pump who hasn't had his hand on your ha'penny, Pearl Munday.'

An ugly expression contorted Pearl's face, vividly reminding Ida of her many unhappy encounters with her sister as a child.

'I'll get my Lenny on you, you old bat,' shouted Pearl, her expensive hat losing its anchorage and slipping forward.

'I'll be waiting for him.' Queenie licked her index finger. Closing one eye, she pointed at Pearl. 'Waiting to curse him so his balls dry up and his fecking teeth fall out.'

Pearl glared at Queenie and Queenie glared back for a moment, then shaking out her dripping coat, Pearl folded it carefully across her arm.

She looked at Ida. 'Make sure you spend all that ten bob on Billy.' Her gaze slid across to Queenie. 'Mental. Bloody mental!'

Straightening her hat, Pearl turned and walked away, under the scrutiny of the Mafeking Terrace residents who were standing on their doorsteps.

Queenie watched her defeated adversary depart for a moment or two then turned and walked back towards Ida.

'You look pretty grim there, Ida,' said Queenie, as she stopped in front of her.

'Do I?' asked Ida, watching her sister negotiate the cobbles in her high-heeled shoes.

'That you do,' said Queenie. 'And don't you be thinking you can berate me for slinging your sister out—'

'I wasn't,' Ida cut in. 'I was just thinking I wish I'd been quick enough to wipe my feet on her coat, too.'

Chapter Seven

'GRAN . . .?' said Billy.

Queenie looked up from the racing page of her newspaper and peered at him over her half-rimmed spectacles.

'How is it you know so much about the horses?'

He was sitting next to her eating the jam sandwich she'd made for him when he got in from school fifteen minutes before and was still in his uniform.

It was the second Friday in November, and just after three o'clock. *Music While You Work* was in full swing and there was still an hour and a half until the blackout curtains had to be drawn, securing the population of London into their miserable dark world.

Billy hadn't lingered after school and Queenie couldn't blame him. The overnight puddles had been thick with ice when she went out for the family's bread that morning and had remained solid all day. Mind you, even though it was cold enough to rot spuds in the ground, it was as warm as a summer's day when compared to the glacial temperature between Ida and Jerimiah.

'Do you write it all down?' He indicated the dog-eared notebook at her elbow.

'Sometimes,' said Queenie. 'But mostly it's all up here.' She tapped her head.

'Eddy Browne's brother says you know the form of every horse,' said Billy, his eyes wide with admiration.

'Well, maybe I do.' Queenie shook out the paper.

'Will you teach me about the horses, Gran?' he asked, spraying crumbs as he spoke.

'You're too young for such things,' said Queenie.

'Please...' Billy whined. 'So I can win lots of money so I can look after Mum and Dad and the rest of the Brogan family.'

Queenie studied the boy's freckled face. If truth be told, Billy didn't have a drop of Brogan blood in him and would have to be told the truth about his birth at some point, perhaps when he was a year or two older. It didn't matter to Queenie, because although Billy was not her grandson by blood, he was in all the ways that mattered.

'All right, lad,' she said, smoothing the newspaper across the kitchen table. 'I'll show you how easy it is to win lots of money.'

'Don't worry, Gran,' he said, with a grin. 'When I'm rich I'll look after you too.'

Queenie suppressed a smile.

'All right, lad, let's see if there's a nag who can make our fortunes in the one o'clock at Newmarket,' she said, adjusting her half-rimmed glasses on the end of her nose.

Wiping his mouth with the back of his hand, Billy rested his elbows on the table and leaned over the racing page.

'Well, Mason Melody looks promising,' Queenie said, glancing down the list of runners and riders. 'He's lasted two races over the distance and been placed in all but one of the previous six.'

'So he's fast,' said Billy.

'He is and Dicky Mullins, who weighs no more than a couple of feathers stuck together, is on his back,' continued Queenie. 'And on top of it all, Mason Melody ran the hooves off the odds-on favourite last time out.' She pointed at the minute BF alongside the horse's name.

Billy studied the letters and numbers for a second then looked up.

'So he's a good bet?' he asked.

'There's worse,' Queenie agreed. 'And he prefers firm to hard.' She tapped the letters f and h under the horse's name. 'And I'd be guessing with the weather being such as it is, Newmarket's track will be as unyielding as a pair of nun's knickers. Your man, Fat Tony, was offering five to one for Mason Melody, and judging by his form, I for one wouldn't have argued with those. So what do you think, lad? Will you chance your pocket money?'

Billy raised his hands and then as his mouth formed soundless words he closed each grubby finger over in turn.

'So, if I put a tanner on Mason Melody I'd get half a crown back,' said Billy.

'You could,' said Queenie.

Billy's eyes lit up. 'I could buy that Airfix model of a Lancaster bomber that's hanging in Feldman's window instead of having to save for it, and I could get four ounces of sherbet lemons, too.'

'That you could,' said Queenie. 'So hand over your money.'

'I've spent my pocket money already, but I have sixpence left from my Saturday fire money.' Delving into his pocket Billy fished out two threepenny bits and handed them over.

Queenie's hand closed around the coins. 'Now, let me tell you, the nag you've put your money on ran in the one o'clock today and was grand until the last furlong when he lost his stride and came in fourth.' She slipped his money in her pocket. 'And now the bookmaker's got your money and you've got to get up in the cold on Saturday morning and light another dozen fires to earn some more.'

Billy's face collapsed. 'But that's not fair.'

'No, that's the sheer foolishness of putting your hard-earned money on a horse.' Grasping his soft childish hand, she shook it. 'And I'll tell you this, lad, and tell you no more: betting is a mug's game. Now eat your sandwich and then if you tidy your room as your mother's been asking you to for a week or more, I'll let you have your money back.'

Billy's scowled and jammed his sandwich in his mouth.

The handle rattled as the back door opened.

'Only me.'

A pushchair containing an infant bundled to the ears in blankets bounced over the threshold as Cathy, Queenie's middle granddaughter, manoeuvred it through the blackout curtain and into the room.

Like her sisters, Cathy was slim and of middling height, although since having her son Peter eighteen months ago, her girlish figure had changed to more womanly curves. However, whereas Mattie, Jo and their older brother Charlie had the dark colouring of Queenie's side of the family, Cathy was fair like Ida's side of the family and had the sweet face of Ida's mother but thankfully not her sour disposition.

She too was wrapped up against the cold in her everyday green coat with chequered scarf tucked around her neck and a knitted beret over her honey-blonde curls.

'Well, this is a nice surprise,' said Queenie, standing up. 'Let me make you a cuppa.'

As always when she walked through her parents' back door into the familiar kitchen, Cathy felt the cloud of despondency that was her constant companion lift a little.

Gran was in the kitchen, there was the comforting smell of supper cooking in the oven and there were peeled spuds and chopped cabbage in saucepans on the rings above. Even the faint smell of bleach from the bucket under the sink, which was brimming with the family's smalls, somehow made her feel better.

She was ashamed that she had once thought her parents' house shabby but having left as a bride just two short years ago, she would now give almost anything to return.

Forcing her sad thoughts away, Cathy closed the back door with her foot.

'Hello, Gran,' she said. 'And yes, please, I could murder for one.'

'I'll not be asking for that,' her grandmother replied. 'Just a wee cuddle from this little darling.'

She held out her thin arms towards Peter who, seeing a bit of fuss coming his way, started wriggling about. Unwrapping her son from the layers of blankets and his coat, Cathy handed him to her gran who tucked him on to her hip.

'Hello, Billy,' Cathy said, unbuttoning her own coat. 'Good day at school?'

He shrugged and carried on munching at his sandwich.

Queenie's arm shot out and gave him a clip around the ear.

'Ow,' he said, putting his hand to his head.

'Your sister said hello,' she snapped.

'Hello,' he mumbled through the last mouthful of sandwich. 'And school's all right.'

'That's better,' said Queenie. 'Now, about your business.'

Billy stood up and, dragging his feet as he went, left the kitchen.

'I hope you haven't been teaching Billy about the horses,

Gran?' said Cathy, as the old woman folded away the newspaper.

'Just what he needs to know,' said Queenie.

She tickled Peter under the chin making him giggle and the little boy tucked his head into her shoulder. She gave him a noisy kiss on the cheek and then stood him on the floor. Peter looked around solemnly for a moment and then sat on the lino.

'Mum in?' asked Cathy, as she gave her son a rattle and his pram reins to play with.

'Not yet,' said Queenie, taking the tea cosy off the pot. 'She's gone to help out at the rest centre and if you're after Jo, she's had to do a double shift as she's got half the ambulance station off with flu. How's that misery of a mother-in-law of yours?'

'Just the same,' said Cathy, battling to keep the cloud of despondency from settling back on her shoulders.

Stan's mother Violet Wheeler was only just fifty but as she wore widow's grey and an expression like she were wearing wire-wool drawers, you'd be forgiven for thinking she was Gran's age.

As her gran poured the tea, Cathy made herself comfortable on the chair Billy had just vacated and watched her infant son playing contentedly at her feet.

'Your mother's taken it upon herself to save all our sugar rations for Christmas, so you'll have to have it without,' said Queenie, putting a mug of tea in front of her.

'That's all right, Gran. I'm doing the same myself and, to be honest, it's been so long since I had a cuppa with sugar in it, I don't know I could drink tea with it in now.'

'But I do have a little treat for you,' Queenie said, picking up the biscuit barrel shaped like Big Ben that was sitting on the table and popping the lid open.

Cathy's eyes lit up. 'Custard creams!' she said, hardly believing her eyes. 'I haven't had one of those for months. Where on earth did you get them?'

Her gran winked. 'That's for me to know and you to wonder.'

Putting her tea on the table and sitting down opposite Cathy, Queenie scooped up her great-grandson and settled him on her knee. Taking one of the biscuits from the tin, her gran handed it to the toddler on her lap and his cheeks dimpled into a smile.

Cathy glimpsed a reflection of his father's handsome face in her son's innocent one and unhappiness pressed down again.

'Have you heard from Stan?' asked her gran, as if she could read her thoughts.

'Yes, I have,' said Cathy. 'The prison governor has granted me a Christmas visitor's pass.'

'Are you taking Peter?' asked Gran.

'Stan's mother moans to high heaven if I ask her to watch him while I pop to the shops, so she'd never have him all day, so he'll have to come with me,' said Cathy.

'I'm sure your mother would be pleased to mind the lad while you're away visiting,' said Queenie, pulling a happy face at the baby who laughed.

Cathy pressed her lips together. It was tempting, especially after the way Stan had been the last time she went to see him, and Peter would be happier with her mum than being strapped in his pushchair and lumped on and off trains all day, but . . .

'Stan hasn't seen him for almost six months,' said Cathy, 'so I'd better take h—'

The handles rattled as someone else opened the door. The blackout curtain billowed and Mattie stepped into the room. She was muffled to the chin in a long berry-red coat with a fur collar and cuffs and a perky little black felt hat to finish off the ensemble. She held a bag of shopping over one arm and balanced her daughter Alicia, also bundled up against the elements, in the other.

'Hello, Gr—' She spotted Cathy and stopped in her tracks.

'Mattie, it's grand to see you,' their gran said, as Cathy regarded her sister coolly across the family kitchen.

'Hello, Cathy,' Mattie said, giving her a warm smile. 'How are you?'

'Fine,' said Cathy, half turning from her and taking a sip of tea.

There was long empty moment as Cathy felt her sister's eyes bore into the back of her head then Mattie spoke again.

'Look, Alicia,' she said, walking over to Queenie. 'Your cousin Peter's here, too. Isn't he getting big?'

Cathy studied the bottom of her mug and didn't reply.

'And how's my best girl,' said Gran, taking Alicia's hand.

The baby, who had Mattie's dark colouring, kicked her legs and wriggled in her mother's arms in response.

'Teething again,' Mattie replied.

'I can't believe she'll be a year soon,' said Gran. 'I've just made a pot so can I get you a cuppa?'

'No thanks, Gran, I'm on my way to see Francesca. I only popped in to drop this off for Mum.' She plonked the shopping bag on the table. 'Lipton had just had a delivery when I got there earlier so I managed to get a couple of tins of pink salmon for her Christmas stash. Tell her I'll pop in later on in the week.'

'Well, I'll no doubt see you then too. Say goodbye, Peter,' said Gran, waving the baby's hand for him.

'Bye-bye,' Mattie replied, doing the same with Alicia's chubby fist. She turned. 'Bye, Cathy. Nice to see you and Peter again.'

Cathy studied a spot on the wall behind her sister and didn't reply. Mattie stood there a moment then left.

As the door slammed, Queenie's sharp eyes fixed on Cathy. 'Don't you think this quarrel you have with Mattie has gone on long enough?'

'I said I'd never speak to her again and I won't.'

'For the love of Mary, Cathy. She's your sister.'

A pang of loss started in Cathy's chest as memories of Mattie, plaiting her hair and helping her buckle her shoes for school, flashed through her mind. It was swiftly followed by the memory of snuggling into her older sister in the old double bed they had shared as children.

Shoving the thoughts aside, Cathy forced herself to hold her grandmother's gaze. 'And if she'd remembered that I was her sister, my Stan wouldn't be rotting in prison.'

Half an hour after leaving her mother's house Mattie was having a coffee with her long-standing friend Francesca Fabrino in Alf's café, while Alicia slept in the pram next to the table.

The café was now owned by Francesca's father Enrico, who had taken it over in April. It had previously been a pie and mash shop so had the typical black-and-white tiled walls of the traditional East End eating house, but Enrico had added a touch of his native Italy by suspending a selection of battered copper pans from the ceiling behind the counter and hanging ornamental plates on the walls. There was also a painting of Ponte Vecchio in Florence, where the Fabrino family came from, on the wall at the far end. It was one of three Florentine scenes painted by Francesca's older brother Giovanni.

On the night Italy had entered the war, Francesca's family had been the victims of a rampaging mob who burnt down their fish and chip bar on Commercial Road; the painting was the only one they were able to salvage.

She and Francesca first met when they were four and a half and had sat next to each other in Miss Gordan's class at Shadwell Mixed Infants School.

Topping Mattie by an inch or two, Francesca had clear olive skin, almond-shaped ebony eyes and straight black hair so long she could sit on it, but today, as she'd only just returned from her job as a sales assistant, it was still pinned up into a tight bun.

They were sitting at one of the corner tables in the café, which was situated half a dozen doors down from the underground station on Whitechapel Road, opposite the London Hospital.

It was about four now and the shop's blackout blinds were already down, the curtain pulled across the door. With just a handful of low-wattage bulbs lighting the interior, the eating house was more like a Chicago speak-easy than a friendly family café. They were in the lull before the evening rush and so, apart from a handful of customers dotted around the tables, she and Francesca more or less had the place to themselves.

'Honestly, Mattie,' said Francesca, looking across at her friend, 'I really thought Cathy would be speaking to you again by now.'

'So did I, Fran,' Mattie replied, feeling a weight pressing down on her heart. 'But she still blames me for Stan being sent to prison.'

Francesca raised an eyebrow. 'I don't see why. It wasn't you who made him get him involved with those Nazi traitors. And she wants to be thankful he's behind bars and not dangling from a rope.'

'Perhaps,' said Mattie. 'But what with us still at odds and Mum not talking to Dad, I'm beginning to dread Christmas.'

Her friend looked amazed. 'They're still not talking?'

Mattie shook her head.

'But it's been ages. I'm surprised your dad's not sweet talked her around by now,' said Francesca, looking astonished, as well she might because Mattie was equally puzzled by her parents' ongoing quarrel.

She sighed.

Reaching across, Francesca placed her hand over Mattie's. 'Don't worry,' she said sympathetically. 'I'm sure they'll work it out soon.'

Mattie forced a smile. 'I blooming well hope so.'

The two friends exchanged a fond look, Francesca squeezing her hand before releasing it.

'Well, do you want to hear my news?' she said.

'Tyrone Power came into Boardman's today and when you served him he fell madly in love with you,' said Mattie.

Francesca laughed. 'Oddly enough, no.'

'Well, what?'

'I handed in my notice because,' picking up her handbag from the floor Francesca rummaged around for a second then produced a manila letter with 'His Majesty's Government' stamped in bold letters across the top, 'I've signed up for war work.'

It was now Mattie's turn to look surprised. 'But I thought your dad wants you to work in the café.'

'He might but I don't,' said Francesca. 'Other women are doing their bit to beat Hitler, so I don't see why I shouldn't.'

'But how on earth did you persuade him?' said Mattie.

Lovely though he was, Francesca's father had a somewhat traditional view of how young and unmarried Italian women should spend their time. It was in the home, cooking and cleaning for their menfolk until they found a suitable – preferably Italian – husband.

'Easy,' her friend replied. 'I told him if I didn't sign up voluntarily for war work now, when the new National Service Act comes in next month I could be drafted into the army and stationed goodness knows where, with hundreds of lonely soldiers.'

Mattie laughed. 'So what have you signed up for, the ATS or the Land Army?'

'Factory,' said Francesca. 'Much as I don't want to serve coffee in the shop, I can't desert Dad altogether, not after all he went through last year.'

Her friend's gaze flickered across the room to where her father was serving late-afternoon coffees and teas behind the counter.

He and his son, like thousands of other men of Italian descent, had been interned for several months but were released just after last Christmas. Giovanni had immediately signed up and there was a picture of him, all chiselled chin and liquid eyes, sitting next to the till at the end of the counter. However, Enrico Fabrino, after spending the best part of last winter in an aliens' internment camp and who had never been hale and hearty, now looked ten years older that his forty-five years.

'Besides,' Francesca gave a light laugh, 'I'd miss you and your family too much if I got posted somewhere up north or abroad.' She took a slow sip of her coffee. 'Talking of abroad, have you heard from Charlie?'

Mattie gave her friend a soft smile. 'I had a letter from him the day before yesterday.'

'How is he?'

'Hot and bored but other than that he seems well enough,' Mattie replied. 'Although, he was in an accident a few weeks back when the ack-ack gun he was towing skidded off a sand dune and nearly took the lorry with it.'

Alarm flashed across her friend's pretty face. 'Is he all right? I mean, he's not hurt or in hospital, is he?'

'No, other than having to wait in the sweltering desert heat for a recovery truck, he's fine,' said Mattie. 'He also asked me if I'd seen Stella.'

'And have you?'

'Not recently,' said Mattie.

She hadn't but unfortunately lots of other people had: dancing with a sailor, dressed to the nines and getting off the night bus. She'd even heard a whisper that her wayward sister-in-law had been to visit Old Mother Connery in Ensign Street to get her out of a bit of trouble.

'Is she still working nights in that dining club up West?' asked Francesca.

'Yes,' said Mattie. 'So at least I see Patrick from time to time as Mum and Gran look after him until Stella collects him.' A smile lifted the corners of her lips. 'He's such a cheeky little chap.'

'And with those dark curls and big brown eyes he looks just like Charlie.' A forlorn expression flitted across Francesca's face and she buried her nose in her coffee cup.

Mattie studied her friend's downturned face as the clock on the wall behind the counter ticked off the seconds.

'You would think I'd have got over it by now, wouldn't you?' said Francesca, raising her eyes after a few moments. 'After all, they've been married for almost a year.'

'It takes time,' said Mattie. 'And I know it's hard, Fran, but you have to find someone else.'

'You're right.' Francesca blinked away the moisture gathering along her lower eyelids. 'After all, there's plenty of fish in the sea.'

'And with your looks, you've certainly got the right hooks to catch them,' said Mattie. 'Why don't you give that blond chap you were telling me about last week a chance?'

'You mean the doctor?'

'Yes, that's him,' said Mattie. 'Next time he offers to take you to the pictures, say yes.'

'I will.' Francesca forced a too-bright smile. 'I might even say yes to that fireman who asked me to the Spitfire fundraising dance at Poplar Town Hall.'

'That's the spirit,' said Mattie.

'In fact,' continued Francesca, chirpily, 'from now on I'm going to—'

The Moaning Minnie on top of the hospital opposite let off a long wail. Everyone in the café stood up and started gathering their coats and bags together before hurrying to the door.

The ack-ack guns a mile away in Victoria Park started booming, shaking the ground beneath their feet.

'Grab Alicia,' shouted Francesca, throwing the last of her coffee down her throat, 'and I'll catch you up.'

Leaving her friend bolting the door, Mattie scooped her dazed-looking daughter out of her pram and wrapped the knitted blanket tightly around the baby. Hooking her handbag on her arm, she headed for the gap at the end of the counter. Francesca returned and the two girls hurried through to the corridor behind. Opening the door under the stairs, Francesca grabbed the torch off the hook and directed the beam in front of them as they descended the stairs.

Like Mattie's own basement, Francesca had equipped half the area beneath the shop with all the things necessary to withstand a long raid, including two truckle beds, extra blankets, a small primus stove and a selection of tinned food, plus a bucket under the stairs discreetly hidden behind a curtain.

Cradling Alicia in her arms, Mattie settled herself at the end of her friend's bed while Francesca lit the hurricane lamp overhead, bathing the enclosed space with a mellow yellow light. The first bomb found its target, followed by a dozen others in quick succession. The cellar shook, dislodging dirt from above and rattling the crates of lemonade stacked in the corner.

Carrying two canvas money bags, Enrico ran down the stairs. He stashed them away and then set about securing the café's stock on the shelves while Francesca came to join Mattie on the bed.

The ground shook again as another bomb, a high explosive one judging by the blast, hit the ground nearby. Alicia stuck her thumb in her mouth and snuggled into Mattie.

'Poor sweetheart,' said Francesca, gazing fondly at her goddaughter. 'She should be tucked up in her own bed not spending the night in a cold cellar.'

'Shouldn't we all?' Mattie replied.

Francesca gave her a wry smile.

The ack-ack guns pounded again, followed by another half a dozen explosions close by rattling the bottles and dislodging more dirt. The ground shook once more, sending the lamp above them swinging wildly and the beams creaked.

With her heart pounding in her chest Mattie looked up, but the steel girders supporting the roof hadn't shifted. She took a slow deep breath.

Another deafening bombardment rocked the earth, the noise of it filling the cellar and stopping all conversation. They sat without speaking until the Luftwaffe bombers above had discharged their payload and there was a lull.

'You know, Mattie,' Francesca said, 'it wouldn't be so bad if Stella was any kind of a wife to him but . . . Well, I mean, it's just not fair, is it?'

Studying her friend's face in the light from the swinging hurricane lamp, and seeing Francesca's brown eyes filled with love and longing, Mattie gave her a sympathetic smile.

'No, it's not.'

And it wasn't. Not one little bit. Because if it were, her brainless half-wit of a brother would be married to the woman who truly loved him rather than to the one who'd caught him with the oldest trick in the book.

'If you could take a deep breath, Mrs Gilbert,' said Dr Osborne, as he held the cone end of his stethoscope against her back.

Ellen did as he asked, and the familiar pain under her rib made itself known.

It was almost eleven in the morning on the third Monday in November and she was in the consulting room of the elderly family doctor. The surgery was in Sutton Street – a stone's throw from where she lived.

Retracting his stethoscope from beneath her blouse, Dr Osborne straightened up.

'Well, your lungs seem to be clear, Mrs Gilbert,' he said, walking around and resuming his seat behind the paper-strewn desk. 'And for that we must be thankful.'

He peered over his spectacles at her, the light from the table lamp reflecting on his bald head. 'So how is the pain?'

As she was an only child, her parents had been quick to find the sixpence needed for a doctor's visit, so Dr Osborne had seen Ellen through various childhood illnesses. He was younger then, with a full head of sandy-coloured hair. At nearly seventy he should have retired years ago, but like so many of the doctors who served the working population of the docks, he regarded his work as a vocation and Ellen, like many others, was thankful for it.

'Bearable,' said Ellen.

He looked puzzled. 'Hasn't the increased dose helped at all?'

'It did,' Ellen replied. 'But it made me very drowsy and, well . . .'

'You don't want to upset Michael?' Dr Osborne replied.

Giving him a pained smile, Ellen shook her head. 'No. He's worried enough already. Is there nothing else I could take?'

Dr Osborne sighed. 'I'm afraid not. If the tumour was just in your bones, aspirin might ease it a little but as it's infiltrated your lungs there's risk of internal bleeding. Aspirin would make that worse so the only thing I can offer you is syrup of morphine.' Resting his elbows on the leather-bound blotting pad in front of him, the elderly doctor steepled his fingers and rested his chin on them.

'Have you told him yet?' he asked, watching her intently.

Pressing her lips together, Ellen shook her head.

'I know, my dear, that Dr Willard said three or four months, but you must understand these things can never be predicted precisely and it could be—'

'I understand, and I want to but . . .' Clasping her hands together, Ellen looked down at her lap.

There was a pause as she struggled to master her swirling emotions then her mouth pulled into a firm line and she looked up.

'I know it's a very hard conversation for a parent to have with their child, but it needs to be had,' the doctor said.

'I'll tell him, Doctor,' Ellen replied, 'just as soon as I have things in place.'

'For his care, you mean, when you're . . .?' Dr Osborne gave her an apologetic look. 'When you can no longer care for him yourself?'

'Yes,' said Ellen. 'I have spoken to the relative I want him to live with.'

Dr Osborne raised a busy eyebrow. 'Haven't they agreed?'

'They are just sorting out the arrangements,' Ellen replied. 'But I'm sure they will . . .' The image of Ida's devastated expression when she realised who Michael was loomed into her mind. 'I would be grateful if you could write me up for some more medicine.'

'Of course.' Unscrewing the top from his fountain pen, the elderly doctor scribbled on a sheet of headed notepaper and then handed it to her. 'I suggest you take a full dose at night at least so you have a decent night's sleep.'

Ellen took it. 'Thank you, Doctor.'

Standing up, she slipped the prescription into her pocket and then took out a florin, which she gave to him.

Pulling out the drawer beside him, the doctor popped it into his cash box then slid the drawer shut.

'Perhaps if they aren't sure, it might be better to consider other arrangements,' he said. 'Barnardo's, for example. In their home at Barkingside the boys live in houses with a house mother and father, just like a real family. They've even got this excellent scheme for children to have a fresh start by being rehomed with families in Australia.'

'Oh, no,' said Ellen. 'I don't want Michael to be sent away to the other side of the world and from everything he's ever known.'

'Well then, what about getting your priest to approach the Poor Sisters of Nazareth on your behalf?' said the kindly doctor. 'I understand they have a number of houses all over the country.'

'Thank you, Doctor, but when the time comes I know the person I've asked to care for Michael will be happy to make him part of their family,' said Ellen, fervently praying that it would be so.

Rummaging around in the money belt concealed under her fur coat, Queenie pulled out a handful of change.

'There you are, me lucky lad,' she said, dropping three silver coins in Brian Murphy's outstretched hand. 'Twelve shillings, all thanks to Colourful Dancer in the three o'clock at Chepstow on Saturday.'

'Thanks, Mrs Brogan,' he replied, his Adam's apple bobbing up and down under his shaving rash. 'And what odds are you offering on Music Man in the midday at York tomorrow?'

It was about three in the afternoon and because it was the first day of the working week, Queenie had been busy, paying out wins from the previous week and taking bets on the coming week's races. She'd been up before five, as usual, to fetch the family's daily loaf from the bakers in the market, if that's what you could call the grey slab of National Bread. Having fed and watered the family and packed them off to their various daytime occupations, she'd taken her notebook, strapped on her money belt and set off on her rounds.

First off, she'd called in at Feilding's to pick up the early edition of the newspaper with Saturday's results, which she studied as she sipped a mug of coffee in Rose's Café. Having noted the runners and riders she would be paying out on she'd headed to the market, paying out winnings to stall holders and taking bets. When the Mason's Arms had opened its doors for its lunchtime customers, Queenie, fortifying herself with half a Mackeson, had continued her work at a corner table, jotting the takings and winning in her trusty notebook.

The pub had closed a few minutes before so now she'd shifted her operation to a quiet if dank corner under the arches at the end of Watney Street, so she could catch the afternoon trade and be ready for the knocking-off whistle at five.

'Seven to four on,' Queenie replied.

'Then I'll have a shilling both ways,' said Brian, handing back one of the coins she'd just given him.

Extracting the pencil jammed under her battered felt hat and pulling the dog-eared notebook from her pocket, Queenie opened it at a clean page. Dabbing the pencil point on her tongue she scribbled the bet down, slid the money back into her belt and fished out a sixpence.

'Ta,' he said, taking it from her. 'I'll see you in the Compasses on Wednesday.'

'That you will, God willing,' Queenie replied as he walked away towards the bustle of the market.

Careful not to brush against the slimy green moss clinging to the brickwork, Queenie opened her ledger and raised her almost invisible eyebrows. *Well, that's a fine day's work and no mistake,* she thought as she scanned down the entries, and she still had the Railway Arms and Dover Castle to visit when they opened at seven.

Covering Watney Street and the roads close by, plus a handful of pubs along the Highway and Cable Street, Queenie only had a small turf compared to Fat Tony's other runners, but it was more than enough to keep her busy. To be honest, you'd think with bombs raining down day and night, life would be enough of a gamble for most but, somehow, knowing you could be here today and gone tomorrow had brought out a sporting streak in everyone. Not that she was complaining.

She pocketed only a ha'penny for each bet she took, but even on a quiet day she walked away with two bob in her pocket. Although not a fortune it was enough for her to put a bit by for her funeral, buy a pound or two of Tate & Lyle from Slim Fred to add to the family's sugar ration when Ida wasn't looking or slip an extra pint of milk into Mattie and Cathy's bags for their wee darlings.

Of course, betting outside the race track was totally illegal, but the landlords of the local pubs were happy to turn a blind eye to her antics. After all, what looked more harmless than a grey-haired granny chewing on her gums and enjoying half a pint in the corner?

Putting her record book back in her coat pocket and

the pencil behind her ear, Queenie settled her old felt hat on her head and started off towards the market. The weak afternoon sun made her squint for a second as she emerged from the shadow of the railway arch. She glanced across at the clock, complete with a kilted highlander with bagpipes, hanging in the off-licence window.

Ten past. She had just short of an hour to spare before the factories turned out and the dock gates opened, and as her bunions were all but murdering her, Queenie decided to take the weight off her feet in the Railway café and have a well-earned cuppa.

Idly wondering if the tooth that had made Mattie's daughter feverish all week had come through yet, Queenie headed up the market but just as she reached Carswell's the Chemist, a woman clutching a paper bag accompanied by a boy wearing school uniform stepped out into her path.

It took Queenie a moment but then she recognised her.

'Afternoon, Ellen,' she said. 'I heard tell you were back.'

Ellen's mouth dropped open as she stared at her.

'Mrs Brogan,' she said, recovering herself. 'How are you?'

'Grand, and yourself?'

It was a stupid question. There was no need for Queenie to gaze into the bottom of a teacup or lay out the cards to see Ellen Gilbert wasn't long for this world. It wasn't so much the jaundiced hue of her complexion or the way her flesh hung lifelessly around her jaw and mouth, it was her eyes. Once so bright, they now had a dull flatness about them as if the soul inside knew it was soon to depart.

'I'm well,' said Ellen. 'As well as I can be.'

They stared at each other for a second then Queenie spoke again. 'And is this young Michael I've been hearing so much about?' Again, it was a stupid question because there was no doubt at all as to who the boy standing beside Ellen was. In fact, with his unruly black curls and broad face, it could have been Jerimiah as a boy and Queenie's heart ached at the sight of him.

'Yes, this is Michael, my son,' said Ellen, looking defiantly at Queenie. 'Michael, this is Mrs Brogan.'

Even though he was just ten, Michael's shoulders were already squaring off, like Jerimiah's at the same age. The faint shadow on his top lip showed; like his father he'd be shaving by the time he was fifteen, and his oversized hands and feet indicated he would match Jerimiah's stature in time. As he looked up at her with Jerimiah's clear dark eyes, the urge to gather him into her arms threatened to overwhelm Queenie.

''Tis my pleasure to meet you,' she said, hearing the emotion tight in her voice. 'I see you're at Greencoat School.'

'Yes,' said Michael, glancing down at the badge with an old-fashioned sailing boat on it. 'But I've only been there a little while.' His eyes darted past them on to the other side of the road. 'Ma, the baker's putting a tray of buns in the window. Can I have one?'

'You can,' Ellen said, handed him thruppence. 'As long as you make sure you eat your tea.'

'Ta, Mum, and nice to meet you, Mrs Brogan,' he shouted over his shoulder as he scooted away.

Ellen's gaze, full of heartbreak and love, followed the boy as he dashed towards the shop on the corner then her attention returned to Queenie.

'He is Jerimiah's,' she said.

'None could argue with that,' Queenie replied.

Ellen let out a long sigh. 'I'm sorry my return has caused your family such a lot of trouble, Mrs Brogan, but I had no choice. I just hope Ida can see that.'

Queenie didn't reply.

Ellen glanced across the road. 'Well, the blackout starts in an hour, so I ought to get Michael home. Nice to see you, Mrs Brogan, and I hope to see you again sometime.'

'I'm sure you will,' said Queenie.

A ghost of a smile flitted across Ellen's face then she turned and crossed the road to join her son. Queenie watched her drag herself wearily across the road to where her son was munching his way through a bun outside the baker's.

Although Ellen's arrival had driven a wedge between her son and Ida, Queenie did have Ellen to thank for one thing. At least this week when she entered the confession box she'd have a sin that she needed cleansing from her soul.

Wicked though it was, she couldn't help but think that if Ellen hadn't been about to meet her maker, Michael, who looked so like his father it hurt, might have been lost to her for ever.

Chapter Eight

'STAND UP, DAISY, and let's see how it fits,' Ida said to the little girl standing in front of her.

Daisy Mullins who, as she'd just informed Ida, was six and three-quarters, drew herself up to her full height.

'What do you think?' asked Ida, looking at Daisy's mother who was standing next to Ida.

It was just after four thirty on a dreary November afternoon. As usual at this time on a Tuesday afternoon Ida was dressed in her serviceable green drill WVS dress and was on duty at the rest centre in the Catholic Club's main hall.

Although the rest centre was paid for by the council it was run by the Stepney branch of the WVS. Most of the space in the hall was given over to rows of camp beds but there was also a canteen and snack bar that was open for hot food day and night. During the daytime a nursery was held in the committee room opposite. Today the crèche was filled with young children while their mothers attended the cooking demonstration being given by a home economist from the Ministry of Food.

Ida was in charge of the second-hand clothing and shoes section, which was squashed at the far end of the hall. It comprised tightly packed dress rails which had been donated by one of the local clothing factories. On the rails hung a variety of daywear that was sorted by size into men's, women's and children's. Pairs of shoes were lined up on the floor beneath. With people pitching up at all hours with just the clothes they stood up in, only the refreshment counter was busier.

Ida had taken her WVS uniform with her to work and come straight to the hall when she'd finished at eleven. Stella was off work with a sore throat so, as she didn't need to collect Patrick, she'd told Queenie that she would go straight to the rest centre to help sort a consignment of clothing from the American Red Cross, which was true. However, the real reason for not going home first was that she didn't want to see Jerimiah; she still couldn't bring herself to say yes to him.

'It's a bit big, isn't it?' said Vera Mullins.

Vera and her three children lived in one of the old cottages in Elm Row near to the Children's Hospital by Shadwell Basin. That's to say, they'd lived there until this morning when they had returned from the shelter at first light and found the home they'd left ten hours before had been turned into a pile of charred beams and rubble with all their worldly possessions crushed beneath.

'Well, she'll get plenty of wear out of it and, to be honest,' Ida glanced along the rail of clothing beside her and the rows of shoes beneath, 'I don't think we've got anything smaller. It's come all the way from America.'

Vera studied her daughter for a few seconds more then nodded. 'You're right. I'll save some coupons if it sees her through a couple of winters. I don't know, my kids seem to sprout up overnight.'

'I know just what you mean,' said Ida, helping Daisy out of her oversized coat and adding it to the bundle of clothes Vera had already selected for herself and her two boys. 'My Billy's grown at least two inches since the summer and the cuffs of his school blazer are halfway up his elbows. I'm going to have to take him along before Christmas to get him some extra clothing coupons.'

'Well, I 'ope you have better luck than the woman opposite me,' said Vera, as Ida secured her bundle with a length of twine. 'Her ten-year-old was one of those early blooming girls and could barely button her school blouse across her but the ruddy pen-pushers at the Town Hall still refused her the coupons for a new one.'

'There you are,' said Ida, handing the clothes to the young mother. 'If you'd just sign for them at the registration table and as soon as the council have found you somewhere come back and get some kitchen equipment.'

'Thanks, Mrs Brogan,' said Vera, taking her daughter's hand.

Hooking her arm through the improvised handle Ida had tied round the clothes, she headed off towards the two truckle beds at the far end of the hall which had been allocated for her and her children until the welfare could find her a place to rent.

Pulling up the chair next to the lines of shoes against the wall, Ida had just opened the next canvas bag to be unpacked when Cathy appeared around the corner of the men's rail, dressed, like Ida, in the forest-green dress of the WVS with the enamel brooch pinned on the collar. She had been helping with the teas all afternoon and had just collected Peter from the nursery.

'Hello, Mum, you still here?' she said, shifting her son into a more comfortable position on her hip.

'Hello, luv,' said Ida. 'Yes. I need to get this lot on the rails before the next batch arrives tomorrow.'

'I thought there were three of you on the clothes,' said Cathy.

'There should be, but Madge West's sister is in hospital after being trapped in her cellar, so she's minding her kids,' said Ida. 'And Peg's got a stinking cold.'

'Do you want me to stay and give you a hand?' said Cathy.

'No, I've only got this bag and I'll be done,' said Ida. 'Are you coming to tea on Sunday?'

'Yes. Stan's mother won't like it,' said Cathy, 'but I need a break from her constant carping.' Peter started to grizzle.

'Peter!' said Ida in a sing-song voice, making a happy face at the baby.

He looked at her solemnly for a moment then started niggling again.

'Well, if you're sure you're all right, Mum,' said Cathy, rocking back and forth to soothe her unhappy son, 'I'll leave you to it and take this young man home for his tea.'

She bent down and gave Ida a peck on the cheek and Ida took her grandson's hand.

'Bye-bye, Peter, see you Sunday,' she said.

Her grandson stuck his thumb in his mouth and curled into his mother's shoulder by way of reply.

'Bye, Mum,' said Cathy.

'Bye, luv. And don't take no notice of Stan's mother,' she called after her daughter.

Cathy walked out of the hall just as Mrs Hardwick, the wife of the Rector of St George's, marched in. As the district organiser for Stepney, Wapping and Shadwell, Mrs Hardwick had originally commandeered the crypt under her husband's church as the central meeting point for the local clothing exchange, knitting circle and packing of parcels for the troops, but after St George's was gutted by an incendiary bomb she had shifted operations to St Bridget's and St Brendan's Catholic Club.

Just short of fifty, with tightly permed mousy-coloured hair, fierce eyebrows and a top lip that a walrus would have been proud of, Mrs Hardwick was all fur wraps, sharp eyes and long-nosed looks.

Not feeling in the mood to be talked down to by the area organiser, and seeing her heading towards the registration table on the other side of the rails of clothing, Ida ducked back behind them.

The record of who had been in and what they'd been given each day was logged by Mrs Crowther, the dentist's wife, and Miss Archer, who looked after her elderly mother. Mrs Hardwick's steel-tipped heels came to a halt and she started quizzing the WVS record keepers about the comings and goings that day.

Ida opened the last sack of donated clothing and started sifting through it. Her mind was half on her task while the other half was running through what she needed in the market the next day, but as she pulled out a pair of blue denim dungarees the conversation of the three women on the other side of the clothes rails caught her full attention.

'Is there anything else?' asked Mrs Hardwick, when the two women had finished speaking.

There was a pause.

'Well, speak up,' barked the rector's wife. 'If it's something that will undermine our efforts here I need to know.'

'It not really to do with the rest centre or any of our activities,' said Mrs Crowther, 'but—'

'But what?' asked Mrs Hardwick.

'Well, you know us, Freda,' said Mrs Crowther in a hushed voice. 'We're not ones to gossip but it's one of our members. Well, her husband, actually, and . . .'

'And some woman in Juniper Street . . .'

Ida's mouth went dry.

'We're talking about Ida Brogan's husband,' said Miss Archer. 'You know the rag-and-bone man with the piebald cart horse.'

'Do you mean the Irishman who has that junk yard under the arches in Chapman Street?' asked Mrs Hardwick.

Ida's mouth pulled into a hard line.

'That's him,' said Miss Archer.

'It's just a rumour, Mrs Hardwick,' added Mrs Crowther, 'but people are saying that he and this woman in Juniper Street are carrying on.'

'Yes,' chipped in Miss Archer. 'And . . .'

'And?' asked Mrs Hardwick.

There was another pause as the blood pounded through Ida's ears.

'Well, people are saying this woman's boy looks too like him to be a coincidence,' said Miss Archer.

'The face off him, in fact,' added Mrs Crowther. 'And everyone says it.'

'What do you expect?' said Mrs Hardwick. 'When all they get for transgressing God's holy ordinance is a couple of Hail Marys and some Latin mumbo-jumbo said over them. They're almost as bad as those greasy Maltese in Wellclose Square. Is it any wonder half of the children around here aren't sure who their fathers are?'

'I can't say I'm surprised,' said Miss Archer. 'Jerimiah Brogan always looked very flash with his collar unbuttoned showing his chest and that red neckerchief of his tied at his throat.'

'And not only that . . .' said Mrs Crowther. 'Have you seen the way he—'

'Mrs Hardwick, ladies,' a man's voice called from the other side of the hall, 'could you spare me a moment of your time?'

'Of course, Doctor,' Mrs Hardwick called back.

There was a shuffling and scraping of chairs then three pairs of high heels clip-clopped away.

With her heart thumping in her chest and tears distorting her vision, Ida stared blindly ahead while the images of Jerimiah and Ellen swirled around in her head once more.

Why was she surprised? Jerimiah and his bit of slap-and-tickle with Ellen must be the talk on every street corner by now. They'd be laughing at her for being such a blind fool not to have realised sooner. And the gossips wouldn't forget it, either. How could they when they only had to look at Michael to be reminded of the scandal?

She stood up, grabbed her coat from the end of the rail and her bag from the floor, and fled the hall.

Twenty minutes later Ida stumbled through the back door of Mafeking Terrace and threw her bag on the table. Resting her hands next to it, she hung her head and allowed the cloud of misery that had been hovering over her since the moment she'd realised who Michael was to engulf her.

Blindly, she dashed through the house and upstairs. She stumbled into her bedroom, slamming the door, and stood staring at the double bed with the patchwork cover she'd made from scraps left over from making her children's clothes. The children she'd conceived and delivered in that bed.

Her children! Hers and Jerimiah's.

She stared at it as memories of warm embraces and private nights swirled around in her head. Then she crossed to the dresser under the window. Pulling out one of the two smaller drawers at the top, she rummaged around under the handkerchiefs and stockings until she felt what she was seeking.

Sliding out the small parcel, she unwrapped the tissue paper and took out the length of scarlet ribbon it contained. Hooking it around her finger, Ida held it aloft.

She'd had it for over a quarter of a century but it had lost none of its vibrant colour. Twisting it back and forth, Ida studied it for a moment then screwed it up in her hand. Holding it in her fist she marched back downstairs to the parlour.

Crossing to the fire, Ida stood for a moment then threw the ribbon on to the glowing coals. The fabric started to curl and shrivel immediately.

She'd saved her pennies for almost a month before she could buy the luxurious satin trim to weave through her hair. She'd been wearing it the night she met Jerimiah at the St Patrick's Day dance and had kept it tucked away ever since.

A faint whiff of hair drifted up as the flames consumed the silk, but Ida couldn't distinguish the red of the ribbon from the red of the flames any longer as her vision was obscured by her tears.

'So that's me booked for next Wednesday, the twenty-sixth, to take you and yours from Assembly Place to Windmill Lane in Stratford,' said Jerimiah, scratching a line under the entry in his work ledger and shoving the pencil back behind his ear.

It was close to five o'clock and he was standing in the area that served as an office at the back of his yard. Although

Samson had finished his day's work over two hours ago, Jerimiah had only just finished unloading the pile of furniture he'd bought for a few pounds that afternoon.

'I'm obliged to you, Mr Brogan,' said Pat Cotton, a wiry chap with a mass of red hair, offering Jerimiah his hand. Pat, who had lived just off Caroline Street until his house and ten others had been flattened two weeks before, worked as a fireman on the Great Eastern Railway and had been on a run to Colchester that night. Thankfully, his wife and three kids had been tucked up safe beneath the ground in Bethnal Green Station. However, unlike many others who'd had to bed down with relatives, as an employee of the Great Eastern Pat had been allocated a railway cottage at the back of the Stratford Depot in Maryland.

"Tis my pleasure to transport you and your lovely family to your new home,' said Jerimiah, taking his hand.

They shook, then, repositioning his knapsack on his shoulder, Pat left.

Locking his record book in the top drawer of his desk, Jerimiah turned off the shaded light and left the office. He checked that the horse had enough hay and water to last until the morning then walked out of the yard, bolting and chaining the gates behind him. Buttoning up his overcoat against the chilly November air, he took his torch from his pocket and shone it on the paving stone beneath his feet.

As always at this time in the evening, the street was full of men and women coming home from work, but as the fog from earlier in the day had lifted, leaving clear skies above, there was an equal number of mothers, children and elderly people making their way to the shelters, carrying their supplies for the night.

Hoping that Ida hadn't already set off for the Tilbury, Jerimiah crossed Chapman Street and, sidestepping a couple of dockers going into the Old House at Home on the corner, headed for Mafeking Terrace.

Since he'd told her about Ellen's condition she'd hardly spoken a word to him. To be honest, he didn't blame her, especially given what he was now asking of her. Most women would have told him straight out where to go but his Ida wasn't most women. He prayed to God she might be able to rescue them both from the hell he'd plunged them into.

Within a few moments of turning into his road, Jerimiah was striding past the empty cold frames and barrel of spuds to his back door. Pushing it open he expected to find the light on and his wife in the kitchen but instead the room was in darkness and the house beyond silent. Letting the blackout curtains fall back into place, Jerimiah flicked the switch and skimmed his eyes over the scene.

The crockery was upturned on the draining board and the kettle looked cold, which suggested no one was home. However, the shopping bag Ida took to the shelter each night was on the table and the Thermos flask beside it had yet to be filled.

'Ida,' he called.

There was a noise from the parlour beyond but there was no answer. Puzzled, he walked through to the other room and switched on the light to find his wife, with her shoulders hunched, feet drawn up beneath her and her face covered by her hands, sitting in the chair.

'Ida,' he repeated.

She didn't answer.

Jerimiah walked over to her.

'Ida, what's happened?' He laid his hand on her hunched shoulder. 'It's not one of the kids—'

'It's not one of our children,' she snapped at him through red-rimmed eyes. 'It's you and *your* son.'

Staring up at Jerimiah, with his tousled black curls, collar unbuttoned and cuffs turned back revealing the soft hair of his brawny arms, rage tore through Ida. Unwinding her legs, she stood up and faced him.

'Everyone's talking about you and Ellen,' she said.

'And who might everyone be?'

'That stuck-up Mrs Hardwick, for one,' Ida replied, as the voice of the rector's wife's replayed in her head. 'I heard her today talking to her cronies, Miss Archer and Mrs Crowther, who couldn't keep their mouths shut if their lives depended on it. We'll be the talk of every WVS canteen and rest centre by this time tomorrow.'

Jerimiah pulled a face. 'People talk. That's the plain truth of it.'

The anger simmering in Ida's chest boiled over.

'It's all right for you,' she shouted, balling her fists together and flaying them at him. 'When this gets out, all your mates down the Catholic Club will be slapping you on the back and winking: calling you a sly dog and then buying you a Guinness. Whereas I'll have to stand in the Sainsbury's queue while people look sideways at me and whisper about my husband and his fancy woman.'

'I haven't got a fancy woman,' he replied in a level tone. 'The truth is, from the moment I saw you, Ida, I've never had or wanted any other woman but you.'

'Except Ellen,' shouted Ida, giving him a scalding look. 'My best friend. Who you went to bed with while I was mourning James.'

Jerimiah's mouth pulled into a hard line. 'He was my child, too, Ida. You weren't the only one who was heartbroken.'

'I suppose that's why you slept with Ellen, was it?' snapped Ida, as the images of him holding her best friend started to play again in her mind. 'Because you were heartbroken.'

A rarely seen thunderous expression hardened her husband's face. 'Can you recall, Ida, what you were about while I was standing in the rain at the City of London Cemetery and laying our baby son in the cold earth?'

Ida bit her lower lip but didn't reply.

'It was two full days before I could persuade you to give me James's body after he died.' Images of tiny fingers and a miniature nose replaced those of Jerimiah and Ellen in Ida's mind. 'You then took to your bed for three weeks, leaving me to care for Charlie and the girls,' he added. 'I spent the days trawling the street for trade to keep a roof over their heads and feed them, fearing all the while I'd come home one day to find the police there to tell me you'd been found floating in London Docks. I was barely sleeping and eating but I was keeping my head above water, just. And it was these arms,' he bellowed, thrusting his hands forward, 'that laid his small white coffin before the altar in St Bridget's and St Brendan's for his requiem mass.'

The image of her baby son lying limp and cold in her arms flashed through Ida's mind, sending pain ripping through her like a raw-toothed saw. Memories and emotions burst up in her. In her mind's eyes she saw her six-day-old son lying in his cot like a beautiful wax doll, his eyes closed and his chest still.

She remembered Jerimiah and Father Mahon coaxing her to relinquish James's motionless body while she clutched him to her milk-filled breasts. She remembered the faces of her children, unsure and fearful as she sobbed uncontrollably.

'Don't think you were the only one to have your heart ripped in two when James died, Ida,' Jerimiah continued, as she remembered the black fog of despair that had enveloped her for countless days. 'I didn't understand but I accepted that the only way you could deal with the pain was to disappear into your own mind. But can you imagine how I felt, Ida? In here?' He punched his chest. 'I wanted to hold you, so we could grieve for our son, our precious son, together. But you shut me out, as if it were my fault James died. As if I should have done something to . . .' Moisture shone in her husband's eyes, but he blinked it away and they fixed on her again. 'Yes, I slept with Ellen; and only once. In a moment of weakness, which I regretted the moment I came back to reason. I'm sorry, truly I am, and if I could change it, I would. But Michael is my son. I won't deny it or him. I know what I'm asking of you, Ida, but will you treat him as your own, like I have all these years with Billy?'

Ida looked up at him incredulously. 'It's not the same, Jerimiah; you know it's not. Michael *is* your flesh and blood whereas neither of us are Billy's real parents—'

Jerimiah's attention shifted from her face to a spot just behind her right shoulder and alarm flashed across his face.

Ida turned to see Billy, dressed in his school uniform, with his grey socks at half mast, his claret and blue West Ham scarf wrapped around his neck, standing in the doorway with a look of utter devastation on his face.

'Billy luv,' said Ida, as a cold hand clutched around her heart. 'Let me explain.'

But Billy didn't. Instead, he stared wide-eyed at her and Jerimiah for a moment then turned and tore out of the house, slamming the back door behind him.

'Billy,' Ida screamed. Dashing past Jerimiah, she chased after her son. 'Billy, come back—' But her words were cut off by the wail of the air raid siren.

'Billy!' she screamed again, racing through the kitchen towards the back door.

Jerimiah got there before her and yanked their coats off the hooks. 'Don't worry,' he said, thrusting her coat into her hands as he opened the door to the low hum of German planes above and searchlights cutting across the sky. 'We'll find him.'

The first bomb hit the ground somewhere close to the Limehouse Cut as Jerimiah turned into Cable Street. Ida, who was just a pace in front of him, staggered as the ground beneath their feet shook. Jerimiah caught her before she collided with the wall.

'There he is,' she shouted, righting herself and jabbing her finger down the empty street.

Jerimiah followed her gaze towards where the Town Hall stood silhouetted against the fiery sky over the City. He saw his son scoot past the steps of the Old Dispensary and even though the night was as dense as pitch because of the blackout Jerimiah could see the boy's white face illuminated by the red blaze of the burning buildings around them.

'Billy,' screamed Ida.

Billy halted for a second but then turned and tore off again. A blast, a little closer this time, rattled their ears as it sucked the air from around them. Instinctively, Jerimiah held Ida to him as scalding air pulsed past them, splattering him with grit and whipping tendrils of her hair across his face.

Ida gripped her husband's arms and looked around him.

'Billy, wait!' she screamed as the low humming from the next wave of aircraft overhead grew louder. 'Billy!'

'It's all right, I'll catch him,' Jerimiah told her, dragging her into a shop entrance. 'You stay here.'

'No,' she said, pushing past him and running after their son.

Jerimiah followed as another bomb found its target and rattled the glass in the shop windows, sending the wires of the barrage balloon overhead squeaking and whining as the air buffeted it.

Keeping Billy in his sights, Jerimiah stretched his legs and pelted past Ida. The sooner he caught the boy the safer for all of them.

The clanging bell of a fire engine slowed him for a couple of seconds as it passed but then he picked up the pace again, closing the distance between him and his distraught son. Another blast reverberated around them as something, probably a warehouse roof, crashed to the ground a street or two south of them, sending flames leaping into the air.

Billy staggered slightly with the impact then seeing Jerimiah gaining on him, he dashed across the road as an ambulance, bell clanging and tyres screeching, roared around the corner, narrowly missing the fleeing boy.

Without breaking his stride, Billy headed for the charred beams and the mountain of bricks and concrete that had only a month ago been the Waterman's Arms public house.

'Billy. Son. Stop!' bellowed Jerimiah, his voice hoarse with the burning air he was dragging into his lungs. 'Let me and your mum explain.'

Scrambling up five foot until he reached the top of the jumble of brickwork and plaster that had been the public house's front wall, Billy turned.

'I ain't your son,' he screamed, his cheeks damp in the red reflection of the blazing buildings. 'And she ain't my mum.'

Wiping the back of his hand across his nose, he turned and disappeared behind the mound of rubble he'd been standing on.

'Billy, come back; it too dangerous,' sobbed Ida, as she reached Jerimiah's side. She went to go after the boy, but Jerimiah caught her.

'You'll never make it across in those,' he said, glancing down at her lightweight court shoes. 'I'll get him.'

Ida nodded. 'All right, but—'

The ack-ack guns half a mile away at the Tower drowned out her voice and she started forwards again. She slipped, and Jerimiah caught her.

'Ida,' he said firmly, setting her upright and gripping her upper arms, 'I'll get him.'

She nodded.

Leaving her on the pavement and with the St James's Gardens searchlights criss-crossing the sky above, Jerimiah picked his way across the jumble of splintered floor joists and shattered concrete towards his son.

Billy was nimble but he didn't have the weight to keep his footing and each time a bomb sent the ground trembling he struggled to remain upright.

Towards the river another bomb exploded, shaking the ground again and sending loosened brickwork tumbling from the half-destroyed walls of the public house.

'Stand still, Billy!' Jerimiah shouted in a voice that would have usually halted the boy at a hundred paces but tonight had no effect.

Instead of heeding his words, Billy leapt across on to another block of masonry, wobbling precariously as he found his balance.

Jerimiah jumped across on to another chunk of concrete. 'For the Love of God, Billy—'

The ear-piercing shriek of a German bomb hurtling its way towards the ground cut off his words as the world burst into a scorching inferno of red and yellow. From what seemed like a long way away Ida's scream echoed across to him. He turned but not before the heat seared the right side of his face and he smelt the unmistakable odour of singed hair.

A blast of air, heavy with the smell of sulphur and evaporated cordite, pressed him backwards before the vacuum created by the bomb's detonation sucked him forward, almost lifting him off his feet in the process. As the shockwave subsided, Jerimiah planted his boots firmly on the rubble.

'Billy!' screamed Ida, stumbling across the debris with her eyes fixed on something behind him.

With his ears still ringing, Jerimiah looked around to see Billy lying like a rag doll across a pile of bricks.

'Mum,' Billy sobbed, as he tried to get up.

'I'm here,' Ida shouted back as she reached Jerimiah.

'We're both here,' Jerimiah added. 'And don't you worry, me lad, we'll soon have you home. You wait here, Ida. I'll fetch him.'

Stepping on to the broken bricks, Jerimiah started towards their son but Ida grabbed his forearm.

'Be careful,' she said, her fingers biting into his muscle despite his thick coat.

Although his burnt skin stung, Jerimiah smiled. 'For sure, me darling.'

Moving as fast as he dared, Jerimiah picked his way across the rubble until he reached the sobbing boy. Bending down, he scooped Billy up in his arms.

'I'm . . . I'm so . . . sorry, Dad,' sobbed Billy, his face buried into Jerimiah's shoulder and his arms like a metal vice clamped around his neck.

'Hush, now. 'Tis forgotten,' said Jerimiah, holding the boy's trembling body closer. 'Now let's get you back to your ma, and home.'

Turning, Jerimiah started back but he'd taken no more than a pace or two when the ominous drone of approaching aircraft started his eardrums vibrating. The first of a dozen bombs fell in an even row behind him, sending flames darting into the sky and buildings a few streets away crashing to the ground. The planes soared over their heads and looped southwards to pay a visit to Bermondsey, Rotherhithe and Surrey Docks on their way back to northern France.

In the peculiar lull that settled over an area once the munitions were spent, Jerimiah heard something like a rusty hinge on a door creak.

He looked up at the Waterman's Arms' only remaining wall looming over them. The space around him shifted an inch or so. Ida screamed but Jerimiah was already moving. Placing his large hand over the back of Billy's head to protect it and grasping the boy even tighter, Jerimiah jumped across from shattered chunk of brickwork to concrete pillar as the wall crashed to the ground.

With blocks of plaster and mortar bouncing around him and dust and grit swirling around his legs as he ran, Jerimiah fixed his eyes on Ida, who stood on the pavement with her hands covering her mouth, a look of horror on her face. He had only a couple of paces to go when something hard and sharp thumped into his back, knocking the breath from him and sending pins and needles down his arm.

Jerimiah gasped and staggered forward into Ida's arms.

'Jerry, are you all right?' she asked.

Stars popped in the corner of Jerimiah's vision and he shook his head to clear them.

'I'm grand,' he said, loosening Billy's arms a little and taking a deep breath. 'And so is Billy, aren't you, lad?'

'I'm sorry, Mum,' said Billy, his tears now damp on Jerimiah's collar.

'I should think so too,' said Ida. 'Making your poor dad—'

'Go easy there,' said Jerimiah, smiling down at her. 'The lad's had a bit of a shock all round, wouldn't you say?'

She hugged Billy, who was still clinging to him, and Jerimiah winced.

'And what of you?' said Ida, looking him over.

'Something whacked me in the back, that's all; I'll be right as rain tomorrow,' he replied, praying it would be so.

Ida's gaze ran slowly over his face.

'Oh, Jerry, I . . . I . . .' In the light of the search beam, tears glistened in his wife's eyes. 'I thought . . .'

Although it ached like billy-o, Jerimiah put his free arm around her shoulders. 'It's all right, luv.'

A low hum could be heard as the next squadron flew up the Thames towards them.

In the dark, Jerimiah pressed his lips on to his wife's hair. 'I think we've all had enough excitement for one night so to my way of thinking a cup of tea is long overdue.'

Ida raised her head and her eyes locked with his for a couple of heartbeats then she forced a smile and nodded. He gave her a squeeze and pain shot down his arm. Ignoring it, Jerimiah adjusted Billy into a more comfortable position in his arms and guided his family towards home.

Reaching forward, Ida smoothed a stray lock of hair out of her son's eyes. 'I'm sorry, Billy, we should have told you sooner but . . . well, I couldn't because . . .'

The words 'I was scared' had stuck in her throat.

'Because Mum wanted to wait until you were old enough to understand,' said Jerimiah.

Ida gave him a grateful look. They had returned to the house about half an hour ago and now she and Jerimiah were sitting on either side of their son's bed. Billy's room was the smallest of the three upstairs rooms and was situated by the turn of the stairs. Billy had shared the room with his older brother Charlie but now he had the ten-by-six room to himself, along with his collection of comics, model soldiers and the Airfix RAF planes that dangled from the ceiling. That said, tonight he'd dug out his old and very worn teddy bear Mr Buttons from the bottom of the wardrobe to tuck under the covers with him.

The all-clear had gone just as they were about to head for the shelter so they'd returned home instead and walked into an empty house. Jo was on duty at the ambulance station and wouldn't be home until dawn and Queenie had yet to return from whichever one of her old cronies she had sat out the evening's air raid with.

After checking her son over and finding his only injury from the night's adventure was a twisted ankle and a few cuts and bruises, Ida had made them each a hot drink: tea for her and Jerimiah and a hot chocolate, with plenty of sugar, for Billy.

'So Aunt Pearl is really my mum,' said Billy.

'Sure enough, she's the woman who gave birth to you,' said Jerimiah.

'Is that why she's always buying me presents?' said Billy.

'Yes,' said Ida. 'Because you're special to her.'

'But if I was special, why did she leave me in the workhouse?' the boy asked.

'Because she . . .'

Ida glanced across at Jerimiah.

'Because, Pearl was very young,' he said. 'And knew she couldn't look after you properly so she wanted to make sure someone who loved you would care for you.'

'Why didn't she just give me to you?' he asked, looking at Ida.

'She was upset and wasn't thinking straight,' Ida replied, trying to keep the revulsion at her younger sister's callousness from her tone.

'Who's my dad?' asked Billy.

Stretching across, Jerimiah ruffled his hair. 'I am, of course.'

'What, like Michael?'

A stab of pain jabbed into Ida's breastbone.

'No, not like Michael,' she replied. 'But in the same way I'm your mum.' Billy opened his mouth to speak but Ida raised her hand. 'Now, my lad, now the Jerries have gone home for the night I suggest you tuck yourself under the covers and get some sleep or you won't be getting that thruppence Dad promised if you scored ten out of ten in your spelling test tomorrow.'

Billy nodded and snuggled down beneath the blankets.

Jerimiah leaned forward and kissed his son on the forehead but as he levered himself up off the bed he gasped.

'Why don't you go and open that bottle of Jameson's you've been saving for Christmas?' suggested Ida.

Jerimiah gave her a weary smile. 'I think I just might.' Rubbing his left shoulder, he walked out of the room.

Ida leaned forward.

'Goodnight, sweetheart.' She kissed the same spot on Billy's forehead where Jerimiah had planted his kiss. 'And remember, me and your dad love you and you're ours as much as Charlie and the girls are.'

Billy nodded and then sticking his thumb in his mouth, closed his eyes.

Ida studied his face for a moment then followed her husband downstairs. Jerimiah had taken off his jacket and waistcoat and was just in the process of pouring himself a second drink when Ida walked in the room. He looked weary and from the stiffness of his movement he was clearly in pain from his brush with the chunks of masonry earlier.

'Is the lad all right?' Jerimiah asked, as she closed the door.

Ida nodded. 'I wouldn't be surprised if he wasn't already fast asleep.'

'Hardly surprising,' said Jerimiah, taking a mouthful of drink. 'Not after the merry dance he led us.'

Ida gave a wan smile.

He replaced the bottle on the sideboard. 'I thought you were a little kind in your explanation in regard to your sister's part in his birth.'

Ida shrugged. 'Perhaps, but I could hardly tell him his mother tried to get rid of him and when that failed, dumped him in Bancroft workhouse before his cord barely detached.'

'You have the right of it there,' he said. 'But perhaps we should have told him before.'

'We should have,' said Ida. 'And I wish I'd listened to you when you said as much but I was . . . I was scared.'

Jerimiah looked puzzled. 'Of what?'

'That Billy would . . . would . . . love Pearl more than me . . . because . . .' Tears welled up in Ida's eyes.

'Why would he?' said Jerimiah. 'Sure, Pearl buys him fancy presents and calls him her "darling" but it wasn't her who sat up for three nights when he had measles, was it?'

'No,' said Ida in a small voice.

The look that always made Ida feel special crept into her husband's eyes. 'In all the ways that matter, Ida, you're Billy's mum, so why would he love her instead of you?'

Ida forced a brave smile. 'You're right but I couldn't face losing him like I lost . . .' A fat tear rolled down her cheek.

Putting down his glass, Jerimiah crossed the space between them in two strides and took her in his arms.

'It's all right, my darling girl,' he whispered softly, pressing his lips to her hair.

His arms tightened around her and feelings she'd not experienced since finding out about Ellen started to steal over her, but she cut them short and disentangled herself from his embrace.

'Sit down and let me look at that shoulder of yours,' she said a little more harshly than she intended.

Jerimiah popped open the buttons of his shirt and stripped it off in one swift movement. Turning one of the upright chairs around, he sat astride it, resting his muscly, hair-covered forearms across the back.

Ida walked around behind him, feeling her pulse quicken, her eyes running over the bulky contours of his shoulder and back.

'Ooow,' she said, wincing in sympathy as her gaze rested on the livid bruise across his right shoulder blade.

'That bad, is it?' asked Jerimiah.

Placing her hands on his shoulder, she ran them gently over his back, enjoying the feel of his skin under her fingertips but then she stopped. Had Ellen enjoyed the feel of his corded muscles under her fingers, too? Ida snatched her hand away.

'You'll be sore for a week or two, I reckon,' she said, looking away. "Truthfully, I don't know if you'll be up to taking the wagon out—'

The back door banged shut and Ida took a sudden step back.

'Well, praise all the saints, the fecking Germans have buggered off early for once,' said Queenie, marching in from the kitchen. She spotted her son's back. 'What in the name of all that's holy happened to you?'

Rising to his feet, Jerimiah took up his shirt. 'It's a lengthy tale but . . .' He briefly told her about Billy.

'It's of no matter and mind, and perhaps we should have told him sooner, but he knows,' Jerimiah concluded wearily. 'Now, as by your own admission, Mother, the Germans have buggered off, I have a mind to do the same. I've a full day ahead of me and I'll be all the happier for doing it after a full night's sleep in my own bed.'

He looked at Ida. 'Ida?' he asked, the softness in his gaze threatening to dissolve her anger and hurt.

Although he'd shrugged on his shirt he hadn't bothered to fasten it and Ida's eyes flickered over the mass of curls on his chest.

'I'll be up in a moment,' she said, wondering if Ellen had raked her fingers through those curls as she had countless times. 'I've to put the porridge to soak first.'

He stood motionless for a second or two and then with a sigh walked out of the room, his heavy footsteps thumping up the stairs to the floor above.

Feeling her mother-in-law's eyes on her, and her pulse racing, Ida headed for the kitchen but as she passed Queenie the old woman spoke again.

'Well, I'll tell you this and tell you no more, Ida,' she said. 'For the sake of your soul and your children's happiness, you and Jerimiah must find yourselves some peace about the lad because he'll forever be Jerimiah's son.'

Chapter Nine

'THAT'S THE LAST of it, Mrs Jessup,' said Jerimiah, setting the fruit crate containing a variety of crockery on the kitchen table.

'Thanks,' said the young woman, her breath visible as she spoke. 'I didn't realise I had so much.'

'No one does,' Jerimiah replied, 'until they have to pack it all up.'

It was just after midday on the morning after he and Ida had dashed after Billy.

Perhaps he was imagining it but Ida seemed to be a little warmer towards him after his brush with the masonry. He'd hoped, in the privacy of their bedroom, he might have had a chance to talk to her further but, unfortunately, the combination of having been awake since five that morning and two generous measures of Jameson's meant he was asleep as soon as his head hit the pillow. He hadn't even heard Ida come to bed and she'd already left for work by the time the alarm went off at six.

Now he was now standing in the very small kitchen of Mrs Jessup's new home. She and her five children had spent the last three hours huddled together amongst all her worldly goods on the back of his wagon while Samson plodded the fifteen or so miles from Bow to Waltham Abbey.

Of course, as the bombed-out houses and factories they passed along their route testified, nowhere was completely safe but with the Germans concentrating their nightly raids on cities and military targets, the small town clustered around the ruins of the ancient abbey was safer than most. It was also nearer to her husband who was one of the ground crew at RAF Dunmow.

While he'd unloaded the last of her crates and boxes, the young mother had already lit a fire and put a kettle on to boil. The youngest of her children, a baby of about a year, was strapped into a highchair by the fire drinking his lunchtime bottle while his siblings, who ranged from about six to twelve, were upstairs squabbling about who was sleeping where.

She was the third family he'd moved in as many weeks and he had two more booked before the end of the month, one to Leyton, another to Brentwood, which was about as far as he could manage in a day, which was a pity as he'd had to turn down a couple who were moving just outside Bishop's Stortford the week before. While Samson still had a few years left in him yet, a full day pulling a loaded wagon, rather than just plodding stop-start around the neighbourhood, took its toll on the horse so perhaps it was as well he was only moving Pat Cotton's family to Stratford next week.

The door opened and the woman's oldest boy burst into the room.

'Guess what, Mum?' he said, his face red with the cold. 'They've got chickens next door. Can we get some?'

'We'll see,' his mother replied. 'But before we think of anything else we need to keep this fire going.'

'I'll leave you to it, then,' said Jerimiah.

'Yes, thank you, Mr Brogan,' said the young woman, opening her handbag. Taking the money from her purse, she handed him three green pound notes and a brown ten-shilling note.

'Can I offer you a cup of tea before you head back?' she asked, as he pocketed the money.

'It's kind of you but no,' he said. 'I want to have meself home and me horse tucked up in his stable before the blackout starts.'

Leaving Mrs Jessop, Jerimiah re-buttoned his overcoat and left the house.

Samson, who he'd left munching his way through a nosebag of oats, shook his head as he saw Jerimiah emerge.

'Right, me old lad,' said Jerimiah, unwinding the reins from the lamp-post in front of the house. 'Let's get ourselves home.'

Holding on to the front seat and stepping on the wheel hub, Jerimiah leapt up on to the front board of the wagon and winced as pain shot across his shoulder again. The biting wind caught his hair as he settled himself on to the seat. Taking his cap from his pocket he flipped it on, turned his collar up and they set off.

He had decided to take a different route home as on their way to Waltham Abbey the A10 had been clogged with army trucks and wagons heading towards various military bases in East Anglia. However, he'd only gone a few miles when he was stopped by an army roadblock.

'Sorry, mate,' the fresh-faced corporal manning the barrier shouted as Jerimiah pulled Samson to a halt. 'We had a big 'un land in the road last night.' He pointed towards a pile of earth down the road. 'The sappers 'ave been at it all morning and should have the temporary road open soon. You might as well get yourself a cuppa while you wait.'

He indicated the café nestled in amongst some old farmers' cottages.

Jerimiah nodded and guided Samson on to the verge. Removing the horse's nosebag so he could graze the winter grass, Jerimiah tied the reins loosely to the hedge and, with his stomach starting to rumble, strolled across to the small eating place.

As you'd expect in the middle of the working day, the café was full. Squeezing his way between the tables of auxiliary firemen and ARP personnel, Jerimiah headed for the counter at the far end.

The woman behind it, a motherly sort with her blonde hair swept back into two rolls on either side of her face, looked up from buttering bread as he approached.

'What can I get you?' she asked, licking butter off her thumb and taking the next slice from the pile beside the bread board.

Jerimiah scanned the blackboard on the wall behind her then gave her his order.

Sticking the knife in the block of butter, the woman turned and called his order through the serving hatch then plonked a mug of tea in front of him. Jeremiah handed over his money and, spotting a table with just one occupant in the far corner, he made his way across.

'Would you be minding a bit of company?' he asked, pulling out the empty chair.

The young man, with a smattering of shaving rash and a Brylcreem quiff, looked up. 'No, mate,' he said. 'Be my guest.'

Jerimiah unbuttoned his coat and sat down while his lunch companion returned to contemplating the bottom of his mug.

Before Jerimiah could unwind his scarf the woman behind the counter had waddled over and set a steaming bowl in front of him. Jerimiah thanked her then glanced at the young man opposite him.

'I guess you'll be waiting for the road to clear, like me,' said Jerimiah, picking up the sugar shaker with its label reminding customers that there was a war on and that they should have only *two spoonfuls per person*.

The young man nodded glumly. 'I've got a van full of stuff I should have delivered to my mate in Spitalfields at first light.'

'When you say stuff, what exactly are you referring to?' asked Jerimiah.

'Potatoes mostly, six sacks, but I've another two of onions and one of green beans,' the young man replied.

'Have you now?' said Jerimiah, jabbing his fork into a piece of meat.

'Yeah, plus three crates of cabbage and two of spinach,' the young man added.

'You've quite a crop there, haven't you?' said Jerimiah. 'Would you mind if I ask you how you find yourself in possession of such treasures?'

The young man's face lit up. 'From my smallholding,' he replied. 'My father died two years back and I've been building it up ever since.'

'Well, all credit to you.' Jerimiah took a slurp of tea. 'But arriving a few hours late to market won't harm them, and sure they'll sell as well tomorrow as today.'

The worried expression returned to the young man's face. 'It's not that. It's my wife. According to the midwife she's overdue and she is terrified of going into labour at night in case there's an air raid. I promised I'd be back before the blackout started. After sitting here for half the day I'll never get back in time.'

165

Well, tell me, Mr . . .?'

'Duggan, Ted Duggan.'

'Tell me, Ted, how much were you hoping to be paid for your van of vegetables?' Jerimiah asked, scooping up the last morsel of stew with his fork.

The man on the other side of the table gave him a wily look. 'Nine, perhaps ten pounds.'

'Well, I'll tell you what, Ted,' said Jerimiah, leaning back to rummage around in his trouser pocket. 'I have six quid here.' He laid a crumpled selection of pound and ten-shilling notes on the table. 'How about I give you that for what you've got on the van and you can be on your way home to warm yourself in front of the fire with your darling wife. What do you say?'

He offered his hand.

Ted's eyes flickered on to the money and back to Jerimiah's face. 'I'd have got at least eight in the market,' he said.

Jerimiah's hand went back into his pocket. 'Let's call it six and a quarter.' He threw two half-crowns on to the paper money.

Ted's eyes went back to the money.

'And you'll be saving yourself a few petrol ration stamps besides,' added Jerimiah.

'I'll tell you what,' said Ted. 'If you can dig out an extra quid and a half from somewhere you can have the lot plus the four hens I have in a crate.'

Looking up from the family's ration books that were spread across the kitchen table, Ida glanced at the clock on the wall.

'I shouldn't worry,' said Queenie, who was sitting opposite her. 'I'm sure he'll be home soon.'

Ida tried to look confused. 'Who?'

'Jerimiah, of course,' said her mother-in-law. 'Your wedded husband; isn't that why you're checking the blessed clock every five minutes?'

'No, it's not,' said Ida, forcing herself to hold the old woman's gaze. 'Now, if you don't mind, I've got to add up the family's rations ready for the weekly shopping on Friday.'

Queenie raised an invisible eyebrow and then returned to reading the evening paper.

It was a lie, of course. With her mother-in-law's attention on the racing results, Ida glanced back at the clock. Twenty past five. Only another hour and she would have to start out for the shelter.

Although she was trying to figure out their weekly rations she was also worried as to where Jerimiah was. Usually by now he'd be getting ready to report for duty with the rest of the Stepney Home Guard. As he wasn't in when she, Queenie and Billy sat down for their tea at half four, she'd plated up his supper of liver and mash and left it above a pan of simmering water, but if he didn't return soon, it would be ruined.

A flutter of anxiety started in her chest.

What if something had happened to him . . .?

Ida shoved the thought aside. After what he'd done she shouldn't care?

Putting aside the thought he could have been caught in a raid, blown up by a UXB or crushed under a collapsing building, Ida turned back to the family ration books.

She'd just finished calculating how many points she would need to make a lamb stew and was now trying to work out if she had enough in her fat ration for a fruit crumble when the back gate banged.

She waited for Jerimiah to come through the door, but when five minutes ticked by and he still hadn't appeared, Queenie gave her a questioning look.

'Perhaps he's in the bog,' said Ida.

'Elsie Mascall thought that when her old man got up in the middle of the night, only to find him lying face down and stone dead in the yard the following morning.'

Ida rolled her eyes. 'It's being so cheerful that keeps you going, isn't it, Queenie?'

Rising from the table, Ida took her coat from the back door. Slipping it on, she took the torch from the pocket and, switching off the kitchen light first, opened the back door.

Directing the beam on the floor she stepped out into the cold yard with Queenie just a pace behind her. Jerimiah wasn't anywhere to be seen but there were a couple of sacks on the flagstones outside the shed and a light and movement within. With Queenie dogging her steps, Ida walked across and opened the door.

Jerimiah had lit the hurricane lamp and hung it on the beam and was in the process of shoving the ancient pushchair that his mother sometimes used, with its mismatched wheels and squeaky axle, behind his gardening tools.

'What are you doing?' asked Ida.

'Making a space for our new guests,' he replied, nodding towards the crate at his feet as he dusted off his hands.

Ida shifted her torch beam on to it and some low cackles started.

'Chickens!' Ida and Queenie said in unison.

Jerimiah grinned. 'I've bedded them down with some straw and some of Samson's oats, so they should be fine until I can knock together a coop tomorrow.'

'But where on earth did you get them?' asked Ida, staring incredulously at the rough wooden crate.

Jerimiah told her about a young farmer with his van load of vegetables and his pregnant wife.

'I don't know if they'll lay but we'll give them a few days to show us their intention, and if not, you can fatten them up,' he concluded.

Ida stared at him and he gave her a nervous smile.

'Well, either way they will certainly help put a decent spread on for Christmas,' said Ida.

'Never a truer word spoken,' added Queenie. 'But look at you, lad,' she said, addressing her strapping six-foot son as if he were five. 'You're all but frozen. I'll sort the girls out while you go and have your supper. Stir yourself, Ida, and get something warm inside your wedded husband before he ends up like Ollie Mascall.'

Giving her mother-in-law another exasperated look Ida stepped out into the frosty air. The sky above was clear with stars twinkling around a bright full moon, a bomber's moon, heralding a German raid for certain.

Jerimiah followed her out of the shed and scooped up the jute sacks as he passed. They walked in silence back to the house.

Hanging up her coat, Ida crossed the kitchen and relit the gas under the kettle. Shaking off his coat too, Jerimiah hooked it on the back door.

Winding the tea towel around her hand, Ida lifted the plate with his dinner off the simmering pot.

'It's liver and potato,' she said, placing it before him. 'And I hope it's not too dry.'

'I'm sure it's fine.' He smiled. 'And I'm glad I got home before you left for the shelter, Ida,' he added in that melting voice of his.

Looking down into his twinkling eyes, Ida's heart thawed a little. She broke his gaze and went back to the stove.

'I'm glad you're home before I set off too,' she said as she poured their tea. 'I want to talk to you.' She turned and found him looking at her expectantly.

'About Jo and Tommy,' said Ida. 'They want to bring the wedding forward.'

Although his friendly smile didn't falter, Jerimiah's shoulders drooped a fraction.

'Do they now?'

'Yes, to Whitsun next year,' said Ida, placing two mugs of tea on the table and sitting down. 'I said I'd mention it to you if I got a chance. For what it's worth, I think you should let them. Despite his brother's being on the wrong side of the law, Tommy's as straight as they come and he's really making something of himself in the army. Jo says he's got another promotion coming his way soon but, more important than all that, he really loves Jo.'

Ida took a sip of her tea and lowered her eyes.

'And that's what really matters, isn't it?' said Jerimiah.

Keeping her gaze fixed on the rim of his plate, Ida didn't answer.

'Maybe I will agree,' said Jerimiah. 'But I have a lot on my mind at the moment.'

Ida's heart thumped in her chest a couple of times and then she raised her head. 'I also want to talk to you about . . .' Taking a deep breath she looked her husband square in the eye. 'About Michael. He can come to live with us after Ellen's gone.'

Jerimiah stared open-mouthed at her for a moment, then let out a long breath.

'Thank you, Ida,' he said. 'Thank you so much.'

'I'm not doing it for you,' she snapped. 'I'm doing it for that poor little boy. And at the end of the day, he is your blood and we've always said family is family.' Tears pinched the corner of her eyes. 'I'll have a word with Billy but now he knows you're Michael's father and half the WVS are talking about it, it's only a matter of time before the girls find out, so we'd better tell them about Michael too and then write to Charlie.'

'Would you like me to drop in on Ellen—'

'No,' Ida said, cutting across her husband. 'I'll call in on her tomorrow. The girls are here for tea on Sunday, so we can tell them then. Goodness only knows what they'll say.'

A bleak expression flashed across Jerimiah's face and the corners of Ida's mouth lifted slightly as they both knew exactly what Mattie, Cathy and Jo would say.

'What about Michael?' said Jerimiah after a long pause. 'We'll have to tell him too.'

Feeling as if she were teetering on the end of a bottomless chasm, Ida gazed into her husband's dark eyes.

'I'll tell Ellen you'll drop by next week and talk to him, and if he's going to be part of the family, perhaps you could bring him around now and again so he can get to know us. He'll be miserable enough when his mother dies without finding himself living with a bunch of strangers.'

Jerimiah gave her a grateful smile. 'Thank you again, Ida. You're a grand woman and I just want to—'

The back door opened, and Queenie stomped in, bringing a rush of cold.

''Tis cold enough to freeze the lake of fire in hell,' she said, closing the door behind her.

'How are the chickens?' asked Ida, grateful for the excuse to tear her gaze away from her husband's unsettling face.

'Well enough,' Queenie answered. 'They're starting to scratch around so I'm going to fetch them some of Albert's bird seeds and find an old blanket to keep them snug.'

She disappeared into her room and Ida's attention returned to Jerimiah. He smiled, and even after all these years he still had the power to send her pulse racing and her stomach fluttering.

For a second it was as it had always been between them and a smile started to lift Ida's mouth, but then thoughts of what he'd done with Ellen cut it short and she looked away.

Queenie reappeared carrying a tartan bundle and a brown paper bag. 'Shouldn't you be picking Patrick up now, Ida?' she said as she marched through the kitchen.

'I should,' said Ida as another blast of cold air signalled her mother-in-law's departure.

Rising to her feet she went to walk past Jerimiah, but he caught her hand.

'Just one more thing,' he said, looking up at her with eyes full of love and devotion. 'I want you to know, Ida, that from the moment I first set eyes on you across the hall at that St Patrick's Day dance wearing that scarlet ribbon in your hair, you're the only woman I've ever loved or ever will love.'

Ida studied the thick knuckles, the twisted veins and the fine dusting of hair across the back of his hand for a moment then she withdrew her fingers and her eyes returned to his face.

Although there was a sprinkling of grey amongst her husband's bristles and the lines around his eyes and mouth were a little deeper, it was the face she'd smiled upon for more than two decades. Still, Ida held her emotions in check as she imagined it must have worn that same wanting expression on it ten years ago when he looked at Ellen.

Chapter Ten

WITH THE PINT of milk she'd just collected from the doorstep in her right hand, Mattie rested her left on the newel post at the end of the banister.

'Breakfast!' she called, looking up the stairs.

'Two minutes, luv,' her husband called back.

The telephone in the hall had rung as Daniel had wiped the last few suds from his chin. That was twenty minutes ago and she knew his toast would have to stay warming under the grill for at least ten more.

It was just before seven thirty on the fourth Saturday in November and Mattie, in her dressing gown and slippers, was like any other wife cooking her husband's breakfast before waving him off to work.

Except she wasn't because unlike most men, her husband was eating the first meal of the day at his own kitchen table rather than in a military canteen somewhere hundreds of miles away from his family.

Not that Daniel wasn't serving his country as much as any other able-bodied man, it was just Major Daniel McCarthy, veteran of the Spanish Civil War, was doing his bit in an MI5 bunker in central London rather than in the army.

They had debated moving out a bit to Leytonstone or Barkingside but Mattie hadn't liked the idea of being that far away from her family so in the end they'd decided to take their chances with everyone else.

They both knew the Luftwaffe would be back as soon as the weather allowed them to fly again, so sinking their savings into the house was a bit of a gamble but . . . well, you had to look to the future.

It also meant that, unlike many other families, and if you ignored the fact they slept in a Morrison shelter in the basement, they had some semblance of normal married life.

Mattie walked back into the kitchen and Alicia, who was munching her way through a chopped boiled egg and soldiers, looked up.

'Dada,' she said, kicking her legs excitedly.

'He'll be down soon, sweetie,' Mattie replied, setting the milk on the table next to the teapot.

She went to the cooker and gave the porridge a stir. Satisfied that it hadn't stuck to the bottom, Mattie was just about to reach for a bowl when Daniel strolled in, with the morning newspaper under his arm.

Mattie's heart did a little double step. Even now, after eighteen months of married life, the sight of him sent her pulse racing.

A little over six foot with dark hair and eyes, a blunt chin and a broad athletic frame, Daniel looked more like a matinee idol than one of the country's top undercover operatives.

Thanks to his mother who came from the Alsace region of France, who their daughter was named for, he spoke French like a native and German like a Frenchman, which was why he was the man in charge of liaising with the resistance cells in Normandy.

Seeing her father, Alicia jigged in her highchair.

'How's my best girl this morning?' he said, crossing the room in two strides.

She offered him a well-chewed piece of her toast by way of reply.

Skilfully avoiding getting butter and jam on his shirt, Daniel kissed his daughter on her dark curls.

'Thank you,' he said. 'But you eat it as I think Mummy's made me breakfast.'

He sat down next to his daughter as Mattie set a bowl of porridge in front of him.

'Is there an egg this morning?' he asked, looking up at her.

'You're in luck,' she replied, enjoying the smell of his freshly applied aftershave drifting up. 'Gran got me half a dozen from the market yesterday.'

'Your gran!' Daniel's well-formed mouth lifted in a wry smile. 'She'd find ice in a desert.'

Leaving him to skim through the headlines while eating his oats, Mattie went to the larder to fetch eggs and her bowl containing their weekly fat ration.

Scraping off a sliver of lard with a knife, she plopped it in the frying pan, lit the gas and within seconds the block of white fat had melted.

Taking the egg from the carton she cracked it on the side of the pan but as she dropped it into the sizzling lard and watched it slide into the fat, her stomach heaved. Mattie put her hand to her mouth and swallowed. She glanced at Daniel who was busy playing a finger game with his daughter, and let out a sigh of relief.

Telling her rebellious stomach to behave, Mattie retrieved her husband's toast from the grill. She put it on a plate, scraped butter across it then flipped the cooked egg on to it. Turning off the boiling fat before the smell could reach her nose, Mattie picked up the plate and carried it to the breakfast table. Placing it in front of her husband, she sat on the chair opposite him and picked up the teapot.

'Anything interesting?' she asked, indicating the front page of *The Times*.

'The usual,' Daniel replied. 'Labour MPs are asking that the conscription powers be extended to cover property, which their Tory counterparts are calling communism by the back door. The government have given the Finns until midnight to stop fighting the Russians or Britain will declare war on them.'

'Who aren't we at war with?' asked Mattie, holding her daughter's Peter Rabbit beaker to her lips so she could drink her milk.

'Well, not the Americans, thankfully,' said Daniel. 'Although they're going to have to get off the fence soon as the talks between them and the Japanese have broken down and there are reports that the Japanese fleet have been sighted off south-east Indo-China. Oh and they're still showing that Arthur Askey film, *I Thank You.*' He looked at her. 'Do you fancy it?'

Mattie pulled a face.

'No, me neither,' he replied. 'But the new John Wayne looks pretty decent.'

Mattie laughed. 'So when do you have time to go to the flicks?'

'Too true.'

'I suppose that was Lennox phoning,' she said, as she refilled his cup.

'I'm afraid so,' said Daniel, spearing a square of yolk-covered toast with his fork. 'A bit of a problem with one of the contacts in France.'

'And he wants you to sort it out,' said Mattie.

'Got it in one.' He gave her an apologetic look. 'It might be another long day if we can't raise him.'

Picking up her cup Mattie raised an eyebrow. 'Well, there is a war on.'

'Are you going around to your mum's later?' Daniel asked.

'I was going to,' Mattie replied. 'But I want to finish my piece on turning shirt collars and cuffs and get it in the lunchtime post. We're around there for tea tomorrow anyway and besides, Jo said you could cut the atmosphere with a knife so she's volunteered for extra shifts at the ambulance station to keep out of the way. She's upset too because she was hoping Mum could talk Dad into letting her and Tommy bring the wedding forward, but she's got no chance if they're not speaking to each other.'

'Poor Jo,' said Daniel. 'Although I can't understand why your dad won't let them get married. After all, Tom's a good chap.'

Stretching forward on her highchair Alicia caught her father's hand.

'Perhaps it's a dad and daughter thing,' said Mattie, watching Daniel struggling to continue with his breakfast with one hand.

They exchanged a fond look then he glanced down at the empty table in front of her.

He frowned. 'Aren't you having anything?'

'I'm not hungry at the moment,' she replied. 'I'll have something later when I've got washed and dressed.'

The telephone in the hall rang.

Putting down his tea and freeing himself from his daughter's grip, Daniel stood up.

'Stay put,' he said. 'It's bound to be for me.' And he left the room.

Listening to the muffled sound of her husband's deep voice in the hall, Mattie raised the cup to her lips and took a sip.

What with feeling queasy and having missed two monthlies now, she was pretty certain she was pregnant again, but they had been disappointed before so, as Daniel had enough on his plate at the moment, she'd decided to wait until her next period was due in another few weeks before giving him the good news.

The low hum of male voices in the Catholic Club bar drifted over Jerimiah's head without making a dent on his consciousness. It was hardly surprising, really, given his brain had so many thoughts crashing against his skull.

It had been a dismal cloudy day but just before the blackout started at five thirty the wind had picked up so now the sky above was clear, which would no doubt herald a night of bombing. On a clear crisp winter night the Luftwaffe pilots only had to follow the moon's reflection off the Thames to find their targets. For this reason, Ida had gathered Billy early and headed off to the shelter, via Stella's, an hour ago.

It was still an hour before he had to report for duty, which is why he was enjoying a pint, dressed in his Home Guard uniform with his rifle propped up against the bar beside him.

The room on the first floor of the Catholic Club had the usual couple of dozen customers leaning against the bar or dotted around the tables. Many, like Jerimiah, were dressed in their khaki or navy Civil Defence uniforms and were either on their way to a night duty or on their way home having completed their day's shift at their air raid shelter or plane spotter posts. There were even a few regulars amongst them who were home on leave.

Pete was, as ever, behind the bar serving beer and good cheer.

He'd served Jerimiah his usual Guinness but after assuring each other that their respective families were well, Pete had left him to his beer and his disquieting thoughts of how Mattie, Cathy and Jo might react to the news that they had a half-brother.

Picking up his half-drunk pint Jerimiah swallowed another mouthful of the dark liquid, enjoying the bitterness at the back of his throat. He was just in the process of taking a second when the bar door opened and Jo's fiancé strolled in.

He'd have to say, if someone had told him a year ago that he'd have allowed Tommy Sweete, kid brother of the notorious gang leader Reggie Sweete, to become engaged to Jo, he would have laughed in their face. Reggie, who was in Wakefield doing twenty years for manslaughter, was a bad lot and no mistake but, credit where credit's due, Tommy was cut from a very different cloth. He was also one of those rare fellas who had a head for figuring out numbers and puzzles and so was in the signals regiment stationed in Bletchley.

Spotting Jerimiah at the bar, Tommy walked over.

'Afternoon, Mr Brogan,' he said, as he reached Jerimiah.

'And to yourself, Tommy,' said Jerimiah.

'Can I get you another?' Tommy asked, indicating Jerimiah's glass.

'No, but if you were to top it up with a half, I'd thank you.'

Jerimiah finished off the last of his drink as Tommy signalled the barman over and gave their orders.

'Well, it's grand to see you,' said Jerimiah. 'But I'm a mite surprised as I thought you weren't back until Christmas.'

'I'm not supposed to be but I've been sent to do a bit of liaison with our post at Hendon,' Tommy replied. 'It's me and two of my team and we're billeted in a hotel near Euston. It's a bit scruffy but the landlady's a good sort and there is a war on.'

'So they tell me,' Jerimiah replied.

Tommy grinned. 'I haven't told Jo so I'm going to surprise her at the end of her shift.'

Their drinks arrived, and Tommy offered Pete a few coppers.

'Put it on my slate,' said Jerimiah.

'Ta very much,' said Tommy, pocketing his money.

'I've had a good week,' Jerimiah replied.

Taking his pint, Tommy took a long swallow. 'Just what the doctor ordered,' he said, smacking his lips. 'I've been dreaming of that.'

Jerimiah gave him an amused look. 'Don't they have beer in the mess where you are?'

'They do,' Tommy replied, 'and some local brew that knocks your head off, but there's nothing so good as being back on your own patch with a pint in your hand, so thanks.' He took another mouthful. 'Jo said you've branched out into removals and second-hand furniture.'

'Needs must,' said Jerimiah. 'I'd never have kept food on the table if I hadn't, but if I'd known I'd be in such demand, I'd have done it a year back.'

'Jo said you're doing well for yourself,' said Tommy.

'I could say the same about yourself, lad,' Jerimiah replied, indicating the single chevron on Tommy's upper arm.

Tommy grinned. 'Yep, I'm aiming to make sergeant by next Christmas.'

Jerimiah took suitably impressed.

Picking up his pint Tommy took a long draught. 'Actually, Mr Brogan,' he said at last, 'it's about me making lance corporal that I dropped by to have a few words.'

Jerimiah waited as Tommy took another drink.

'It's about me and Jo,' Tommy went on.

Jerimiah frowned. 'What about you and Jo?'

Alarm flashed across Tommy's face. 'Oh, nothing like that, Mr Brogan,' he said hastily. 'It's about bringing the wedding forward a year. Jo had a word with her mum and so I thought perhaps Mrs Brogan might have mentioned it to you.'

'She said you and Jo were talking about some such,' Jerimiah replied.

Tommy cleared his throat. 'I know you said we had to wait until Jo was twenty at least but, well . . . I'm being transferred to London in the New Year and as she's nineteen soon—'

'In four months,' corrected Jerimiah.

'And I have almost seventy pounds in the bank, which is enough for a deposit on a house in Bethnal Green or Bow,' continued Tommy, 'and with my promotion I'll have enough to support myself and Jo, if not in luxury then at least in comfort, so I . . . that is *we* were wondering if you'd consider agreeing to us getting married the week after Whitsun in May.'

'Were you now?' said Jerimiah.

'Yes, we were,' said Tommy firmly. 'After all, Cathy was eighteen when she got married.'

'I know, lad,' he said wearily. 'But I've weightier matters on my mind at present which are requiring my attention so—'

'All I ask is that you think about it, Mr Brogan,' Tommy cut in, looking Jerimiah square in the eye. 'I love Jo and she loves me and we want to face whatever the war and life throw at us together; we want to face life holding fast together as man and wife.'

Jerimiah held the younger man's gaze for a second then he nodded. 'I'll think about it.'

Tommy's shoulders relaxed a notch. 'Thank you, Mr Brogan.' He finished the last of his beer and glanced at his watch. 'I ought to get my skates on.'

'Will we see the two of you later?' asked Jerimiah.

'Er . . . no There's . . . a . . . a nice restaurant around the corner from the hotel so I thought I'd treat Jo to supper,' he said, looking innocently at Jerimiah. 'Thanks again, Mr Brogan.'

Leaving his empty glass on the counter, Tommy strolled back across the bar and out through the door.

Jerimiah watched the door swing back and forth a couple of times then raised his glass to his lips.

Holding fast together as man and wife, he thought as the creamy foam slid over his tongue. That's how he would have described him and Ida just a few short weeks ago but now, although he was relieved that Ida had agreed to care for Michael, he wondered if the lad would forever stand between them.

Cathy had just got to the end of her row when a bomb landing somewhere south of them shook the corrugated iron arching over her.

'God preserve us,' warbled her mother-in-law, Violet Wheeler, drawing the blanket covering her even tighter to her whiskery chin.

Swapping her needles into the other hand, Cathy started her next row without bothering to glance her mother-in-law's way.

According to the alarm clock hooked on a nail over the door it was half past nine. She and her mother-in-law were where they had been every night for almost a year and a half, tucked up in the cramped Anderson shelter at the bottom of their garden while the Luftwaffe rained down death from the sky above.

The siren had gone off two hours before, just as they were bedding down for the night. Although she hadn't gone potty like some people who'd hung curtains around a painting of a window, complete with views of pastoral scenes, Cathy had tried to make their nightly abode as homely as possible. She'd put up a few photos and books on the shelves that Stan had fixed next to the low entrance. There was a crate of tinned food for emergencies and she'd even managed to squeeze in a small table on which were placed a teapot and mugs.

She and Stan had got married the day before war broke out. Her new husband had spent their first weekend as a married couple digging out the ground and setting up their Anderson shelter, swearing all the time that they wouldn't need it. Well, he was wrong about that and lots of other things, too.

Cathy laid her knitting aside and swung her feet off the narrow bunk where she'd been sitting. 'I'm making a cuppa; do you want one?'

'I thought you'd never ask,' said Violet, giving her a sour look from under her helmet of curlers and a thick hairnet. 'I could die of thirst waiting for you.'

From your lips to God's ears, thought Cathy.

Another blast shook the earth, showering them with grit from the cracks between the corrugated sheets overhead.

Violet shrieked again. Thankfully, in his cot at the foot of her bunk, Peter continued to sleep peacefully, like the baby he was.

Without bothering to look at the old woman, Cathy poured the boiling water from the Thermos flask into the pot.

'You know I like mine in a cup,' said Violet, her gnarled, blue-veined hands closing around the china mug.

Placing her mug of tea on the floor, Cathy climbed back on the bunk bed and picked up her needles and wool again.

'I don't know how you can sit there knitting when any moment we could be blown to kingdom come,' said Violet.

Humming quietly to herself, Cathy looped the wool around the needle and slipped the stitch. Her mother-in-law's eyes flickered on to the knitting in Cathy's hand.

'That's Stan's jumper, isn't it?' she said.

'It was,' said Cathy. 'It'll be a pair of socks for Billy's Christmas box soon.'

'You can't do that; Stan might need it,' said Violet.

'Not at the moment, he——' Cathy bit back the words but it was too late.

'No, he won't, will he?' spat Violet, giving her another hateful look. 'No, because my poor Stan is locked up in prison thanks to that bloody sister of yours. If she'd had any kind of family loyalty she would have given Stan the nod.'

'Perhaps if he hadn't got himself mixed up with a bunch of Nazis in the first place he wouldn't have needed anyone to give him "a nod",' Cathy snapped back.

The ack-ack guns fired off another round, shaking the sides of the shelter again.

'He was only trying to save us going to war with

Germany,' Violet shouted over the booming guns.

'Yes,' Cathy yelled back, 'by helping a dozen German spies to land in Wapping.'

A bomb found its target nearby and the hurricane lamp swung back and forth, casting angular shadows on the rippled wall of the shelter.

'It's your fault my Stan's locked up like some common criminal.' Violet jabbed a bony finger at Cathy. 'I told him not to marry you. "Your father was head porter at Spitalfields," I said, "and what's hers? An Irish tinker, that's what. You're too good for the likes of her and her kind."' Stan's mother warmed to her theme.

Cathy swapped her knitting needles across and wound the wool around her finger.

'"She's only marrying you so she's got a meal ticket," I told him,' Violet went on.

'But would he listen?' whispered Cathy.

'But would he listen?' snapped Violet.

'No, he wouldn't,' Cathy muttered.

'No,' said her mother-in-law. 'No, he wouldn't.'

'Common,' said Cathy under her breath.

'Common,' echoed Violet. 'That's what you and your tinker family are, as common as muck.'

The ack-ack guns half a mile away in Shadwell Park let off an earth-shaking round. Cathy's ear drums vibrated as her mother-in-law let out a piercing shriek. In his cot at the foot of her bunk, Peter jolted awake and joined in.

'For goodness' sake,' snapped Cathy. 'You've woken Peter with all your bloody caterwauling.'

Putting aside her knitting, she got up and went to her son. He was all flushed faced and bright eyed, having been abruptly woken from a deep slumber.

'It's not my fault I suffer with my nerves,' whined Violet. Cathy ignored her.

'Stan would understand. He was always considerate of my nerves,' continued her mother-in-law. 'Not like some I could mention.'

Bending into the cot, Cathy picked up her son and his blanket, then scrambled back on to the bed. Wrapping the baby-blue cover her mother had crocheted around him, Cathy settled her son in her embrace.

Another bomb landed close by and the shelter shook again. Peter, whose eyelids had just started to flutter down, jumped in Cathy's arms and started crying again.

'For God's sake, can't you shut that child up?' snivelled Violet, clasping her hands together on her chest as the ack-ack guns pounded again.

Ignoring her mother-in-law, Cathy started humming 'Hush-a-bye Baby' while rocking Peter gently in her arms.

A series of bombs thumped to the ground but further away this time, judging by the rumble. Peter stuck his thumb in his mouth and his eyes closed as he drifted back to sleep.

'Stan will have a few things to say to you when he gets home about the way you treat me,' moaned Violet. 'I wish you and him had never got married.'

As the Shadwell ack-ack guns let off another round, Cathy pressed her lips to her son's downy head and heartily agreed.

Chapter Eleven

'SO, GIRLS,' SAID Ida, with a heavy sigh, 'now you know everything.'

It was Sunday afternoon and three days since she'd told Jerimiah she would take Michael after Ellen passed on. As usual on a Sunday afternoon, Ida was sitting in the back parlour. The best crockery was out on the sideboard next to plates of sandwiches, with either spam or pilchard fillings, and an eggless cake was displayed on the stand.

Jerimiah was sitting next to her on the sofa, Billy had been sent around to his friends for the afternoon and Queenie had tactfully withdrawn to her room for an afternoon nap. However, rather than listening to the Sunday after-dinner play and knitting while Jerimiah dozed in one of the fireside chairs, as was her usual Sunday-afternoon custom, Ida had spent the last thirty minutes, give or take, explaining the situation involving Michael to their three daughters.

Well, explaining wasn't really the right word. Scandalising them was more like it, for the three sisters had sat open-mouthed and wide-eyed as she and Jerimiah told them everything.

'I know it's a bit of a shock,' said Ida in conclusion. 'But there it is.'

Two pairs of brown eyes and one pair of blue shifted from her face and bore into their father sitting beside her. For all she told herself it was his own fault he found himself having to confess his transgression, as he sat under the blistering scorn of his daughters' gazes for the past half an hour Ida found pity for his plight tugging at her heart.

'Shock?' Jo gave a hard laugh. 'I should say. Yesterday I had two brothers and today I have three. I'd call that a bit more than a blooming shock, wouldn't you, Mum?'

Ida's youngest daughter was sitting on the footstool between her two sisters on the other side of the fire. She'd come straight from her morning shift at the ambulance depot and was still in her uniform.

'How could you, Dad?' asked Cathy. 'And with Mum's best friend.'

She was sitting to the left of Jo, in Ida's easy chair, while Peter, bless him, played on the rag rug by her feet with a handful of wooden bricks.

'And after the way you went on about separate rooms when I go and see Tommy.' Jo gave him a mocking look. 'Talk about people in glass houses.'

'Don't talk to your father like that, Jo,' snapped Ida. 'Your dad made a mistake.'

'A mistake, Mum, is putting the wrong coin in the gas meter or getting on the wrong tram not—'

'So you didn't know about Michael, Dad?' cut in Mattie.

She was sitting on Queenie's rocking chair with a sleeping Alicia tucked in the crook of her arm.

'No, I didn't,' said Jerimiah, his voice rumbling over his women folk. 'But now I do and that Auntie Ellen is dying we can't just pretend he doesn't exist.'

'No, we can't,' Ida replied, hoping only she could hear the hesitation in her voice.

Gratitude warmed Jerimiah's eyes.

Feeling her resolve to never forgive him waver a little she gave him a cool stare in return.

Several seconds ticked by and then Jo spoke. 'So when is he moving in?'

'It's difficult to say but probably after Easter sometime,' said Ida. 'He and Billy can bunk in together.'

'Well, that explains a lot,' said Jo. 'I wondered why Billy's been more lippy than usual lately.'

'I'd noticed that, too, Jo,' added Cathy. 'He even had the blooming cheek to call me an old nag when I asked him to wipe his feet when he came in my kitchen the other day. What's he got to say about having a new brother?'

'I'd guess he won't be too thrilled,' added Jo. 'After all, he's never been much good at sharing, has he?'

'Well, he'll have to get used to it, won't he?' said Jerimiah. 'And I'm sure he'll be glad to have someone to play with.'

The three girls didn't look convinced, which was hardly surprising. Although she didn't like to admit it, Ida had possibly let Billy get away with things sometimes.

Retrieving a brick that her son had knocked out of reach, Cathy gave Mattie a sideways glance.

'Considering you're always the first to give everyone the benefit of your wisdom, I'm surprised you haven't put in your tuppenceworth yet,' she said, overlooking her vow never to speak to Mattie again and giving her a sharp look.

'There's nothing to say, is there?' Mattie replied, matching her sister's belligerent stare. 'Whether we like it or not Michael is our half-brother and his mother is dying. And what would you have Dad do? Send him to an orphanage?'

'I knew you'd take his side,' said Cathy.

'I'm not taking anyone's side,' Mattie replied. 'But if Mum's agreed to care for Michael after Auntie Ellen dies then I don't see there's any more to be said.'

'*Auntie Ellen*,' sneered Cathy. 'I don't know how you can call her that after what she's done to Mum.'

'The woman's dying, Cathy!' said Mattie, looking hard at her sister. 'Have a bit of compassion, will you?'

'What, like you did,' countered Cathy, 'when you stood back and let my Stan walk into a trap—'

'That's enough, all of you,' Ida snapped. 'Your dad made a mistake.'

Jo opened her mouth to speak but catching the look on her mother's face she closed it again.

'None of you has had to go to school barefooted or shivering because you didn't have a proper coat and that's more than most children around here can say. None of you has had to go to bed hungry because we didn't have the money for food and you haven't had to sit in the dark for want of a copper for the meter, and you know why?'

Ida looked from Cathy to Jo and then Mattie but none of them answered.

'I'll tell you why, shall I?' she continued. 'Because your dad has been out on that wagon in all weathers to keep a roof over your heads and food in your bellies and that's because he's the kind of man who puts his children first. Now, if I'm willing to care for Michael because of who he is then I don't see how you three, Charlie and Billy can say otherwise. Family is family, and I'd thank you to remember that and do what we always do: stick together. Do you understand?'

The three girls nodded.

'Good.' Fixing a smile on her face, Ida rose to her feet. 'Now, perhaps if someone wouldn't mind knocking on your gran's door to let her know we're done, I'll put the kettle on.'

Leaving her family chatting in the lounge, and with pain like a vice pressing against her temples, Ida went through to the kitchen. Going to the stove she lit the gas and moved the kettle she'd filled an hour before over the heat. She went to the sink. Resting her hands on the cold enamel, she stared through the strips of gummed paper criss-crossing the glass of the window. The sun had gone behind the houses to the back of them already, but the warm pink and white streaks of the frosty evening still illuminated the paved area of the backyard. As she studied the familiar space, with the zinc bath hooked on the wall and the old mangle alongside it, tears sprang into her eyes but a movement behind her made her blink them away. She looked around.

Jerimiah was standing in the doorway, looking at her with such longing in his eyes it squeezed her heart.

'You all right, luv?' he said softly, crossing the space between them in two strides.

'Yes, I'm fine,' she lied.

'Thank you again, Ida.'

She shrugged. 'As I said before, I'm not doing it for you. Now go and join the girls and I'll be in with the tea in a moment.'

His dark eyes searched her face for a second or two then a heart-rending smile lifted the corners of his mouth.

Ida forced herself not to smile back.

They stared at each other for a couple of heartbeats then Jerimiah turned and went back into the parlour. Ida resumed her contemplation of the yard. Her eyes skimmed over the four chickens picking in the dirt, safe in their coop made from old doors and a bent Morrison shelter that Jerimiah had picked up somewhere on his travels. Like everyone else with a square of earth in their backyard, he had already started to prepare the troughs ready for planting up spring greens and onions. She'd watched him as, wrapped in his sheepskin jerkin and bent low, he'd sifted the soil then filled the variety of troughs and barrels dotted around the wall.

She'd been washing up at the sink when he came in and he'd put his cold hands on her neck, making her giggle and squirm. He'd told her he knew a way she could warm him up. She'd refused at first, citing potatoes to peel, but as the house was empty . . .

She recalled how the hair of his chest had tickled her nose as he arched over her and her fingers dug into the corded muscles of his upper arms. Was that only eight or nine short weeks ago? Although she should say a thousand Hail Marys for even thinking it, she wished Michael had never been born. But soon he would be sitting across the breakfast table from her, the living proof of Jerimiah's betrayal.

With the rumble of a bomb landing on the dock half a mile south of her, Mattie lay staring up at the steel sheet of metal above.

Her husband Daniel lay beside her, his head crammed against the mesh at the top of their Morrison shelter while his feet rested upright on the bottom.

Their daughter Alicia, with her teddy Mr Blue, was tucked into the cot her father had made for her on Mattie's side of the metal cage. This meant she had to lie at an angle with her feet wedged between the side of the cot and her husband's muscular calves. However, it was neither her awkward position nor the Luftwaffe that had driven sleep from her mind.

It was probably close to two in the morning and although she'd been dog tired when she'd returned home from Sunday tea with her family, the moment her head had hit the pillow, sleep had fled.

The ack-ack gun on the Isle of Dogs sent the ground trembling as they let off another round skyward. Mattie sighed and rolled on to her side. In the mute glow of Alicia's Noddy night-light she gazed through the wire lattice at the twelve-by-twelve basement space that was the McCarthys' nightly shelter.

Following the instructions in the government leaflet on setting up a refuge room, Mattie had set buckets with sand by the door to deal with incendiary bombs, added a first-aid kit to deal with any casualties and found two enamel jugs, which she filled with fresh water each night in case they were trapped. There was even a bucket in the far corner hidden by a curtain that served as a toilet. Although the shelter took up most of the available space, Mattie had tried to make the subterranean room as comfortable as possible. There were a couple of old easy chairs either side of the paraffin heater, a coffee table plus a primus stove for boiling a kettle, a selection of books and a wireless, so once she settled Alicia to sleep Mattie could have a bit of company.

The ack-ack gun pulsated again. Taking the blankets with her, Mattie shifted back into her original position then rolled towards her husband to see that he too was awake.

'You too?' whispered Mattie, looking at her husband in the dim light.

'Been trying to get to sleep for hours,' he whispered, the whites of his eyes highlighted in the low light.

She gave him a sympathetic smile. 'Problems in France?'

He nodded. 'Isn't it always? But there're no prizes for guessing what's keeping you awake.'

'I keep thinking about poor Mum,' said Mattie quietly. 'I know she put a brave face on it, but I could see she was holding back the tears. She must be heartbroken.'

'Who wouldn't be?' Daniel replied in the same hushed tone. 'But I have to say I'm very surprised at your dad.'

'Me too, and if it wasn't for the fact Ellen's dying we would never have known.'

'I suppose you have to give her credit for that,' said Daniel. 'After all, rather than causing trouble when she found out she was pregnant, she moved away.'

Mattie frowned. 'I suppose, and I can't really blame her for coming back now. I know how I'd feel if I were dying and had to leave Alicia, but I also know how I'd feel if I found out you'd had a child by someone else.'

Daniel's arm tightened around her and he tucked her into his strong body.

'You don't ever have to worry about that, my darling.' He kissed her.

Another bomb shook the ground as they exchanged a fond look.

'It's Jo I feel sorry for,' Mattie continued, when the shock-wave had settled. 'She's the one living there with all this going on.'

'Well, it might work in her and Tommy's favour and per-suade your dad to let them get married,' he said. 'And it's not as if this Michael will be the first cuckoo in the Brogan family.'

Mattie shifted towards him more and gave him a querying look. 'What do you mean not the first cuckoo?'

Her husband gave a low laugh. 'Really, Mattie, haven't you ever noticed how much your dad looks like Father Mahon?'

'Father Mahon and Gran!' said Mattie, looking incredu-lously at her husband. 'Don't be ridiculous!'

'Scoff if you like but I'm just saying there's a very strong resemblance, that's all.' Daniel pressed his lips on her forehead.

Alicia cried out and her parents lay still.

'I wish I'd got home before she went to bed,' Daniel whispered as his daughter's breathing returned to its normal rhythm.

'It can't be helped,' Mattie whispered back.

'I know, but I miss seeing her.' He kissed Mattie again, his lips lingering a little longer. 'And you.'

'And I miss you, too,' she replied softly as another bomb crashed to the ground. She kissed him lightly on the lips. 'Well, at least you're here with me and Alicia.'

In the half-light, an emotion she couldn't interpret flitted across the strong angles of her husband's face and then he smiled. 'I'll tell you what,' he said, snuggling her closer, 'Lennox owes me a few days off so why don't we ask Jo to babysit so you and me can get ourselves togged up in our glad rags and go dancing up West?'

Mattie's eyes flew open. 'Goodness, we haven't been dancing since August,' she said, already running through the dresses in her wardrobe.

'I know, that's why I suggested it,' said Daniel.

'Oh, Daniel.' She kissed him hard on the lips. 'I'd love to. We might even get a chance to talk properly, too, without the telephone and a one-year-old interrupting.'

That odd emotion crossed his face again but then he smiled and as his arm tightened around her, he rolled her on to her back.

'I love you,' he whispered, gazing down at her.

Reaching up, Mattie ran her hand over his face, enjoying the feel of her husband's rough night-time bristles under her fingers.

'And I love you,' she whispered back.

They lost themselves in each other's eyes for a moment then Daniel's mouth captured her with a kiss that didn't need explaining.

As his hands slid over her body, Mattie closed her eyes and sighed. Yes, an evening up West dancing would be absolutely wonderful, but what would be even more wonderful would be the look of sheer delight in her husband's eyes when she told him he was going to be a father again.

Chapter Twelve

ON THE CORNER of Juniper Street, Ida stopped, glanced in the window of Woodman's, and adjusted her green felt WVS hat.

Satisfied it sat at the right angle, she took a firmer grip on the bulging shopping bag she was carrying and set off down the road. There were two women in aprons and curlers loitering outside number 7 and as Ida approached they looked around.

'Yes,' said the older woman, giving Ida the once-over.

'I'm looking for Mrs Gilbert,' said Ida.

'Upstairs at the front.' The woman flicked her ash on the pavement and turned back to her conversation. 'It's on the latch.'

Breathing through her mouth to reduce the odour of boiled cabbage and cat, Ida pushed open the front door and walked in. She held her coat so it didn't brush against the grubby walls, climbed to the first-floor landing and walked the few steps to the front-room door.

Ignoring her hammering heart, she clenched her fist and rapped on the central panel.

'It's open,' a woman's voice called from inside the room.

Taking a deep breath, Ida grabbed the handle and walked in. Ignoring everything else in the decrepit room, her eyes fixed on the woman sitting with her feet up in the fireside chair.

It was Ellen, who she'd sat on the kerb with as they played with their dolls, who she'd fought alongside against the playground bully, who she'd drunk her first gin with in the Stratford Regal and who had been there when she married Jerimiah; but this Ellen was a paler, thinner, greyer version of her life-long friend.

Even though it had only been a little over a month since she'd seen her, it was clear that Ellen Gilbert wasn't long for this world.

'Ida, it's you.' Relief swept over Ellen's weary features.

'Yes, it's me,' said Ida, putting the full shopping bag on the nearest chair to ease her aching arm.

Ellen's eyes flickered over her. 'I see you've signed up for the Civil Defence.'

'Well, we all have to do our bit,' she replied, as images of the other woman's night of passion with her husband flashed through her mind.

Ellen held her gaze and the clock on the sparse mantelshelf ticked off the seconds.

'What am I thinking of?' said Ellen, gripping the arms of the chair and starting to rise. 'Let me make you a cup of tea.'

'No, it's all right,' said Ida, adjusting the shoulder strap of her handbag. 'I'm on duty at the clothes exchange in the Catholic Club at two.'

The clocked ticked halfway around the dial again and Ellen spoke.

'It's so good to see you after all this time.'

Ida gave her a chilly look. 'I wish I could say the same.'

Ellen sighed. 'I understand. I know how much the discovery of what happened between me and Jerimiah years ago has upset you but—'

'*Upset*,' cut in Ida with a bitter laugh. 'I'm not upset, Ellen. I'm devastated.'

'I didn't want to come between you and Jerimiah,' said Ellen. 'As soon as I knew I was carrying Michael I moved away because I didn't want you to know.'

'Well, I know now,' said Ida.

Closing her eyes, Ellen took a long deep breath and then opened them again. 'I'm dying, Ida,' she said, her voice tight with pain. 'And I will rest in peace if I know Michael is with people who will love and care for him. As a mother yourself, wouldn't you want the same?'

'I would,' said Ida with a heavy sigh. 'Which is why I've agreed to take him when the time comes. We told the girls yesterday and Jerimiah will be writing to Charlie.'

Tears welled up in Ellen's eyes as she stared at Ida then she covered her face.

Ida stood, with her arms at her side, watching the woman who had once been more of a sister to her than her own flesh and blood sob her heart out. A small part of her wanted to go and comfort her while the rest of her enjoyed the other woman's pain.

After a moment Ellen pulled herself together and looked up. Her colourless lips lifted in a weak smile. 'Thank you, Ida,' she whispered. 'Thank you for doing me this last kindness.'

'I'm not doing it for you,' snapped Ellen. 'And I'm not doing it for Jerimiah, either. I'm doing it to save a ten-year-old boy from being put in a children's home. Have you told him – about your condition, I mean?'

Ellen shook her head. 'Not yet. I was waiting until I knew if . . . if you would agree.'

'Well, you'd better, and soon, by the looks of you,' said Ida. 'Jerimiah will be by tomorrow after school to tell Michael that he's his father. And he better start to get to know us, too, so when the time comes . . .'

'That's a good idea,' said Ellen.

She smiled warmly, inviting Ida to do the same, but instead Ida pressed her lips together and glanced at her watch.

'I ought to go.'

'Of course. And thank you again, Ida.'

A feeble smile flashed across Ellen's face briefly showing the shadow of the laughing young woman she'd once been.

With an odd feeling of loss aching in her chest, Ida stared at her one-time friend for a moment then, as unexpected tears pinched her own eyes, she turned and fled the room.

'Anything else, luv?' asked Ruby, who was standing on the other side of the counter.

Ida shook her head. 'Just a tea, thanks.'

Grasping the metal teapot in both hands, the owner of Kate's Café on the Highway poured her a cup.

'There you are,' she said, placing it in front of Ida. 'One cup of rosy lee. Sugar's on the table.'

With the one o'clock hooter calling factory workers back to their benches there were plenty of empty tables so, taking her tea, Ida made her way over to a seat in the window.

Sitting with her back to the other customers, she cradled her cup in her hands and stared across at the charred remains of St George's Church, gutted by an incendiary bomb six months before.

Thankfully, she had an hour to kill before she needed to be at the Catholic Club. Time enough, she hoped, to get the chaotic thoughts in her head in to some sort of order.

Yes, Michael was coming to live with them and no doubt in time the children, even Billy, would come to terms with it and accept Michael as their own. But what about her and Jerimiah? What about their life?

It was a stupid question really because they were married. Married until death parted them. But she could think of dozens of women who loathed the men they were married to. Was that her fate now?

Closing her eyes, Ida sent a silent prayer heavenward then opening them again took a gulp of tea.

Gazing out of the café window her attention was drawn to the front window of Fontaine's, the hairdresser's on the other side of the road.

Manny Fontaine, who had been perming and tinting the locks of his many clients for as long as Ida could remember, had met his maker three months before when the pub where he was having a quiet drink suffered a direct hit. The salon had been taken over by a nice young woman called Maria and her husband, who already owned two salons: one in Roman Road and the other in Mare Street. Now, instead of the black-and-white photos of flat-eyed, cherry-lipped society women with tightly crimped curls, there were colour photos of smiling women with their hair tumbling over their shoulders or sporting bouncy bobs.

Ida adjusted her focus and looked at her reflection in the café window. She turned her head and studied the tightly pinned bun squashed under the brim of her hat for a second then, swallowing the rest of her tea, she stood up and strode out of the café.

Having delivered four crates of corned beef, six of haricot beans and the same of dried milk to a grocer in Roman Road and lifted twice his body weight in second-hand furniture, by the time Jerimiah walked through his back door just before five he was all in. It didn't help that he'd been on patrol until midnight the night before and, even though he had been totally exhausted by the time he'd tumbled into his cold bed at one, he'd been unable to sleep, instead he'd stared at the ceiling thinking about Ida, and calling himself all the cussed bastards under the sun.

Pulling the blackout curtain aside he stepped into the kitchen. His mother was stirring the pots on the stove.

'How's you, Ma?' he asked, shoving his cap in his pocket and unwinding his scarf.

'Not so bad, boy,' she replied. 'Can I get you a brew?'

'I'd murder for one,' he said, hanging his overcoat behind the door. 'Isn't Ida back yet?'

Pouring his tea, his mother shook her head. 'No, and it's as well I'm still in command of me faculties or you'd have no supper either.'

She placed his drink on the table and Jerimiah sat down. Closing his cold hands around the warm cup, Jerimiah listened to the BBC telling the country that the army were just ten miles from Tobruk and that the Germans were attacking Moscow. As the weather forecast started, Jerimiah glanced up at the clock again.

'I wonder what's keeping her?' he asked.

As if to answer his question the back door opened and the blackout curtain billowed as Ida stepped out from behind it.

Well, that's to say it was Ida but looking very different from the woman he had last seen. Ida had always had naturally curly hair so she'd never needed to perm it and although there were a few grey hairs at the temples, for the most part her hair was the same rich brown colour as when he'd first set eyes on her across the dance floor. Even now the thought of its softness under his lips sent a thrill through him.

However, with a house to run and a family to care for, she had taken to wearing her hair in a tightly pinned bun at the nape of her neck. But now, in its place, was a mass of bouncy shoulder-length curls swept back Rita Hayworth style and held in place by a tortoiseshell comb above each ear.

If this wasn't enough to hold his attention, she was also wearing lipstick, and a bright red one at that.

'Jesus, Joseph and Mary,' said Queenie, looking Ida slowly up and down. 'Look what the cat dragged in.'

Ignoring her mother-in-law, Ida looked at Jerimiah.

'Sorry I'm late,' she said, taking off her coat. 'I was late getting to the relief centre so I stayed on to help sort things out.'

'That's all right, me darling,' he said, gazing in amazement at his transformed, and very attractive, wife.

'It is no such thing, Ida Brogan,' contradicted his mother. 'A man should have his dinner on the table ready for him when he walks in the door.'

'Ida's entitled to have her hair done if she's a fancy to, Mother,' said Jerimiah. 'And I think you look grand, Ida, so you do.'

'I just fancied a bit of a change, that's all,' she said, shaking her head slightly and setting her curls bouncing.

A faint flush coloured Ida's cheeks and she gave him a shy look.

'Grand, is it?' said Queenie. 'More like mutton dressed up as—'

'Didn't you say you were after giving Prince Albert's cage a bit of a clean, Ma?' cut in Jerimiah, giving his mother a pointed look.

Giving him the look that as a child would have been swiftly followed by a clip around the ear, Queenie's toothless mouth clamped shut and she stomped out of the room. Leaving his tea untouched on the table, Jerimiah stood up. 'Can I pour you a cuppa, Ida?'

She looked astonished for a moment but then took the seat opposite him. 'Yes, that would be nice.'

Taking the pot his mother had just made Jerimiah poured his wife a cup of tea.

'Truth be told, I've not been in long myself,' he said, placing her drink in front of her and resuming his seat. 'I've been hard at it all day but I've been well compensated for my aching back.'

Sliding his hand into his pockets he took out a handful of green and brown banknotes plus some silver and placed it on the table between them.

Ida's eyes opened in amazement.

'And that's just this afternoon's,' he added. 'Take it.'

'What, all of it?' she asked.

'It's yours as much as mine,' he said. 'And with this new points system coming in soon you might pick up a few treats to add to your Christmas stash.'

'Well, it would help,' said Ida, scooping it up.

'Also,' Jerimiah continued, 'honest to God, Ida, what with moving people, local deliveries and the second-hand furniture, I've got so much work I can't keep up with it so I was wondering if you could give your notice at the solicitors and help me run the business. In fact, I'm going to put in for a telephone after Christmas. I can't keep giving out Mattie's number and expecting her to run around every five minutes with messages.'

'All right,' said Ida. 'I can't say I'll be sorry not to have to get up at the crack of dawn to spend hours on my knees scrubbing floors. Besides, I'll have my work cut out here when . . .'

Lowering her eyes, she took a sip of her tea then looked back at him. 'I went to see Ellen today and told her we'd take Michael when, you know . . .'

Letting out a breath he didn't know he was holding Jerimiah's shoulders relaxed.

'Thank you, Ida.'

Pain flitted across her face and she gave him a sharp look. 'And I told her you'd be round tomorrow afternoon to tell him who his . . .' Ida couldn't bring herself to say more. They stared at each other for a moment then the compère on the wireless announced *Can I Help You*.

Ida finished the last of her tea. 'I've to collect Patrick at six so I ought to be getting ready for the shelter. Is Billy back yet?'

Jerimiah shook his head and Ida pursed her lips.

'That's twice this week I've told him to be back by four and he hasn't been,' said Ida.

'I'm sure he'll be back any moment,' said Jerimiah.

'Well, he'd better be here soon if he knows what's good for him,' she said, 'or he'll get the rough edge of my tongue.' Her eyes flickered over him. 'And shouldn't you be making tracks, too?'

'You're right; I should be getting my uniform on, but,' reaching across the table Jerimiah closed his hand over hers, 'before we part I want to tell you again, me darling, what a rare beauty you are in all ways,' he said, hoping she could see the love and gratitude reflected in his eyes.

The colour returned to Ida's cheeks. She removed her hand from under his and stood up, staring down at him for a moment or two with chilly indifference but then her eyes warmed a fraction.

'Weren't you always the master of the blarney, Jerimiah Brogan?' she said.

Hope flickered beneath the hard lump of unhappiness in his chest as Ida held his gaze for a heartbeat then left the room.

Leaning forward, Jerimiah rested his elbows on the table and covered his face with his hands. Maybe, just maybe, in spite of everything that was now between them, they could find their way back to each other again.

'How are you getting on with your homework, Michael?' Ellen asked, walking into the lounge carrying a tray with two cups of tea and a plate of jam sandwiches.

Her son, who was sitting at the table and still wearing his school uniform, looked up from the books spread out in front of him. 'The arithmetic was easy, but I'm a bit stuck on filling in the capitals of the Empire.'

It was nearly three thirty in the afternoon the day after Ida had come to see her. Michael had drawn the blackout curtains when he'd come home ten minutes ago so with the coals glowing in the grate and the low-wattage light overhead, Ellen's living room was both warm and cosy. As *Children's Hour* wouldn't be on the wireless for another hour, Michael had decided to make a start on his homework.

'Do what you can and I'll help you when I've had my tea,' she replied.

Michael turned his attention back to his book, the lock of black hair that never would stay where it was put falling over his forehead as he looked down.

Resisting the urge to reposition it, Ellen put his tea and the plate of sandwiches next to him and took her tea. Settling herself in the armchair, Ellen put her feet up on the fender as her son devoured his afternoon snack.

The fire crackled and the clock on the mantelshelf ticked off the minutes. Ellen felt her eyelids grow heavy but just as they were fluttering down there was a knock on the door and Michael looked up from his studies.

'It's open,' Ellen called, praying it wasn't Mrs Crompton after her rent.

Jerimiah stepped in and removed his leather cap. 'Afternoon, Ellen.'

A warm glow spread through Ellen. 'Afternoon, Jerimiah.'

Jerimiah's attention shifted to his son. 'Hello, Michael.'

'Hello,' Michael replied, twiddling his pencil back and forth.

'You look frozen, Jerimiah,' said Ellen. 'Can I get you a cuppa?'

'A tea would be most welcome,' he replied. 'But not if it's putting you out at all.'

'I've just made one,' she replied. 'Make yourself comfortable and I'll fetch it. Two sugars, isn't it?'

'Not any more.' Jerimiah tapped his flat stomach. 'At my age I have to watch me waistline.'

Her eyes slid over him, her heart beating a little faster at the sight of his broad chest, long legs and firm features. As if he could sense her feelings, Jerimiah broke from her gaze.

Tilting his head, he looked at the school atlas on the table. 'Am I right in thinking that's geography homework I see?'

'Yes, Miss Farley wants us to list all the capitals of the British Empire by Friday,' Michael replied, pointing to his exercise book. 'I have most of them, like India and Burma, they're easy, but I get the African ones like Togoland and Southern Rhodesia muddled . . .'

'Well now,' said Jerimiah, pulling out the upright chair next to the boy, 'let me see if I can be of some assistance.'

Ellen went into the kitchen and poured another cup of tea. By the time she returned to the lounge, Jerimiah and his son were deep in conversation, their black curls side by side as they studied the atlas.

'One cuppa,' she said.

They looked up at her with the same eyes and the same smile and a lump formed in her throat.

'Do you know what, Mum?' said Michael. 'Mr Brogan has an encyclopaedia with twenty-nine books in his house.'

'I know,' said Ellen, as she pictured the bookcase that had always taken pride of place in Ida's back parlour.

'How come?' asked Michael.

'Because Mr Brogan and his wife Ida are old friends and before you were born I used to live across the street from them.'

'Have you got children?' Michael asked.

'That I have,' Jerimiah replied. 'Two boys and three girls.'

Michael sighed. 'I wish I had brothers and sisters. My dad died when I was a baby.'

Jerimiah raised his eyes and looked at Ellen.

Jerimiah ruffled the boy's hair. 'I'll tell you what, Michael, I'm just on my way back to my yard so how do you fancy coming and giving me a hand bedding my horse Samson down for the night in his stable?'

Michael's eyes lit up. 'Can I, Mum? Please.'

Ellen smiled. 'I don't see why not. As long as you're back by six so we can get to the shelter.'

'Don't worry, I'll have him back by then,' said Jerimiah.

'See if you can find all those capitals before I've finished my drink, and we'll go.'

Michael's eyes lit up again. Gripping his pencil firmly, he turned back to his studies.

Jerimiah's eyes grew soft as they rested on him for a moment or two then they returned to Ellen.

'So, how have you been?'

'All the better for what Ida told me yesterday.' She glanced at Michael deep in his studies. 'Are you going to—'

'Yes I am,' he replied, then looked down as he drank his tea.

A sad smile lifted Ellen's lips as she watched his averted face. He didn't want to be here with her, she knew that, but she was happy he was.

They sat in silence while the clock ticked a minute and their son's pencil scratched across the paper. After a few moments, Michael shut his book and looked up eagerly.

'You done then, lad?' asked Jerimiah.

Michael nodded.

Draining the last of his tea, Jerimiah rose to his feet, his thigh muscles moving effortlessly as they took his weight.

'Well then, get your coat.'

Jumping down from his chair, Michael dashed to the door and wrenched his duffel coat from the hook.

Holding the coat open so Michael could get his arms in, Jerimiah opened the door.

'Bye, Mum,' Michael shouted, dashing out.

'Have a nice time,' she called after him, as her son's footsteps thundered down the stairs.

'I'll get him back in good time,' Jerimiah said as he followed him.

'Bye, Jerimiah,' said Ellen softly. 'Lovely to see you.'

He forced a smile and left.

Silence descended, bringing desolation in its wake, but Ellen pushed it away and forced happiness to take its place.

And despite everything she was happy. Happy because not only would Jerimiah take Michael into his family, but he would love him, too. Ellen knew he would. He would love his newly discovered son because Jerimiah was a man who loved. And that's why she would love him until her last breath.

Resting his hand gently on his son's shoulder, Jerimiah guided Michael along the pavement to the lamp-post where he'd left Samson.

'He's big, isn't he?' said Michael, standing by the horse's head and looking up.

'Sixteen hands.' Jerimiah patted the beast's neck affectionately. 'But as gentle as a lamb.' Taking the last nugget of that day's carrot from his pocket, Jerimiah gave it to the boy beside him. 'Put it on the palm of your hand and hold it out flat.'

Michael did as instructed and Samson snuffled it up.

The boy laughed and wiped his hand down his trousers. 'It tickled.'

Jerimiah smiled. 'That's his whiskers. Tell you what, Michael, instead of sitting on the wagon, why don't you ride on his back?'

The boy's eyes lit up. 'Can I? Like a cowboy?'

'Sure you can.' Grasping the lad under the arms, Jerimiah lifted him up. 'Swing your leg over.'

Michael did, and Jerimiah lowered him on to the horse's back. Flicking his ears, Samson turned to see who was astride him and then blew through his nose.

'He doesn't mind, does he, Mr Brogan?' asked Michael, eyeing the horse warily.

'No, he don't mind,' said Jerimiah. 'And don't worry, I'll walk beside you.'

Jerimiah loosened the reins from the lamp-post and, taking it as his signal to head home, Samson stepped off.

'Rest your feet on the shafts and hold on to the clump of hair at his shoulders,' said Jerimiah, noting that Michael's ankles already dangled below the wagon's shafts.

'So,' said Jerimiah as Samson got into his pace, 'how's school been this week?'

Having recounted coming top in his spelling test and how he'd been picked instead of some other boy for the football team to play Morpeth School the following week, Michael finished by confessing he'd been sent to the headmaster for fighting in the playground. He'd avoided the cane as it was his first offence but he'd had to do a hundred lines instead.

By the time they'd turned into Chapman Street, Michael was rolling with Samson's stride like Roy Rogers and Jerimiah was up to date with all the happenings at school. As they reached the yard gates, Michael turned the conversation to other things.

'What are your children called, Mr Brogan?' he asked, as Jerimiah unfastened the chain and padlock.

'Charles, Matilda, Catherine and Josephine, known as Charlie, Mattie, Cathy and Jo, they are all grown up, and then there's William, known as Billy, who's a few months older than you,' Jerimiah replied.

'Are they named after saints like I am?' asked Michael.

'My girls are rare treasures, so I named them after empresses,' he replied, aware that at the moment he and his three 'rare treasures' weren't on the best of terms.

'What about Charlie and Billy?' asked Michael, as Jerimiah led Samson into the yard.

'I wanted to call Charlie, Charlemagne but Auntie Ida put her foot down and Billy already had his name when we collected him,' said Jerimiah.

That wasn't strictly true. Billy had been listed as 'male infant 17' in the workhouse but the matron in charge of the babies, a motherly woman, named all of her charges alphabetically. Had Billy arrived in her care a day earlier he might have been called Victor.

Michael gave him a quizzical look and Jerimiah gave him a sanitised version of how Billy came into the world, which seemed to satisfy the boy.

Holding Samson by his halter, Jerimiah manoeuvred the horse so the wagon was flush against the wall, then he lifted Michael down.

'Right now, cowboy,' he said, setting the lad on his feet. 'Help me un-tack Samson. I'll hold the shaft if you undo those big buckles.'

Michael nodded as Jerimiah gripped the smooth wood and the lad started picking at the leather, a lock of his thick black hair flopping over his brow as he bent to his task.

Michael released the strap and Samson plodded away towards his stable. Jerimiah lifted the shaft back to rest on top of the wagon.

'Can you fill his trough with some feed while I remove the rest of his tack?' asked Jerimiah.

Michael nodded and went to the sack while Jerimiah relieved the horse of the last items of strapping and hung them on the hook. When he came back Michael was stroking the horse's neck while Samson munched his way through his supper.

Jerimiah smiled and put his arm around the boy's slender shoulders. 'You've done a good job there, son,' he said, feeling the word embed itself in his heart. 'Let's sit down and rest a while.'

He led him over to the bales of hay stacked in front of the office and they sat down, his son's feet skimming the ground.

Jerimiah turned to face him. 'Michael, do you remember much about your dad?' he asked quietly.

'Not much,' said Michael. 'I don't think he liked me, though, because I can't remember him ever talking to me and the only time I can remember him doing something other than sit by the fire with a glass of beer in his hand was when he got very angry and swiped me around the head. He went to hit me again but Mum stepped in so he hit her instead and called her names then stomped out of the house.'

Anger flared in Jerimiah's chest, but he held it in check.

'Perhaps that's why Mum named me after my granddad, Mum's dad,' Michael continued. 'And she named me after St Boniface instead of me dad; Mum said he was a bishop in the olden days. '

'He was, in the eighth century. He was martyred. But your mum didn't name you after him. She named you after me. My second name is Boniface, too, and that's why she gave it to you, Michael, because,' Jerimiah drew a breath, 'you're really my son.'

Michael's eyes opened wide and he stared up at Jerimiah.

'But how, when you're married to Auntie Ida?' he asked.

Jerimiah coughed. 'I'll explain all that to you when you get older,' he replied, shifting his position slightly. 'All that matters is that you're my son and no matter what happens I'll always look after you.'

He watched as emotions crossed back and forth across his son's face as he took in the news of his true parentage.

'So, Charlie, Mattie, Cathy, Jo and Billy are . . .?'

'Your brothers and sisters,' said Jerimiah.

Joy flooded Michael's face. 'I have brothers and sisters!'

'You have,' laughed Jerimiah, caught up in his son's happiness. 'And that's why your mum came back so we could all get to know each other.'

Michael jumped down. 'I've got brothers and sisters!' he repeated, springing up and down on the balls of his feet. 'I always wanted brothers and sisters, Mr Brogan!' He stopped bobbing and looked uncertainly at Jerimiah.

They stared at each other for a heartbeat then Jerimiah smiled, 'Perhaps "Dad" would be better now.'

He opened his arms and Michael rushed into them. Hugging his son to him, a lump formed in Jerimiah's throat as the fatherly love flooded through him.

Chapter Thirteen

'AND YOUR MUM'S cough is a lot better, Stan,' said Cathy. 'The doctor said if her chest is clear when he calls next week she can stop the eucalyptus inhalation.'

Her husband Stan, sitting on the other side of the wire grille that divided prisoners from their visitors, grunted by way of reply.

It was the last Thursday in November and she was sitting in the visiting room of Bedford Prison. According to the large-faced clock over the door it was just after two in the afternoon, although it was difficult to know as the windows were set so high that hardly any of the winter sunlight penetrated the gloomy interior.

The custodial building had been constructed a hundred or so years ago and, like Pentonville and Wandsworth, had separate wings for inmates depending on the severity of their crime. Its large entrance gate was flanked by two mock medieval towers and high brick walls surrounded the buildings and exercise yard within.

What should have been an hour-and-a-bit journey had in fact taken over two and a half due to a bomb destroying one of the lines out of St Pancras the night before. Having arrived much later than she'd planned, Cathy had then had a damp half an hour walk through the town to the prison.

She'd arrived three-quarters of an hour earlier and, after being frisked by a miserable-looking prison matron and having Peter's pushchair all but dismantled to ensure she wasn't trying to smuggle contraband or a jemmy into the prison, she and a handful of other bedraggled wives and children were led through the echoing stone corridors and into the visiting room.

Her son, wrapped up to his chin in a crochet blanket, was sitting on her lap chewing on a Bikiepeg while she was trying to have a conversation with Stan. Trying because she reckoned she'd have more chance of getting blood out of the prison stonework.

Cathy forced a smile and they lapsed into silence.

As it was only a few weeks to Christmas the visiting room was packed. There were a dozen or so other women sitting either side of her and staring through the criss-crossed grille at their loved ones. At the far end, a couple of the children started squabbling, causing a big-boned woman with arms like a wrestler's to stand up and belt both of them around the head. The fighting siblings lapsed into silence just as one of the babies in the room started grizzling.

Cathy looked back through the mesh at her husband.

Stanley had just turned twenty-nine and stood a fag paper below five foot ten.

After eighteen months in prison, his slender frame had toughened to wiry and even with his hair cropped and wearing the shapeless buff-coloured prison uniform, he was still a handsome chap. Well, he would be if he lost that sulky expression.

'I was surprised how near the prison is to the train station,' said Cathy, having racked her brains and come up with nothing else.

'Is it?' asked Stan.

'Yes,' continued Cathy. 'Just a short walk.'

An ugly expression twisted Stan's mouth. 'Well, I

wouldn't know, would I? The only place I walk every day is around the poxy exercise yard.'

'Language, Stan, please.' She looked pointedly at Peter.

He shot another angry look at her through the wire. 'I thought you were here to visit not nag.'

'I'm not nagging,' said Cathy. 'I just don't want Peter to pick up bad language now that he's started talking, that's all.'

'Talking, is he?' said Stan, giving his son a disinterested look. 'Well, I ain't heard him say a dicky bird since you walked in.'

'He's just shy, that's all,' said Cathy, giving her son a quick hug. 'He called your mum "nanny" as clear as day yesterday.'

'Has he said "daddy" yet?' asked Stan.

'No, not yet, but it'll come,' said Cathy.

'I don't see how,' Stan replied. 'When he don't know who I am.'

'Of course he knows who you are,' Cathy replied. 'I have your picture next to his bed and I tell him to wave you goodnight. Peter.' Her son looked up. 'Give Daddy a wave like we do when you and teddy go to sleep.'

With the teething peg still in his mouth he looked at her solemnly for a moment then waved at the portly prison warden keeping an eye on proceedings, baton in hand, by the door.

'See, I told you,' Stan barked. 'My own son doesn't know me from Adam.' An ugly expression contorted his face. 'And do you know why?'

Cathy did but she didn't answer.

'Your poxy sister,' Stan continued. 'If she'd had any regard for you, she would have tipped me the wink before the bloody police and MI5 arrived instead of helping them spring their bloody trap.'

'Perhaps if you hadn't got involved with those Naz . . . those people then you wouldn't have been arrested in the first place,' said Cathy.

'That's right,' Stan shouted, 'blame me.'

The officer, who was tapping his baton on his leg, moved to stand behind Stan. A sullen expression dragged down the corners of Stan's mouth and he slumped back in the chair.

'Look, Stan, I've come all this way in the freezing cold to see you and all you've done is sit there with a face like thunder and have a go at me. If you're going to carry on like this I won't bother in future.'

'You won't have to,' said Stan, 'because I'm being let out.'

'But you've only served eighteen months,' said Cathy, feeling a flutter of anxiety in her chest.

Stan gave her a sour look. 'Well, you don't sound too pleased. '

'Of course I'm pleased,' said Cathy, in a hollow tone. 'It's just a bit of a surprise given you were sent down for a five-year stretch.'

'Well, it's thanks to this new call-up act,' said Stan. 'If we're between eighteen and fifty, passed fit and the governor signs the chit, we can transfer to the army.'

'That's good then, isn't it?' said Cathy.

'I suppose,' said Stan grudgingly. 'But I'd rather be walking out of here a free man than to fight for that bloody warmonger Churchill.'

'And us,' said Cathy, pulling her coat a little tighter around her to keep out the chill. 'You'll be fighting for me and Peter, too.'

Stan shot her another belligerent look. 'Well, I wouldn't need to, would I, if your bloody sister hadn't interfered,' he snapped. 'There would have been none of this death and destruction if people had listened to Mosley and joined with Hitler but no. That Jew-loving Churchill and his cronies wanted a war so now . . .'

As he rabbited on, Cathy hoped that once the prison governor had heard Stan's views on the Jewish conspiracy to control world finance and the importance of keeping the Aryan blood pure, he might think twice about signing his release chit.

'Right then.' Jo took a mouthful of tea. 'Shall I show you what I've got so far?'

'Fire away,' said Cathy, who was sitting opposite her feeding bitesize chunks of bun to Peter who was sitting in his pushchair next to her.

It was the Saturday after Cathy's visit to her husband in prison and the two sisters were sitting at a table at the back of Boardman's restaurant. They were surrounded by shoppers all on the same quest as Jo and Cathy: to find something, anything, to give to their loved ones at Christmas. And it was a quest. Toys were in short supply because all the metal had gone to build aeroplanes. Books were as plentiful as hen's teeth because the wood was needed to construct army camps and – something never mentioned by the Ministry of Information – coffins. There were hardly any cigars because the troops had priority. There was a shortage of beer as the hop fields had been given over to growing vegetables and there were no toiletries, china ornaments or any other fripperies as all the factories that used to make them were now making shells and bullets. If by some miracle you did manage to buy or even make something to give to your nearest and dearest for the festive season, you had to wrap it in old newspaper because there was no wrapping paper either.

And the cafés and restaurants weren't faring much better as food was in such short supply, but because it didn't require coupons and the fixed price for a basic meal was a shilling, Boardman's cafeteria was doing a roaring trade.

Therefore, after a bit of standing around holding their trays, she and Cathy had nabbed a table at the back and now their empty lunch plates had been stacked to one side and they had cups of tea cooling in front of them.

It was Jo's first day off for over two weeks and she was enjoying wearing civvies for a change – tartan slacks with an Aran double-knit jumper under her winter coat, to be precise. Although they hadn't had a bombing raid for most of her last tour of duty, the ambulance station had been busy helping with the evacuation of casualties to country hospitals so the local ones were ready for the next wave of injuries that were sure to arrive once the Luftwaffe returned. And they would, any day now, especially now the Germans had been pushed back by the Russians. After all, Hitler had to make sure someone was punished for his failure and more than likely it would be London again.

Jo had arrived at Cathy's house at nine and found her sister having a row with her mother-in-law who clearly expected Cathy to be scrubbing the already spotless house from top to bottom instead of gadding off in search of Christmas presents.

They'd walked up White Horse Lane and arrived at Stepney Station just as a number 25 pulled up. After half an hour of bumping over debris, winding around shell craters and rattling over the wrought iron of Bow Bridge, they'd arrived at Stratford Broadway.

Having had a quick cuppa and given Peter his mid-morning rusk in the Co-op's café, they'd decided to split up to search for bargains and meet up at one for lunch. Now they were comparing their purchases.

Jo delved in her shopping basket and pulled out a roll of handkerchiefs tied with a narrow pink ribbon.

'I've got these for Mum,' she said, laying them on the table. 'I was after something a bit fancier but that's all they had. If I embroider IMB in the corner and a different flower on each, Mum will love them.'

'I'm sure she will,' said Cathy. 'I managed to get her this on the market.' She pulled a pack of six bath cubes from her shopping bag and laid them on the table. 'They're Lily of the Valley.'

'Just right for when she's having a soak in the tub at St George's baths,' said Jo. 'You were lucky to get them; I was looking for something like that for Mattie.'

'Well, they were on the stall opposite the pie and mash shop,' said Cathy. 'What are you giving Tommy?'

'Something to make his eyes pop but he won't be able to unwrap it in front of the family, that's for sure,' giggled Jo.

Cathy's eyes stretched wide. 'You're so naughty.'

'I know but we are getting married soon, so who cares.' She frowned. 'At least, we will be if I can wheedle Dad into giving his consent.'

'Well, if you take my advice, don't rush into it,' said Cathy. 'Because marriage isn't what you imagined it might be.'

Jo gave her sister a sympathetic look. 'I take it the visit to Stan didn't go too well.'

'No, it didn't,' Cathy replied. 'He spent the whole time with a face like a smacked arse and moaning about everything. Well, what Mattie and that hero bloody husband of hers did, mostly. Now I don't say he's altogether wrong on that score, but you think he could have just given it a rest, for once.'

Actually, Jo thought Cathy was completely in the wrong about Mattie and her husband, Daniel, who'd nearly died stopping a bunch of Nazis landing in London Docks. But as Cathy already had a pig of a life living with Stan's whingeing mother there was no point adding to her woes by pointing out that Stan was lucky to be in prison and not dangling on the end of a rope.

'And to top it all,' her sister continued, 'the train back was delayed by an hour so after fighting my way through St Pancras with the pram and Peter screaming for his dinner I had to wait another half an hour for a bus to Liverpool Street before squeezing on to a number fifteen for the final leg of the journey. It was six thirty by the time I walked through the back door. I tell you, I know he's my husband and all that, but if he's going to be like that every time I visit him I don't know that I'll bother again.'

'Well, you won't have to if they parole him into the army and ship him off to North Africa,' said Jo.

'No, I won't, will I?' said Cathy, looking positively jolly at the prospect of her husband being sent to face the enemy a thousand miles away in the desert.

'Mum mum,' said Peter, stretching his chubby hands towards the currant bun just out of his reach.

Cathy broke off another chunk and handed it to him. 'Anyway, let's not talk about my miserable husband. What are you getting Gran?'

'The same as you, probably,' said Jo.

'Gin,' they said in unison and laughed.

'Afternoon, girls. Having fun, are we?'

Jo looked up to see her sister-in-law Stella standing there.

Like them, Stella was wrapped up against the damp November weather but rather than a three-year-old coat and utility trousers like Jo's, her brother's wife was dressed in a sleek, mid-calf-length bright blue coat with an astrakhan collar and matching cuffs, which if she hadn't got from some black market spiv, then Jo was the Queen of Ireland. Although Jo and Cathy were wearing a little powder and lipstick, Stella was made up as if she was about to paint the town, with heavily made-up eyes and crimson lips.

'We were.' Jo looked at her watch. 'Patrick not with you?'

'No, I left him with the woman opposite,' Stella replied. 'She'll get him ready for when your mother picks him up for the shelter later as I've got to be in work early.' She glanced at the box of bath cubes on the table. 'I suppose you're out doing a bit of Christmas shopping.'

'We are,' said Cathy. 'I suppose you're out doing the same.'

'I might pick up a few bits if I see something,' Stella replied. 'But I buy most of my presents up West, at Selfridges, Derry and Toms and Harrods, if I want something really special.'

'Is that where you got Charlie's present, then?' asked Cathy, giving her sister-in-law an innocent look.

Stella blinked. 'Charlie?'

'Yes, Charlie,' said Jo, 'your husband, surely you remember him.'

'Of course I remember him, you cheeky cow,' snapped Stella, a pink flush creeping up her throat.

'Well then, you'll know that the closing date for getting presents to servicemen before Christmas was last Wednesday,' said Jo, giving her hateful sister-in-law the sweetest of smiles.

'Yes, of course I did. I sent mine the day before.' Stella flicked a speck of something from her sleeve. 'But what

I really came over to ask was, how's your dear little brother?'

'Billy's fine,' said Cathy.

Matching Jo's syrupy expression, Stella smiled. 'No not Billy, the other one,' she clicked her fingers. 'Oh, what's his name?' She clicked them again.

'Michael,' said Jo.

Stella beamed at her. 'That's it, Michael. How could I forget with everyone talking about him?' She gave a tinny laugh. 'Well, him and your father.'

Cathy's lips pulled into a hard line. 'Michael's fine, thank you for asking.'

'I bet it was a bit of a shock finding out you've got another brother,' Stella continued.

'More a surprise, I'd say,' Jo replied, holding her smile. 'But we're all looking forward to getting to know him.'

'That's nice. All one big happy family,' said Stella. 'Although I'm sure your mother's not too impressed to find her husband got her best friend up the duff. From what people have been telling me, Ellen what's-her-name had always been after your dad so you can't really blame him if she was offered on a plate, I suppose.'

Cathy's face darkened, but as she opened her mouth to reply, Jo kicked her under the table.

'I'm sure you're right, Stella,' said Jo, her sugary smile turning to sickly syrup. 'After all, everyone knows you're the expert about offering it on a plate.'

The pink flush colouring her sister-in-law's throat turned to puce.

'Well, it's been grand to see you, Stella,' said Jo, not bothering to suppress her amusement, 'but don't let us keep you.'

'No, don't let us keep you,' repeated Cathy.

Jo picked up her cup and Cathy did the same then both sisters looked away.

Out of the corner of her eye, Jo saw Stella hover next to them for a second or two before spinning on her heels and stomping away.

'Tart,' said Cathy, when their sister-in-law was out of earshot.

'First-class bitch, don't you mean?' said Jo.

'Yes, best in show,' agreed Cathy. 'Do you think she really did send Charlie a present?'

'Course she didn't,' said Jo. 'The last day to post to servicemen wasn't last Wednesday but the Monday before, and I know Mattie and Mum sent off Charlie's Christmas box at least a week before that. Charlie'll be lucky if his dear wife gave him a second thought, let alone a present.'

'Poor Charlie, being tied to the likes of her,' said Cathy. 'I don't know why she ever married him.'

'Because Francesca wanted him,' said Jo.

Cathy looked surprised and Jo laughed.

'Surely you knew.' Her sister shook her head. 'Well, you must be the only one who doesn't. Well, you and that daft brother of ours anyway, great big lummox that he is. Poor Francesca's been mad for Charlie since school and when Stella saw it, she set her sights on him just to spite her.'

'But why?'

'Because, as we've already established, our sister-in-law is a bitch,' said Jo.

Having finished his last piece of bun, Peter stretched up for another.

Jo broke off a bit and offered it to him. His small hand closed around it.

'What do you say?' asked Jo, pulling a smiley face at her nephew.

'Ta,' said Peter.

Jo released it.

'You're not really going to be there tomorrow when Dad brings Michael home, are you?' asked Cathy as Jo wiped her fingers on her handkerchief.

'Of course, I am,' said Jo. 'So is Mattie. And you ought to be there too, Cathy, for Mum's sake.'

'I don't know how she can even bear to look at Dad after what he's done,' said Cathy, 'let alone welcome his . . . his . . .'

'Neither do I,' said Jo. 'If it were Tommy I'd, well, actually I don't know what I'd do, but as Mattie said, if Mum can forgive Dad and accept Michael then we should too. After all, whether we like it or not, Cathy, Michael's not going away.'

Ida glanced at the clock on the mantelshelf for the second time in five minutes and noted that it now said ten to three. Mattie, who was sitting across from her on the sofa, caught her eye and gave her a reassuring smile. Ida tried to return it but only managed a nervous twitch of the lips.

There was a thump in the room above and Ida looked up.

'Do you want me to give Billy a shout?' asked Mattie.

Ida shook her head. 'Let him play in his room until they get here. He'll only fidget if he has to wait.'

'You know Cathy would have been here, Mum, if Mrs Wheeler didn't have one of her rattily chests again,' said Jo, who was sitting next to her sister with her niece Alicia on her lap.

'Of course,' said Ida, hoping she sounded convinced.

The truth was, Cathy didn't want to be here and, to be honest, neither did she. She didn't want to be sitting here waiting for her husband to arrive, with the best china all laid out on the table, fish paste and liver sausage sandwiches cut into triangles on her oval serving plate and a ginger cake on her mother's glass stand.

In fact, she'd go further than that and say she didn't want Michael, she didn't want Ellen, she didn't want people looking sideways at her in the market or when she walked into church. In fact, in moments when everything pressed down on her so hard she felt she was about to be crushed by it, despite her resolve of only a few days after visiting Ellen to try to recapture what she and Jerimiah had, just at this moment Ida didn't want him either. But then you can't always get what you want, can you? So here she was, on the last day of November, sitting in her own back parlour waiting to greet Jerimiah's son by another woman.

'Fecking rattily chest, my cods,' said Queenie, who was sitting in her son's chair next to the fire. 'The woman's no more than a hippo . . . hipto . . . hapocontitics or whatever the bejesus word is.'

'Hypochondriac,' laughed Mattie.

'That's yer man,' said Queenie, her dentures clicking softly as she spoke. 'Fecking bog crazy the woman is.'

'I hope you're not going to start swearing when the boy gets here,' said Ida.

Queenie glared at her. ''Tis no more than he'll hear walking around the dock and I'm at liberty to swear in my own house, am I not?'

Ida could have pointed out it was her house Queenie was swearing in but she didn't because although the old woman would tear her own lung out rather than admit it, she was anxious, too.

Ida knew this because, contrary to her usual practice of putting them back into the jar on her window sill after church, her mother-in-law still had her false teeth in, and she'd forgone her lunchtime Guinness and a double gin chaser and opted for a small port and orange instead.

The back door opened, and Ida's heart thumped painfully in her chest.

'Anyone at home?' Jerimiah called from the kitchen.

Ida opened her mouth to speak but her tongue didn't seem to be working so no words came out.

'In here,' called Mattie, giving her another sympathetic look.

Ida stood up and turned to face Jerimiah as he ushered Michael into the room.

Jerimiah smiled. 'Hello, luv,' he said quietly, his eyes soft and brimming with gratitude.

Ida forced a brittle smile. 'Hello.'

Stepping behind the lad, Jerimiah laid his large hands on the boy's slender shoulders. 'Ida, you'll remember Michael.'

Feeling a band of steel gripping her chest, Ida's gaze shifted down. Credit where credit's due, dressed in his Greencoat school uniform with a dazzling white shirt, properly knotted tie and polished black lace-up shoes, Ellen had kitted her son out perfectly for a Sunday-afternoon visit. However, what cut Ida to the quick was just how closely the boy resembled his father.

'Hello, Michael,' Ida forced out over the lump clogging her throat.

Putting his rolled-up cap in his blazer pocket, the boy

stepped forward. Holding his arm across his stomach, he bowed. 'Hello, Auntie Ida. Nice to meet you again.'

Jerimiah's hands returned to their resting place and then he expanded his gaze to include the rest of the room.

'Everyone,' he said, his deep voice reaching every corner of the room, 'this is Michael.'

'Hello, Michael,' said Ida's two daughters sitting on the sofa.

'Where's Billy?' asked Jerimiah.

Billy replied before Ida could by bursting through the door.

He too was dressed for a Sunday family tea but unlike Michael he was blazerless, his tie was skewed sideways, one sock was at half mast and the front of his shirt had come adrift.

He stopped in front of Michael and the two boys gave each other the once-over.

'Are you Michael?' asked Billy.

'Yes. Are you Billy?'

'Yes,' said Billy. 'Have you got a train set?'

'No,' Michael replied.

'Well, I have and it's a big one,' Billy replied. 'The best one in the shop and it cost three quid.'

'I've got all the RAF Airfix planes,' said Michael.

'Perhaps you two can swap notes on your toys when we have tea.' Jerimiah guided Michael across the room to the sofa. 'Michael, this is Jo.'

'Hello, Jo,' the boy said, and she smiled at him.

'And this is Mattie,' Jerimiah continued.

'Hello, Mattie.'

She smiled at him and took her daughter's hand. 'And this is my little girl Alicia.'

Michael looked down solemnly at the baby who looked solemnly back up at him.

A sad look crossed Jerimiah's face. 'I have another daughter Cathy but she—'

'Couldn't be here,' cut in Ida. 'Because her mother-in-law is poorly.'

'You'll meet her another time, Michael,' said Jerimiah, giving Ida another grateful look. 'And this,' he said, turning the boy towards Queenie, 'Is my ma, your gran.'

Rising from her chair, Queenie stared at her grandson for a long moment then her wrinkled face lit up with pure joy.

'We've already met,' said Queenie. 'Hello again, Michael.'

'Hello, Mrs Brogan,' the boy replied.

'Gran will do, I'm thinking,' said Queenie.

Michael's expression matched the old lady's and he smiled. 'Hello, Gran.'

The raw-tooth saw cut deeper into Ida's heart.

Wiping a rarely seen tear from her eye, Queenie flung her arms around the unsuspecting lad and dragged him to her.

Looking bemused, Michael stood awkwardly while she kissed his forehead and smoothed his hair as Billy watched with amusement.

'Did you know I have a parrot?' she asked the lad as she released him.

'Yes, I did,' said Michael, his eye lighting up excitedly.

'It's a grey one and I feed him if Gran's not around,' chipped in Billy. 'Gran lets him out sometimes and he flies around.'

Michael's eyes opened even wider. 'Can I see him flying?'

'Perhaps after tea,' said Ida. 'We don't want him shi—' She caught Queenie's amused expression. 'Making a mess on the tea.'

'And what a tea,' said Jerimiah, a little over jollily. 'Auntie Ida's put on a grand spread for us, hasn't she, Michael?'

The boy nodded. 'Thank you, Auntie Ida,' he said, looking artlessly across at her.

Ida forced a smile. 'That's all right, Michael. Why don't you tuck in?'

Billy started forward, but Ida checked him with a look.

'There's fish paste or liver sausage,' said Mattie, standing up and going to the table.

'And ginger cake to follow,' Queenie added.

Jerimiah handed the boy a plate. 'Why don't you take what you fancy, Michael? And then sit on the pouffe between the girls and your gran.'

'I'll go and make the tea, then,' said Ida.

Leaving the family choosing their sandwiches, Ida fled to the kitchen. Without pausing she relit the gas under the kettle she'd boiled half an hour before and while it came back to the boil she spooned tea into the pot.

The kettle started whistling. Taking it off the heat, Ida made the tea and returned to the parlour just as Queenie finished telling them yet again about Kinsale, the small port south of Cork where her family originated from.

Putting a bright smile on her face, Ida walked in.

'Who's for tea, then?' she asked, holding up the teapot.

'Everyone, I'd say,' Jerimiah replied, giving her his usual easy-going, relaxed smile now. 'How many sugars, Michael?'

'Two please,' the boy replied. His eyes shifted to the shelves of grey books with gold lettering on them. 'Is that the encyclopaedia you were telling me about, Dad?'

Dad!

The word burst over Ida, taking the breath from her lungs and sending her head spinning as her mind shouted it over and over again in her head.

Although she'd known in her head that Jerimiah was Michael's father for over six weeks, hearing the boy call him dad had suddenly burnt the knowledge into her heart. And it hurt. It hurt like hell.

'Mum,' someone said from afar.

The floor started to shift but Ida pushed the sensation aside. She blinked and found Mattie standing in front of her, looking worried.

'You're spilling the tea, Mum,' she said, glancing down at the pot Ida was holding.

'Sorry,' said Ida, somehow managing to keep her voice even. She shifted her attention past her eldest daughter on to Michael standing quietly behind her. 'How many sugars did you say, Michael?'

Chapter Fourteen

'STAND STILL WHILE I do your hair,' said Ellen, dipping the comb in her son's washing water and running it through his dark curls again.

'But, Mum,' he said, bobbing on the balls of his toes, 'the latest copy of *Boy's Own* is out today and if I don't get to Feldman's soon they'll all go.'

It was just after eight in the morning and the BBC news announcer was informing the country of Germany's struggle to advance on Rostov.

It was the first Monday in December and they had left the shelter just after the all-clear had sounded at six. When they'd returned home, the embers in the grate had still been glowing so Ellen had added fresh coals and the replenished fire had soon taken the chill off the room. While Michael had splashed about like a puppy in a puddle getting himself washed and dressed for school, Ellen had cooked him his fried bread and egg, which he'd bolted down in two minutes flat along with his cup of sugary tea.

'There you are,' said Ellen, cocking her head to the side and admiring her son. 'All ready for school. Gather your books together while I fetch your sandwiches.'

Grabbing his satchel from the back of the chair as he passed, Michael scooped his buff-coloured exercise books out from amongst his annuals and comics, crammed them into the bag and buckled the flap. He returned just as Ellen was folding down the edges of the paper bag. Placing her son's mid-morning snack in the OXO tin, she handed it to him.

'There you are,' she said.

'What is it, Mum?'

'Fish paste.'

Michael pulled a face.

'It'll keep you going until the end of the morning.' Ellen ruffled his hair. 'But make sure you eat all your dinn—' She gasped.

Alarm shot across her son's face. 'Mum!'

'I'm all right,' she said, taking slow breaths so as not to aggravate the sawing pain under her rib.

'Do you want your medicine?' he asked, his anxious eyes searching her face.

She shook her head. 'No, it just caught me unawares, that's all. Now come on, my lad,' she said, forcing a cheery smile. 'You'd better get your skates on if you want to get there before the bell goes.'

Shoving his lunch tin in his satchel, Michael slung it over his shoulder and then, giving her a quick peck on the cheek, dashed to the door.

'Bye, Mum,' he called over his shoulder as he tore out. 'See you tonight.'

Before Ellen could answer, the pain cut into her again. Holding her side, she focused on the lamp overhead and breathed slowly, hoping the agony would fade. It didn't. In fact, if anything the movement of her ribcage made it worse.

Curling into the pain that was now slicing through the left side of her body, she staggered over to the sideboard. In truth, she'd already taken a spoonful of the painkiller not an hour before and shouldn't really have another until midday, but she needed to do something. Leaning on the solid wooden cabinet to steady herself, Ellen poured out half the measure of morphine and swallowed it down.

Putting the bottle down, she took a couple of deep breaths then staggered back to her chair. Flopping in it, she closed her eyes and listened to the early-morning sounds: the letterbox rattling and empty bottles chinking together in the crate as the milkman passed on his way back to the dairy.

There was a knock at the front door and Ellen heard Mrs Crompton, the landlady, open the door downstairs. As the faint melody of *Music While You Work* from next door's wireless drifted through the wall, Ellen smiled and embraced unconsciousness.

Searing pain brought her back to the here and now, dispelling the warm drowsiness of oblivion in an instant. She didn't know how long she'd been lying there, but the sun was now high enough to have crested the house opposite, so she guessed it must be about ten or so. Feeling as if she was being torn apart from the inside out, Ellen cried out in pain. Gripping her side, she tried to sit up in the chair but the torturous sensation in her side bit deeper and she flopped back, fighting for breath.

She was dying. She knew it. She wished Michael was here with her but better perhaps that he wasn't. No ten-year-old child should have to watch his parent depart this life.

No. Although all her love and joy in this world was centred around her darling son, Ellen was glad he wasn't with her now.

The agony speared her again, causing sweat to spring out on her forehead. She tasted blood and realised she'd bitten through her lower lip. If only she could ease this pain a little, she could prepare herself properly to meet her maker.

Her gaze drifted to the bottle of medicine still sitting uncorked on the sideboard. Taking a deep breath, she gripped the arms of the chair again but her legs wouldn't support her so she shuffled forward and slid on to the floor. Now on all fours, Ellen waited until the blackness threatening to engulf her mind receded a little, then she crawled, inch by inch, towards the sideboard.

With the pain in her side throbbing mercilessly, Ellen's fingers felt the rough planks of the waxed floorboards as she crept across the room. Finally, she reached her goal but as she tried to rise up, pain swept over her, causing black spots to crowd into her vison. From what seemed like a long way away, Ellen heard the front door being opened again and footsteps on the stairs.

There was a knock. Hope flared in Ellen's chest. Forcing the blackness in her head aside, she tried to call out, but nothing came.

There was a second knock.

She had to answer. Stretching up, Ellen curled her hand around the edge of the open cutlery drawer but as she pulled on it to rise, it shot out. Ellen screamed as the drawer crashed to the floor, scattering knives and forks across the room.

Exhausted, she crumpled on to the floor, her cheek resting on the colourful strands of the rag rug in front of the hearth.

Gazing across the dusty floorboards, and with the agony in her side overwhelming her mind, Ellen waited for the angels to come and take her soul to heaven.

The door opened but instead of seeing a white robe and a pair of golden sandals, the last thing Ellen saw before oblivion overtook her was a pair of slender legs in lisle stockings and a pair of stout brown lace-up shoes as Ida Brogan stepped into the room.

*

Taking the last mouthful of her tea, Ida put the cup back in the saucer balanced in the palm of her hand and placed it on the bedside locker next to the hospital bed.

As it was now nearly midday the half a dozen nurses, dressed in the London Hospital's distinctive uniform of lilac pinstriped dress and lacy cap, had finished their morning tasks and had already set the central table for dinner. Now, half of them were pinning up paper chains at the windows while the rest were dressing the artificial Christmas tree with stars made from pipe cleaners.

The staff nurse in charge that morning, who was doing her last check of the ward before the dinner trolley arrived, stopped at the bottom of the bed. She walked to the bottle of blood hanging upside down on the stand by Ellen's head. She checked the rubber tubing dangling beneath and examined the needle in the back of Ellen's left hand. She then went back to the end of the bed and took a pen from under the bib of her pristine starched apron.

'Mrs Gilbert looks a bit better?' she said, unhooking the clipboard at the end of the bed and jotting something down.

'She does,' Ida agreed.

Although she still looked like she was two breaths away from being a corpse, Ellen did look ten times better than she had when Ida found her collapsed on the floor.

'Did Dr Muir speak to you?' asked the nurse.

'Yes,' said Ida. 'He came by just after the porters brought Mrs Gilbert back from theatre.'

The nurse glanced at her upside-down fob watch. 'She went down at eleven, so she should be awake soon.' She raised her head. 'She's a lucky woman. If you hadn't found her, well . . .' She let the sentence hang unfinished. 'I'm on duty until six so if you need anything just get one of the student nurses to fetch me. I'm Nurse Sullivan.'

'I will,' said Ida.

Picking up Ida's empty cup, Nurse Sullivan continued on her way.

Leaning back in her chair, Ida recrossed her legs and then turned her attention back to Ellen, who was lying peacefully in the hospital bed. As if she knew she was being watched, Ellen opened her eyes. She gazed around for a second or two and then spotted Ida.

They looked at each other for a moment then Ellen spoke. 'Where am I?'

'In the London on Charrington Ward,' Ida replied.

Panic shot across Ellen's waxen face. She tried to get up on her elbows but she collapsed back, exhausted.

'Michael!' she whispered. 'I have to—'

'Don't worry about Michael,' cut in Ida. 'Your landlady said she'd fetch him from school during the dinner break and bring him up here.'

Ellen relaxed back and let out a long sigh. 'Thank you.'

She shifted and must have felt the crêpe bandage secured tightly around her chest because she put her hand on it.

'The doctor said you'd sprung a leak, which meant your lungs were filling up with blood,' Ida explained. 'They drained two pints in theatre before it stopped. The almoner came along while you were under. She said that given that they couldn't just leave you bleeding there's a good chance, if you apply to the hospital's charitable trust, they'll write off the fee.'

The double doors swung open and Michael dashed in.

Seeing his mother lying in the bed, he ran over and threw himself across her.

'Mum, Mum,' he mumbled, clinging tightly to her.

Ellen's unfettered arm closed around him.

'It's all right,' she whispered, pressing her lips to his forehead.

A solitary tear escaped from the corner of Ellen's right eye and trickled down her cheek as sadness and love mingled together on her face.

A lump formed itself in Ida's throat.

The ward door swung open again and Mrs Crompton walked in. Leaving mother and son clinging to each other, Ida went over to her.

'Thank you for bringing him,' said Ida.

'S'aright, least I could do given how she is,' said the landlady. 'But I can't stay because I have to get my Jim's dinner.' She gave Ida a conspiratorial wink. 'You know what men are like. I told Mrs Deeks from number seven on my way here,' Mrs Crompton continued, 'and she said if you can get him back to her by five, she's happy to take Michael to the shelter with her as usual.'

'I'll bear it in mind,' said Ida.

The landlady adjusted the shopping bag on her arm. 'Well, I'll be off.'

She turned to leave but after a couple of steps turned back.

'By the way, I thought it best just to tell Michael 'is mum had taken a tumble.' She looked past Ida to where Ellen and Michael clung together. 'Breaks your heart, don't it?' she said, a sorrowful expression deepening the lines on her face.

Ida forced a smile but didn't comment.

Mrs Crompton left and Ida rejoined Ellen and Michael.

'I was just telling Michael that we are old friends,' said Ellen, looking beseechingly at Ida.

Ida paused for a heartbeat then smiled. 'Yes, we are,' she said, looking into the boy's young face that was so much like Jerimiah's. 'We used to go dancing together.'

Michael laughed, and a fond smile lifted the corners of Ellen's bloodless lips.

'Did you?' asked Michael, looking incredulously from his mother to Ida and back again.

'Yes, we did,' said Ellen, pretending to scowl at him.

The boy laughed again and hugged his mother.

Holding her son close, Ellen closed her eyes. The bitter-sweet expression returned to her face for a moment then she looked at Ida.

'Although, Mrs Brogan was always lighter on her feet than me,' she added softly.

As Ida held her old friend's gaze, images of them as girls on a Friday night flashed through her mind. How they'd giggled as they eyed up young fellas, freshly shaved and flush with their weekly wages, lolling against the bar in the Regal. She remembered their wonder at the plush gilt and velvet of the dance hall and how their legs flew and skirts swirled as they'd danced the turkey trot. The smooth sensation of their shoes gliding across the polished dance floor in the tango and then dashing across Stratford Broadway in the rain to catch the last tram home.

A pang of longing for those happy days when she and Ellen were thick as thieves and twice as bold bubbled in her chest.

'But your mum picked up a tune quicker,' Ida replied.

She and Ellen stared at each other for several moments then the undulating wail of a siren filled Ida's ears.

The nurses pottering about the ward stopped mid-task and started directing the patients who could walk to leave their beds and chairs and evacuate the ward. Nurse Sullivan appeared wearing a tin helmet with a W painted in white on the front. Standing on a footstool she blew her whistle.

'There is limited space in the hospital basement,' she shouted in a strong, clear voice. 'And priority is given to the sick so visitors who are within walking distance of their own shelters are requested to make their way there now.'

Two of the student nurses marched over to Ellen's bed.

'Right, Mrs Gilbert,' one said briskly, kicking off the bed's brake, 'let's get you tucked away safely.'

Fear flashed across Ellen's sallow face.

'Don't worry, Ellen,' Ida said, taking the boy's small hand in hers. 'I'll take care of Michael.'

Scooting past the man leading the sing-song, Michael dived behind the old pram and crouched down. Holding on to the curved steel of the handle, he peered out from behind it to where David Manny, a skinny boy with a crop of ginger hair, stood counting out loud with his hands over his eyes.

He'd heard people moaning about Tilbury Shelter, but he couldn't understand why because it was blooming brilliant. Firstly, there was a proper canteen, so you didn't have to bring your own food, and secondly, there was all sort of things going on, like draughts tournaments and talks about the ancient Egyptians, but the best thing about the massive space under the warehouse was there were lots of boys his own age. Of course, they'd given him the once-over when he arrived, but Billy, Auntie Ida's son, had told them he was his brother, so they let him join them.

He still wasn't quite sure how he was Billy's brother, but his father said he'd tell him when he got older. He didn't mind how, really; he was just glad that Billy was his brother. And not only that but now he had three sisters and a big brother too. Plus, and perhaps the best thing of all, Mr Brogan was his father.

He and Auntie Ida had only got as far as Commercial Road when the all-clear sounded so instead of going to the shelter they had gone to pick up Billy and their blankets before setting off again. They'd collected a baby along the way too, and arrived at the shelter just as the WVS canteen started dishing up supper. After a big plate of sausage and mash, Billy's mum had sent them off to play. He'd been doing that ever since.

He didn't know exactly what time it was, but he did know it was ages past his bedtime and that he hadn't had so much fun since he couldn't remember when.

He spotted Billy on the other side of the shelter, tucked in behind a pillar, and waved. Billy grinned and beckoned him over. Michael glanced across at David, who was searching behind a pile of crates, and then dashed across.

'Let's hide in there,' said Billy, pointing at a half-size door in the wall.

'What is it?' asked Michael.

Billy shrugged.

Michael cast his eye over it and bit his lip.

'Unless you're scared,' added Billy.

'I ain't scared,' Michael replied, shoving the other boy. 'Just wondered if your fat head would get through the hole.'

Billy grinned again, his teeth flashing white in the dim light above.

Keeping low, they scurried across to the door and went through. The door led into what must have been a storeroom so leaving the door open to let the light through the boys tucked themselves out of sight.

With their backs on the wall and their arms resting on their knees, Michael and Billy caught their breath.

'It pongs a bit,' said Michael, wrinkling his nose.

'It's the marge in the basement,' Billy informed him. 'It's gone off.'

He rummaged around in his pocket then pulled out his handkerchief and unwrapped it.

'Want a gobstopper?' he said, holding out the cloth containing two fat balls.

'Ta,' said Michael, popping the nearest one in his mouth.

'Do you think the Luftwaffe will come tonight?' asked Michael as he sucked the fluff off his sweet.

'Perhaps they will if the fog goes,' said Billy. 'But when I get bigger I'm going to join the army like Charlie and kill lots and lots of Germans.'

'Me too,' said Michael. Then he asked, 'Who's that baby that your mum collected on the way here?'

'Patrick,' said Billy. 'He's Charlie's boy.'

'Why don't his mum take him to the shelter?'

'Cos she works at night in a West End club,' Billy explained.

Michael looked astonished. 'She's a singer!'

'No, she's a tart,' Billy replied. 'At least, that what my mum calls her.'

'I like your mum,' said Michael, without thinking. He did, too. Although when he'd met her at the hospital she'd looked like a right dragon, but as they'd walked back to her house she'd asked him what his favourite lessons at school were and laughed at the knock-knock joke he'd heard on the radio that morning. She'd even bought him a pennyworth of chips in the fish shop on the way back to her house.

'She's all right, I suppose,' said Billy. 'But you know she ain't my real mum.'

'Isn't she?' said Michael, looking surprised.

'No, she's not,' Billy replied. 'Pearl, her younger sister, is my real mum. She wears nice clothes and is very rich. It was 'er who bought me the Hornby train set.'

'Did she?'

Billy gave him a smug look. 'And the model Spitfire hanging from the ceiling.'

'That too?' asked Michael, unable to hide his awe. 'She must be loaded.'

'She is,' Billy replied. 'In fact, I reckon she's richer than some of those toff tarts who talk posh and swank about up West.'

'We had a girl down our street who had a baby but didn't want it and— Ow,' Michael yelled as Billy punched him. He rubbed his arm. 'That hurt.'

'Well, don't say it,' Billy replied.

'Say what?'

'That Aunt Pearl didn't want me,' Billy replied, his eyes shining bright in the dim light of their hiding place. 'Because she did. I know she did because she always buys me nice presents.'

'Why did she give you to your mum, then?' Michael asked, feeling slightly bemused by it all.

Billy shot him an angry look. 'I told you she ain't my mum.'

Michael sighed. 'All right, keep your hair on, but why?'

'Because . . . because she did,' snapped Billy. 'That's all. But I bet one day she'll come and fetch me back and I tell you something: she wouldn't always be smacking me for nothing like you know who does.' He thumbed over his shoulder to where Ida was feeding the baby a bottle.

'Does your mu— Auntie Ida smack you a lot?' Michael asked, as a chorus of 'Roll Out the Barrel' drifted through the open door.

'All the time,' said Billy. 'What about yours?'

Tears sprang into his eyes. Pretending to wipe his nose, Michael dashed them away with the back of his hand. He shook his head. 'When I was little but not for a long time.'

'That's cos you're a mummy's boy,' said Billy.

'I'm not,' shouted Michael, grabbing hold of the other boy's arm.

Billy shook him off and scrambled to his feet. 'Mummy's boy, mummy's boy,' he mimicked in a falsetto voice as he scrambled back through the tiny doorway.

Left alone in the cubby hole, Michael closed his eyes. An image of his mother lying in the hospital bed with a tube in her arm materialised in his mind and his eyes stung again. Resting his forearms on his knees, he hung his head as all the fears about his mother that he'd kept at bay for months surged up and whirled in his mind.

Billy called something to him, but Michael didn't hear him because loneliness pressed down on him. The smell of the rancid margarine below filled his nostrils as an empty painful space opened in his chest, stopping his breath and making his heart pound. Scrambling to his feet, he stumbled towards the low entrance and, heedless of the rough concrete scraping the skin from his knees, crawled back into the main part of the shelter. The jumbled sounds of babies crying, children laughing and people talking and singing hit him like a wall as he emerged.

He turned left and then right and back again, his gaze searching for something he couldn't define. Someone called his name, but he ignored it and ran stumbling over the ends of blankets and baskets, crashing into people.

An ARP Warden with white hair and a bushy moustache stepped in front of him, arms outstretched. Michael dodged to the side but didn't see the child's toy in his path and tripped. He put his hands out to stop his fall but before he hit the ground a pair of motherly arms scooped him up.

'It's all right, Michael,' said the woman's voice as he was enveloped into a soft warm bosom. 'Shush, shush, sweetheart, you just have a good cry.'

So, clinging on to Billy's mum for all he was worth, Michael did.

Putting her foot on the axle, Cathy pushed down on the pram's handle and lifted the front wheels clear of the back step.

'Is that you, Cathy?' Mrs Wheeler called from the front room.

'No, it's bloody Jack the Ripper,' muttered Cathy, shutting the door behind her.

'Cathy!' the old woman screamed again.

'Yes, of course it's me,' she shouted back, pulling the blackout curtain aside and wheeling the pram in.

Peter, who was sitting up amongst the pillows and blankets, looked anxiously up at his mother and stuck his thumb in his mouth.

Unbuttoning her coat, Cathy hooked it on the back of the door then went to the kettle on the stove. It was cold.

Cathy's mouth pulled into a hard line. God forbid her mother-in-law should drag her fat arse out of the chair and boil it in readiness for supper.

Filling the kettle, she put it back on the gas and lit it. The blue flame spluttered a little and then flickered into life. Well, half-life really as they'd just had a note from the gas board informing them that a proportion of the domestic gas supply was being diverted to factories until further notice.

'I hope you haven't scraped the paint off the door bringing that pram in like you did yesterday,' her mother-in-law called out.

Cathy didn't reply.

'I said—'

'I heard you,' snapped Cathy.

Sending a withering look towards the front of the house, Cathy unstrapped Peter from his harness. Taking off his woolly balaclava and coat, she lifted him out of the pram and carried him through to the front room.

Stan's mother was sitting in her usual place by the fire. She gave Cathy a look that could have stripped paint.

'What time do you call this, then?' the old woman snapped.

Cathy glanced at the clock. 'Seven thirty.'

'And you should have been home hours ago to get me my supper,' the old woman added.

'And I would have been if they hadn't diverted the bus from Stratford because of an unexploded bomb in West Ham Lane,' Cathy replied.

'But I've been waiting for my tea,' moaned Mrs Wheeler. 'You know I like it at five o'clock prompt.'

'Well, you should have got it yourself, shouldn't you?' Cathy replied, setting Peter on the floor by his box of toys.

'And the air raid siren went off at two,' the old woman continued.

'I know. I was in Boardman's and had to carry Peter down two flights of stairs to their basement,' said Cathy.

'Well, you wouldn't have had to if you'd stayed home instead of gadding about enjoying yourself and spending money,' Mrs Wheeler replied. 'You know I don't like being alone during a raid.'

'Well, you were all right then, weren't you?' said Cathy. 'Because the all-clear sounded after thirty minutes because it was a false alarm.'

Her mother-in-law's sour look deepened. 'You've got no consideration for my nerves and I'm going to write to my Stan and tell him.'

'You do that. Anyway,' her eyes flickered to the two empty cups on the coffee table and then back to the miserable old woman, 'you haven't been alone, have you?'

'As it happens, Mrs Fisher from number seven popped by.' Mrs Wheeler gave Cathy the sweetest smile. 'She'd heard something when she attended mid-week communion at St Dunstan's this morning, something she felt it her Christian duty to tell me about . . .' A glint of pure delight lit the old woman's pale eyes. 'Your father and his bastard son.'

Cathy's heart lurched uncomfortably as her mouth went dry.

'I always knew your family were a bunch of rogues and ne'er-do-wells,' Mrs Wheeler continued with glee, 'but I didn't think even *your* father was an adulterer and fornicator, too.' She jabbed a bony finger at Cathy. 'I warned my Stan – begged him, in fact – not to get himself mixed up with you and your bog-trotting family but would he—'

Turning on her heels, Cathy marched out of the room.

'Where are you going?' Mrs Wheeler screamed after her.

Cathy didn't reply. Fury coursing through her veins, she crossed to the door and all but ripped Peter's coat and hers off the hook.

She threw them on to the pram and then, ignoring her outraged mother-in-law, she marched upstairs. She stripped the top two blankets from her bed, folded them into a manageable size, then carried them back downstairs and tucked them at the end of the pram.

Grasping the handle, she kicked off the brake and shoved it through the door into the front room.

Mrs Wheeler glared at her. 'I've told you before not to bring that thing in here.'

Cathy ignored her.

Peter's bottom lip started to tremble and, looking fearfully at his mother, he let out a piercing wail.

'For goodness' sake,' said Mrs Wheeler, holding her forehead dramatically. 'Can't you keep that child from making a racket for once?'

Bending down, Cathy scooped up Peter from the floor. She kissed his tears away then bundled him into his coat.

'Where are you going?' asked Mrs Wheeler as Cathy strapped him back into his pram.

'Out,' snapped Cathy, slipping her son's hat on and swathing him in blankets.

'Out!' shouted her mother-in-law. 'Out where?'

'Anywhere as long as it's away from you,' Cathy replied, shoving her arms in her coat sleeves.

'But you haven't made me my supper,' said her mother-in-law, looking incredulously at her.

'No, I haven't, have I? And I'll tell you something else.' Cathy gave her a tight smile. 'I'm not going to. Not today, not tomorrow and never again. I've had it up to here' – she placed her finger on her eyebrow – 'with you and your whining. As far as I'm concerned, you can starve to death. And I'm not spending another night listening to you snoring and farting either, so you can have the shelter to yourself; I'll be making my own arrangements from now on.'

A hateful expression contorted the old woman's face. 'You wait. I'll write to Stan and—'

'I couldn't care less what you tell Stan,' snapped Cathy. 'But I'll tell you this, my dad's not perfect but he's not a traitor to King and country, so if you want to gossip to the neighbours, you can talk about your Nazi-loving son.'

Gripping the handle firmly, Cathy pushed the pram out of the parlour and into the kitchen, scraping the wheel hub along the sideboard door as she passed.

As a fretful baby started niggling a couple of arches away, Michael stirred in his sleep. Ida put aside her knitting and, stretching across, tucked his blankets a little closer around his shoulders.

She was in her usual spot under the second arch from the back, on the right-hand side of the old warehouse. Like many others who used the shelter nightly, she was flanked on both sides by old sheets strung across the washing lines that hung between the pillars to give them a bit of privacy.

Most of the nightly activity had stopped now as children settled to sleep and their parents had a hot drink and listened to the BBC's nine o'clock news.

Michael was lying beside Billy on what had been one of the loading platforms. Both boys were wrapped in blankets against the cold and Ida's covers were neatly folded ready for her to slip beneath when the warden turned off the lights at ten. Of course, Patrick had been fast asleep in his pram for hours and would probably wake her in the wee small hours for another bottle but, with a bit of luck, she'd get a solid four hours either side before people started getting ready for work at six.

Satisfied that Michael had settled again, Ida rested back in her deckchair and took up her knitting. It was one of Jerimiah's old jumpers – it had worn through at the elbows and neck, but there was still enough good wool in it to make Billy a sleeveless pullover.

Taking a needle in each hand, Ida drew out the unravelled wool from the ball ready to start a new row. A smell of something so faint she could barely catch it drifted up and an image of Jerimiah flashed into her mind.

How could she forgive him? And even if she did somehow manage that, could she go further? Could she rekindle her love for Jerimiah? She didn't know.

Her eyes drifted back to the sleeping boy and she thought of his mother.

Perhaps it was impossible. But if she was to have any hope of loving Jerimiah again then she must stop torturing herself by imagining them together.

It wouldn't be easy, not by a long chalk. It might even be impossible, but if they were ever to rebuild their shattered marriage she would have to try.

She studied Michael's peaceful face for a second more then she wound the wool around her finger and slipped the point of the knitting needle behind the first stitch.

She had only just purled half a row when the sheet on the other side of the two sleeping boys parted and a pram was wheeled through.

'Cathy,' said Ida, as her daughter appeared behind the pram. 'What are you doing here?'

'Hello, Mum,' said Cathy, giving her a quick peck on the cheek. 'I'm getting away from my witch of a mother-in-law.' And Cathy recounted her argument with Mrs Wheeler.

'So if you don't mind, Mum, from now on me and Peter are going to squeeze in along with you?'

'Of course I don't mind, luv,' said Ida. She stood up and shifted her beach chair across to give her daughter room to move. 'I'm glad of the company.'

Cathy put Peter's pram alongside Patrick's.

'Billy looks like butter wouldn't melt in his mouth when he's asleep,' said Cathy, smiling at her young brother curled in a blanket with his eyes shut.

'Yes, looks are deceiving, aren't they?' said Ida. 'He's been a right handful recently. I had Mrs Yates from Arlington Street knocking on my door on Monday complaining about Billy throwing stones at her window and frightening her bedridden mother. She's threatening to call the police if she finds him doing it again and I don't blame her.'

'I hope you gave him a good telling-off,' said Cathy.

'You bet I did,' said Ida. 'He stormed out and when he'd gone I found my best cup lying in half a dozen pieces in the backyard. I'm not surprised he's acting up,' she continued, 'not after finding out that Pearl's his real mother and now having Michael on the scene. He's unsettled, that's all; I'm sure he'll sort himself out soon.'

'I hope you're right,' said Cathy. 'But you ought to tell Dad.'

'I would if he didn't already have half the world sitting on his shoulder.'

Cathy gave her a sour look. 'Well, whose fault is that?'

She spotted the boy sleeping next to Billy and looked at her mother in astonishment. 'Don't tell me that's . . .?'

'Yes,' said Ida.

She resumed her seat as Cathy lifted out the blankets she'd draped across the end of Peter's pram and set them out alongside Ida's.

Ida pulled out the Thermos flask of tea from her basket and poured herself and Cathy a cup.

'Where did you get that old thing?' Ida asked as her daughter set Stan's striped fishing stool next to her.

'In the shed.'

Ida handed her one of the flask's two Bakelite cups. 'Lucky for you there's a spare.'

Cathy grinned. 'Thanks, Mum.'

Cathy took a sip and then set the cup down. Delving into her basket, she found her tapestry bag and pulled out her knitting, but after half a row she paused.

'He looks just like our Charlie,' said Cathy.

'And your dad,' Ida added flatly.

Cathy gave her a nervous look. 'I didn't want to mention it.'

'It's the plain truth.' Ida shrugged.

'But how come you've got him, Mum?' her daughter asked, glancing at the sleeping boys again.

Ida told her about finding Ellen and the dash to hospital.

'I know you're being a good Christian and all that, Mum,' said Cathy when she'd finished, 'but I don't know how you can even look at him let alone take him on as one of us.'

'It's not Michael's fault, is it?' said Ida, glancing at the boys and lowering her voice. 'You can't blame him for how he got here, can you?'

'No but—'

'And what would you do if it were Peter, Cathy?' Ida added in the same muted tone. 'Let him be taken to a children's home to be brought up by strangers? Can you imagine what it's like for him seeing his mother so sick?'

'Does he know?' Cathy asked under her breath.

Ida glanced at the sleeping boy and shook her head.

'But the poor lad's worried sick about her; he knows something's not right. He sobbed his little heart out earlier, he did. And when all's said and done, he's our flesh and blood, and flesh and blood take care of their own, don't they?'

Cathy opened her mouth to answer but before she could, the wail of the air raid siren penetrated the shelter's doors.

Mutters of 'bloody Jerry', 'sodding hun' and worse went around the vast area below ground as the ack-ack guns on the Isle of Dogs started pounding.

Peter started grizzling so Cathy put aside her knitting and stood up.

As her daughter comforted her fretful son, Ida's gaze shifted on to Michael's sleeping face. Now she'd got to know him a bit Ida had to admit he was a nice little lad, polite too. Credit where credit's due, Ellen had done a good job bringing him up. And flesh and blood did take care of their own; where would they be if they didn't? But, she wondered, would she ever be able to look at him without imagining all too vividly how he'd got here?

Chapter Fifteen

THE TRUMPET PLAYER blasted out the last note of 'Dancing in the Dark' and Daniel swirled her around as the music stopped. Mattie, like everyone else on the dance floor, applauded.

'Shall we sit the next one out?' Daniel asked, as the bandmaster raised his baton again.

Mattie smiled up at him. 'Yes, let's.'

Slipping his arm around her waist, Daniel guided her through the couples on the dance floor and back to their table.

Another bomb found its target nearby, sending the bottles stacked behind the bar at the other end of the club jiggling while the chandelier dangling above the dance floor bounced a couple of times. But as everything stayed upright, and no drinks were spilled, everyone continued as they were.

It was the first Thursday in December and, although she wasn't certain, Mattie thought it must be close to midnight. They were in the Excelsior Club just off Shaftesbury Avenue, and despite there having been a full-scale air raid going on since nine that evening, the basement was packed with people enjoying a meal and a dance.

Even with bombs raining down all around, the theatres and night clubs in the West End and Soho were as busy as before the war started. More so, in fact, as after a year of nightly raids, Londoners had decided enough was enough of doom and gloom and now the capital's nightlife was as gay as ever.

It had been a wonderful evening and Daniel had certainly pushed the boat out. They'd started with cocktails in a bar near St James's then headed to the Coliseum to see *Me and My Girl*, followed by dinner near Trafalgar Square and now dancing. It had been a perfect night and she planned to top it all by finally letting him in on her happy secret.

Reaching their table, Daniel pulled her chair out and a smile lifted the corner of Mattie's mouth in anticipation of his joy at learning he was to be a father again.

'Thank you,' she said, tucking her skirts under her and sitting down.

He resumed his seat opposite.

'Another drink?' he asked.

'Perhaps a small one,' said Mattie.

Daniel raised his hand and the waiter sped over and took their order.

'It's a good band, isn't it?' said Mattie, her foot tapping in time with the beat.

'Not bad,' Daniel replied.

The waiter returned and placed their drinks on the table. Daniel picked up his whiskey. 'To us.'

'To us,' Mattie repeated, raising her glass too.

'Have you had a good evening?' Daniel asked, as she took a sip of her G&T.

'Wonderful.'

An expression she couldn't interpret flashed across his eyes for a second then he smiled.

'I'm glad, and can I say again you look absolutely gorgeous,' he said, his gaze confirming his words.

'Thank you.' Resting her chin on her hand, Mattie leaned forward. 'And can *I* say you look pretty good yourself, Major McCarthy.'

She gave him a sultry look, expecting to see the usual spark of anticipation, but instead the odd emotion returned for an instant before it vanished once more.

Reaching across, he took her hand. 'Mattie,' he said softly, 'I love you.'

'I love you, too,' Mattie replied. 'And guess what I—'

'I've been ordered back to France,' he cut in.

Something akin to ice water replaced the blood in her veins as she stared across at him.

'When?' she asked, struggling to control the fear and emptiness pressing down on her.

'I'm not sure yet but I'm guessing in a week or so,' Daniel replied.

'So soon?'

'I'm afraid so,' said Daniel. 'With the Germans embroiled in Russia and our forces taking on the Italians in North Africa, the top brass want to make sure our allies in the French resistance don't feel neglected.'

'I understand,' said Mattie.

He squeezed her hand. 'I'm sorry it's just before Christmas.'

'We'll have others, lots,' Mattie said. 'After the war.'

Daniel's eyes held hers for several heartbeats and then he lifted her hand and pressed his lips to her fingers.

She wanted to scream, No! Not again! It's not fair! Why you? Why now? Tell them to send someone else. Let them go behind enemy lines and risk being shot as a spy. But she didn't. She couldn't. Daniel had to do his duty and she had to do hers by not making it any harder for him. Somehow she smiled back as she willed her mind to memorise every curve and line of Daniel's beloved face.

Putting down her drink, Mattie placed a hand on his arm. 'Daniel, can we go home?'

Ten minutes later, after Daniel had paid the bill and they'd retrieved their coats from the cloakroom, Mattie emerged from the club on Daniel's arm.

The glowing red sky to the south of them indicated that the docks and factories on the river had borne the brunt of the Luftwaffe's attack that night. Although the air was heavy with the smell of charred wood, brick dust and sulphur, and bells clanged loudly as fire engines sped to the next call, the humming aircraft engines overhead indicated the German squadrons were heading back to their bases in France and Belgium.

Taking Daniel's arm, Mattie tucked herself into her husband's side and they started up Shaftesbury Avenue towards Tottenham Court Road.

'We're too late for the tube but we should find a taxi in Oxford Street to take us home,' said Daniel, shining his muted torch on the pavement just in front of their feet.

'I hope so,' said Mattie, sidestepping a pile of rubble in her path. 'I don't fancy walking back to Stepney in these shoes.'

Daniel laughed.

A fire engine streaked past them and, turning the corner, they were confronted by two other fire appliances and a heavy rescue team working to stem a fire in one of the office blocks on the west side of the street.

'We can cut through to Charing Cross Road,' said Daniel, guiding her into one of the narrow alleyways that ran through Soho.

From the smell of ammonia and the open doorways with young women loitering in them, it was clear they had left the glamour of theatreland and were now in the less salubrious part of Soho.

Keeping his torch trained on the flagstones, Daniel quickened his pace and very soon they were at the end of the cut-through, but just as they reached Charing Cross Road an ARP warden stepped into their path.

'Sorry, mate,' he said, stretching his arms to block them. 'There's an unstable wall around the corner and the demolition team are just about to bring it down, so if you could step inside for a moment.'

He indicated a door flanked on either side by photos of naked women with ribbon banners and stars covering strategic areas.

Daniel pushed open the door, which had the words 'BonBon Club' painted diagonally across it, and Mattie walked in.

'I've never been in a strip club before,' she giggled, her aching heart lightened a little by their ludicrous situation.

'It's not something I do unless under orders,' said Daniel as they emerged through the blackout curtain into the brash lights of the foyer.

There were half a dozen people like them, who'd clearly been directed into the club for shelter, plus a girl in a skin-tight stylised uniform with a neckline so low Mattie was surprised her breasts stayed within it. A bulldog of a man in a dinner suit with a shaved head and no neck stood to one side.

Everyone was milling about looking at the ceiling and floor, which was hardly surprising as the photos of naked women here were considerably larger than the ones on display outside; what's more, the girls in these photos had lost their banners and stars.

'Honestly,' Mattie said, turning to stare at her husband's chest. 'I don't know where to put my face.'

'Well,' said Daniel, looking over her head at something behind her. 'I think you should take a look at this.'

Mattie turned. Her eyes rested on the photo on the wall behind her and her mouth dropped open.

Billed as 'Salome from the Mysterious East', and stark naked except for a veil and some bangles, stood Mattie's sister-in-law Stella.

Grasping the edge of the bucket, Queenie tipped the contents into the chickens' pen and the four hens dashed out of their hutch.

It was just after dawn, but she'd been up since four. Firstly to fetch the bread for the family's breakfast and then to gather worms from the park for the hens. She'd returned just as Ida got back from the shelter at six thirty so she could care for Patrick until Ida got back from the yard before lunch.

Having Ida in the yard each morning had certainly helped Brogan & Sons removal and delivery business grow. She was not only there to take requests from people moving house or needing goods delivered, she was also able to sell the furniture. Things had picked up to such an extent that there was talk of taking on a strong lad to help, and Jerimiah was waiting to hear back from the Post Office about the telephone he'd applied for.

'There you are, girls,' said Queenie, setting down the pail and watching the birds pecking at the wriggling creatures on the flagstones.

The hens were a gift from the saints, so they were. It had taken them a few days to sort themselves out but then they'd started laying, and now Queenie had taken over their care, she collected at least three eggs each day and sometimes four.

The back door opened and Billy stepped out with Michael just a step behind him. Both were dressed in their school uniform, navy in Billy's case and green in Michael's, with their satchels strapped to their backs and doorstops of bread and marge in their hands.

'We're off, Gran,' shouted Billy through a mouthful of crumbs.

'Have you got your lunches?' Queenie asked.

'Yes, Mrs Brogan,' Michael replied. 'And our homework.'

A warm glow started in Queenie's chest.

It had only been a few days since Ida had come home from the shelter with Michael in tow but it already felt as if he'd been there for ever and the sight of him filled a slightly bigger place in her heart each time she saw him.

'Is Patrick still asleep?' Queenie asked.

'I think so,' Billy replied.

'Be off with you then, you pair of cheeky-faced rascals,' said Queenie, waving them away.

They waved back and then, grinning and jostling each other, they raced across the yard to the back gate. Michael reached it first.

'I'd thank you to leave it on its hinges,' Queenie shouted as the boy tore it open.

'Oh, Gran, Prince Albert escaped when I gave him his cuttlefish and he's in the kitchen,' Billy called over his shoulder as he disappeared after his friend.

The gate crashed shut and they were gone.

With her lips pressed together and hoping she wouldn't have to explain to Ida about how there was bird shite all over her cooker again, Queenie marched to the back door but as she opened it, a flurry of grey flapped over her head.

261

Swooping across the space, the parrot landed on the edge of the chickens' run and he puffed up his feathers. The hens stopped scratching in the dirt and, throwing back their heads, started dancing about.

'You have the right of it there, girls, so you do,' said Queenie, watching the hens strutting about. 'Although, more often than not, they're more trouble than their daily meat, a fella does have his uses from time to time.'

The back gate opened again.

Turning around, Queenie saw Mattie, looking like she'd not slept for a week, pushing her Silver Cross pram into the yard.

Mattie forced a smile. 'Morning, Gran.'

'And to you, me darling,' Queenie replied. 'You're early this morning.'

'I know,' Mattie replied, unbuckling Alicia from her straps and lifting her from the pram. 'Is Mum in?'

'Not yet,' Queenie replied.

Tears sprang into Mattie's eyes. 'Daniel's been ordered back to France.' And she started to cry.

Queenie crossed the space between them and put her arms around her. Alicia, caught between them, started to wriggle in protest so Queenie took the little girl from her mother and settled her on her hip then she tucked her hand in the crook of Mattie's arm.

'Your ma will be home soon so let's go indoors and I'll put the kettle on.'

Twenty minutes and a cup of sugary tea later, Mattie finally finished telling Queenie how Daniel had broken the news of being sent back undercover to France. Alicia and Patrick, who'd woken up just as they walked through with the tea, played with a couple of wooden spoons.

'I know he hasn't any choice,' Mattie concluded, 'and I couldn't be prouder of him, but my heart's fair breaking at the thought of him in such danger. Especially as . . .' She looked away and blew her nose.

'As you're having another baby,' said Queenie softly.

Mattie gave her a sad little smile. 'How long have you known?'

'When you and Daniel had tea with us a few weeks back and you went green at the sight of the pilchard sandwiches,' Queenie replied. 'I take it you didn't tell him?'

Mattie shook her head. 'He'll have enough to worry about without me adding to it.'

Queenie didn't say otherwise.

Draining the last of her tea, Mattie put her cup down on the floor and Queenie's gaze flickered on to it.

'And you don't need to read my tea leaves,' said Mattie, guessing her thoughts, 'because I know Daniel will be coming back to me and Alicia.'

'And his little lad,' said Queenie, faintly sensing her still forming great-grandchild.

Mattie gave her a long-suffering look. 'Gran . . . really.'

'Just calling it as the sight shows me,' said Queenie.

Her granddaughter rolled her eyes.

The door opened and Ida, still in her coat and unwrapping her scarf, came in.

'Mattie, I saw it was your pram.' She saw her daughter's tear-stained face. 'Sweetheart, what's happened?'

Mattie had just finished retelling her story again by the time Queenie came back in with the next round of tea. She was now sitting in her father's chair on one side of the fire with Alicia on her lap and Ida sat on the opposite side with Patrick on hers.

'Well, orders is orders,' said Ida, taking the cup Queenie offered her and placing it on the top of the mantelshelf, out of Patrick's reach. 'And it was very thoughtful of him to make sure you both had a night to remember while you're apart.'

'It was lovely night,' said Mattie. 'But Mum, Daniel's posting wasn't the only thing I discovered.'

Closing the door behind her, Stella Brogan yawned and then stretched her eyes to wake herself up.

She had arrived home only twenty minutes ago, barely enough time to replenish her make-up and change out of her high heels and cocktail dress into something more suitable to walk along Commercial Road to Mafeking Terrace, three streets away.

Truthfully, she was so tired she reckoned she could have slept even if a hundred-pounder went off on the pillow beside her, but it was gone one o'clock now so she daren't leave Patrick with Ida much longer. The last thing she wanted was to have her mother-in-law poking her nose in as to why she was late. If she put Patrick in his cot and shut his door so she couldn't hear him, she should be able to get a couple of hours' shut-eye before Ida came to collect him.

She yawned again, and a smug smile spread across her lips. Missing a night's sleep had been worth it, though. Commander Julian Moncrief of His Majesty's Navy had been most generous, as the five green pound notes added to the cash box hidden under the pantry's floorboards testified.

When Ida had agreed to look after Patrick, Patrick had been just six months old and a grizzly little bugger who woke her most nights, so Stella had been more than happy to dump him on his doting grandmother while she worked in the ball bearing factory and had a laugh with the girls on the assembly line.

A full week's work at the factory comprised five twelve-hour shifts but she'd told Ida it was six, so she could have a night to enjoying herself up West. She'd gone with a couple of local friends at first but soon got in with a more sophisticated set and it was after a particularly wild night in some private club somewhere that she'd been offered the job in the BonBon Club. The owner, Tubbs Harris, had seen her potential and offered her seven quid a week on the spot. What with that, tips and the occasional payment to take a serviceman's mind off the war for an hour or two, she was accumulating a tidy sum.

She turned the corner of Mafeking Terrace and gazed down the too familiar street at the women on their knees scrubbing a white half-circle on the pavement outside their front door – a sign that the woman of the house was not only a diligent housewife but also respectable.

Stella's lips curled up in a sneer. Ha! Who wanted to be respectable when life was so much more fun when you weren't?

Ignoring the disapproving looks from the women kneeling on their front steps, Stella shook out her hair, raised her chin and wiggled down the pavement towards her mother-in-law's house.

Walking past the front door, she slipped down the side alley. Lifting the latch on the back gate, Stella walked through and into the paved yard behind the house. Of course, letting yourself into a house by the back door was so common but then what else did you expect from a rag-and-bone man's family?

Crossing to the door, Stella paused for a moment to stretch the sleep from her eyes – she was supposed to look as if she'd just woken up rather than exhausted after a night partying – and entered the house.

'Only me,' she called.

'We're in here,' her mother-in-law replied from the parlour.

Giving the kitchen with its rickety table and chairs and dresser full of mismatched crockery a contemptuous glance as she passed, Stella walked through to the family's main living area.

If the kitchen was ramshackle then the front room, with its collection of armchairs, dusty books and cheap ornaments from long-forgotten days at the seaside, was positively decrepit but what really brought Stella up short when she walked in was that both Ida and Queenie were in the room.

Both were sitting in their respective chairs, both had their arms folded across their bosoms and both were wearing a face like they'd been sucking the juice from lemons. Between them, playing with a pile of bricks on the hearth, was her son Patrick, who seeing her walk in, reached up for his grandmother.

Without taking her hard eyes from Stella, Ida picked him up and settled him on her knee.

Forcing a friendly expression on her face, Stella smiled at the two women.

'Sorry I'm a bit late,' she said, 'I didn't get in until three and forgot to set the alarm.'

Ida gave her a tight smile. 'Busy night?'

Stella nodded. 'The club was chock-a-block with service personnel and by the time I left I was totally exhausted.'

'I bet you were, Salome,' said Ida.

Stella's heart lurched.

'Who?' she said, trying to look puzzled.

'The BonBon Club off Charing Cross Road, isn't it?' her mother-in-law continued. 'Where you work?'

'Who told you?' asked Stella.

'Never mind who told us,' said Ida. 'Is it true?'

'Of course it's true,' Queenie replied. 'You only have to look at her face to see that.'

'All right,' said Stella, shaking her hair and giving both women a hateful look. 'I'm a dancer, what of it?'

'Dancer!' scoffed Queenie. 'That's a fecking posh word for a floozy who takes her clothes off in front of a load of men. Stripper is what everyone else calls it.' A sweet smile lifted her wrinkled face. 'Salome,' she said in a falsetto voice, wriggling her hands around Arab-style. 'Fresh from the Exotic East! Fresh from giving a sailor a tuppenny one up against a dock wall, more like.'

Stella glared at the old woman who matched her furious stare.

'How could you?' asked Ida, pressing her lips on to Patrick's dark curls. 'And what do you think Charlie will say when he finds out? God only knows why my boy didn't see through you from the start.'

'Because her tits stopped him seeing what she was really like,' said Queenie. 'Sure aren't all men fecking eejits when it comes to their cods?'

'Well, you certainly know that, don't you, Ida?' Stella replied. 'After all, everyone knows what Jerimiah's cods were thinking about with Ellen Gilbert!'

The colour drained from her mother-in-law's face but Stella's enjoyment of it was cut short as Queenie jumped up and stormed across the room. The old woman raised her gnarled hands and before she could stop herself, Stella took a step back.

'Oh, hear me, spirits,' Queenie warbled in that ridiculous quivery voice she used when she pretended to talk to the so-called other world. 'Hear my call—'

'I've had enough of this,' snapped Stella.

Snatching Patrick off Ida's lap, she grabbed his coat that was lying on the end of his pram.

'I don't give a shit what you think,' she said, bundling her son into his outer clothing. 'And I don't care what Charlie thinks neither. We could all be dead and gone this time next week, but in the meantime, I'm not going to sit around worrying about it. I'm going to have some fun and enjoy myself, whether you like it or not, and if you want to collect Patrick and take him to the shelter, you can but if not I'll find someone else—'

'No, I'll take him,' Ida cut in.

'Well then, I'll have him ready as usual,' said Stella, plonking her son in the pram.

She looked at Queenie. 'And as for you, you mad old woman, they ought to lock you in the barmy farm and throw away the key.'

Grabbing the handle, she kicked off the brake and then pushed the pram back through into the kitchen.

'Curse you, Stella Miggles,' Queenie screamed after her. 'Curse you and may the furies crush your wicked—'

Stella slammed the door and headed across the flagstones towards the gate but as she opened it, a gust of wind whirled past her and a shiver ran up her spine.

Queenie's words started to return to Stella's mind, but she cut them short. *Load of old claptrap*, she thought. Pushing her son's pram out of the yard and down the side alley, she walked home.

Chapter Sixteen

THE LOW HUM of the people sitting beside their loved ones and talking softly drifted down Charrington Ward and roused Ellen back to consciousness. Realising the pain had lessened, and she was not in heaven yet, she breathed out slowly, relieved the shot the nurse had given her a little while ago had worked.

Each day it was more difficult to fight the pain, but she suffered it because it gave her one more precious day with Michael.

There was a faint scraping sound beside her and Ellen raised her eyelids a fraction to see Ida, dressed in her WVS long coat and felt hat, sitting by the side of her bed. She had the latest copy of *Woman's Weekly* open at the Christmas recipe page on her lap, but she wasn't reading it. Instead her chin rested on her chest and her eyes were closed. Ellen wasn't surprised.

The air raid siren had gone off at six the night before and the whole area had been bombarded until the sun crested the horizon. Like those sheltering in the reinforced hospital basement, Ellen doubted Ida had had more than a few hours of snatched sleep before heading off to work.

Ellen opened her eyes fully and her gaze ran slowly over her old friend. A wry smile lifted her lips. Friend! Ida would hardly call her that now. And she was sorry for it, truly she was. She almost wished Jerimiah had married someone else then she would not have had to deceive her dearest friend, but he hadn't, he had married Ida.

Even now, with death hovering on her shoulder, Ellen didn't regret what she'd done. How could she when Jerimiah had released all of her pent-up need for him that night and given her Michael? His son.

Something clanged further down the ward. Ida jumped and opened her eyes.

'You're awake,' she said, pulling herself up straight. 'Did it work?'

Ellen looked puzzled.

'The jab the nurse said she gave you just before the visitors' bell rang,' Ida explained. 'She said you'd been in a lot of pain.'

'Oh, yes,' said Ellen. She glanced at the magazine. 'Planning the Christmas dinner?'

Ida rolled her eyes. 'I would if I knew what I'll be getting from the butcher. All he could get me last year was an ox heart.'

'I suppose you've asked him for a turkey.'

'Yes, me and everyone else,' Ida replied.

There was a pause and then Ellen spoke again. 'How was Michael this morning?'

'Fine,' said Ida. 'He and Billy have formed their own gang in the shelter and he's learned all his spellings for the test this morning, but I'm sure he'll tell you all about it when he comes in later. I've put his name down with Billy's for next week's children's party in the shelter. Dr Robertson from Greenbank surgery is going to be Father Christmas.'

A lump formed in Ellen's throat but she swallowed it down.

'Michael will love that,' she said, forcing a smile.

'And I've told Father Mahon you'd like him to visit,' said Ida.

Someone further down the ward called out for a nurse and Ida turned to see the cause of the commotion.

Ellen's gaze ran over her old friend's profile and a pang of sadness pressed down on her.

'Thank you, Ida,' said Ellen.

Ida shrugged. 'I'm sure the good father's happy to come.'

'No, I mean for taking Michael in,' said Ellen.

'Well, I couldn't leave him to fend for himself, could I?' said Ida.

'Some would,' said Ellen. 'Especially—'

'Well, not me,' Ida cut in. 'Besides, he's been no trouble.'

A nurse hurried past them down the middle of the ward. Ida's gaze followed her for a moment then she looked back at Ellen.

'You've done a good job raising him,' she said, looking straight at Ellen.

'Thanks, Ida.'

'It couldn't have been easy by yourself,' her old friend continued.

Ellen smiled. 'Is it ever easy raising children?'

Ida laughed softly. 'You're right about that but credit where credit's due: Michael's a good lad.'

'Thank you,' Ellen repeated. 'But it must be a difficult situation having him at home with you and Jer—'

'As I said, he's been no trouble,' Ida cut in, her eyes bright as they fixed on Ellen.

An image of Michael in his school uniform waving her goodbye loomed into Ellen's mind. It lingered there a moment before an image of him in the same uniform weeping at a graveside replaced it.

Tears sprang into her eyes.

'It's not fair,' she sobbed, as the tears flowed unchecked

271

down her cheeks. 'Why did I have to be the one who got this bloody cancer? Why is God punishing me?'

Ida didn't reply.

'I've only got Michael and I was happy with that, watching him take his first steps, tucking him in bed at night. I thought I'd see him grow into a man,' Ellen continued. 'See him meet a nice girl some day and get married. But I won't. All I'll be to his children is a woman in a fading photo because—'

Images of what she would never see, never do and never have overwhelmed Ellen and stopped her words. With grief enveloping her, she closed her eyes. Feeling numb, empty and alone, a minute or perhaps ten passed and Ellen's heart filled with sorrow she couldn't tell.

'Mrs Gilbert,' a man's voice broke into her thoughts.

'Yes,' whispered Ellen, without opening her eyes.

'I'm Dr Rutherford,' he continued. 'If you recall, I spoke to you yesterday.'

She nodded.

'Good,' he said. 'As I mentioned then, because of the shortage of beds, we are evacuating our long-stay patients, so we've arranged for you to be moved to Brentwood.'

Ellen's eyes flew open.

'Brentwood!' she gasped, staring at the young doctor standing at the foot of her bed. 'But that's miles away. My son!'

'I'm sorry,' the doctor replied. He gave her a cheery smile. 'Just until you get back on your feet.'

'But . . . but I need to be with my son,' Ellen said. 'Can't I go home?'

He pulled a face. 'You could if you had someone to care for you but at the moment, Mrs Gilbert, you're really much too frail—'

'It's all right, Doctor,' interrupted Ida. 'I'll take care of her.'

The air raid warden at the ARP post in Turner Street was just chalking up the time the blackout started that evening when Ida walked past, having left Ellen's bedside twenty minutes earlier. She was due on duty at the rest centre at three thirty and should have gone straight there but she had somewhere else to go first.

Waiting until a couple of army trucks packed with soldiers had rumbled past, Ida crossed the road and hurried down Anthony Street.

Greeting the odd acquaintance and ignoring snide whispers as she went, Ida continued on towards the railway arches. Within minutes she'd turned the corner of Chapman Street and was crossing the road in front of her husband's yard.

She paused and then, sending up a quick prayer he would be back from his afternoon rounds, grasped the handle of the small access door and turned it.

The door opened, and with her heart hammering in her chest, Ida went in.

Jerimiah was adjusting Samson's harness, but he looked around as she stepped through the door.

Pleasure lit his face and Ida's heart did a little double beat in response.

'Hello,' she said. 'I hoped you'd be back.'

'Well, back I am, and have you heard the news about the American fleet?' he asked, leaving his task and strolling towards her.

'Yes, it was on the midday news,' said Ida. 'And it's splashed all over the late papers.'

'And mark my words. We'll be at war with the Japs too by the end of the day and then the Yanks will declare war on Germany and Italy, joining us in the fight.'

'Well, about bloody time,' said Ida.

Jerimiah smiled. 'I'm sure Churchill said the same thing, especially as it won't just be spam and powdered egg they'll be sending us from now on but men and machines.'

'I just keep thinking of those poor lads, though, on the ships,' said Ida. 'Because whenever I hear of casualties, I always think of our Charlie.'

'I know,' he said, giving her a soft look. 'So do I.'

Still,' said Ida, with a sigh, 'at least we don't have to worry about standing alone any more.'

'Perhaps not,' he replied. 'But we have to worry about Burma and Singapore because I bet you a pound to a penny that old Tojo has got his beady eyes on our Far East territory.' He tilted his head. 'Now, pleased though I am to see you, shouldn't you be at the rest centre this afternoon?'

'I'm on my way there now,' she said. 'But I had to come and tell you first.'

'Tell me what?'

'I've just come from the hospital and . . .' She told him what the doctor had said, and what she had offered.

'Are you sure?' he asked, looking down at her incredulously.

She wasn't but . . . Forcing herself to keep her eyes on her husband's face, Ida nodded.

'I'm sorry,' she hurried on. 'And I know I should have asked you first but . . .'

'When?'

'Early next week,' Ida replied. 'Jo can move in with Mattie.

With Daniel going soon it will help her cope and it won't be
. . .' She forced a smile. 'When all's said and done, Jerimiah,
I can't stand by and let Michael be separated from his dying
mother.'

Jerimiah raked his fingers through his hair. 'If you're
sure?'

'I am,' said Ida, as firmly as she could.

A tender look crept into his dark eyes and he smiled. Ida's
heart started to melt and she was tempted to return it but
instead, taking a deep breath, she spoke again.

'Before we bring Ellen home from hospital there's
something else you have to do.'

Although it was only just three o'clock in the afternoon, the
pale December light was already failing when the Greencoat
school bell rang.

Jerimiah, who had been parked up opposite the main
entrance on Dalgleish Street for about ten minutes, fixed
his eyes on the wrought-iron gate as the first few pupils
streamed through them.

After a minute or two of watching gangs of boys and girls
heading home, he spotted Michael in the middle of a small
group of lads making their way towards him.

Taking his feet down from the running board, Jerimiah
jumped off the wagon and gave a loud, two-tone whistle.

Michael looked across and after saying something to
his companions he hurried over. 'Dad,' he said, looking the
image of Charlie at the same age. 'What are you doing here?'

'Waiting for you,' said Jerimiah. 'Your mum asked me to
fetch you.'

Fear flashed across the boy's face. 'Is she all right?'

'Yes, she is,' Jerimiah replied. 'In fact, Auntie Ida popped in to see her this afternoon and she had a long chat with your mum about how well you're doing at school but also . . . also about your mum coming home from hospital.'

'Is she coming out soon?'

'Next week,' said Jerimiah.

Michael's face lit up. 'She's going to be out for Christmas?'

'She is,' said Jerimiah. 'But I tell you what, instead of standing here, as Auntie Ida is doing her bit at the rest centre and you don't have to be at the shelter until six, why don't we take a ride on the wagon and have a little chat? I'll even let you drive the horse?'

Michael's eyes stretched wide. 'Can I?'

'Of course,' said Jerimiah. 'Climb up.'

Putting his foot on the wheel hub and grabbing the rails, the lad scrambled up on to the front seat. Jerimiah bounded up after him and sat beside him on the plank of wood.

Sensing the shifting weight behind him, Samson pricked up his ears and shook his head.

Jerimiah unwound the reins and handed them to the lad. 'Shake them so they touch his rump,' he said, pulling the brake lever back. 'He'll know what to do.'

The horse took up the strain and the wagon rolled forward over the cobbles, towards the Seamen's Mission and Commercial Road at the bottom of the street.

As they navigated their way between the dock lorries and carts, Michael told him about how he'd scored twenty out of twenty in the test to identify enemy aircraft and then gave a blow-by-blow account of how he had bested one of the bullies in a playground fight. However, as they passed under the railway bridge into the relative quiet of Maize Row, Jerimiah took his courage in his hands and shifted the conversation to what he really had to tell the lad.

'About your mum . . .' said Jerimiah.

Michael looked up.

'Because she's still not well, when she comes home from hospital, she won't be going back to the rooms in Juniper Street but coming to our house instead,' said Jerimiah, reaching out and pulling the right-hand rein to avoid the wheels rolling into a hole.

'Does that mean we'll be spending Christmas with your family?' said Michael.

'Yes, it does, and don't worry,' Jerimiah ruffled the boy's hair, 'we'll make sure Father Christmas knows where you are.'

Michael grinned.

'In fact,' continued Jerimiah, 'Auntie Ida wants you and your mum to stay with us from now on so she can help you look after her.'

'Will me and Billy still share a room?' asked Michael.

'For now,' Jerimiah replied. 'And you'll still get to go to the Tilbury Shelter as you've been doing and you'll be able to see your mum every morning when you get back. You could help Gran with the chickens, too. Would you like that?'

Michael nodded and forced a smile. 'Yes.' He offered Jerimiah the reins. 'Could you drive?'

Jerimiah took them back and Michael stared at the horse's rump as they ambled along the narrow path by the waterway, which was littered with fallen masonry and twisted shrapnel from the German planes' nightly visits.

Leaving the lad to his thoughts, Jerimiah guided Samson between the debris and they plodded on. The pungent mixture of salt and sewage wafted into Jerimiah's nose as they emerged from the dankness of the Minories and Blackwell Railway arch and the Regent Canal lock gates came into view.

They reached the first of the three locks and Samson, sensing his stable was only half an hour away, picked up his speed. The evening fog was now swirling up from the river as the pale winter sun sank behind the warehouses that lined Shadwell Basin. The wagon rolled into Narrow Street and Michael spoke again.

'Mum's not going to get better, is she, Dad?' he said softly, looking up at Jerimiah.

'No, she's not, son,' Jerimiah replied, pulling the horse to a halt and letting the brake lever go.

As the wagon creaked beneath them, Michael's dark eyes, a reflection of his own, held Jerimiah's for a heartbeat before the lad threw himself into his arms. Jerimiah hugged him tight as his heartbroken son sobbed against his chest.

'That's why your mum came back to Stepney,' said Jerimiah, smoothing Michael's springy black curls. 'So me and Auntie Ida could look after you and so you could get to know your brothers and sisters and be part of the fam—'

A screech cut through Jerimiah's words and set his ears vibrating as a squadron of Stukas hurtled earthwards from the clouds. A bomb crashed to the ground somewhere close to Horseferry Road on the other side of the cut, sending flame and debris shooting high into the air. Another plane, flying so low it looked as if it would hit the water, screamed towards them.

Hugging Michael tightly and shielding the boy with his body, Jerimiah flung himself from the cart and landed on the cobbles as a shell whizzed past, leaving a smell of sulphur behind it. Blinding light and fire exploded around them. Samson screamed and reared in his shafts and something bit into Jerimiah's leg. There was an ear-splitting crash as a pulse of air sucked the breath from him. Samson shrieked again, then with sparks flying from his wildly thrashing hooves, he sank to the floor in a tangle of legs, tail and mane as something hot and sticky splashed Jerimiah.

'Dad!' A muffled voice broke through the clanging noise in Jerimiah's head.

He tried to raise himself up, but a pain shot up his leg. Tasting bile at the back of his throat, blackness engulfed him.

'You look like you've got in a bit of a tangle there, sweetheart,' said Ida, pausing the trolley filled with dirty mugs. 'Would you like me to give you a hand?'

The little girl, a pretty thing of about eight or nine, was sitting at the end of the camp bed. She looked up from her knitting.

'Yes please,' she replied, offering Ida her tangled wool.

Ida was in the main hall of the Catholic Club and had just finished doing a round of tea. Although it wasn't much past four in the afternoon, the women and children who'd arrived at the rest centre that morning after last night's bombing were already bedding themselves down for the night. She didn't blame them because with a third-quarter moon and a clear frosty sky, it was only a matter of time before the Germans arrived.

She'd asked Cathy to collect Billy and Patrick and meet her in the Tilbury at six. By which time, Jerimiah would have told Michael, bless his poor little heart, everything about his mother's condition, and brought him to the shelter to join them.

Some would think them unfeeling to tell the poor lad, but the truth of it was Ellen had only a few weeks, perhaps less, on this earth so better he be prepared than wake up one morning and find her gone.

Tucking her skirts under her, Ida sat down next to the child. 'You're Ivy Roberts' oldest girl, Wendy, aren't you?'

The little girl nodded.

'What are you making?' asked Ida, taking the needles with grey wool hanging from them.

'A scarf for me dad,' Wendy replied. 'He's in the navy. I wanted to make him socks but Mum said to start with something simple first. Mum's upstairs with my sister seeing if the women from the council can find us somewhere.'

'When were you bombed out?' said Ida, holding the needles towards the light to see better.

'Two nights ago,' Wendy replied. 'The whole street was flattened and the rescue men had to dig us out of our shelter in the garden. Tina wouldn't stop screaming so me and Mummy had to keeping singing nursery rhymes to stop her.' The little girl's shoulders sagged, and her lower lip started to tremble. 'I wish Dad had been there.'

'Last year two of my daughters were trapped after a bombing raid,' said Ida, holding the wool taut while she picked up a dropped stitch.

The little girl looked up. 'Were they?'

'Yes, and they said they were really scared.' Reaching across, Ida smoothed a stray lock from the child's forehead. 'I'm sure your dad will be very proud of you when he realises how brave you were and how you helped your sister not be afraid.'

Wendy gave her an achingly plucky little smile and Ida smiled back.

'You'd dropped a couple of stitches a few rows back and knitted where you should have purled but I've got it all back as it should be,' she said, finishing off the purl row.

'Thank you, Mrs . . .' said Wendy as Ida returned her needles.

'You can call me Auntie Ida.' She stood up. 'And I ought to get these cups washed ready for our cocoa later.'

Taking hold of the trolley handle again, Ida pushed it back towards the kitchen area, but she'd only gone a few yards when someone called her name.

She looked up and saw Flo Tatler standing on the bottom step scanning the room.

'Over here,' shouted Ida, waving across the heads of people sitting on the camp beds.

Looking relieved, Flo hurried over.

'Thank goodness; I thought I'd missed you,' she said, her hand on her substantial bosom as she caught her breath. 'The ARP information officer at Shadwell has just sent a runner across with the news.'

'What news?' asked Ida.

'Your husband's been shot. He's been taken to the London.'

With her mind showing her images of Jerimiah's body riddled with a dozen bullet holes, lying dead on a marble slab, Ida couldn't remember running up Sutton Street or dashing across Commercial Road. She only just registered an air raid siren going off as she tore up Jamaica Street towards the old hospital on Mile End Road, but when she burst through the door and into the casualty area, her senses screamed back to life as the noise of women crying and children screaming hit her like a blast of hot air.

What had once been the waiting area had long been turned into a field hospital. Trolleys with people swathed in bandages or clutching damaged limbs had replaced the rows of chairs and now, in the wake of an air raid, there were people on the floor too.

The nurses and doctors, in their white helmets with a red cross painted on the front, moved between the injured. Sadly, the trolleys with screens closed around them showed that the doctors hadn't been able to help everyone.

With the smell of surgical spirit clogging her nose, Ida's gaze scoured the faces but couldn't see the one she sought.

A young woman with pale hair and blue eyes, wearing a ward orderly's overall, went to hurry past, but Ida caught her arm.

'I'm looking for Jerimiah Brogan,' she said.

'Check the board,' the young woman said, nodding towards the blackboard propped up on a chair.

Her heart hammering in her chest, Ida skimmed down the long list of names and all but wept when she found Jerimiah's third from the bottom.

It had 'PR' next to it. Ida looked around and spotted a door at the far end with the words 'Plaster Room' painted on it; she made her way over.

A nurse rushed out and Ida caught the door before it closed and went in.

There were a dozen couches with people resting on them, but Ida's eyes and very soul fixed on Jerimiah: he lay at the far end of the room, his eyes closed and covered in blood.

With her knees threatening to buckle beneath her, Ida made her way over. As she came within a few feet of him, Jerimiah opened his eyes.

'It's all right, me darling,' he said, getting up on his elbows.

Her gaze ran over him and she spread her hands. 'But . . .'

'The blood's Samson's,' he said, looking bleakly at her. 'A lump of shrapnel from the bomb passed right through him; killed him stone dead, which I count as a blessing.'

He looked away but not before Ida saw tears shining in his eyes.

'I'm sorry,' she said. 'I know you were very fond of him.'

'He was a good horse,' Jerimiah replied, still studying the wall, 'with years left in him.'

He swallowed and then turned back.

'Two blessings, if the truth be told,' he continued, 'because if the shrapnel hadn't hit Samson first it would have taken my right leg clean away rather than giving me a puncture wound that will ache like billy-o but will heal.'

Ida's gaze shifted from her husband's blood-covered face to his leg to see it swathed in a thick bandage.

'Why didn't you take cover when the Moaning Minnie went off?' she asked.

'Because it didn't,' Jerimiah replied. 'My guess is the Jerries kept themselves behind the clouds until they reached Barking Creek and then came at us. The metal went straight through the muscle, but the doc says I'll be as right as rain in a week or so, which is more than can be said of me poor Samson.'

A feeling like cold water washed over Ida as horror gripped her.

'Where's Michael?' she gasped, looking frantically around at the other patients.

Michael answered for himself.

'Auntie Ida,' he shouted, bursting through the door she'd just walked through.

Letting go of the matronly WVS woman's hand, the boy dashed over and hugged her.

She'd have to sponge that blazer and get the shirt in to soak before they left for the shelter but other than that, considering what he'd been through, Michael looked quite cheerful.

'There you are, Mr Brogan.' The WVS woman handed Jerimiah a cup and saucer then smiled at Ida. 'Your son wanted to get his dad a cup of tea and the nurses let him wash his hands and face in their sluice. I'm sorry I couldn't do anything with his uniform but—'

'That's fine,' Ida cut in, resting her hand lightly on the boy's shoulder. 'I'll give it a good soak when I get home.'

The WVS woman smiled and ran her gaze over Ida's green uniform. 'Well, you know how it is, Mrs Brogan, so if you'd excuse me.'

Ida gave her a wan smile and her hospital colleague left.

Ida turned her attention to the boy beside her.

'Are you all right, Michael?' she asked, looking him over.

He nodded. 'My knee's a bit sore from where I landed but nothing else, but . . .' Tears welled up in his eyes. 'They got Samson.' He sniffed and wiped his nose with the back of his hand. 'I hate them.'

Reaching out, Ida put her arm around the boy's slender shoulder. 'He didn't suffer and he's in heaven now.'

'I know,' Michael replied. 'But I still hate the Germans.' He sniffed again. Pulling her handkerchief from her pocket, Ida handed it to him and he blew his nose.

'It was a Stuker,' Michael said. 'Came soaring down just like this.' He swooped down with his hand. 'And Dad grabbed me and . . .'

For once, hearing the word 'Dad' on Michael's lips didn't twist Ida's guts.

In fact, the moment she'd heard Jeremiah say, 'It's all right, me darling' in that soft Irish lilt of his, her mind cleared of all emotions except one: love. Love for the man she'd given her heart to the moment she'd set eyes on him. That love had been sorely tested these last weeks but it had not been broken.

And it was a special once-in-a-lifetime love that had brought her and Jerimiah through good times and bad, the worst being the loss of their sweet darling James, but would it hold firm when Ellen was under their own roof?

Chapter Seventeen

JO HAD JUST closed the drawer that now contained her underwear when her sister Mattie walked into the bedroom carrying two cups of tea.

'I've put Alicia down for a nap so I thought I'd come and give you a hand,' she said.

'Thanks, Mattie,' Jo replied. 'I've just about finished but I'm dying for a cuppa.'

It was the second Thursday in December and Jo had finished work at midday. However, instead of catching up on some sleep at home, she had made herself a quick sandwich, which she'd eaten while packing her clothes and other bits and pieces. Then, with a suitcase in each hand, she'd walked the half-mile to her sister's house at the back of St Dunstan's Church.

Taking the cup from her sister, Jo sat on the bed.

'You know, I thought you were coming just after lunch,' said Mattie, sitting beside her.

'Yes, sorry,' Jo replied. 'I was intending to but Tommy phoned the ambulance station last night and asked me to move his lorry.'

'His lorry?' said Mattie. 'I didn't know he had one.'

'Well, it's his brother's really,' said Jo. 'But he won't need it where he is so Tommy's got it. The Civil Defence at the Town Hall had been using it but they don't need it now, so he asked me to take it to his mate's garage at Bow Common to store it until he gets back at Christmas in two weeks two days' time.'

Mattie laughed. 'Missing him, are you?'

'More than I can say.' Jo sighed.

'Young love,' said Mattie. She took a sip of her tea. 'I hope you'll be comfortable in here.'

'I'm sure I will,' Jo replied, looking around.

Although this was the smallest bedroom, her sister's spare room was at least as large as her room at home. It was furnished with a double bed, a wardrobe and a dressing table, but there was still plenty of space for Jo to move around. The small two-bar electric fire glowing in the old cast-iron grate was also very welcome as the weather had recently turned decidedly wintry.

'And I won't have to put up with Billy's constant back chat,' Jo added. 'He's turning into a right terror.'

'Well, he's had a lot to cope with, what with finding out where he really came from and having Michael move in,' said Mattie.

'I suppose so,' Jo said, as her sister sat beside her. 'I still think it's a blooming cheek to have her come home to us, though, don't you?'

'A bit,' Mattie agreed. 'But where else could Mum and Dad put her?'

'But why do they have to put Ellen Gilbert anywhere?' Jo said, blowing across the top of her cup. 'After what she's done to poor Mum... If it had been me, I'd have left her in hospital. It's bad enough having Michael living there without having Dad's floozy moving in too.'

'You make it sound like Dad's been carrying on with Ellen for years,' said Mattie.

'How do we know he hasn't?'

'Jo!' Mattie gave her a big-sister don't-be-silly look.

'All right.' Jo sighed. 'I know he hasn't but I still don't

see why Mum agreed to look after her.'

'For Michael's sake,' said Mattie. 'Poor little lad.'

'And that's another thing,' said Jo. 'I don't know how Mum can agree to take him on after Ellen goes.'

'She's doing it for Dad, I suppose,' said Mattie. 'And when have you ever known her not help a child?'

'Mum's too soft-hearted,' said Jo. 'Especially after what Dad's done. I can barely speak to him, I'm so angry.'

Her sister raised an eyebrow. 'Are you sure that's not because he hasn't given you an answer about bringing the wedding forward yet?'

Jo took a sip of tea. 'Perhaps.'

'Well, at least he's still here,' said Mattie, giving her a pointed look.

Jo's anger vanished in an instant as she imagined her father lying white and cold in his coffin.

'Yes, he is, thank God.' Jo crossed herself and her sister did the same.

'I'm sad about old Samson, though,' said Mattie. 'What's Dad going to do without him?'

'He says he'll use the hand cart for local deliveries and he's hoping to hire one of the Truman Brewery horses for a few days next week so he can move the people he's already got booked in but he's still waiting to hear if there's one he can have,' said Jo.

Mattie took a mouthful of tea. 'Well, as Mum said: Dad's always provided for his family.'

The image of the coffin flashed through Jo's mind again. 'I suppose that's why she's offered to care for Michael and nurse Ellen,' she said. 'If you love someone then you have to forgive them because you couldn't live without them.'

'No,' whispered Mattie. 'You couldn't—'

Jo looked at her sister and saw tears in her eyes.

'Oh, Mattie,' she said, slipping her arm through her sister's, 'I'm sure Daniel will be back before you know it.'

Mattie placed her hand on her rounding stomach and gave Jo a brave little smile. 'Hopefully, before—'

'Did someone say my name?'

Jo looked around to see her brother-in-law, dressed casually in flannel slacks, open-necked shirt and cardigan, stroll through the door.

Mattie blinked away her tears and smiled at her husband.

'Yes, I was just saying to Jo that it will be nice to have someone to talk to about knitting and cooking instead of football and cricket,' she said.

Mattie and Daniel exchanged a loving look.

'Did Mattie tell you she's had another article accepted?' asked Daniel, shifting his gaze to Jo.

'No,' said Jo, looking admiringly at her sister.

'Yes, *Woman at Home* this time,' he continued. 'Something about chopping up men's clothes.'

Mattie gave her husband a make-believe exasperated look. 'It's about how to make a child's dress out of a man's shirt.'

'And she drew the diagrams herself,' her-brother-in-law concluded, looking at his wife with undisguised pride.

Jo looked even more impressed.

'As I said before, I might as well put my six years slaving over a sewing machine in Gold and Sons to good use,' said Mattie.

The phone downstairs rang.

'I'll get it,' said Daniel.

Mattie's eyes followed him as he left the room, then she turned back to Jo and gave a too-cheery smile.

'Well, that's another good thing about living here with me and Alicia,' said Mattie. 'You and Tommy can phone each other any time you like.'

Jo matched her sister's cheery expression. 'We certainly can.'

With her gaze on her sister's lovely face, Jo sent up a small prayer of thanks to the Virgin Mary and all the saints in heaven. Even if she and Tommy had to wait to get married, at least he was serving King and country in Buckinghamshire and not behind enemy lines in France.

Glancing around the quiet yard one last time, Jerimiah switched off the light. He opened the door cut into the left-hand gate and, ducking, stepped through into Chapman Street. Locking it behind him, he turned westwards and strolled towards the solidly built Victorian hall situated halfway down Gravel Lane. Pushing open one of the hall's half-glassed doors, he walked in.

As one of the few halls in the area with a sprung dance floor, it had been the place where bridal celebrations, wedding anniversaries and lively wakes had been held before the outbreak of hostilities. It was still a busy place full of people but now it hosted first-aid classes and an ARP post. It was also the headquarters of Jerimiah's Home Defence platoon, which is why he was stopping off there on his way back home.

At the far end of the hall, nurses from Munroe House ran a baby clinic on a Friday afternoon. They were just finishing off so their patients could get home safely before the light went and the Luftwaffe arrived.

In the opposite corner, a handful of ARP wardens were gathered around the blackboard where their shifts were chalked up, while in the serving hatch a couple of motherly WVS women were handing out tea and jam tarts to anyone in need of them.

With Christmas just under two weeks away the hall had a decidedly festive appearance, mainly due to the fact that someone had clearly sneaked off with an axe to Epping Forest as there was a six-foot Christmas tree in the far corner with homemade papier-mâché baubles dangling from its branches and a grubby-looking one-eyed fairy on the top.

Sidestepping out of the way of a toddler dragging a stuffed dog on a length of string behind him, Jerimiah headed for the small committee room next to the stage. He stopped in front of the door, knocked and on hearing the command to enter he turned the handle and went in.

Marching smartly past the oval committee table laden with maps and books, he came to a halt next to the man wearing full battle dress and a major's crown on his epaulettes.

Jerimiah did a quick stand-to and saluted.

Major Algernon Hitching-Wells looked up from his paperwork.

Like Jerimiah, the man in charge of the Wapping Home Guard had fought in the last war. However, while Jerimiah was wallowing in the mud at the bottom of a trench in the Somme, Captain Hitching-Wells, as he was then, was slumming it in a chateau outside Albert as a member of Field Command.

Perhaps it was just as well, as the major was well over six foot tall and would have been a gift to a German sniper. Although he was nearer to seventy than sixty,

Hitching-Wells still had sparse grey hair and an impressive moustache. The younger son of a middle-ranking aristocrat with no real prospects, he'd signed on as a wet-behind-the-ears lad of sixteen and had been fighting the foes of the Empire ever since. He'd fought Boer settlers across Natal and Swaziland, the tribal rebels in the Punjab and Bengal and, for a brief stint, the Boxers in Peking. He'd even been in one of the regiments involved in the Easter Rising in Dublin but as three-quarters of the men under his command in the Home Defence were of Irish descent he and they felt it better for morale if that wasn't mentioned.

'Stand easy,' said Wapping's commanding officer. He glanced at his watch. 'I didn't expect to see you, Brogan. I wasn't expecting you back on duty for another week.'

'I'm not reporting for duty, sir.' Jerimiah clasped his hands together behind him and stepped his feet apart. Before he could stop himself, he winced.

'Leg playing you up?' asked Hitching-Wells.

'Now and again,' Jerimiah replied.

'Well, I suppose it's to be expected; after all, it's less than a week since you copped it.'

'Indeed,' Jerimiah replied. 'But I'm hoping it will be as good as new in a week or two.'

'Good, good. I suppose you've come to tell me when you're coming back, then,' said Hitching-Wells, laying his fountain pen down on the table.

'No, I'm afraid not,' Jerimiah replied. 'I've come to tell you I'm resigning to—'

'Resigning!' spluttered Hitching-Wells, his plentiful moustache waggling back and forth rapidly. 'What sort of lily-livered, namby-pamby talk is this then, Brogan? Good

God, man, you've only been nicked by a bit of flying metal not lost a leg.'

'I know that, sir,' said Jerimiah, acutely aware of the throbbing in his thigh. 'I've been shot before – twice, in fact – and survived, but it's the National Service Act.'

'I don't see what that's got to bally-well do with anything,' snapped his commanding officer.

'Well, for one, I'm now counted in the numbers of those eligible to be called up for the services and as such I have to register like every other man under sixty, which I did three weeks back,' said Jerimiah. 'Most men of my age are sent off to serve in supply depots and in the transport division so as to release younger fighting men from non-combative duties and, although I'm more than happy to do my bit, I've got a family who rely on me so I can't take the chance of being posted miles away.'

'Well, just tell the pen-pushers at the conscription office you're a reserved occupation,' said Hitching-Wells.

Jerimiah raised an eyebrow. 'I can't see the mandarins at the Ministry of War accepting that being a second-hand furniture dealer and a one-man delivery service is a reserved occupation, can you, sir? Especially as the act scraps nearly all the categories for exemption.'

Leaning back, Hitching-Wells regarded him down his long nose and smiled. 'Well now, Brogan, I still have a couple of old army chums in Whitehall so—'

'Thank you, sir, very kind indeed,' cut in Jerimiah. 'But I've made up my mind to join the National Fire Service as an auxiliary.'

Hitching-Wells' moustache started waggling again. 'Have you, by Jove?'

'Yes, sir,' Jerimiah replied, keeping his eyes fixed on his commanding officer's flushed face and bulging eyes. 'In fact,

I've already sent in my application. I'll be glad to fulfil me duties over the next few weeks, as you've men away visiting family, but as soon as I've got a start date for the Fire Service I'll be handing in my corporal's stripes.'

Hitching-Wells glared while Jerimiah maintained his pleasant expression for a long moment.

'Very well,' said the major, looking down and picking up his pen again. 'Dismissed.'

Jerimiah did a quick salute at the bald patch on top of his commanding officer's head then, turning on his heels, he marched out of the room.

When he emerged from the hall and back into the street, he found that the light had all but gone so turning up his collar he headed for home. Even though the Fire Service's three pounds ten shillings a week covered only the rent and half of Ida's housekeeping, it would keep the wolf from the door until he'd figured out some other way to support his soon to be expanding family.

Holding the edges of chicken wire together, Ida threaded the two-inch length of thick fuse wire around the adjoining sections. She picked up Jerimiah's pliers and twisted the wire together. Satisfied it was firmly in place, she repeated the process until the two-foot-tall structure stood unaided in the middle of the kitchen table.

It was Monday afternoon, just after four, and the house was quiet. Jo had moved to Mattie's and Queenie was at the pensioners' matinee at the Troxy so Ida had the house to herself, which was just as well because, what with one thing and another, her nerves were stretched to breaking point.

Ellen was being sent home tomorrow and despite what she'd told Jerimiah and everyone else, she really wasn't sure about the whole thing. The other thing worrying her was Jerimiah. Well, not so much him, all six foot of himself, as much as her feelings towards him once Ellen was under their roof.

For weeks she'd raged and riled at him and many a day she'd felt that if she never set eyes on him again it would be a thousand days too soon. However, after nights of jolting awake with the image of Jerimiah lying on a hospital trolley, covered in blood, still in her mind, Ida decided she would have to suffer it somehow because a world without Jerimiah wasn't a world she wanted to live in.

Putting aside these fraught thoughts and emotions, Ida leaned back and admired her handiwork for a moment then picked up the spool of industrial fuse wire. She was just about to start snipping off another two-inch length when the door opened and Jerimiah stepped in, bringing a blast of cold air with him.

'Hello,' she said, laying down the cutting tool and wire. 'You look frozen. Would you like a cuppa?'

'I most certainly would, luv,' he said, unwinding his scarf and unbuttoning his coat.

'How's your leg?' she asked, watching as he limped to the table.

'Cold's got into it a bit but not bad otherwise,' he said, giving her a cheerful smile.

'Perhaps you shouldn't be pushing yourself so hard yet,' said Ida, moving to the stove and relighting the gas.

'I only did a couple of local deliveries,' he replied. 'Light ones, that's all. Enough to pay the rent.' His gaze ran over the wire structure standing in the middle of the table. 'I hope you don't mind me asking, Ida, but what on earth are you making?'

'A snowman,' she replied. 'To put the Christmas presents around instead of a tree. There was a thing on the news yesterday about wood being diverted to the war effort so there's no wrapping paper or books, so it stands to reason there won't be a Christmas tree in the market either. I thought I'd make a jolly snowman instead. I got the chicken wire and the fuse wires from the builders' merchant this morning and a couple of rolls of cotton wool in the chemist. I'll make the eyes and hat out of scraps and poke a couple of sticks through for arms. I've just got to squeeze it in for his shoulders and waist and then prop him up in the corner.'

Jerimiah looked impressed. 'What a grand idea.'

'I thought so and if I've got any cotton wool left, I'll stick it on the window frames like mock snow,' she said. 'With the newspaper chains strung across the room, and stars cut out of milk bottle tops pinned to the ceiling, it will be just as jolly as every other Christmas.'

'I'm sure it will be.'

'I've just got to hope Ray Harris comes good and finds me something to roast or we'll all be sitting down to spuds and cabbage on Christmas Day,' she said.

'And if we are, then I'm sure it will be the grandest spuds and cabbage anyone ever tasted,' he replied.

Ida raised an eyebrow. 'As I say: full of the blarney.'

Jerimiah smiled, and Ida smiled back.

They remained like that for a couple of heartbeats then the kettle started to whistle. Ida switched off the gas and went over to the kitchen dresser. Taking the tea caddy, she spooned tea into the pot but as she snapped the tin lid back in place, she stole a look at her husband, who was resting his head back with his eyes closed.

He always looked tired and cold after a day out on the wagon at this time of year but today he was frozen raw and was positively grey with weariness. And despite all his denials, by the way his was rubbing his leg, he was in pain, too.

'Perhaps you should ease up a bit, Jerry,' she said, pouring water on to the leaves. 'After all, it's only a week since the accident and you don't want to have the wound start bleeding again, do you?'

'Honestly, Ida, I'm fine—'

'If it's the rent you're worrying about, I could always go back to Naylor, Corbet and Kleinman's,' Ida continued. 'I've heard the woman who replaced me has signed on for factory work after Christmas—'

'No, Ida,' he cut in. 'You work hard enough running this house and feeding the family, on top of helping me with the business, without spending every morning scrubbing other people's floors, plus when Ellen arrives tomorrow you'll have all that on your plate too.' He studied her closely. 'Are you sure you want to do this?'

'Yes,' Ida said, hoping he couldn't hear the quiver of doubt in her voice. 'It wouldn't be fair on Michael if she weren't here with us.'

Jerimiah nodded. 'I won't lie to you, Ida,' he said with a sigh. 'It's going to be a bit tight until I can replace Samson but I've done something about that. I didn't want to say anything to you until I knew that it was going to work out, but last week I applied to the Auxiliary Fire Service and I got their reply this morning. I've been invited for a fitness assessment and interview next Monday.'

Ida frowned. 'I don't much like the idea of you dashing into a burning building,' she said, pouring out his mug of tea.

'"Tis no more than I do most nights helping the fellas in the heavy rescue,' he replied. 'Except I'll be wearing a fire-proof jacket and breathing equipment rather than a battle jacket with a neckerchief tied over my nose and mouth.'

'Well, I suppose that's something,' she conceded, trying not to imagine him running into an inferno as she stirred in the milk and two sugars. 'And if you're part of the Fire Service you're less likely to be called up into the army. I remember the last time, being at home with Charlie as a newborn and worrying myself witless not knowing if you were dead or alive in a trench somewhere.'

'On top of which,' continued Jerimiah, as she placed his drink in front of him, 'I'll get paid the standard ARP rate of three pounds ten shillings. It won't be as much as I've made recently by moving folks but if I can keep the second-hand furniture going until I can hire a horse from the brewery in the next week or so, I'll be able to pick up where I left off.'

'I've still got over a fiver in the pot from the money you gave me a few weeks back if that would help,' she said.

She went to pick up the pliers again but before she could, Jerimiah stretched across and placed his hand over hers.

'That's grand but that's yours for our family's Christmas.' He gave her that sideways smile of his that always set her heart dancing. 'And don't worry, sweetheart, we've been through worse and survived, haven't we?'

Ida smiled.

He was right. They had survived the trials and heartache of raising a family amidst grinding poverty; in fact, it had bound them together in a way an easy life would not have done. However, although Michael was a lovable lad, now Ida knew how he came into being, would those bonds of love between her and Jerimiah stretch wide enough?

Bending over the double bed, Ida smoothed the candlewick counterpane again despite having already done it three times and there being no crease in it.

She glanced at the alarm clock sitting on the bedside cabinet. Jo had forgotten the clock when she'd moved out, but she expected Mattie would have a spare.

Next to the clock stood two images: one of Michael as a baby, which Ida had first seen on Ellen's mantelshelf, and the other of him in his school uniform with Ellen standing proudly beside him.

It was just after two in the afternoon and a day since Jerimiah had come home and told her he was joining the Fire Service.

She'd returned home from the shelter that morning when the dawn blackout ended at seven. Due to the fog that had come up from the river, the Germans had ceased bombing at midnight-ish so she and the rest of those sheltering in the Tilbury had had a full six hours' sleep before the warden woke them. It was something she was heartily thankful for as she had a very busy day ahead.

After seeing the boys off to school, Ida had had her usual hour's forage around the market to see what was on offer. She had managed to get some flour, a quarter of suet and some raisins in Sainsbury's plus the family's Christmas tea ration at the Home and Colonial and a couple of oranges that had just come off the lorry in the market. With a bit of luck, with just over a week until Christmas Day, they might stay fresh enough for her to pop in the boys' Santa stockings.

She'd also got a decent bit of beef skirt at the butcher's for that night's tea, and she'd reminded him again that whatever joint he got for her for Christmas dinner, it needed to be large enough to feed eight adults and two growing lads.

She'd returned just as the eleven o'clock pips heralded the news and after eating a pilchard sandwich and bolting down two cups of tea, she'd set to work on the bedroom that Jo had vacated. She cleaned, polished and changed the sheets then turned down the blankets and slid the invalid slipper pan and old newspapers discreetly under the bed for when they were needed.

Glancing around the spotless room, Ida looked out of the window through the gaps in the brown paper pasted across the glass and noted that although at this time of day people were usually tucking into their midday meal, there were a great number of her neighbours smoking and chatting and loitering around their doors.

The back door slammed but Ida kept her eyes on the top of the street.

'Just meself,' Queenie shouted from below.

'I'm upstairs,' Ida called back.

'I take it they're not here yet, then?' her mother-in-law replied.

Ida opened her mouth to shout 'no' when an ambulance, rolling over the cobbles at the regulation five miles an hour to avoid damaging the tyres, turned the corner.

'Just arrived,' said Ida, her heart thumping in her chest.

Casting a final glance around the room, she went downstairs and met Queenie at the bottom.

'I've relit the kettle,' Queenie said.

'Ta,' Ida replied. 'I'll make a pot once I've settled her . . .'

A lump stopped her words so instead she opened the door just as the ambulance, that's to say a battered-looking Post Office van with a big red cross painted on the side, pulled up at the front door.

The neighbours, who had been trying to look busy polishing door knobs and sweeping front steps, ceased their tasks and turned their attention to the vehicle parked outside Ida's door.

'Number twenty-five?' asked the round-faced driver as he got out of the cab.

'Yes,' said Ida.

He nodded and went around the back of the ambulance.

Clasping her hands together and ignoring the audience on the other side of the road, Ida waited.

After what seemed like an eternity but was in truth a moment or two, the two ambulancemen reappeared carrying a stretcher, with Ellen lying on it. Her lips were tightly drawn and she opened her eyes briefly as she was lifted down but thankfully, not long enough to see the look of shock on Ida's face.

It had only been a few days since Ida had last seen her but from the putty-grey skin, hollow cheeks and sunken eyes, it was clear, even in the fading light, that the tumour eating away at Ellen was getting the upper hand.

Taking a deep breath, Ida stepped forwards.

'Mrs Gilbert is in the room at the top of the stairs on the right,' she said to the driver who was holding the front of the stretcher. 'Everything is prepared, if you'd like to take her up.'

'Ta, missis,' he replied. 'Her bag and stuff are on the front seat.'

With the stretcher bouncing as they walked, the two ambulancemen trudged past her and into the house. Opening the driver's door, Ida dragged the carpet bag out and followed them in.

Queenie, who was still standing in the hall, closed the door behind her. 'You go and do what needs doing upstairs, Ida, and I'll make the tea.'

Ten minutes later, having settled Ellen in the bed, the two ambulancemen left the room and thumped back downstairs.

'Well then,' said Ida, as the front door slammed below, 'I think that's the last few bits from the hospital packed away. Queenie is making a cuppa. I expect you're dying to see—'

Ida pressed her lips together. *Bugger!* 'Michael should be home from school soon,' she added quickly. 'I know he's really looking forward to seeing you.'

A hint of a smile lifted the corners of Ellen's bloodless lips. 'Me too,' she whispered.

'We don't leave for the shelter until half past five, so you'll have a good hour or more with him before we head off,' said Ida.

Ellen acknowledged her words but her eyes remained closed.

There was a long pause with just the ticking of the clock breaking the silence then they heard the sound of the back door slamming, followed by footsteps running upstairs.

The door burst open and Michael charged in. Ellen's eyes opened.

'Mum,' he shouted, dropping his satchel and throwing himself on her.

Pain shot across the dying woman's face, but she didn't cry out, instead her arms closed around her son and she pressed her lips to his dark curls.

'I'll go and see where that tea is,' Ida said, forcing her words over the lump that had formed in her throat.

Ellen's eyes fixed on her and tears shimmered in them. 'Thank you, Ida,' she croaked, as she clung to her son.

Feeling tears pinching the corners of her own eyes, Ida turned and left the room. In the dim glow of the landing light's 40-watt bulb, she grasped the banister above the stairwell. Resting her hand on the smooth wooden rail, Ida let her shoulders sag and her head fall forward. She stayed motionless for a long moment then, wiping her face with the heels of her hands, made her way downstairs.

She met Queenie carrying a tray at the bottom of the stairs. Ida forced a smile as the old woman passed her but as Queenie put her foot on the first step she turned and gave Ida a rare look of admiration.

'You've got a grand big heart, so you have, Ida Brogan,' she said. 'A grand big heart.'

Chapter Eighteen

'HELLO, ME LOVE,' said Mo Flint, as she spotted Queenie tucked against the glass partition between the public and snug bar in the Railway Arms. 'Me and Sam were just talking about you.'

'Kindly so, I hope,' said Queenie.

'Is there any other way for such an old friend of me mother's, God rest her soul?' Mo replied.

She crossed herself and Queenie did likewise.

It was an hour after two on Thursday afternoon and two days after Ellen had arrived. Queenie was in the public house situated on the corner of Library Passage, a stone's throw from St George's Town Hall.

Queenie and Mo's mother Doreen had come from the same village and were distantly related a few generations back, a fact they'd established when Mo's brother Brian ended up in the same class at school as Jerimiah.

Mo and her husband Sam had been the landlady and landlord of the Railway Arms for about ten years, while Brian had gone to America.

'What can I get you?' asked Mo.

'Do you need to ask?' said Queenie, giving her a pitying look.

The landlady laughed. 'A small one?'

'Would be grand,' Queenie replied.

Taking a half-pint tumbler from the rack above, Mo held it under the Guinness spout and pulled on the pump.

She and Queenie exchanged news of who'd died and who'd survived the previous week's bombings until there was a creamy head sitting on the top of the glass.

'Also,' said Mo, sliding it across the counter to her, 'I heard what your Ida's doing for that poor Gilbert woman. Pure saint she is, and everyone around here says so especially as . . . you know . . .'

Queenie picked up her glass. 'I have no argument with you on that score, Mo.'

'How is the little lad?' asked Mo.

'Bearing up, despite having a multitude of troubles on his shoulders at such a tender age,' Queenie replied.

'Well, God bless his little heart and Ida too,' said Mo. 'If it had been me, I would have ripped Sam's balls clean off.'

Queenie opened her purse but Mo raised her hand. 'On the house.'

Raising her drink in thanks, Queenie took a sip of the velvety brew. She spotted a quiet table in the corner and headed in that direction. She'd no sooner set her rear in the chair than the door opened and Paddy Leary slipped into the bar.

He too was an acquaintance from long ago but unlike Mo, who'd settled into a steady occupation, Paddy had plumped for a more precarious way of making a living. This ranged from digging roads and seasonal farm work to hooking up with travelling fairs during the summer months. He spoke to anyone, knew everyone and would sell you anything, which is why she'd sought him out.

He glanced around and acknowledged her with a nod of his head. After ordering and receiving a drink, he came over.

'How's me darling Queenie today?' he said, taking the seat opposite her.

'Well enough,' she replied. 'And all the better if you have news for me about my Christmas surprise.'

'That I have.' He shifted his chair closer. 'But you've no time to tarry. Red Colin said he'll hold them until Sunday but no longer as they're shifting north on Monday.'

Queenie's gnarled hand closed around his arm. 'You're a grand fella, Paddy, so you are.' Grasping her glass, she finished her drink in one and stood up. 'Now, if I'm to be there and back in a day, I'd better shift meself and be about me business. My regards to anyone you speak to who knows me and I'll see you around.'

Placing the glass back on the counter and giving Mo a quick wave, Queenie ambled out of the pub and into the cold crisp winter's afternoon.

'So that's a tanner each way on Neapolitan Lad in the one thirty at Cheltenham tomorrow,' said Queenie, her breath escaping in puffs of steam as she spoke.

'That's right,' said Jim Eccles, wearing his blood-stained butcher's apron and with a soggy roll-up dangling from his lips. 'And I 'ope as how I have better luck than I did last week with TomTom.'

Queenie wrote the bet in the dog-eared notebook then, sticking the pencil back behind her ear, she took his money and slipped it into her pocket.

He touched his forehead and then turned and walked away.

Queenie was standing in her usual place on Thursday afternoon in the narrow alleyway that ran behind the Angel and Trumpet and had been for the past half an hour. The old

Victorian pub was situated at the bottom of Durham Row, which ran alongside St Dunstan's graveyard.

Although it was a forty-five-minute walk from the Railway Arms, it was worth suffering her corns pinching as the public house was just round the corner from Stepney High Street shops and, with only a week until Christmas, everyone was out looking for bargains, and then for a way to pay for them. In addition to her usual punters, Queenie had had a number of women carrying on the local tradition of placing a bob or two on one of the Boxing Day meetings.

Queenie stamped her feet to get a bit of blood in them. She gave a small prayer of thanks that it wasn't raining and that she'd put on two pairs of socks that morning.

'Queenie Brogan?'

Queenie turned to find two young men she'd never seen before standing in the shadows behind her.

They were in their late twenties, above average height and clean shaven. Both were wearing civilian suits, gabardine macs, with the collars turned up, and their fedoras pulled down.

'Well now, that depends,' she replied.

'On what?'

'Who's asking and what you might want with her.' Queenie gave them the once-over. 'You're a bit old for your mother to dress you the same, aren't you?'

The man on the right, with black eyebrows and hair, glanced at his mate. 'We ain't twins.'

'Well, there's a thing,' said Queenie, giving them a mocking look.

Irritation flitted across the other man's ice-blue eyes for a second but then he gave her a friendly smile.

'These utility suits are all the blooming same,' he laughed, inviting her to join him.

She didn't.

'Perhaps a couple of handsome young men like yourselves should have stayed in your uniforms,' she said.

'We ain't in the army,' said the dark, low-browed individual.

'We're gas fitters: reserved occupation.' The blond's gaze flickered on to the book in her hand. 'And we're after a little flutter.'

'On a horse that is,' said the other, his voice booming between the closely spaced houses surrounding them.

Queenie glanced in both directions along the alleyway but, thankfully, could see no sign of PC White, the beat officer. Chalky was one of the old sort of coppers who didn't leave the station if it was wet, and he could smell a cup of tea brewing a mile off. That said, there was a new Superintendent at Arbour Square Police Station who'd been cracking down on folks making a bob or two by their wits so you couldn't be too careful.

'Keep your voices down,' she said in a low voice. 'Or are you after having every magistrate in London hear what you're about, you eejit.'

A flush burst across the dark-haired man's face and he looked as if he was about to reply but a glance from his chum silenced him.

'We heard you were the person to see for the best odds,' said the blond.

Queenie returned her attention to him. 'Now where would you hear such a thing?'

'From John.'

'Which John?'

'John Burton from the Red Lion,' he replied. 'We're staying in digs opposite. He said Queenie Brogan gave the best odds in the area, so we thought we'd search her out.'

'We were in there last night,' added his darker, and denser, companion.

'How's his wife?' asked Queenie. 'Have they sent her home yet?'

'I hope not,' said the sharper blond. 'The last I heard, she was in West Ham cemetery. Now do you want to take our money or not?'

Casting her eyes over them again, Queenie chewed her lips for a moment and then spoke again.

'What's taken your fancy then, lads?' she asked.

'Wayward Fellow,' said the fair-haired chap. 'Running in the twelve thirty tomorrow at Newmarket. Red Mick down the Waste is offering evens. What odds are you giving?'

Taking her pencil from behind her ear, Queenie opened her book. 'Six to four,' she said, skimming her eyes across the line of figures and symbols next to the horse's name.

'Is that your best?'

'It is.' Looking at them expectantly, she dabbed the end of her pencil on her tongue. 'So what do you want to place on it? A shilling? Or perhaps two? At those odds you might even consider half a crown both ways to cover your stake.'

The two men glanced at each other and the blond gave a curt nod.

'Queenie Brogan,' he said as his dark-haired friend grabbed her arm firmly with both hands, 'I am arresting you for—'

'Get your hands off me, you great lummox,' Queenie screamed, trying to snatch her arm back.

'In contravention of the—'

'Me heart,' said Queenie, clutching at her chest and coughing.

'Street Betting Act of 1906. You are not obliged to—'

'I'm going,' croaked Queenie, keeping half an eye on them as she swayed.

'Say anything,' the blond officer continued, giving her a cool look. 'But anything you do say—'

'Tell me dear son,' Queenie staggered back and braced herself against the church railings, 'and my darling grandchildren—'

'May be given in evidence,' concluded the fairer officer of the two.

'Yeah,' said the dark-haired officer. 'Who's the eejit now, you old cow?'

The two plain-clothed officers sniggered.

Queenie's toothless mouth pulled into a hard line and she straightened up. 'Evidence, is it?' she shouted, as she struggled against the officer holding her. 'I'll give you evidence to put in your little book. You fecking pair of gobshites tricked me. Led me astray, you did.' She raised her hand to the sky. 'The very saints in heaven must be weeping at the way you brace of savages have led a feeble old woman, who was doing no harm to no one, down a path of iniquity.'

She placed her hand dramatically over her face and her shoulders shook. She stood like that for a moment or two then peered through her fingers at the two officers. They were both regarding her impassively with an expression of boredom on their faces.

Queenie lowered her hand.

'Have you finished?' asked the fair police officer.

Queenie glared at him by way of an answer.

'Good,' he continued. 'Now are you going to walk to the station or should I call the hurry-up wagon?'

'With nothing on at all!' said Francesca, looking across the table at Mattie with disbelief in her large dark eyes.

'Not a stitch,' said Mattie, handing Alicia, who was sitting on her lap, half a biscuit. 'If I hadn't seen it with my own eyes, I wouldn't have believed it.'

It was just after three and she and Francesca were having their weekly get-together in the Dunstan Tearooms on Stepney High Street.

Although they'd met in Rose's Café in Watney Street for as long as Francesca could remember, Mattie had suggested they meet here for a change a couple of weeks ago.

The café was much like any other in the area, with a counter at the back and a dozen tables with flowery tablecloths dotted around. The eating house, like everywhere else, was doing its bit for the war, and the walls were covered with posters urging people not to waste food or encouraging women to come into the factories.

It was just around the corner from Mattie's house and she'd suggested the change in venue not only because of her condition but also because it was further from the area where her parents lived, which meant she didn't have to put up with people's sideways glances and overhear her parents' and Ellen Gilbert's names being whispered.

The Brogan family had always provided their neighbours with a sprinkling of juicy gossip over the years but her mum taking in not only Michael but also the woman who'd had a fling with her husband had had tongues wagging nineteen to the dozen.

They'd been there for a full half an hour already so had exchanged their day-to-day news – how Jo was settling into Mattie's and how Francesca's dad's café was faring and how difficult it was to find presents for everyone with hardly anything in the shops. Having got all the run-of-the-mill family news out of the way, Mattie had just told her friend about coming face to face with a poster of her stark-naked sister-in-law in a Soho strip club.

'How could she?' asked Francesca. 'How could she take her clothes off in front of a load of men on a stage?'

'It beggars belief, I know,' said Mattie. 'But there it was, for all to see.' Spreading her hand out, she waved her fingers across her from left to right. 'Salome from the Mysterious East; although it didn't say if that was East Ham or East Tilbury.'

Unhappiness replaced disbelief on her friend's face. 'Poor Charlie. Whatever will he say when he hears?'

'We're not going to tell him,' said Mattie. 'Not while he's facing God only knows what in North Africa. He'll find out soon enough, but we don't want him upset when he needs his wits about him to give the Germans a good hiding.'

'I think you're right,' said Francesca. 'Making sure Charlie comes back in one piece is all that matters.' She sighed. 'It's so unfair.'

'I know,' said Mattie. 'Everyone knows what she's like and he might be my own brother, but Charlie hasn't got the brains of a rocking horse if he can't see you're a thousand times better in every way than blooming slack-knickers Stella.'

'Everyone tells me I should try to find someone else but . . .'

'I know, because I couldn't.'

Daniel had left two days ago and although she'd managed to wave him off with a cheerful smile, she had sobbed for three hours straight as soon as the door closed.

Francesca gave her a sympathetic look.

'I wonder if she ever loved him like I . . .' She turned and gazed out of the window.

Stretching across, Mattie closed her hand over her friend's. Then Francesca frowned.

'Mattie,' she said, her focus on some commotion in the street, 'isn't that your grandma?'

Chapter Nineteen

'FOURTEEN DAYS AND a five-pound fine,' said the magistrate, scrubbing a line across the name of the fourteenth miscreant he'd administered justice to in the past hour. 'Next!'

The man, who'd been caught selling a stolen ration book, shuffled out of the dock and into the clutches of the waiting prison warden.

Jerimiah glanced at the clock above the door behind him, which was now showing almost twelve. He wasn't surprised he had the devil of all headaches because by rights, after pushing a cart for twelve hours and being on patrol with the Home Guard all night, he should be in bed not sitting in the visitors' gallery of Thames Magistrate Court.

The court had been built a quarter of a century ago out of the same solid red brick as Arbour Square Police Station, which adjoined it. However, unlike the police station, and with its high-ceilinged, oak-panelled interior and marble floors, the court did its best to make the magistrates, solicitors and barristers feel at home by mimicking a well-to-do town house or country residence.

Jerimiah pressed his lips tightly together. He took a long even breath to settle his mounting fury and his pounding head. His attention shifted to the Thames Court's magistrate, Sir Randolph Ewing JP, complete with black robes and horsehair wig, sitting beneath the gilded, lion, unicorn and quartered shield of the Crown.

As old as Methuselah, Sir Randolph was one of the old-time magistrates who, Jerimiah suspected, would have sentenced the midwife who'd slapped him at his birth to five years' hard labour had he been able. Sir Randolph had no time for the new-fangled notion of evidence and preferred to think that anyone brought before him was guilty, and he sentenced accordingly.

The door to the cells below opened and a prison officer marched back in with the next law-breaker: Jerimiah's mother.

Queenie shuffled across the space between the prisoners' door and the dock as if she was about to depart from this life: every step brought forth a contorted expression of agony. Gripping the wrought-iron railing, she climbed the three steps to the dock as if scaling Everest then swayed a little before grabbing the front edge as if her life depended on it. With her head hung low, she turned slightly. Her eyes skimmed the gallery above until she saw Jerimiah.

The clerk of the court in front of the magistrate's bench rose to his feet with the charge sheet in his hand.

'Philomena Ursula Brogan?' he said, looking at Queenie.

Queenie gave a little nod but didn't raise her head.

'You are charged that at three thirty on the eighteenth day of December in . . .'

She stood with her shoulders sagging as he read out the charge.

'How do you plead?' he concluded.

'Guilty,' she whispered then gripped her chest and coughed.

Sir Randolph regarded her coolly over his half-rimmed spectacles. 'Mrs Brogan.'

She looked up.

'I'm surprised to see you're still alive,' he said, resting his elbows on the bench and weaving his fingers together in front of him. 'Because when last we met, just a few months ago, you seemed convinced you weren't long for this world.'

'Well now, sir,' said Queenie, giving Sir Randolph a sweet smile, 'who of us can fathom the ways of the Almighty? But I'm sure St Peter will be greeting me at the gates of heaven very soon, especially' – clutching her chest, she coughed again – 'after a night in a cold, damp cell.'

She sent another accusing look at the two young officers waiting near the witness box to give evidence.

The magistrate looked at his clerk. 'Wasn't Mrs Brogan given bail?'

The clerk of the court cleared his throat. 'I believe it slipped the minds of the arresting officers.'

'Well, then,' Sir Randolph replied, in an uncharacteristically pleasant tone, 'as I don't want you to expire in the dock and clog up the wheels of justice, we'd better get you dealt with and on your way.'

'Thank you, sir,' said Queenie, in her little-old-lady voice. 'May the Lord and all his saints above bless your generous nature.'

The magistrate gave a tight smile and then, turning to the clerk sitting in front of him, raised a bushy eyebrow.

'Mrs Brogan has been up on the same charges three times this year and four times last year and was given a fine on each occasion, your worship,' the clerk explained.

'How much on each occasion this year?' asked the magistrate.

'Five pounds the first, rising to eight the second and ten on the last occasion. Mrs Brogan was convicted of the same offence in October,' the clerk replied.

'Thank you, Turner.' Sir Randolph looked at Queenie again. 'Well, Mrs Brogan, it seems the penalties I've imposed thus far have had little effect on your lawless ways.'

'There is the option of a custodial sentence, Your Worship,' the clerk pointed out.

Queenie blanched.

'Indeed,' said the magistrate. 'And perhaps it would make Mrs Brogan think twice the next time she's tempted to flout the law of the land, but I'm not sure someone in Mrs Brogan's poor health would survive the journey.'

'I wouldn't, sir,' Queenie said hastily. 'I have learned me lesson, good and proper this time, honest.'

Sir Randolph smiled. 'I'm sure you have but just in case you haven't, this should remind you.' His congenial expression disappeared in an instant as his acerbic one returned. 'Thirty pounds and a suspended sentence of twenty-eight days bound over for a year. Seven days to pay. Next!'

Thirty pounds! The blood pounded through Jerimiah's ears. Rising from the hard, wooden bench, his mouth pulled into a hard line as he made his way downstairs to the cashier's office.

'There you are, Mr Brogan,' said the court cashier, handing Jerimiah the receipt for the payment of his mother's fine. 'And I'll wish you a merry Christmas.'

It was half an hour since his mother had been sentenced and Jerimiah had been waiting in the queue in the cashier's office, which was on the right side of the main entrance.

Forcing a smile, Jerimiah tucked the slip of paper in his wallet, which he then returned to the pocket of his work trousers. Stepping aside, the person behind him in the queue took his place.

Squeezing past those still waiting, he walked back into the court's entrance hall.

It was now midday or thereabouts, so those who had been dealt with that morning had mostly left, which was just as well as the waiting area was already packed with smartly dressed but anxious-looking locals who were on the afternoon list. Sprinkled amongst them were a handful of wide-boys and spivs dressed in wide-lapelled American-style jackets and well-heeled solicitors and barristers in dark tailored suits.

Scanning the crowd and not finding his mother, Jerimiah's temples started to throb again but thankfully, as the black blobs at the edge of his vision began to gather, the door leading from the cells opened and Queenie walked out with her carpet bag hooked over her arm.

She looked around and, spotting Jerimiah, trundled across the space between them.

'Forgot me, my arse,' she said as she reached him. 'Those bloody wet-behind-the-ear coppers didn't bail me on purpose.'

'Is that right?' said Jerimiah.

'Yes,' she replied, putting her hand in the small of her back. 'And it's done for my old bones, I can tell you.' Her gaze flickered up to the painted sign above Jerimiah's head. 'You've not paid the fine already, have you?'

'And why would I not?' he replied, as an image of the thirty hard-earned pounds he'd just handed to the court clerk flashed through his mind. 'I'll no more be able to pay it in seven days as I am now.'

'Well, I've no more liking than you for giving my money

to the law but they caught me unawares,' she said.

Jerimiah gave his mother a mocking look. 'Well, that's a surprise, isn't it, considering you're forever boasting you can spot a copper, in uniform or out, a mile off?'

'I can,' Queenie replied. 'But they weren't rozzers from around here and I didn't cop on to them as—'

'Well, you "not copping on" has cost me thirty quid,' he cut in, as his temples pounded again. 'Thirty fecking quid! That will take me half a year to put back in the savings jar.'

His mother gave him a querying look. 'Are you quite fair and fine, son?'

'As good as any man would be who's got a brutal head for being awake for thirty hours straight,' he replied, glaring down at her.

She looked contrite. 'Well now, sorry I am for—'

'Haven't I got enough on my plate, Ma?' he cut in. 'With no horse, three daughters barely speaking to me, Billy causing havoc, plus a lad who I'm now looking out for and the woman I betrayed my darling Ida with dying in the front bedroom . . .'

An image of Ida, lovely generous Ida, with her open heart, ready smile and welcoming arms, materialised in his mind. He'd lost her. He knew it. Perhaps not in body, as they'd vowed before God and his saints 'till death do us part', but he'd lost the twinkle in her eyes at a shared joke, lost the gentle caress of her hand as she passed the back of his chair, lost the warm body to curl into at night. But most of all, and what cut him to the very heart, was that he'd lost her love.

The black cloud that had hovered over Jerimiah from the moment Ellen had walked into his yard all those weeks ago suddenly engulfed him. A band of steel tightened around his chest, clogging his breath and capturing his words.

With his head pounding fit to rupture, Jerimiah covered his eyes with his hand.

Queenie laid her hand on his arm. 'Now then, son, don't you fret yourself. I've a plan that will see us all rolling in clover and—'

'I don't want to hear it,' he shouted, shaking her off. 'I've had enough of your schemes and plans and smart ideas because they always end up with you in the dock and me out of pocket.'

Out of the corner of his eye, Jerimiah saw the people near to them take a step or two away.

Queenie frowned, and her bottom lip jutted out. 'So you'll not hear me out, then?'

Fixing his mother with a look that would give grown men the urge to empty their bladders, Jerimiah loomed over her.

'No, Mother, I have no interesting in hearing whatever cock-eyed, hare-brained eejit idea you've cooked up in that barmy brain of yours,' he yelled, his fists balling tight as he matched her livid expression.

She didn't blink, and her angry expression deepened. 'There's no necessity for you to bellow at me like a loon, Jerimiah. I'm not deaf, you know.'

'Good, so hear this,' he replied. 'If you cost me the price of a horse again, I'll put you in the harness and have you pull me wagon around the town.'

His mother glared furiously up at him for a couple of seconds then she looked away.

'Well, now I know where I stand,' she said, adjusting the bag on her arm.

He gave her a tight smile. 'Yes, you do, Mother.'

'Then I'll be about my business,' she said.

'As will I,' Jerimiah replied.

She glared at him for another moment then turned and marched through the crowd, which parted before her, across the black-and-white tiled entrance hall and out of the double front doors.

Jerimiah waited for a few seconds. With his temper still simmering and his brain hammering in his skull, he straightened his leather cap and followed her out.

After placing the last jam tart in the bottom of her battered Peek Freans biscuit tin, Ida pressed the lid on firmly. Taking it to the dresser, she placed it with the other tins containing the rest of her morning's efforts.

With Christmas Day only six days away she'd been chopping, mixing and rolling all morning in preparation for the big day. The last batch of mince pies were just finishing off in the oven, filling the kitchen with a fruity aroma.

Well, in truth, a fruity and carroty aroma as she'd had to grate some of the vegetable in with the mixture to make it go further. In fact, the housewives of England should give daily thanks for carrots as, along with potatoes, they seemed to be the food substitute of choice in all the recipes printed in magazines and government information leaflets. Pretending one food was in fact something else had become a bit of a pastime. Ida reckoned that she had a 'substitute' something or a 'mock' something else every day. The mock duck was in fact moulded sausage meat and the mock cream for the mince pies was reconstituted dried milk, marge and sugar whipped together. The Christmas cake had mock marzipan, made from ground haricot beans and almond essence. However, given there would be eight adults in the house on Christmas

Day and only one toilet, Ida drew the line at using liquid paraffin as a substitute fat in the pudding.

Getting the faintest whiff of burning, Ida hurried across to the stove, grabbing the tea towel from the back of a kitchen chair as she passed.

Winding it around her hands she opened the oven. She'd just pulled out the baking tray when the back door opened and Jerimiah walked in. She'd not seen him since the night before when she'd left to collect Patrick from Stella at five and she hadn't set breakfast for him as he was going straight to court from the Home Guard HQ when he got off patrol at eight.

Jerimiah could usually pass for a man ten years younger, but not today. Today, with two days' growth of beard, dark smudges under his eyes and lines etched around his mouth, he looked every day of his forty-four years.

'Hello, luv,' he said, unwinding his scarf.

'I thought you'd be back ages ago,' said Ida, shutting the oven with her knee.

'So did I,' he said, ripping off his coat. 'Is my mother in?'

Ida shook her head. 'She came in about an hour ago while I was giving Ellen lunch upstairs,' she replied, putting the tray of pies on the table. 'I called down to her, but she didn't answer as she was in her room feeding her parrot. I saw her through the landing window rummaging around in the shed out back but by the time I got downstairs she'd gone out again. What happened at court?'

Her husband's mouth pulled into a grim line. 'I'll tell you what happened . . .'

Ida stood open-mouthed while he recounted his mother's brush with the magistrate.

'Thirty pounds!' she said when he'd finished, as thoughts of the rent book and gas meter loomed in her mind. 'But I've got the butcher to pay as well as getting the last-minute things from the market and then there's the—'

'I know, me darling,' he said, suppressing a yawn. 'But you're not to fret. And that's why I popped in to the yard before coming home.'

Stepping across to his coat, which was hanging behind the door, he pulled a battered Oxo tin from the pocket then walked across to where she was standing.

'There's almost fifteen pounds in there,' he said, handing it to her. 'Plus, I've a bob or two still owed to me from others. It should tide us over until I start in the Fire Service in a few weeks.'

Ida stared at the tin in her hand for a moment then looked back at her husband's haggard face. 'But you need ready cash for the auctions?'

'Until I get another horse there's no point me buying a stick of furniture as I can't move anything worth trading on the hand cart,' he replied.

'I thought you were hiring one of the brewery's horses,' said Ida.

'So did I but the government bought half of the brewery's drays for farm work and the brewery need the horses they have left to deliver the Christmas and New Year orders, so I've not a chance of anything for a week or more.'

Memories of the lean years after the American crash, when she and Jerimiah went hungry to feed four small children and keep a roof over their heads, flashed across Ida's mind.

'But don't worry,' he said, seeing the look on her face, 'we'll get by. We always have.' His dark eyes grew warm as he gazed down at her. 'Trust me, Ida, and I'll get us through.'

They stared at each other for a moment then Ida smiled, and Jerimiah smiled back.

Then he yawned.

Without thinking, she put her hand on his arm. 'Why don't you catch a few hours upstairs before the boys come home, Jerry?' she said, enjoying the feel of the soft hair on his forearm.

He shook his head. 'I'll be grand if I just put me feet up for an hour or so in the chair but,' his hand closed over hers, 'I could murder a cuppa.'

Ida laughed. 'I'll bring it through.'

He yawned again and ambled into the front room.

Relighting the gas under the kettle, Ida quickly put the tea in the pot while the water came to the boil. She poured the scalding water over the leaves then taking one of the large mugs from the dresser, she filled it from the pot, adding a splash of milk as he liked it and a generous two teaspoons of sugar.

Holding it high she walked through to the parlour.

'One cuppa—' She stopped.

With his feet up on their old threadbare pouffe, Jerimiah was sprawled in his chair with his head back and his eyes closed.

Treading lightly across the rag rug in front of the fire, Ida crossed the small room and placed her husband's hot drink on the floor next to the leg of his chair. Then she straightened up. Running her gaze over the familiar contours of her sleeping husband's face, she smiled. Bending over, she pressed her lips on to his forehead.

'Come on, you two, or you'll be late for Junior Club,' said Ida, as she dragged the back wheels of the pram up the last few steps up to the shelter's main door out on to the street.

It was Saturday, the day after Queenie had appeared in court and just five days before Christmas. It was also the morning after a night of some of the heaviest bombing they'd had for some time. The all-clear had sounded half an hour ago at six and those who worked on a Saturday had already left the shelter. Ida and her family were heading home too.

Ida had a full day ahead of her. With the whole family descending on them for Christmas, once she'd packed the boys off to the Shamrock League's Saturday-morning boys' club and seen to Ellen, she intended to clean the house from top to bottom.

'Coming, Auntie Ida,' Michael shouted from the bottom of the stairs.

'Where's Billy?' Ida asked.

'I don't know; I told him to come,' Michael replied.

Ida pressed her lips together and was just about to go back down the stairs when Billy appeared from behind the lower door of the shelter.

'Where have you been, Billy? I told you ages ago we were going,' said Ida.

'Don't go on,' he replied, giving her a truculent look. 'I'm here now, aren't I?'

Resisting the urge to tear him off a strip, Ida took a deep breath. She'd hardly slept a wink last night. However, while most people had been kept awake by the Luftwaffe, Ida had the situation with Jerimiah and his mother to thank for her broken night's sleep.

Although her mother-in-law had a tongue that could cut through steel and her antics would try the patience of the

Lord himself, she couldn't remember the last time Jerimiah had lost his temper with her.

It wasn't any wonder, though, given what he'd been through in the last few weeks. With a mountain of household bills stacking up, they had no hope of finding the twenty-five pounds for the quarterly rent on the yard, let alone the same again for a new horse.

Reaching the landing at the top of the shelter, Ida looked at the baby sleeping in the pram. He looked so like his father Charlie it made her heart ache with the memory. She tucked the crocheted blanket around Patrick a little tighter and pushed the pram towards the entrance.

'Well, Ida, it looks like we've survived to fight another day,' said Ted Mitchell, Tilbury Shelter's senior ARP warden, as he held the door open for her to manoeuvre the front wheels through.

'Praise Mary,' said Ida, crossing herself hastily. 'Although there were times last night when I was expecting to find myself at heaven's gates, I can tell you.'

'You and me both, girl,' said Ted. 'Jerry did us good and proper last night.'

He indicated the scene outside and as Ida took in the sight that greeted her, her chin dropped.

She'd known that the Germans had taken full advantage of the clear winter sky from the relentless explosions and the constant shaking of the ground, but now, in the red glow of blazing buildings and the mellow yellow of the dawn light, she could see the full horror of the night raid.

The block of flats across from the entrance had been three storeys tall and home to at least forty families when she'd gone down into the shelter the evening before; now it was a pile of rubble. And it was the same all along the street. At the far end of the road a fire engine shot water in a high arch into what was left of the bonded warehouse.

'St John's copped it,' Ted went on, nodding towards the black smoke billowing skywards. 'According to the copper who went by a while back, they're still digging out survivors. And there's nothing but a hole in the ground at the Sidney Street telephone exchange. If you ask me, it's because our boys are giving them hell in the desert at Benghazi. Your Charlie's out there, ain't he?'

'Yes,' said Ida, a lump forming in her throat as she glanced at Charlie's son asleep in the pram. 'He's part of the gun crew on a twenty-five-pounder.'

Ted grinned, showing a set of large, uneven teeth. 'Well, I hope he gives the bloody Hun a right pasting.'

Ida forced a smile then looked down the stairs again. 'Billy, Michael!'

The two boys, who'd been milling around with some other lads, clattered up the stairs.

'About blooming time,' she said, as they skidded to a halt in front of her. 'Now let's get home before we freeze to death.'

Billy shoved Michael. 'Race you,' he shouted as he tore off.

Having regained his balance, Michael pelted after him.

Ted chuckled. 'I was just like that at their age. Full of beans.'

'Full of mischief,' said Ida. 'And I've got them under my feet until they go back to school in two weeks.'

'Well, boys will be boys,' said Ted.

'See you tonight,' said Ida, pushing the pram after them.

'God willing,' he replied, touching the brim of his tin hat as she walked past.

As the road was blocked to vehicles, Ida guided the front wheels of the pram into the middle of the street. Picking her way between rubble and blackened beams strewn across the road, she followed the two boys, who jostled each other and laughed as they searched for shrapnel with German markings to add to their collections.

Although Billy, who had a September birthday, was a full ten months older than Michael who had been born the following July, they were both in the same school year, and due to move into secondary school next September. As soon as they went back after the New Year she would have to see about getting their names down.

She and Jerimiah hadn't been able to afford to send the eldest three children to grammar school but they had managed to scrape the money together for Jo's Coburn Girls School outfit. She and Jerimiah were hoping to do the same for Billy, if he passed the entrance exam, and send him to one of the local grammars, but now they would be funding Michael too. Although Raines was the nearest school, just the other side of Commercial Road, most of the pupils and teachers had been evacuated to Essex. Therefore, Ida had decided to apply to Parmiter's Boys School, behind the Bethnal Green Museum.

It was a bit of a trot from Watney Street but if both boys got into Parmiter's, then she would take Billy, Michael and Patrick to the Bethnal Green Tube shelter from September.

'Mind yourselves,' Ida shouted, as the boys hopped from one block of fragmented brickwork to another. 'I don't want to have to get the iodine out when we get home.'

The boys, their arms windmilling wildly as they wobbled on what had been a door arch, grinned then jumped down and sped on.

They were waiting for her by the steps of the Town Hall, talking to a couple of the ARP messengers standing by their bikes. As she drew close Billy and Michael waved their goodbyes and the boys peddled away on the bicycles.

'Me and Michael are going to be messengers,' Billy announced as she joined them.

Ida raised an eyebrow. 'Are you now?'

'Yes, when we're old enough,' Michael joined in. 'And then we're going to join the army like Charlie.'

'I've been telling him how Charlie stayed to the end at Dunkirk cos he was loading wounded soldiers into ships.' Jumping, Billy adopted a boxing stance with his fists raised. 'And we've decided that we're going to call ourselves the Brogan Brothers.'

The Brogan Brothers! An emotion she couldn't name ran through Ida.

'Yeah,' Michael shouted, copying his brother's stance. 'The Brogan Brothers smash Hitler's face in.'

'And Göring.'

'And Himler,' added Michael.

'And—'

'And you two will be late for club if we don't get a move on,' cut in Ida, bumping the pram down the kerb.

They crossed the road and carried on but as Ida and the boys walked under the railway arch and into Watney Street, they stopped dead.

The glass from every shop, house and pub window lay shattered on the pavement and blackout curtains fluttered from upper-floor windows in the chilly morning air. Store owners crunched shards underfoot as they emptied their gaping shop windows of display stock to avoid it being looted.

A temporary ARP information post had been set up by Myer's shoe shop and the warden sitting behind the desk was checking the list of casualties under the gaze of an anxious-looking crowd of people, many still carrying their night-shelter paraphernalia.

'Where did it fall?' Ida asked the woman auxiliary constable standing guard in front of the blown-out shell of the market's Post Office.

'On the paper works in Tarling Street,' the officer replied. 'High explosive, by all accounts; it only just missed the railway bridge. Plus a land mine blew up the Pipe and Drum alongside.'

'Many dead?'

'Dozens,' the officer replied. 'And double that carted away to hospital, which must be chock-a-block by now as the bloody Krauts hit us hard last night. They hit the Sidney Street telephone exchange, too, so we've been running around like blue-arsed flies cos all the lines are down.'

'Ida!'

She looked around to see Jerimiah climbing over the broken trunk of a telephone pole that was lying across the roadway.

His khaki Home Guard uniform was now red with brick dust, which was also crusted in his hair and smeared across his face. He hurried towards her, limping occasionally as he clambered over the debris strewn across the road.

As always when she saw him each morning after another night of deadly bombardment, she sent a small prayer of thanks that he was still whole, but when Billy and Michael ran happily to him, Ida's heart squeezed a little.

'Your leg playing you up?' Ida asked as he reached her, his arms around each boy's shoulder.

He grinned, his teeth flashing white through the grime on his face. 'Bit stiff, that's all.'

'Have you finished?' Ida asked.

'No, I've just come back to make sure you and the boys were all right,' he replied. 'I'll have a quick cuppa and then head back to give a hand at St John's. The mother superior and the three nuns from the school are still under all the rubble. It was bad all over. The Royal Dock had it bad as usual as did the Surrey and Bermondsey on the other side of the river, but I had a quick recce of our road and, thank God, other than a crack across me ma's window, and a dozen tiles from the roof, our house seems to have escaped the worst of it. I had a quick check on Ellen – she seemed a little shaken but fine too.'

'Praise Mary,' said Ida.

'You all right?' he asked, casting his eyes over her.

She nodded. 'And as always he slept right through the lot.' She indicated Patrick still fast asleep after his morning feed.

Jerimiah gazed down at his grandson and a soft look crept across his face, causing Ida's heart to squeeze again.

He raised his head. 'We'd better get him and the boys home and out of this cold. Ma will have the kettle on by now.'

They set off and, after navigating the shell holes and lifting the pram over a fallen garden wall, they arrived at the bottom end of Mafeking Terrace. Seeing a couple of friends who'd just returned from the Turner Street Shelter, Billy and Michael scooted across the road.

'Five minutes, lads, and then home,' Jerimiah shouted after them.

Ida turned into the cool dampness of the side alley and wondered how Ellen's nerves had held up during the night. Parking the pram in the backyard, she lifted Patrick as Jerimiah opened the back door and held it open for her.

She stepped in and through the blackout curtains, with Jerimiah just a pace behind her, and they both stopped dead.

The kitchen was freezing; there was no kettle simmering on the stove, no porridge bubbling in the pot and no smell of newly baked bread in the air.

Jerimiah and Ida looked at each other for a moment then Jerimiah strode through the house and knocked on his mother's door.

'Ma!'

There was no answer. He opened the door and went in. Prince Albert squawked a couple of times and Ida heard the bird's cage rattle on its stand, then Jerimiah came out again and gave her a bleak look.

Ida put her hand on his arm. 'I'm sure your ma'll be home any minute now,' said Ida.

'No, sorry, mate,' said Bert Fallow, the landlord of the Boatman, as he pulled a pint. 'I ain't seen Queenie since last week.'

Jerimiah forced a smile. 'Thanks, Bert.'

There was still an hour to go before last-orders at ten and the bar was packed with people enjoying a quiet drink. And it was quiet because for once there were no German planes in the sky above.

The sirens had gone off at six and, when the first bombs hit the ground twenty minutes later, everyone thought the evening was shaping up to be a rerun of the night before but, despite it being a clear crisp night, after a couple of runs, the Luftwaffe squadrons headed back to northern France and left East London in peace.

When the all-clear sounded at nine, Major Randolph Hitching-Wells had marched the rest of the Home Guard company back to the Methodist Hall but Jerimiah had forgone his cocoa and biscuits to continue his search for his mother.

To be honest, knowing his mother's wandering ways, he hadn't been too worried about her at first so after he'd thrown down his breakfast and a cup of hot sweet tea, he'd gone back to help dig the Mother Superior's body out from the rubble that had been St John's Church. Even when he'd got back at ten he hadn't been too alarmed and, having been up almost thirty-six hours by then, had fallen asleep before his head hit the pillow.

Unbeknown to him, while he slept, Ida had popped to the Town Hall to check the lists of dead and injured. Mercifully, Queenie's name wasn't on any of them so all through tea he'd expected her to walk through the back door. However, when she still hadn't appeared by the time Ida set off for the shelter with the boys, an uneasy feeling coiled in the pit of his stomach.

Unease changed to anxiety after he'd asked around the market and discovered that the last time she'd been spotted she was walking past Wickhams Store heading towards Bow. Realising no one had seen hide nor hair of her for over twenty-four hours, he began searching for his mother.

He'd started in her usual haunts along Cable Street and around London Docks and Shadwell Basin but with no success. He'd even tried the shelter in St Patrick's crypt to see if any of her old pals who attended there had seen her but with no luck.

He was now standing in the Boatman public house which was situated at the Limehouse end of Wapping High

Street. A squat, black-beamed Tudor pub squashed between lofty Georgian warehouses, the Boatman wasn't one of his mother's regulars but he'd been everywhere else he could possibly think of. Well, everywhere except the morgue at London Hospital.

'Can I stand you a half of the good stuff while you're here?' asked Bert.

Pushing his unsettling thoughts aside, Jerimiah shook his head. 'I've got to get on.'

'Chin up, Jerry. She'll pitch up soon.' Bert grinned. 'Take more than bloody Hitler to finish off your old ma.'

Jerimiah forced a smile and prayed he was right. Shouldering his rifle, he made his way through the drinkers and, pushing aside the heavy curtain hanging in a loop around the door, left the pub. He tucked the collar of his battle tunic around his neck, pulled his sheepskin jerkin a little tighter and headed towards the grey forbidding walls of the Tower at the other end of the cobbled street.

The searchlights on Tower Green streaked across the sky, criss-crossing each other from time to time in the icy night sky. Crunching his hobnailed boots through newly formed puddle ice and shining his torch on the ground, Jerimiah marched between the silent warehouses looming over him. The ever-present smell of charred wood and brick dust drifted up his nose as fire engines and ambulances passed him on their way back to their bases.

After twenty minutes of trudging along, deep in thought, he reached the entrance to Tilbury Shelter. Greeting Ted the main ARP warden who was standing outside with a roll-up dangling from his lips, Jerimiah lowered his head and went in.

It was now close to lights-out at ten, and other than someone's wireless playing softly in the background, all the evening activity had ceased. Children lay curled up in blankets while their mothers sat in a huddle a little way off drinking cocoa and chatting quietly.

In the dim lights hanging above, Jerimiah picked his way between the camp beds and deckchairs to the arch where Ida set up camp each night. He saw her sitting in the small fold-up chair she brought down with her each night. On the old loading-bay ledge alongside her were Billy and Michael, fast asleep and wrapped in blankets. A little way from them he could see Peter also asleep clutching his teddy, while Patrick slept in his pram. His attention returned to Ida, with her head bowed in concentration over her knitting.

Although she drew the line at wearing the all-in-one siren suit the government was forever urging people to adopt, Ida had taken to wearing trousers in the shelter. And very nice they looked too, drawing the eye to her womanly hips and rear. However, her familiar curves were currently hidden away under the forest-green winter coat he'd bought her three years ago. A lock of her dark hair, secured under a tartan scarf tied in a turban, escaped and he watched her tuck it back behind her ear. He'd seen her do the same a hundred times over the years, while sitting by the fire, writing her shopping list or reading to the children.

Sensing someone watching her, Ida looked up. They gazed at each other for a couple of heartbeats then she set aside her knitting and stood up.

'Any luck?' she asked, her breath escaping in little puffs as she spoke.

He shook his head. 'I've asked everywhere and no one seems to have seen her since yesterday afternoon.' He raked his fingers through his hair. 'I tell you straight, Ida, if she's not home in the morning, I don't know what I'll do.'

All the guilt he'd kept bottled up about the argument he'd had with his mother in the court suddenly surged up and gripped his chest. Pressing his lips together, Jerimiah looked up and studied the ceiling.

'I'm sure she'll be back tomorrow,' Ida said softly. 'But if she's not, I'll come with you and we'll look for her together.'

Leaving his contemplation of the iron girders above, Jerimiah lowered his head and met Ida's gaze. With her lovely, dark eyes large in the dim light of the shelter, she smiled encouragingly up at him.

They stood for a couple of heartbeats then a voice cut between them.

'Hello, Dad,' said Cathy, holding an enamel mug in each hand. 'We don't often see you down here.'

Wearing a scarf tied in a turban around her head and her winter coat wrapped over her siren suit she, like her mother, was ready for a night in a subterranean concrete bunker.

Dragging his eyes from Ida's face, Jerimiah smiled at his daughter. 'Hello, luv. I just popped down to let your mum know how the search was going.'

'Any luck?'

Jerimiah shook his head.

'I hope she's all right,' said Cathy, looking concerned.

'Course she is,' he replied, forcing a cheery smile. 'It would take more than Hitler to see off your gran. In fact, if he had the brains he was born with, Churchill would be sending her over to Germany to sort the lot of them out.'

'You're right there, Dad.' Cathy laughed. 'I've just got me and Mum a Horlicks. Do you want one?'

'No, I'm fine,' he replied. 'And I ought to get back before Old Hitching-Wells puts me on a charge for being AWOL. I'll see you and the lad on Christmas Eve for the Mass, will I?'

'I wouldn't miss it,' Cathy replied.

Placing the mugs on the floor between hers and her mother's chair, she went to check on her son.

'Poor Cathy,' said Jerimiah quietly, watching her tucking the blanket under Peter's chin. 'Stuck in that house with Stan's miserable mother.'

'I know,' Ida replied. 'But what can she do? Stan's army pay isn't enough to keep her and it's hard enough for her to hold her head up as it is with everyone knowing Stan's inside without her adding to the gossip by leaving him.'

Aching for his beloved daughter locked in an unhappy marriage, Jerimiah forced a smile. 'I suppose you're right.'

'And although she's got to put up with his cow of a mother,' continued Ida, 'at least Stan's not there and not likely to be for many a long day.'

The overhead lamps flickered on and off, signalling ten minutes until lights-out. Jerimiah turned his attention back to Ida.

'Looks like Jerry's gone home so you should have a quiet night,' he said, smiling warmly at her.

'Let's hope,' she replied, smiling back.

They stood gazing at each other for a long moment then Jerimiah pulled himself up straight. 'Well, I'll be on me way.'

'Yes, and I'd better bed down,' Ida replied.

They smiled at each other again. Jerimiah turned to leave but as he did, Ida caught his arm.

'Mind how you go,' she said softly.

Although he longed to hold her, Jerimiah contented himself with placing his hand over hers.

'To be sure I will,' he said, enjoying the feel of her hand under his. 'And I'll be seeing you, me darling, in the morning.'

Chapter Twenty

'WELL, THIS IS the last victim who matches the description of your mother, Mr Brogan,' said the green-coated attendant, lifting the sheet.

Ida felt Jerimiah tense as they looked down at the old woman lying on the floor at their feet. She was covered in dust, and the right side of her head was caved in. Her jaw was out of kilter and sat at an odd angle to her cheeks and although someone had straightened her clothes, her stockings were shredded and a shoe was missing. But whoever this poor old soul was, she wasn't Queenie.

It was now Tuesday, the day before Christmas Eve, and three days since they'd arrived back to a cold house and found Queenie gone. They had spent any free time they had on Sunday making enquiries locally then after Jerimiah's interview at the local Fire Brigade headquarters on Monday morning they had spent the rest of the day visiting all the hospitals and temporary morgues in the area. After sifting through the recently deceased in the London, the Jewish and the East London Children's Hospital, whose cellar had been drummed into use, they still had not found her. They'd even visited the temporary morgue in the basement of the Old Dispensary in Cable Street but without luck before they had to head home to get tea for the boys and check on Ellen again before going back to the shelter.

Tuesday morning found them standing in St Andrew's Hospital morgue just down from Bow Bridge. They'd already been through the property of the handful of unidentified deceased the council had taken to the Manor Park Cemetery for cremation without recognising any of the items recovered. Now they were working their way through the fresh crop of corpses delivered by the Luftwaffe the night before. Mercifully, the temperature within the vaulted stone space under the hospital's west wing was close to freezing as some had been here since the day before.

Jerimiah let out a long breath. 'It's not her.'

The attendant, a young chap with acne, let the sheet drop. 'I'm afraid that's the last of them.'

'Thank you,' said Jerimiah flatly.

He looked away but not quickly enough to hide the moisture gathering in his eyes.

'Thank you,' Ida repeated. 'You've been very helpful.'

'Of course, the heavy rescue fellas are still digging up bodies, so it might be worth you ringing through to the WVS desk later and seeing if they've brought in someone fitting your mother-in-law's description. That's, of course, if the Post Office blokes have pulled their fingers out and fixed the phone lines by then.' The young man's face brightened. 'You could have a shifty at the body parts – arms and legs, you know – we keep them out the back, lots of people find their nearest and dearest like—'

'I think we might give that a miss,' cut in Ida, feeling Jerimiah tense at the suggestion.

'Okey-dokey,' the young man replied.

The double doors at the far end of the basement swung open and two men in dust-covered dungarees and tin helmets with HR painted on the front hurried in; they were carrying a stretcher between them.

The young man glanced over his shoulder then back at Ida. 'I should . . .'

She gave him a tight smile.

'And I hope your mother turns up safe, Mr Brogan,' the young man added in a tone that wasn't convincing.

Jerimiah didn't move for a second then he turned to Ida. 'We might as well go home,' he said.

'Don't you want to go to Plaistow Hospital?' she asked.

He shook his head. 'I'll pop around to the Town Hall again later but if we've heard nothing by midday tomorrow, then I'll jump on the tram to Plaistow.' He gave her a heart-wrenching smile. 'I'm guessing you've probably got a thousand things to do so we'd best head back.'

Ida gave half a laugh. 'A thousand and one but if—'

'Let's go home, Ida luv,' he said, tucking her hand more firmly in the crook of his arm. 'I think we've seen enough dead bodies for one day.'

Jumping off the running board of the number 15 bus as it slowed at the traffic lights, Jerimiah turned up the collar of his greatcoat and turned towards St Bridget's and St Brendan's on the other side of the road.

He waited until a couple of army trucks, brimming with fresh-faced soldiers, passed then he crossed the road. Walking between the sandbags stacked to shoulder height on each side of the door, Jerimiah opened it and entered the dark interior of the church.

It was now almost three thirty, a few hours since he and Ida had returned from the Andrew's morgue, and as it was still an hour until Father Mahon started evening prayers, there were only a few people dotted in the pews.

Slipping into the back row on the right, Jerimiah wedged himself against the pillar at the far end. Resting his forearms on his thighs and clasping his hands together, he closed his eyes then bowed his head.

Other than celebrating weddings and baptisms or commiserating with those mourning a newly departed soul, Jerimiah left the day-to-day communion with the heavenly realm to the Brogan women. And while he readily acknowledged the existence of the Almighty, he tried not to bother him too much because, with the world as it was at the moment, the Lord had enough on his plate without Jerimiah adding to it. However, given that Queenie, one of the Lord's most fervent devotees, had been missing since Friday, he felt it was time to call on divine help. Truth be told, his mother was probably already with the saints, but if she wasn't, then perhaps they wouldn't mind giving him a bit of a hand to find her.

But his mother's fate wasn't the only worry threatening to crush him.

Although, after what he'd done to her, it might be beyond the powers of even Our Lord and his Mother to have his darling wife love him as she once had, and take Michael as her own, he did know that if there was any woman on God's earth who could, it was his Ida.

Deep in his dispiriting thoughts, Jerimiah was vaguely aware of people leaving and entering the church but the sound of a pram's wheels as they rolled over one of the air vents in the aisle jolted him back to the here and now. He looked up to see Mattie putting the brakes on Alicia's pushchair and slipping into the family's usual pew, halfway down on the left.

Taking down the kneeler that was hooked in front of her, Mattie knelt down. She rested her arms on the back of the pew in front of her, clasped her hands together and bowed her head.

Jerimiah watched her for a few moments, pondering on the fact that no matter how old they were, when you saw your child in pain, all your heart wanted to do was kiss it better. He made the sign of the cross then stood up and sidestepped out of the pew.

Alicia spotted him and started waving her arms as he approached, and Jerimiah's heavy heart lightened a little.

As he reached where Mattie was kneeling, she looked around and smiled.

'Dad,' she said, sitting up on the pew and sliding along so he could sit beside her. 'We don't often see you here during the week.'

'Well, you know how it is, luv,' he said.

She pressed her lips together and nodded, her eyes bright with tears.

'Don't worry, he'll be back,' said Jerimiah.

'I know,' she said. 'I got a telegram from him this morning saying the same. I suppose he would have phoned but the domestic telephone lines are still down.' Placing her hand on her stomach, she gave him a brave little smile. 'Still, at least I'll have something to keep me busy until he does.'

'Oh, me darling girl.' Happiness washed over Jerimiah's bruised spirits. 'Have you told your mum?'

She nodded. 'I met her in the market just now. And Jo and Gran know too.'

'But not Daniel?' he asked.

Mattie shook her head. 'He's got enough on his mind,' she replied, a tear sparkling in her eye.

Jerimiah put his arms around her. He drew her close and she snuggled into him.

Pressing his lips into his eldest daughter's hair, he closed his eyes and added another request to his already long list.

She remained in his embrace for a few moments then Alicia started fretting at being left out, so Jerimiah unclipped her from her straps and lifted her on to his lap.

'No news of Gran, then?' Mattie said, as Alicia curled her little fingers around his large one.

Jerimiah sighed. 'No, 'fraid not. I've even been over to Hackney Hospital, but no luck. I've got a few errands to run first thing tomorrow but then I'll head off to the Wanstead to sift through unidentified belongings—' From nowhere a lump choked off his throat and moisture blurred his vision. Mattie put her hand over his, and Jerimiah forced a smile. They sat there together in silence for a few moments then Mattie patted his hand and stood up.

'Well, Jo's in at six so I ought to get back and get the tea on,' she said.

'Me too,' said Jerimiah, rising to his feet. With Alicia still in his arms, he stepped out of the pew.

'Time to go home and see Auntie Jo, Alicia,' Mattie said, holding her hands out.

The baby started wriggling and Jerimiah handed her over but just as Mattie sat the little girl back in the pushchair, the vestry door opened, and Father Mahon walked out.

Spotting them he hurried towards them.

'Good afternoon, Father,' said Mattie.

'And to you, my dear, and my favourite angel,' he said, bending forward to tickle Alicia under the chin. 'But it's you I'm glad to get sight of, Jerimiah. Any news of Queenie?'

'I was just telling Mattie that—' He stopped. 'What's the matter, luv?' he asked, puzzled at the astonished expression on his daughter's face as she looked at him and Father Mahon standing side by side.

'Oh, nothing, Dad,' she laughed. 'Just something Daniel mentioned a little while ago.'

Blowing on his hands in an attempt to get the blood flowing back into them, Jerimiah picked up the next buff envelope.

It was almost three thirty in the afternoon on Christmas Eve and he was sitting in his improvised office at the back of the yard. The two-bar electric fire was plugged in but, as he didn't have a shilling to spare for the meter, he hadn't switched it on. He'd left the double gates open to let in as much daylight as possible but, as the arch was north facing, he'd been forced to switch on the table lamp so he could see what he was doing.

Thankfully, his wound had healed well but it was still slowing him down, although this wouldn't have been too much of a problem had he not lost Samson.

He'd managed to honour most of the work he'd had in the book by calling in favours from his pals in the Shamrock League, but he'd carried out the local deliveries on his own with the hand cart, which had aggravated the wound and kept Jerimiah awake for two nights with the pain of it.

But that wasn't the only thing that weighed heavy on his mind. There was still no news of Queenie, and he was fast coming to the conclusion that although there was no doubt she would eventually be found, when she was, it would be dead under a pile of rubble.

Putting aside his unhappy thoughts, Jerimiah ripped open the envelope in his hand and took out the letter.

It had 'Stepney Borough Council' printed in bold black letters across the top, but the rest of the print was red. It was from the Rates Department and was the final demand for November's outstanding payment. He studied the sum of £3 17s 9d for a moment then placed it on top of the other half-dozen outstanding bills.

The pile of bills sat to the left of another stack of paper of about the same height, containing requests for Jerimiah to deliver a crate load of stock or move a family to a new address. And that was the rub. Without being able to act on the right pile he could do nothing about the left one. It had been problem enough with a horse, but he'd have scraped by, that was until he'd had to shell out thirty pounds in Thames Magistrate Court. As things stood, he'd be out of the yard and out of business by the end of January.

He picked up the next envelope but before he could open it, Tommy, Jo's fiancé, strolled across the yard and into the covered area of the arch. Like three-quarters of the country's adult population, he was in uniform, which in his case was khaki battle dress and a greatcoat with the Royal Signal Regiment's badge depicting Mercury, the messenger of the gods, pinned to the side of his beret.

Seeing Jerimiah tucked away in his cubby hole, the young man strode towards him. Jerimiah rose to his feet as Tommy opened the door.

'Hello, lad,' he said, extending his hand. 'Nice to see you home.'

'Nice to be here, finally,' Tommy replied, taking it. 'I was supposed to be back yesterday but the line got hit by a land mine just outside Leighton Buzzard and they only managed to get it up and running late last night, so I caught the mid-morning train back today.'

'Does Jo know you're back?' Jerimiah asked.

Tommy nodded. 'I caught her at the ambulance station when she finished at one and we had a bite to eat in the pie and mash shop before she went home to help her mother and Mattie. I said I'd meet her later in the Boatman before she goes to Midnight Mass.'

'Well then, boy, you've got time to join me in a splash of Irish,' Jerimiah said. He resumed his seat and, taking the lid off the zinc bucket beside him, he pulled out a bottle of Jameson's. 'Fetch those over.' He indicated two enamel mugs on the top of the door-less dresser that he used as a filing cabinet. 'And then pull up a seat.'

Picking up the cups with one hand, Tommy dragged the straight-back chair over to the desk with the other and sat down.

Jerimiah poured a generous measure into each mug, handed one to Tommy and raised the other. 'Merry Christmas.'

'And to you,' said Tommy.

Jerimiah took a mouthful, enjoying the smooth feel of the whisky sliding down, and Tommy did the same.

'Any news on your mother?' Tommy asked, crossing one long leg over the other. Jerimiah shook his head and told him how he and Ida had searched for her everywhere they could think of. 'I'm sorry,' said Tommy when he'd finished. 'But if she's not amongst the dead and injured then she might still turn up.'

'Not if she's buried under ten tons of rubble or trapped in a basement,' Jerimiah replied.

'The ARP will find her,' Tommy said. 'We once dug out one family who'd been buried for six days and after a cup of tea they were as right as rain.'

Jerimiah forced a smile and didn't point out that being buried for days in the cold and wet wasn't something recommended for pensioners.

'So how's it all going?' continued Tommy, glancing at the pile of bills.

'A bit slow,' Jerimiah replied. 'But I'm sure it'll pick up after Christmas when I get another horse. I suppose you've come to ask me about marrying Jo, again.'

'As it happens, no,' said Tommy. 'I'm here about the horse.'

Jerimiah gave a hard laugh. 'Don't tell me you've got one.'

'No, I haven't but...' Leaning forward, Tommy rested his arm on the desk. 'I have something that'll be ten times more useful ... my brother's lorry.'

'I thought you were renting it to the heavy rescue at Canning Town depot,' said Jerimiah.

'I was, but the government have sent them four new trucks, fully fitted and complete with lifting gear,' said Tommy. 'They wrote thanking me for my contribution to the war effort and asking me to remove my lorry from the depot as soon as I could. I got Jo to shift it to my mate's garage off Bow Common Lane, but he won't want it holding up his business. It's a three-ton Bedford. Reggie bought it two years back from Maguire and Sons, the coal merchants. It's mine now as he's hardly going to use it in HM Wakefield and I'm offering it to you.'

'Are you not going to sell it?' said Jerimiah.

'It's not worth it,' said Tommy. 'With the domestic petrol ration being scrapped and the commercial allowance being cut it's only worth a fraction of its real price and besides,' he grinned, 'I thought you'd have better use for it.'

Jerimiah regarded his daughter's fiancé coolly.

'And what would you be asking for in return?' he asked, as an image of Jo in her ambulance uniform flashed through his mind.

'Well, the Town Hall were hiring it from me for three and nine,' he said. 'But you can have it for a straight two quid.'

'Is that all?' Jerimiah asked warily.

'Well, if you could keep it in good order, I'd be grateful,' said Tommy, giving him an artless look. 'But as you're Jo's dad, I'm happy with two quid. What do you say?'

Thinking of the three pounds he spent each week on fodder, Jerimiah extended his hand. 'Done.'

Tommy took it.

'And I'm mighty grateful,' Jerimiah added.

Tommy and he looked squarely at each other for a second then they shook hands.

'And if you're lucky,' continued the young man, 'there might be a gallon or two in the tank so that should tide you over until you get your commercial ration book sorted out at the Town Hall.'

'Tell your mate I'll be collecting it on Saturday,' said Jerimiah, mentally running through the jobs he could now say yes to.

'I will, Mr Brogan.' Tommy glanced at his watch and stood up. 'I've a few errands to run so I ought to be heading off but I'll be at yours in time to see you carve the turkey tomorrow.'

'Turkey!' scoffed Jerimiah. 'You'll be lucky. I think Ida's managed to get a joint of lamb, so we might have a slither each if I'm careful with the knife.'

Tommy laughed and then his expression grew sober. 'I do hope you get good news about Queenie soon.'

Jerimiah gave his future son-in-law a grateful smile then slapped him on the upper arm.

Grinning, the young man turned but as he grabbed the handle of the office door, Jerimiah spoke again. 'Tell me, Tommy, why did you not ask for my consent in exchange for the lorry?'

Tommy considered Jerimiah levelly. 'Because we're going to be family sooner or later, Mr Brogan, and family don't take advantage of each other.'

'*In nómine Patris, et Fílii, et Spíritus Sancti,*' said Father Mahon.

Keeping her head bowed and her eyes fixed on the end of the bed, Ida crossed herself.

It was just quarter past five and she was standing at the foot of what had been her three daughters' bed. Ellen was lying in it now with Father Mahon kneeling beside it saying mass and giving her the host. Although it had been touch and go last week, when Ellen had developed a wheezy cough, it looked as if she would make it past Christmas, which for Michael's sake was a mercy. There was no good way for a child to lose a parent but to do so at Christmas would be doubly cruel.

She'd left Michael and Billy downstairs listening to *Children's Hour* while she came up to Ellen with Father Mahon.

He'd arrived half an hour ago, just as she had finished closing the curtains in readiness for the blackout. While listening to Father Mahon's familiar voice run through the Latin prayers, Ida had sent her own prayer heavenward, asking that for Jerimiah's sake Queenie be found safe and well. As she'd already said, for a child to lose a parent at Christmas would be doubly cruel.

'Amen,' whispered Ellen. She started to make the sign of

the cross but on the downward stroke her hand rested on her chest. Hand! A bag of skin with bone inside would be more the truth, and the rest of her was the same. There was barely a shred of flesh on her and the skin was pulled so tight across her nose and cheeks it was a wonder her bones hadn't sliced through. In fact, she was so frail Ida could move her with ease, but she was equally terrified that she would break a bone in the process.

Leaning on the bed, the elderly priest tried to stand. Ida went to assist.

'I'm obliged to you, my dear,' said Father Mahon, as Ida hooked her arm in his and he struggled to his feet. 'A cassock isn't the easiest of garments to negotiate.'

'Thank you for coming, Father,' said Ida.

Picking up his home communion set, Father Mahon placed his hand lightly on Ellen's forehead, closed his eyes for a moment then retracted it.

Leaving Ellen lying peacefully, they left the bedroom and closed the door behind them. They made their way quietly downstairs to the small hallway. Taking down the priest's long overcoat from the hall stand, Ida held it out for him and he shrugged it on.

'You know, Ida, I'm surprised she's still with us,' said Father Mahon, taking his scarf from his pocket and wrapping it around his neck.

'It's Michael,' said Ida. 'She can't bear to leave him. I'd be the same if I had to leave my kids.'

He nodded. 'Any news of Queenie?'

'I'm afraid not . . .' She told him about their continuing search. 'Of course, there's a chance she's lost her memory and is in a rest centre somewhere, but we can't do any more until Friday.'

Father Mahon pursed his lips. 'How's Jerimiah?'

'Holding up,' Ida replied. 'But he and Queenie had an almighty bust-up when he collected her from court, so he blames himself that she went off.'

The elderly priest frowned. 'Well, we must pray for both their sakes that she is found soon.'

'Amen to that,' said Ida.

'Will you be at church later?' asked the priest, shoving his hands in his gloves.

'Me and all the family,' said Ida, opening the front door.

Father Mahon's wrinkled face lifted in a kindly smile. 'And I'll have the joy of seeing them together in a pew.'

'Good day to you,' said Ida as he stepped out into the chilly street.

'And to you, my dear. And, Ida . . .'

'Yes, Father.'

'It's a rare and charitable thing you're about with caring for Ellen there,' he replied. 'In following the Lord's teachings on loving one another you're a humbling example to us all.' He raised his hand. 'God bless you.'

He smiled and for a split second, as she gazed down at the old man in the fading winter light, Jerimiah's face flashed through her mind. She tried to catch the thought that had caused it, but as the priest turned and headed along the street, it vanished.

'Right you are, then,' said Jerimiah, shoving his pencil back behind his ear and his order book in his overcoat pocket. 'I'll pick your delivery up Monday first thing and I'll have it to you by ten at the latest.'

'Thanks, Jerry,' said Winnie Miles, a jolly round-faced woman of his own age with fluffy blonde hair.

Usually at this time on Christmas Eve he would have been savouring a pint in the Catholic Club. However, since Tommy had left his yard three hours ago, he'd been steadily working his way through the delivery requests that had been sitting on his desk. Having just booked in the delivery for Winnie, he now had a full order book for every day next week and three for the following.

He was in the back room of Miles of Thread, the haber-dashers and wool shop in Ben Jonson Road.

'Have a nice Christmas,' said Winnie.

'And you,' he replied. As he turned to pick his way between the bales of yarn and racks of knitting needles, something caught his eye. It was a card of scarlet satin ribbon, about an inch wide, lying on its side on the second shelf. Reaching across, he slid it out.

'Can you sell me a couple of yards of this?' he asked, handing it to Winnie.

'Sure.'

She walked back into the shuttered-up shop and Jerimiah followed her. Holding the card in one hand, Winnie unravelled the shining scarlet ribbon and then measured two lengths against the metal ruler fixed to the edge of the counter. Taking a pair of shears from her apron pocket, she snipped it through.

She wound it up and held it out for him. 'I'm sorry, we're clean out of bags.'

'Don't worry.' He took it and then fished around in his trouser pocket for change. 'How much?'

Winnie raised her hand. 'On the house.'

'No, I have to pay for it as it's my wife's Christmas present,' he replied, pulling out a handful of coppers and silver.

'Thruppence then, if you insist,' Winnie replied. 'But I hope you're buying her more than a length of ribbon or you'll be in trouble.'

Jerimiah grinned. 'Don't you think I know that after all these years? No, this is a little extra.' He slid it into his inside breast pocket. 'Thanks again and I'll see you Monday.'

'I think that's just about everything for tomorrow,' said Ida, surveying the pots and pans with peeled vegetables soaking in cold water, and the kitchen table which had every serving plate and dish she possessed squeezed on it.

'I should think so,' Mattie laughed, who was standing beside her. 'I can't imagine there's much left in the shop.'

'Well, there's my joint of beef at Harris's, for a start. He swears he didn't have one but I bet he's keeping it for someone who'll pay him double, blooming racketeer,' said Ida.

It was seven o'clock on Christmas Eve and she and the two girls had been hard at it for the past three hours, getting the food they'd been buying, storing and preparing for the past few weeks ready for the family's big day tomorrow.

'What did you manage to get in the end?' asked Jo, as she walked in from the back parlour carrying Alicia on her hip.

'A scraggy shoulder of lamb,' Ida replied, eyeing the roasting tin with a clean tea towel draped over it, 'which I'm sure won't stretch to the eight of us plus the boys and two toddlers, three if Stella doesn't turn up.'

'Well, we've enough potatoes and carrots to fill us up,' said Jo, as she set the infant on the floor.

'Not to mention the plum pudding and fruit pie with proper custard,' added Mattie.

'Well, you have to thank the girls outside for that,' said Ida. 'It's their eggs that went into it.'

'And don't forget the spread you've made for tea, Mum,' Jo continued. 'There's so much of it I doubt I'll have to eat until 1942.'

Mattie laughed, and Ida joined in.

'Are those two boys still playing nicely in the other room?' asked Ida.

'Billy's is but Michael's gone up to sit with his mother,' said Jo.

Ida rolled her eyes and surveyed the table again. 'I really wanted to have some more mince pies but I couldn't—'

'Mum,' said Mattie, placing her hand on her arm. 'It's fine. Honest.'

'The main thing is we'll be together,' said Jo. 'And those who aren't, Charlie and Daniel, will know we will be thinking of them.'

'Yes, we will,' said Mattie, a little too brightly. 'Until they're back home again.'

Ida and Jo exchanged a look.

'Tell you what, Jo,' said Ida. 'While I just have a quick check of the cold keep why don't you put the kettle on?'

'Good idea, Mum,' said Jo. 'And you,' she looked pointedly at her sister, 'can put your bum on a chair and rest up from all your dashing about.'

Mattie laughed but did as her sister suggested.

Leaving her daughters chatting in the kitchen, Ida took the large torch from the hook by the door and ducked behind the blackout curtain.

The cold keep, where Ida kept her milk, butter and

anything else that would turn in the heat of the kitchen, sat against the wall of the yard that never got the sun. It was, in fact, a double-sized butler's sink that Jerimiah had brought home years ago. Its lid, which was half of someone called Sven Kristiansen's gravestone, sat firmly on top and even in the height of summer it could keep milk fresh for two days.

As she stepped out into the freezing air, the chickens, sensing someone in the yard, started clucking softly.

An unexpected pang of sadness welled up in Ida's chest. Although she'd have driven the Angel Gabriel to strong drink, Ida had to admit, despite her sharp tongue and explosive temper, Queenie's disappearance had left a large hole in the Brogan family, and in Jerimiah's life.

Shoving the old slab of granite back, Ida shone the torch into the space below and counted the eight pints of milk. She checked the sack of potatoes was still upright and the seal was still tight on the butter crock then she repositioned the lid and went back inside.

Jo was pouring the tea.

Alicia, who had now perfected pulling herself up, grabbed hold of the back of one of the kitchen chairs, lifting the front legs from the floor. Mattie scooped her up before she toppled it on herself.

'You shouldn't be lifting in your condition,' said Ida, glancing at the pronounced roundness of her eldest daughter's stomach.

'I'm fine,' Mattie replied, settling her daughter on her hip.

The back door opened again, and Jerimiah stepped out from behind the curtain. Although his face was pinched with the cold, his eyes were bright and with a sparkle in them she hadn't seen for many weeks. His gaze flickered around the room then locked on her.

His expression changed somehow and a warm feeling spread through her. Feeling suddenly at peace, Ida smiled, and Jerimiah smiled back.

Although he always felt the burdens of the day grow a little lighter when he walked into the comforting warmth of the family's kitchen, tonight Jerimiah felt it doubly so.

There was a meaty smell of his supper being kept warm in the oven and, as always, there was a cup of tea either just about to be made or brewing. But most importantly, and something until recently he had to admit he'd not realised was so precious to him, there was Ida.

They continued to look across at each other for a heartbeat then, conscious of Jo and Mattie regarding their parents strangely, he widened his gaze to include his two daughters.

'Evening, me dears,' he said, unwinding his scarf and taking off his donkey jacket. 'I can see you've all been busy this afternoon.'

'We have,' said Jo. 'But Mum should take most of the credit as she's been putting stuff by and baking for weeks. Me and Mattie have only helped get it all out.'

'I know,' said Jerimiah, gazing at his wife again. 'Where would we be without her?'

Jo and Mattie exchanged a glance and Ida waved his words away with the tea towel.

'Go away with yer old blarney, Jerimiah Brogan.' She shrugged off his compliment but not quickly enough to stop a blush colouring her cheeks. 'I suppose you're after a cuppa, as always.'

'I'm gasping for one, so I am,' he replied.

She held his gaze for a second or two longer then turned and took down his large mug from the row of hooks over the dresser.

'Any news on Gran?' asked Mattie.

The pall of sadness hovering over him, despite his conversation with Tommy, pressed down again and Jerimiah shook his head.

'Not yet,' he said.

Mattie put her hand on his arm. 'I'm sure she'll be found fit and well soon.'

Jerimiah forced a smile. 'I know.'

He doubted it but there was no point telling the children that before Christmas. Alicia clapped her hands and Jerimiah switched his mind to happier things.

'Hello, me darling child,' he said, taking her from her mother.

He kissed her, feeling her baby-smooth cheek under his lips. She responded by giving him a damp kiss in return.

'Is Father Christmas going to bring you something nice?' he asked her as he held her in one arm.

'The Board of Trade Allocation of Raw Materials and the LCC Price Regulation Committee permitting,' said Mattie.

Jo caught his eye. 'Did Tommy catch you, Dad?'

'Yes, he did, and pleased I was to see him,' Jerimiah replied.

He and Jo exchanged a knowing look. She picked up her and her sister's cups.

'Let's go through to the parlour, Mattie,' she said.

Jerimiah handed Alicia back and both girls left the room.

'Well, you're certainly full of Christmas spirit,' said Ida, placing his mug on the table. 'I suppose that's Tommy plying you with Guinness at the Catholic Club to get you to change your mind about him and Jo getting married.'

'Well, you see, now that's where you're wrong,' he said, picking up his drink, 'because Tommy dropped by the yard and . . .'

As he told her about his conversation with Tommy and the dozen or so visits he'd done on his way home, Ida's eyes grew wider and wider.

'So, you see,' he concluded, 'Brogan and Sons are back in business.'

'Oh, Jerry, I'm so glad you're up and running again,' said Ida, when he'd finished. 'So I suppose you'll be off to the Catholic Club to celebrate after your supper.'

'I'm not,' he said. 'I thought it would be nice if we all went to Midnight Mass together as a family.'

Crossing the space between them, Jerimiah took her small hands in his large work-worn ones.

'And I hope and pray it's us, Ida, me and you, who are up and running, because without you nothing makes any sense,' he said, fighting the urge to take her into his arms. 'What do you say, Ida? Is it still me and you against the world?'

She glanced down at his large work-roughened hands holding hers for a moment then her eyes returned to his face.

'Jerry, I—'

'Mum, Dad,' shouted Billy as he burst through the parlour door into the kitchen.

'Come and listen, there's a bloke on the wireless talking about the army in North Africa where our Charlie is.'

*

358

'I hope everyone's ready,' said Ida, bringing her coat into the back parlour and laying it across the back of the sofa. 'Because if we don't leave in ten minutes, all the pews will be taken and we'll end up standing at the side.'

'Almost,' said Jo, trying to comb Billy's hair into place despite his best efforts to stop her. 'I've just got to get my coat on and Mattie's gone to the bog.'

'Are the babies wrapped up warm enough?' Ida asked, glancing at the two prams parked next to each other in front of the glowing embers of the fire.

'Alicia is and Patrick is too now Mattie's put another blanket on him,' Jo replied. 'And once we get in the church, they'll be warm enough. What time is Stella collecting him tomorrow?'

'Goodness only knows,' said Ida, 'but I told her to come before one or not at all as we'll be sitting down to dinner then and won't be opening the door.'

The kitchen door opened and Mattie came in. 'Sorry, Mum, but I had to go.'

'Course, luv,' said Ida. 'Is your dad still out there?'

'Just filling up the girls' feeding trough and covering them with an extra blanket to keep the frost at bay,' Mattie replied.

'Well, while he's doing that I'll just pop up to check on Ellen,' said Ida. 'Billy, stand still so your sister can comb your hair!'

Leaving the family to get themselves ready to go to the Christmas Eve midnight service, Ida made her way upstairs to the bedroom at the front of the house. She'd lit a small fire earlier to keep out the night chill so the room was warm and dimly lit by the bedside lamp.

Ellen, who was as colourless as the sheet beneath her, lay with her arms out of the covers, her eyes closed. Michael was lying propped up against the headboard beside his mother. He was wearing his school trousers and a thick Aran sweater. An old copy of the *Hotspur* lay open on his lap.

He looked up as Ida came in.

'Is your mum all right, Michael?' she whispered.

Ellen looked up.

'I'm sorry; I didn't mean to wake you,' said Ida.

'You didn't,' whispered Ellen. 'I wasn't asleep.'

'Well, we're just getting ready to go to church and I wondered if Michael would like to come to Midnight Mass with the rest of the family,' said Ida.

The boy's eyes lit up. 'Can I, Mum?'

'Of course you can,' said Ellen. 'As long as you behave properly.'

'I promise,' said Michael.

'Go and get your coat on, then,' croaked Ellen. 'And you can tell me all about it in the morning.'

Giving her a peck on the cheek, he bounced off the bed and dashed out of the room.

A sad smile lifted the corners of Ellen's pale lips as her son's footsteps thumped down the stairs. 'He already thinks of himself as part of your family.'

'But he will always be your son, even when—' Breaking from Ellen's sunken gaze, Ida cast her eyes around the room. 'Right, you've had your medicine, you've got a fresh set of sheets and nightdress . . .' Her gaze flickered over the crocheted blanket discreetly covering the commode. 'Is there anything else you want me to do before we leave for church?'

'Just one thing,' Ellen replied, her sunken eyes holding Ida's. 'Give me your forgiveness.'

Long buried emotions of love rose up in Ida's mind as did

memories of walking arm in arm on sunny days and girlish secrets shared.

She looked down at the dying woman. 'You were my friend, Ellen, my best friend, dearer to me than my own sister and yet you . . .'

A ghost of a smile flitted across Ellen's face. 'I know,' she whispered. 'And I'm sorry for how I've hurt you but I couldn't help myself. I had a chance to love him, just once, and, God forgive me, I took it. You don't understand how much I loved him and still do. I loved him from the first moment I saw him as a girl of six or seven. Even then, when I barely understood what love between a man and a woman was, I dreamed I'd be his bride. I dreamed of the children, too, three boys and three girls, all tall and dark with his lovely grey eyes. Those lovely grey eyes that looked at you, Ida, then saw no other woman.' Tears shimmered in Ellen's dark-shadowed eyes. 'I had to smile as you married the man I loved. Had his children.' A solitary tear ran down her right cheek. 'What I did was wrong, I know that, but I can't regret it because it gave me Michael. His son. I understand if you can't forgive me, because if Jerimiah were mine, I couldn't forgive any woman who dared to touch him either, but please, please, forgive him. Forgive Jerim—'

Ellen grabbed her chest as a paroxysm of coughing gripped her. Ida paused for a couple of heartbeats and hurried to her.

'It's all right,' she said, putting her hand beneath her friend's head and lifting it. 'Just take a couple of deep breaths.'

Taking the invalid cup beside her, she offered Ellen a sip of water.

She swallowed a few mouthfuls and the spasm subsided. Ida went to place the china vessel back on the wooden surface, but Ellen's skeletal hand caught her wrist in a vice-like grip.

'He loves you,' she gasped, fixing Ida with a piercing gaze. 'He always has. So I beg you, Ida, don't let your hatred of me destroy that.'

Guiding Billy and Michael forward, Ida prodded them into line and they knelt down on the padded carpet at the altar rail. Adjusting the sleeping Patrick on her shoulder, Ida got on her knees and stole a glance along the line of those waiting for the host.

Next to her was Billy so she could poke him if he didn't behave. The other side of him was Michael, with his hands out already. Both of them were in their new clothes and with their hair brilliantined into a neat order. Next in line was Cathy, in her thick brown woollen coat and tangerine-coloured felt hat, with Peter, wearing a new coat at least two sizes too big, standing in front of her, watching with wonder the candlelight as it played on the rich gold fabric of the altar cloth and church silverware. Jo, in a smart new winter suit with a fur collar and pillbox hat, knelt next to her sister with Mattie, in her red coat and holding Alicia, on the other side. Beside her was Jerimiah.

He, like the rest of the family, had his best togs on, which in his case was his best suit, paisley waistcoat and freshly laundered red Kingsman neckerchief tied at its usual jaunty angle at his throat.

Father Mahon's white and gold chasuble swept across her vision and Ida turned to face the front as he started distributing the host to the family, starting with Jerimiah.

Shifting the sleeping baby's weight, Ida closed her eyes and waited while he stopped in front of each Brogan family member in turn.

She opened her mouth when the priest got to her and she felt the wafer rest on her tongue then dissolve. She heard the heavy fabric of Father Mahon's vestments rustle as he laid his hand on Patrick to bless him.

Waiting until the priest had passed, Ida crossed herself then looked at Jerimiah to find him looking at her with a bleak expression on his face. She knew why: because Queenie wasn't kneeling at the communion rail with them. Ida's heart ached for his pain.

With his lips pulled tightly together, Jerimiah stood up. The rest of the family did the same but as Mattie tried to rise, Alicia started fussing. In one fluid movement, Jerimiah scooped his granddaughter effortlessly into his arms. The toddler put her arms around his neck and snuggled into him, her head resting against his jaw.

Leading the family back down the aisle, Jerimiah waited until Mattie had taken her seat then he handed Alicia back, but not before Ida caught tears shimmering in his eyes.

He looked across at her. Ida held his gaze for a second then Jerimiah turned and marched towards the front door. Laying Patrick back in his pram, Ida followed.

She found him standing on the pathway by one of the old family memorials about three or four yards away from the church porch, watching the thick Thames fog swirl around the stone post, their wrought-iron gates long gone to help the war effort.

In the dim light seeping beneath the church shutters Ida studied her husband for a moment then stepped forward and slipped her arm through his.

'I shouldn't have shouted at her,' he said, still staring ahead into the murky atmosphere.

'You shouldn't be too hard on yourself,' said Ida. 'You'd been up for hours; you were dead on your feet.'

'I know but she's my mother,' he persisted. 'Sometimes, I grant you, she would try the patience of St Peter himself, but I shouldn't have hollered at her like that in front of everyone.'

'I bet she gave you as good as she got, though,' said Ida softly.

A wry smile lifted the corners of her husband's mouth. 'She always did but then she'd never have survived being married to me da if she hadn't. Raised me practically single-handed she did, with him away with the drink and out of work more often than he was in it. Did you know when I was a baby she scrubbed the abattoir's aprons to buy me extra food?'

Ida did, of course, and of the many sacrifices Queenie had made to raise her only son.

Clearing his throat, Jerimiah blinking a couple of times then stared into the impenetrable atmosphere.

Tucking herself into him a little closer Ida squeezed his arm. He patted her hand but didn't look at her. They stood in silence for a moment or two then he spoke again.

'I can't believe she's gone—' He broke off, covering his eyes with his hand.

Reaching up, Ida put her arms around him. Jerimiah lowered his head on to her shoulder and he clung to her, his massive shoulders shaking with emotion.

The opening bars of the last hymn began, but as the

organist piped out his jolly notes a less harmonious noise – a rolling squeak – could be heard.

Jerimiah raised his head from Ida's shoulder and looked around. The puzzling noise, like a rusty hinge, grew closer and as she and Jerimiah peered into the London fog an eerie shape started to take form. Ida's jaw dropped in disbelief as the ghost of Queenie emerged from the swirling pea-souper, but as she drew closer it became clear this wasn't her mother-in-law's spirit but the old woman herself.

It was no wonder Queenie looked like an apparition because in addition to her fur coat she had what appeared to be a horse blanket secured with a broad belt around her and Charlie's old school balaclava under her floppy felt hat.

She was also pushing the battered pram Ida thought had been thrown out years ago, on which sat something covered with a flowery bedspread.

'Ma?' said Jerimiah. 'Is it you?'

'Of course it's me,' the old woman snapped back. 'Who do you think it is, Maeve the Mystical?'

'But we thought you were dead,' Jerimiah continued.

'Dead! Now why in God's name would you think I'd be dead?' she asked.

Jerimiah frowned. 'Perhaps because no one's seen hide nor hair of you for days.'

Queenie waved away her son's words. 'Sure, son, if I were dead wouldn't I come back and tell you I was?'

'Well honestly, Queenie,' said Ida, suppressing a smile, 'when you walked out of the fog I thought you had.'

'Well, I'm not dead, that's for sure,' said the old woman. 'And I tried to telephone Mattie twice to tell you where I was but the sweet telephone girl on the other end couldn't get through.'

'And where exactly were you?' asked Jerimiah as people started filing out of the church behind them.

'Gran!' shouted Mattie, hurrying across with her pram. 'Thank goodness,' she said, hugging the old woman.

Leaping the graves of the long dead, Billy and Michael tore over.

'Thank goodness you're back, Gran,' shouted Billy. 'Cos Prince Albert's been missing you.'

'So have we,' added Michael, earning himself the tenderest look from his grandmother.

Jerimiah's frown deepened. 'As I was saying—'

'Look, Cathy; it's Gran,' shouted Jo as she and Cathy, with Peter in his pushchair, joined the little family group.

'Gran, you're alive,' laughed Cathy, as she and Jo sandwiched the old woman between them.

'Look, Dad,' Jo said, her eyes shining with joy in the dim light. 'Gran's alive.'

'I think we've established that,' said Jerimiah, his voice rising a notch or two. 'But what I'm still trying to get to the bottom of is where in the name of all that is holy your dear old Gran has been these past five days.'

'Chasing Red Colin,' Queenie replied. 'I'd have been there and back by Friday night if it hadn't been for those eejit coppers.'

'There and back from where?' asked Jerimiah.

'Hackney Flats, where he was camped,' she replied. 'I tell you I've had a rare time of it because by the time I got there on Friday he'd moved his vardo to Wanstead. Some kindly soul offered me a berth so after trying to telephone Mattie I got me head down for the night. I cadged a ride to Woodford Wells on Saturday only to find he'd shifted that morning to Harlow. As no one wanted to disrespect

366

the Sabbath I enjoyed their hospitality until Monday.' Her wrinkled face lifted on a fond smile. 'Right grand company they were, too, with a fiddler who knew the old tunes. It took me right back, I can tell you . . .' She caught sight of her son's face. 'Anyway, on Monday one of the young fellas was going north and he offered to drop me in Roydon and finally, with me legs aching and feet murdering the rest of me, I caught up with Red Colin on Monday afternoon. I tried to telephone Mattie again but still couldn't get through so as Paddy Leary, who was on the site with his cousin's family, said he was after coming back to see his sister I asked him to tell you where I was.'

'Well, he didn't,' Jerimiah barked. 'And while you've been out having a rare old time and enjoying "grand company", me and Ida have traipsed around every hospital this side of the Roding River searching for your corpse and—'

'You weren't to know the telephone exchange was out of action,' cut in Ida. 'Or that Paddy Leary didn't do as he said he would.'

'I'll skin him alive, so I will, when I catch up with him,' said Queenie.

'Anyway, we're just thankful you're safe and well, aren't we?' she asked, giving her husband a meaningful look.

Pressing his lips together, Jerimiah's nostrils flared for a second then he let out a long breath.

'Yes, we are, Ma. We're mighty thankful you're back with us and not in heaven giving St Peter a headache,' he said. 'But tell me, why the hell were you chasing all over Essex after Red Colin in the first place?'

'To fetch himself.'

She dragged the threadbare quilt off the pram to reveal an old budgie cage in which was a brightly coloured cockerel, who seeing the world revealed around him, threw back his head and let out a couple of cock-a-doodle-doos to herald his arrival.

'Eggs is all fine and fair for supper, but,' Queenie winked, 'to my mind a leg of chicken is better.' She threw the blanket back over the bird. 'Now, I don't know about you grand folk, but as I've had to walk all the way back from Forest Gate I'd thank you if we could start making our way home.'

'Good idea,' said Ida.

'But before we do,' Queenie unhooked something dangling from the pram's handle, 'as that swindler Harris has probably done you out of the joint you were after, I thought you might find these useful.'

Queenie handed her two brace of large fat rabbits, still in their fur.

Ida stared at her Christmas dinner saviours for a moment then looked back at her mother-in-law. 'Where on earth did you get them, Ma?'

Queenie's face lifted into a wrinkled smile and she winked once more. 'I found them.'

Chapter Twenty-one

'WELL, THAT'S THE last one, I think,' said Jerimiah, dressed in his best suit and sporting the new sky-blue neckerchief Cathy had bought him for Christmas at his throat. 'And it's for Gran.'

It was just before two thirty on Christmas afternoon and the whole family was gathered in the back parlour. Well, squashed would probably be a better way of describing it because with eight adults and two boys and three toddlers squeezed into the fifteen-by-twenty back living room, you could barely see the rug covering the floor.

Ida had tried to make the family's main room as festive as possible, which, given the shortages of practically everything, had been a struggle this year. Especially as when she brought the cardboard box of decorations down from the loft she found the mice had munched their way through all the Chinese paper lanterns. Luckily, the concertina bell had escaped their teeth and was now hanging from the central light. What with that and the paperchains made from strips of her *Woman and Home* magazine draped across the room and the milk bottle tops cut into stars thumbtacked to the ceiling it looked very festive. Even having Mr Frosty, as Michael and Billy had christened her cotton-wool snowman, sitting in the corner instead of a tree didn't mar the Christmassy feel.

Because they were intent on keeping an eye out for Father Christmas, Billy and Michael hadn't actually gone to sleep until well after one on Christmas Eve, so there had been a hope amongst the adults that they might sleep in, but no such luck: both boys were up before the sun. They'd devoured their oranges and read the comics Ida had stuffed into their socks hung up on the bedpost then they started jumping about. Jerimiah had gone into them at six and agreed that they could open one present each as long as they played quietly after that.

Not fully awake, Jerimiah had crashed back into bed and gone straight back to sleep, so he didn't hear Queenie getting up to feed and water the lads then taken them out in the yard while she tended to the chickens and checked the new addition to their number.

Ida must have fallen back to sleep at this point too because the next thing she heard was Mattie and Alicia arriving at nine o'clock.

Hurrying downstairs, Ida found Queenie had already skinned and jointed the rabbits and had put them in their largest pot to simmer on a low gas along with diced carrots, pearl barley and two chopped onions that she'd also 'found' in her travels.

After a mad scramble to get ready and having made Ellen comfortable, Ida and the rest of the family headed off for the ten o'clock Christmas service, arriving with a few minutes to spare to find Jo and Cathy already in their usual pew.

On coming out of church Jerimiah had disappeared to the Catholic Club to meet Tommy for a pint but much to Ida's surprise instead of having to wait on their return before dishing up the meal as they had last year, the two men strolled back in just after *Workers' Playtime* started at twelve thirty.

Ten minutes later, the table had been pulled out and covered with two freshly laundered sheets. While the girls had laid the table, Tommy brought in half a dozen bottles of beer from the cold keep they'd been saving for the day and Jerimiah carried in the chairs. Ida and Queenie drained the vegetables and put them in the tureens and as the one o'clock news started Ida carried through the rabbit stew. That was an hour and a half ago and while they waited for the King's speech at 3 p.m. they had been handing out the presents.

Jerimiah handed the soft package Ida had wrapped in the back page of *Woman and Home* to his mother. She was sitting on her chair, with her dentures in and her feet dangling. Taking it, she read the inscription written on the paper before opening her present and holding up a pair of ivory-coloured long drawers.

Billy and Michael, who were sitting cross-legged in front of the bookcase, put their hands over their mouths and started sniggering but after a severe look from Jerimiah they contented themselves with just grinning at each other.

'I used number-two needles with two ply,' said Ida, more than a little pleased with her work. 'They'll keep you nice and snug in this cold weather.'

'That they will,' said Queenie, admiring her new bloomers.

To be honest, most of the gifts had been knitted, like Billy and Michael's scarves and gloves and Tommy's long socks, or sewn, as with the palm-sized lavender pillow with lace around the edges that Mattie made her sisters for their underwear drawers.

As Pearl was in some funk hole in the country quaffing champagne and eating black-market turkey and would be none the wiser, Ida had split the money she'd given for Billy between the two boys. After scouring every shop down Roman Road, the Waste and Stratford she'd finally found two sets of die-cast knights in armour to go in the castle Jerimiah had knocked up out of an old fruit crate at his yard.

Her mother-in-law gave her a sweet smile, which Ida, sitting in the fireside chair opposite, returned.

Well, when all's said and done, it was supposed to be a time for peace on earth, wasn't it?

She caught sight of her two eldest daughters on the sofa and frowned.

As there was a lack of places to sit Jo said she was quite happy to share the easy chair with Tommy to save space. She was now perched on her fiancé's lap with her legs draped over the arm of the chair, leaving Mattie and Cathy to share the sofa. They were sitting, with their babies on their knees and their nephew Patrick, who seemed to have been abandoned by his mother, between them.

Although Mattie who was amusing her daughter with the soft-bodied doll Jo had bought her looked happy and relaxed, the same couldn't be said of Cathy, who had wedged herself as far as she could away from her elder sister.

Given that Cathy was stuck in a miserable marriage and lumbered with Stan's shrew of a mother, Ida could forgive her middle daughter's sour face but perhaps next year she might try to recall the angel's tidings.

Out of the corner of her eyes Ida caught a movement and she looked around.

'Are you all right, Ellen?' she asked softly.

'Yes . . . I'm fine, Ida,' she whispered. 'It was good . . . of you . . . to ask me . . . to join you.'

Ellen, almost swamped by the dressing gown she was wearing, was sitting in the low armchair just behind Ida in the corner with her feet up on the pouffe and a knitted shawl draped across her legs.

'It is Christmas,' Ida replied. 'And I'm sure Michael's happy you're down here with him.'

Ellen forced a smile that stretched the tissue-like skin across her cheeks to its limits.

She was no more than a bag of bones now and so breathless she could barely move without collapsing. Although you could never say with any certainty, Ida would be surprised if her old friend saw January out.

When the family had returned from church Ida had popped up to check on Ellen and it was then she asked if she'd like to come down for dinner. Ellen didn't feel able but after Ida had helped her with a bowl of rabbit stew Ellen said she'd like to watch Michael open his presents, so Jerimiah had carried her down.

To be honest, she'd only thought to ask Ellen to join them for Michael's sake. After all, it wasn't fair for him to have his last Christmas memory of his mother be one of her gasping for breath on her death bed. However, once Jerimiah had settled Ellen in the corner it seemed right somehow to have her with them.

'Oops, I nearly forgot,' said Jerimiah, bringing Ida's mind back from its sombre thoughts.

He drew a small box wrapped up in pink tissue paper from the inside pocket of his waistcoat and surveyed his family. 'Santa left one more gift.'

His gaze shifted to Ida and his eyes grew tender.

'It's for a woman worth more than all the gold in Solomon's mine, the biggest diamond ever found and every pearl in the ocean.' He offered her the gift. 'Me darling girl, Ida.'

There was a collective ahh while Tommy let out a loud wolf whistle.

Although Ida's lips were threatening to curl into a smile, she rolled her eyes. 'You and your old blarney, Jerry!'

He smiled and then his eyes locked with Ida's for a couple of heartbeats before she lowered them.

Unpicking the wrapping paper to save it, Ida took out a small navy box with 'R&S Garrard' stamped in gold across the top. She opened it and her eyes stretched wide. There sitting in the centre of the velvet backing was an enamel four-leaf clover with diamantes around the leaves and a pearl in the centre.

'Oh, Jerimiah,' she said breathlessly. 'It's beautiful.'

'Pin it on, Mum,' said Mattie.

Ida fixed it on the left side of her best dress and gazed down at it in admiration for a moment then back at her husband. 'It's lovely. Really lovely.'

'You'll have to take Mum out somewhere special now, Dad, so she can show it off,' said Jo.

'And so I shall, don't you worry,' he replied. 'But perhaps she might want to wear it first at yours and Tommy's wedding.'

Jo stared at him for a moment then leaping from Tommy's lap she dashed across and threw herself into her father's arms.

'Oh, Dad, you're the best,' she said, hugging him.

Tommy rose to his feet and offered Jerimiah his hand. 'Thanks, Mr Brogan.'

'My pleasure,' Jerimiah replied, shaking his hand. 'And I've told you before, son, it's Jerry. And, Jo me luv,' he said, patting her back, 'if you're after me walking you down the aisle I'd be obliged if you'd stop strangling me.'

Jo let him go and then turned to her sisters who had also risen to their feet to congratulate her and Tommy.

'Dad?' said Billy.

'Yes, son,' said Jerimiah, looking down at the lad.

'Why didn't Father Christmas leave Mum's present with Mr Frosty with all the others?' he asked.

Everyone laughed.

Queenie caught Ida's eyes and looked pointedly to the left. She glanced around to see Ellen with her eyes closed and her lips drawn. Standing up Ida went over to her and gently put her hand on her old friend's arm.

Ellen opened her eyes.

'Do you need your medicine?' Ida asked quietly.

Ellen nodded. 'If it's not too much trouble.'

Giving her arm a gentle squeeze Ida looked across at Jerimiah, who was enjoying a glass of Scotch with Tommy.

She caught his eyes and he swallowed his drink down.

'Ellen needs to go back upstairs,' she told him as he joined them.

Seeing his mother in some distress, Michael came over, too. 'Mum?' he asked, looking anxiously at her.

'It's all right, sweetheart,' Ellen said, forcing a smile. 'I'm just a bit tired, that's all.'

'Shall I come up and keep you company?' he asked.

Ellen shook her head. 'No, you stay and enjoy the fun with Billy. I'll be fine once I've have a little snooze.'

'We're going to listen to the King's speech, Michael. Do you want to sit with me by the wireless, so you can hear?' asked Mattie, reaching out her hand.

'Go on,' mouthed Ellen.

Michael hovered for a second or two and then went to join the rest of the family.

'Ready?' asked Jerimiah.

Ellen nodded.

In one swift movement he scooped her effortlessly into his strong arms and her brittle ones wound around his neck. As he settled her in his arms Ellen gazed up at him with pure adoration. Raw emotions burst through Ida, but instead of the soul-destroying jealousy and fury that had shredded her heart for the past three months it was pity that brought a lump to her throat.

As the BBC announcer drew the whole country and Commonwealth together in readiness for the King's Christmas Broadcast, Ida opened the door and Jerimiah carried her dying friend upstairs.

Half an hour later, having given Ellen a dose of painkiller and helped her back to bed, Ida draped the shawl back over the commode and then turned back to the woman lying peacefully.

'Better?' she asked.

'Yes, much,' Ellen whispered.

A raucous shout came up from below followed by the deep rumble of Jerimiah's laugh.

A ghost of a smile lifted Ellen's colourless lips. 'They sound like they're having a good time,' she said softly.

Ida nodded.

Ellen's eyes shifted downwards from Ida's face. 'It's a lovely brooch.'

'Yes, it is, isn't it?' Ida replied. Glancing down, she studied the diamantes as they twinkled in the bedside light for a moment. Then, with tears pinching the corners of her eyes, she looked up. 'Now, if you need any—'

The morphine had done its job and Ellen was asleep. Ida

watched her for a few seconds then smoothing out a wrinkle in the counterpane she turned and quietly left the room.

Another roar came up from downstairs and Ida smiled, but instead of making her way downstairs to join the family she crossed the landing and went into her bedroom.

The fog from the night before had returned so although it was only just before four it was already dark outside. Ida closed the curtains and switched on the bedside light on her side of the bed. Taking the stool in front of her dressing table she went and set it down in front of the wardrobe. Stepping up on it she rummaged around amongst the boxes full of family mementoes and documents on top until she found what she was searching for.

Taking down a battered oval tin, Ida put it on the bed and then sat down beside it. After studying the faded image of a country hunt taking refreshments at a thatched inn for a moment she flipped off the lid.

She took out the tiny lawn cap no bigger than her clenched fist. It had yellowed with the passing years, but she could still make out the whitework daisies she'd embroidered over a decade ago around the edge. She held it for a moment then set it aside and took out the lemon matinee coat with duck buttons and the matching leggings and bootees.

Placing the newborn's jacket in one hand, Ida smoothed it with another for a moment then laid that with the bonnet then picked up the six-inch strip of gauze ribbon. It was crinkled in the middle where the knot had been tied and as her gaze ran over it her heart ached with a pain that would be part of her for ever.

A tear she hadn't realised was there escaped and dropped on to the frayed slither of cotton tape and as it spread in the weave the door opened.

Ida looked around and saw Jerimiah.

'I came to see if you're all right, luv,' he said, giving her a concerned smile.

'Yes, I'm fine,' she replied.

His gaze flicked to the contents of the tin on the bedspread and then back to Ida.

'You sure?'

Brushing her cheek with her finger, Ida gave him an open smile. 'Yes, I'm fine, but,' she patted the quilted bedspread next to her, 'you can keep me company for a bit if you like.'

Shutting the door Jerimiah came and sat next to her. He picked up the bonnet.

'I never got over how small the children were when they were born,' he said, the satin ties dangling around his wrist as he turned the cap on his fingers.

'You wouldn't say that if you'd been pushing them out,' said Ida.

'I don't suppose I would, especially not Charlie.' A wry smile lifted the corner of his mouth. 'What was he again?'

'Nine two,' Ida replied. 'And almost a day arriving.'

A sad looked passed across Jerimiah's angular face. 'And now he's a thousand miles away fighting in the desert.'

'And will be back before we know it,' said Ida, praying it would be so.

They sat quietly together for a long moment then he spoke again. 'What else?'

Glancing down, Ida smoothed her skirt. 'Oh, you know. This and that.'

'James?'

Without raising her eyes, she nodded, as the pain of holding their much-wanted, much-loved lifeless son in her arms surged up in Ida.

'I know it was terrible for you,' Jerimiah said softly.

Ida looked up.

'For both of us, Jerimiah,' she said. 'And that's what I've been thinking about us. All we've been through and all we have. Our children and our grandchildren, too.'

'And a new one on the way,' he said.

'And another one, too, by next year with Jo talking about a Whitsun wedding,' said Ida.

Looking up at the ceiling, Jerimiah groaned. 'You're making me feel old.'

Ida's eyes ran over him and she smiled. 'I'm glad you said Jo and Tommy could get married.'

He laughed, and it rolled over Ida like a warm blanket. 'Well, even I'm not strong enough to stand against Jo when she's set her mind on something.' His eyes twinkled as they danced over her face. 'She takes after you for that.'

'And I've been thinking about Michael,' said Ida.

Apprehension flickered across Jerimiah's face.

'He's a lovable little lad and already a part of this family,' Ida said quickly. 'And more importantly, Jerimiah, he's your boy.'

'He is,' her husband replied firmly.

'And none could doubt it,' said Ida. 'But you asked me yesterday if it was still me and you against the world.' She looked him squarely in the eye. 'And it is. We'll face life together as we always have.' One corner of her mouth rose slightly. 'To be honest, I can't see my life any other way, Jerimiah, than beside you.'

They stared at each other for a couple of heartbeats then stretching across the baby clothes on the bed, Jerimiah took her hand.

Raising it to his mouth he pressed his lips on her fingers,

his breath warm on her skin. They lingered there for a moment then he raised his head.

'I love you, Ida,' he said, those dark grey eyes she'd fallen into the first time they met capturing her heart all over again.

'I love you too, Jerimiah,' she replied, knowing that despite everything she did.

He smiled and, her world restored, Ida smiled back.

They sat there spooning each other like a couple of fresh-faced youngsters rather than an old married couple for what seemed like hours then Jerimiah spoke again.

'Well, wife,' he said, giving her that half-smile of his that always made her glow, 'is there anything else on your mind?'

'Nothing, I don't think other than I love my present,' said Ida, touching the brooch with her fingers again.

'Well, that's a great weight off my mind, I can tell you,' he joked. 'Although, I wish it could be emeralds and diamonds. Oh, and I nearly forgot.' He rummaged inside his waistcoat and pulled out something red. He handed it to her.

'I don't know if you recall but you were—'

'Wearing a scarlet ribbon in my hair when we met,' she said, gazing down at the coil of scarlet ribbon that had unravelled in her hand and remembering the fate of the original one. Images of their life together since that St Patrick's Day dance flashed through her mind then she looked up.

And there he was beside her as always, the father of her children, the man she could totally rely on, who was the backbone of the family and who could drive her to wild fury at times, but the man she loved above all others, Jerimiah Boniface Brogan.

Tears, happy ones this time, sprang into Ida's eyes.

'Oh, Jerry,' she mumbled, flinging herself into her husband's arms.

His strong arms embraced her and the warmth and familiarity of his body engulfed her and happiness welled within her. In truth, it was more than happiness, it was more than contentment, it was the deep, deep unshakable confidence in his love.

Feeling his lips on her forehead, Ida looked up.

Jerimiah gazed down at her with all their history and his love shining from his eyes then he lowered his head and pressed his lips to hers.

A jolt of excitement shot through Ida and she kissed him back, enjoying his experienced hands caressing her back and hips. After a moment he raised his head.

'I don't feel old now, do you?' he asked, his vibrant voice resonating through her.

'No,' she said, giving a look very like the one she'd given him at the St Patrick's Day dance all those years ago.

His arms tightened, but just before his lips touched hers again the bone-jarring wail of the Moaning Minnie on top of the Town Hall cut between them.

Reluctant to leave the magic of her husband's embrace, Ida didn't move as the air raid siren ran through a couple of warning cycles and then the bedroom door burst open.

'Dad, Dad,' shouted Billy, as he and Michael dashed into the room. 'There's an air raid!'

'Is there?' Jerimiah roared over the incessant noise.

Ida rolled her eyes at him and slipping the scarlet ribbon into her pocket, stood up.

'Start getting your things together, boys, and I'll be down.'

The two lads dashed out on to the landing and ran back downstairs, the sound of their feet clattering like thunder on the stairwell.

Ida took Jerimiah's hand. 'Come on, we've got a houseful downstairs to get to the shelter.'

'I know,' he bellowed, putting his hands on his thighs as he stood up.

Ida turned to leave but he caught her around her waist and drew her back to him, he went to kiss her but placing her hands on his broad chest she held him off.

'Later, I promise,' she hollered, kissing his bristly chin.

He kissed her forehead and grinned down at her.

'I'll hold you to that,' he bawled.

He kissed her again then let her go and marched towards the door.

'Right now, everyone,' he shouted, 'make sure . . .'

Ida smiled as she listened to her husband taking the stairs two at a time.

When you come to the realisation that when you kiss your family goodbye in the morning there is no guarantee you'll see them again in this world, then it tends to focus your mind on the only thing that really matters: love.

Acknowledgements

As always, I would like to mention a few books, authors and people, to whom I am particularly indebted.

In order to set my characters' thoughts and worldview authentically in the harsh reality of 1941, I returned to *Wartime Britain 1939–1945* and *The Blitz*, both by Juliet Gardiner; *The East End at War by* Rosemary Taylor and Christopher Lloyd; *London's East End Survivors* by Andrew Bissell; *Living Through the Blitz* by Tom Harrison; and *The Blitz* by Cecil Madden to give me a feel for those dark days.

I also reread *Wartime Women* by Dorothy Sheridan; *Millions Like Us* by Virginia Nicholson; *Voices from the Home Front* by Felicity Goodall; *A Wartime Christmas* by Mike Brown; *The Wartime House* by Mike Brown and Carol Harris and *Ration Book Diet* by Mike Brown, Carol Harris and C. J. Jackson to help me construct Ida's day-to-day struggle to provide for her family during a time of rationing and shortages.

As always, I've sprinkled Fullerton family wartime stories and anecdotes throughout *A Ration Book Childhood*, along with stories from *The Wartime Scrapbook* by Robert Opie.

I would also like to thank a few more people. Firstly, my very own Hero at Home, Kelvin, for his unwavering support, and my three daughters, Janet, Fiona and Amy, who listen patiently as I explain the endless twists and turns of the plot. I'd also like to thank the Facebook group Stepney and

Wapping living in 60s early 70s, who this time helped me get the Tilbury Shelter correct and shared their families' wartime experience.

Once again, a big thank-you goes to my lovely agent Laura Longrigg, whose encouragement and incisive editorial mind helped me to see the wood for the trees, and her colleague Julia Silk who has supported me marvellously this year. Last, but by no means least, a big thank-you to the wonderful team at Atlantic Books, Jamie Forrest, Karen Duffy, Patrick Hunter, Sophie Walker and Poppy Mostyn-Owen, for their support and innovation. And finally to my lovely editors Sara O'Keeffe and Susannah Hamilton who again turned my 400+ page manuscript into a beautiful book.

Author's Note

As it became clear during the summer of 1939 that war with Germany was almost inevitable, the British government's Committee for Evacuation began the largest movement of people in modern times.

It was believed that on the declaration of war Germany would launch gas attacks against the civilian population. Therefore, to limit the casualties from such attacks, almost a million school-age children, infants and pregnant women were moved out of cities to safer locations around the country.

Although the scheme was voluntary the Ministry for Information produced a great deal of propaganda urging mothers to send their children to safety. Many women, fearful for their children's lives, signed up to have their children evacuated.

Today, because of mass communication, we are used to regional dialects and cultures very different from our own. But in those days many poorer East London children from tight-knit, working-class communities found themselves amongst strangers in a totally alien culture. What's more, many people living outside the large industrial cities regarded city children as dirty, dishonest and just a step up from feral.

On arrival, children were lined up in the village hall and people picked their evacuee. Siblings were often separated and older children, who could be useful around the house, were favoured over younger ones who were regarded as more demanding.

However, despite their misgivings, many East London mothers took the government's advice and on 31 August 1939 the mass evacuation of children from London and other major cities began. Not wanting to be judged as poor parents, mothers did the best they could to equip their children for what lay ahead.

In addition to their gas masks and identity cards, the government recommended that children take the following items with them:

2 vests
2 pairs socks
2 pairs knickers or pants
6 handkerchiefs
A petticoat, a gym slip, a skirt, blouse and cardigan for girls
Two pairs trousers, a cardigan and jumper for boys
School uniform (if they had one)
An overcoat
Wellingtons and plimsolls
Plus: soap, flannel, towel and toothbrush

Mothers also packed their children off to the country with their favourite toy and sandwiches for the journey.

I can't imagine what it must have felt like to take your children to a railway station and hand them over to a complete stranger. They had no idea where their children were going or when they would see them again. However, by Christmas 1939, as the predicted gas attacks had failed to materialise and with not a bomb having dropped, people started to fetch their children home. Many never returned to their evacuation placements. Even at the height of the Blitz people decided it was better to face the danger together.

Billy Brogan is loosely based on my Uncle Bob who had just turned thirteen when war broke out in 1939. With his brothers, Arthur, Jimmy and George, in the army, Bobby decided he'd had enough of school so, by his own admission, he spent the days roaming the streets with his gang, collecting shrapnel, exploring bomb sites, getting up to mischief and generally having a brilliant time. My grandmother, living only a few minutes' walk from London Docks, was right in the thick of the Blitz in 1940, but she decided, like Queenie, to take her chances up top and never bothered to go to the public shelters when the air raid siren went off. As the war progressed, Bobby signed up for fire watch on one of the local factories and on his fifteenth birthday in 1941 he started his apprenticeship with the Post Office's telephone division.

Although he was eligible to be called up in the summer of 1944, he was by then a qualified telephone engineer and so he remained in civilian life until National Service was brought in in 1948 after which he served in Malta, Egypt and what was then Palestine.